EXIT VISA

EXIT VISA

LEGEND OF THE CUP SERIES

BOOK TWO

DYAN DUBOIS

LUMINARE PRESS
WWW.LUMINAREPRESS.COM

Luminare Press
442 Charnelton St.
Eugene, OR 97401
www.luminarepress.com

LCCN: 2022901643
ISBN: 978-1-64388-869-9

For Rajinder

Table of Contents

CHAPTER ONE

Bombay, 1975

Askara's transition from 1975 freewheeling California life to conservative Bombay life came at a cost. She felt caged, not by Darian, but by the cement city of seven million people. Askara felt she was swimming in thick water, trying to catch her breath, but she sank a little more with every gulp. She had not developed the love and fascination for Bombay that Darian had hoped for in the six months since she had moved there. The nagging thought that their Tahoe quickie marriage at The Chapel of Mountain Love in Nevada had not been valid didn't help her mood. She looked forward to making it real, but for now they settled for posing for their parents' sakes until they could marry on their holiday in Kashmir.

Gradually she substituted hiking for yoga, Thai take-out for Bombay *Usal*—her new favorite food—and heated political discussions for polite party conversations. She even attempted to make Usal, but the dish didn't taste right. Askara got lost somewhere between the tiny beads of coriander seeds, minute sesame seeds, and the pungent dried flower bud of the clove tree. By the time she added cardamon, cinnamon, and the other fragrant spices, having followed the recipe exactly, the dish never tasted like the Usal lentils she loved at the nearby eatery.

At dinner, Darian joked because she had not developed the Indian cook's sense of smell that guided proper melding. Askara's temper flared.

"What?" She dropped her chapati in astonishment. "Are you serious?"

"Of course not. Besides, there's no need to master Indian cooking unless you want to. We have a cook. Do what makes you happy, Askara."

Askara shrugged. "I'm bored. I like to work. Wish I'd hear about the photojournalism gig I applied for." She walked to the window. Black rolling clouds descended on the Indian Ocean, turning green water gray. The wind picked up. Palm trees swayed like seductive belly dancers. "Monsoons?

Darian joined her at the window. "Looks like they've arrived…a bit late this year."

"Monsoons fit a schedule?" Askara said and smiled. "How droll."

"June tenth is the traditional start."

The sky darkened; thunder cracked overhead. Darian rushed to shut the bedroom windows and returned to the kitchen. Huge splats of rain rolled down the dusty glass, leaving a yellow trail. "The rain's more fun to watch than to navigate. Look at those women down below."

Askara leaned out until her nose pressed into the iron-work scroll that protected the window screens. Two women in saris grappled with umbrellas. Another gust and the spines flipped inside out, making an upward V that caught the downpour. The women threw down their umbrellas, and with newspapers held overhead, they rushed under a shop awning.

"The air feels thick," Askara commented, watching insects appear from nowhere to stick to the screens, gripping with tentative antennae like they were searching for a pulse. "How long do the monsoons last in Bombay?"

"Until September. July and August are the worst, with almost nonstop rain, very little sunshine, and water-logged streets. Flooding suspends the rail service at times. As much as twenty-eight inches of rain in a month, not my favorite time to be in Bombay. That's why we'll leave—business travel for me, pleasure for us."

Askara mulled over Darian's statement, her face tight with consternation. She wanted to hear about her journalism application to cover Madagascar's Walking the Dead ceremony, not go on a business trip for Dalal Industries. Her instructor at San Francisco State had recommended she enter the call for entries funded by the Christian Coalition of Catholic Churches, whose representative had delivered the flyers to him, asking for his best students to apply. He informed Askara he had written an excellent recommendation for her. She knew she had a good chance because she wasn't as far from Madagascar as someone in the States and because she had traveled in third-world countries and had learned the ropes. She hoped her slim portfolio was bolstered by her work for Mr. Ramsey, especially since he had listed her as a contributing author on his jewelry book.

"So, you typically escape Bombay every summer? We could live in California during the summer. That would be fun."

"Every monsoon season. Summer is March to May for us. The monsoons are a special category. You'll see. People wait all year for the rains. They dance in the street when the first drops fall. But as time goes on, the humidity and heat become oppressive, the insects obnoxious, and the gray seems never-ending."

"You like this way of living?"

"I do. An acquired taste, I'm sure. But remember, I haven't lived in Bombay my whole life. The rains make a good time to take a break. A little goes a long way when it comes to heat, humidity, and inevitable blackouts. Every AC and swamp cooler pulls on our antiquated system. So, we will leave. Maybe Singapore and Thailand for business. How does that sound?"

"And Madagascar?"

"Sure. I've never been there. Such a diverse environment, highly unique; I would like to see it. From there we could go to South Africa. I have a school friend who lives in Cape Town and wants Dalal to set up an enterprise there."

"Always the hustler."

"Excuse me? Businessman. What is a Walking the Dead ceremony anyway? Why would Catholics be interested?"

"It's not traditional Catholicism, at least not what I think of as traditional. I guess the original people there, the Malagasy, honor their dead by exhuming a relative's remains. They wrap the deceased in a new silk shroud and parade the remains around the village, explaining the events since the relative died, to involve them in the community again. Doing this brings blessings from the ancestors.

But buying expensive cloth means only the well-to-do can afford to honor a relative in this way. It's a big deal to the people, like a form of life insurance for their heirs, you know, having the ancestors watch out for them from the spirit world, protect them. I'd never heard of it before. I looked it up to fill out my application."

"That's Catholicism? Sounds pagan."

"Must be if a coalition of Catholic churches wants an article for their international magazine on the ritual. The Vatican sends priests to South America to verify accounts of spontaneous healing and visions of Christ and things like that. Why not cover this? The ceremony fuses Madagascar beliefs brought from Indonesia and Catholic beliefs brought by French Catholic missionaries in the 1600s."

"Catholic missionaries traveled everywhere in that era, Askara, either the French or the Spanish, even the Portuguese, and then the Protestants escaped to America. Christians were on the move, intent on domination."

"I think they saw it as spreading the word, Darian."

Askara stood at the kitchen window and let the monsoon thunderclaps rumble through her while she watched excited people in the streets rush for cover. She saw a golden stain of marigold offerings bob on the waves, no doubt in thanks for the rain. She ran to the hall closet, pulled out her camera, and attached the telephoto lens to capture her first monsoon in Bombay. Stepping onto their small balcony, Askara documented the mayhem of exultation, chaos, prayer, and people diving for shelter as others danced in the rain, stalled traffic at roundabouts, meandering sacred Brahman cows nibbled grass by the sides of congested roads, and black cloud fists beat the sky. She recalled Ramsey, her ex-boss in California who loved to watch the street scene below Max's Café in downtown San Francisco. Street theater, he called it. Maybe she could learn to love this too?

She decided to send Ramsey copies of these Bombay photos, a memento from the first monsoon season of her newly married life. Despite all their work hassles, Askara enjoyed their bond. Seth Ramsey was like the slightly sleazy uncle who entertains everyone with crazy stories at holidays, never brings a dish, dresses like an actor, and makes the day memorable. Askara thought of him fondly, knowing he won the San Francisco First Book Award because of her help.

Askara checked for her mail daily, but none came. She grew despondent; the thought of a new career in photojournalism seemed to fade. She had counted on getting the job assignment through her instructor. How else would she secure such a helpful reference when no one in Bombay knew her? Darian had plenty of contacts in the business world, true, but she didn't want to establish herself based on being the wife of so-and-so. A hollow victory is no victory at all. She wanted to earn her own salary.

⚓

WHEN DARIAN RETURNED FROM WORK TO SEE ASKARA practicing chapatis, he realized how bored she was. She hadn't complained; she rarely did, but her demeanor spoke loudly. The rain pounding down all day, every day, had turned the streets into rushing garbage rivers, leaving her trapped inside.

"Did you practice yoga today, Askara?"

"Yes, but I've forgotten some of the points the swami told me. I'm not doing some of the asanas correctly. I can feel it. That's a drag. But he left Bombay for the hills and said we would resume our lessons when he returns in September."

"Well, let's get out of the city for a quick change of scene. How about a short trip to see the Ajanta and Ellora Caves? They're only two hundred miles northeast of Bombay. The advantage of going now, in the monsoons, is fewer people go at this time, but the view of the Western Ghats is great, with flowing streams, waterfalls, and lush green hills. What do you say? We'll get a nice hotel room and spend a couple of days seeing the area."

"What's special about the caves?"

"The Ajanta Caves are monasteries and halls cut with primitive hand tools from a huge wall of rock. They date back to two centuries before Christ. They're Buddhist caves, about thirty of them, with elaborate sculptures carved from the rocky hillside. The jungle covered them until the early 1800s when a British officer on a tiger-hunting party discovered them by accident. That is like someone finding the Koh-i-Noor diamond in the dust"

"That would be an amazing find."

Darian continued, "Cave wall paintings depict the lives and births of Buddha and other deities. Monks and pilgrims would retreat to the caves in the monsoons. Ellora Caves, about sixty miles from Ajanta, have Hindu, Jain, and Buddhist art from ancient times. We might need two days at each, I think. You should take lots of photos, if they let you, and submit an article to travel magazines here in Bombay. I don't like seeing you so glum, waiting to hear on that Madagascar thing."

"I'm not *glum*. Sounds great. I'd love to go. When?"

"Let me tie some things up at work. I'll make our bookings for the day after tomorrow. Does that suit you?"

"Sure. Would that book vendor on the main road have information on them? I'd like to do some research first."

"I would think so. The caves are popular tourist destinations. Let's take a look. I'll get the car and pull around the front for you."

"No, let's walk. I want to experience the rain."

Darian looked at Askara and smiled. "Your choice, madam."

Askara suited up in her version of rain gear, sandals, and a nylon shell. Darian humored her, knowing his new leather shoes would bleed orange into his socks. When they arrived, Askara was surprised to see the shop was no more than a lean-to with a canvas cover under an adjoining building's roof. The books stacked on a pallet looked miserable.

"How does he keep them dry?"

"They're not, exactly, but this is a street vendor's display. Down the block, the bookstore is indoors. Let's go."

When they walked into the store, the smell of musty, slightly dank books mixed with Nag Champa incense made for a heady mix. Askara enjoyed the scent, but Darian wiggled his nose and rolled his eyes. He quickly asked for the tourist book area.

The shopkeeper, delighted to speak in English, led Askara to the Ajanta and Ellora Caves section. He stood next to her, flipping pages so fast she couldn't see them, and told her stories of his visits. He recounted how he had gotten the bookstore because of a tip from the fortune-teller, the same man who usually sat on the street corner. He advised him since he was a lover of books to set up shop, and people will come, even from *Amerika*.

"You did what a fortune-teller told you? That's interesting. How has it worked out?"

"Very good; my family and I are living above. My employee runs the outdoor shop on the street. We are doing well. Rain is slowing business outside but pushing people inside. And the fortune-teller's fame is bringing them in daily. People are knowing him. Many come and speak to him and see my shop and buy, just as he said they would. Since ten years, I am keeping shop here. Very very nice."

"Where's the fortune-teller now? The monsoons must drive him away."

"No, he is being busy in the backroom. He works small duties for me. In exchange, he gets a corner of my book storage room. Are you wanting to see him?"

"Sure," Askara said. "What kind of fortune-telling does he do?"

"Good, madam, he is being very clever. He reads your hands and your eyes."

Askara caught Darian's attention and motioned for him to join her. He shook his head *no* and turned to search the books on the shelf in front of him. When Askara entered the small room, the incense was so thick it left a gray pallor hanging in the still air. The storekeeper spoke to the swami seated cross-legged on a small carpet in front of an altar with a picture of the pot-bellied Hindu god Ganesha. Askara recognized the elephant god, a bringer of good luck.

"I will translate unless you are knowing Hindi?"

"Thank you. I don't know Hindi."

The fortune-teller motioned for Askara to sit on a small stool opposite him. He asked her to extend her hands, palms up, to rest on her knees. He sat quietly and studied the lines, then looked into her eyes and back to her hands before he spoke.

"Swami says you are going on a journey where many others have gone before. You will learn something about yourself that you do not know. You have a guru who tells you things you don't remember. Someday you will listen and act with knowledge. Someone in a cave will speak to your heart, and you will follow. You have many lifetimes behind you, none ahead. Special people pull you along on a journey that ends here in Mother India. But you go many places. You tie up old debts to gain freedom. You will not have children, but children will come to you for help.

Often you will have trouble recognizing yourself. You do not see who you are or who you have been with ease. That will change. Duty rules your life now. A man stands next to you to help."

Askara watched the fortune-teller light another candle and stick of incense. He waved the smoke over her until she felt she would choke. Her eyes watered. She smiled at the old man and said, "Thank you," not knowing what to say or ask.

The shopkeeper told her, "One hundred-and-one rupees fee." She fumbled in her travel belt to produce the exact amount, handed the payment to the swami, nodded in respect, raised her hands in namaste, and walked to the storefront to join Darian.

"How was it?" Darian whispered.

"Not sure. I'll tell you later."

After a few minutes of fumbling through the Ajanta and Ellora Caves section, Askara picked out two tourist guides. They raced home through the downpour, Askara's face red with laughter. Darian admired her ability to throw peoples' stares to the wind. She looked wild and free, her hair a tangled halo. After drying off, she gave Darian a quick overview of the reading, telling him it made no sense, not even down to the payment of one-hundred-and-one rupees.

Darian laughed. "That's for good luck. People consider those numbers are a good omen."

———— ✿ ————

ASKARA SPENT THE NEXT FEW DAYS PORING OVER THE tour guides, taking notes, and questioning if she could turn their trip to the caves into an interesting article, considering everyone and their relatives had done the same piece before, for centuries. She didn't give much thought to the fortune-teller's reading. It made no sense, but he was a kindly man, one she enjoyed supporting.

Something surfaced that did give her pause, an image that rattled around in her imagination from an obscure article she had read in an old *National Geographic* in California. In Indonesia, after a burial ceremony, the Bubonic plague had broken out in a small village within days, almost wiping it out. The government responded quickly to contain it. Scientists from around the world came to investigate. Images from her art history books of the Black Death, the scourge of the Middle Ages, haunted her. "How safe is the Walking the Dead ritual?" she wondered.

CHAPTER TWO

Ajanta and Ellora Caves

S eeing the massive yellow ochre rock wall towering above the monsoon-invigorated vegetation made a distinct impression on Askara. The tour guide pointed to the monk's halls and living quarters—windowless cells, dark gaps between rock column teeth. Darian took her by the hand and led her up the path, something she enjoyed, although she focused on the tour guide when he said the paintings inside depicted Buddha in different lives and rebirths as well as other Buddhist deities.

She hurried to enter first, pulling Darian along. Askara assumed it would be like trying to see the *Mona Lisa*. She was wrong. The small crowd, dwarfed beneath the massive rock, didn't affect the vast cave's acoustics or obstruct the views.

They wandered from cave to cave and found a consistent pattern: monks' small cells surrounded a large communal room for eating, studying, and prayer. The *chaitya*, a columned prayer hall, always ended with a dome-shaped *stupa*, the symbol of Buddha's presence. The guide said the stupa represented the transition from earthly life to the cosmos, important for Buddhists. In Cave 19, when the light from a high-arched window illuminated the stupa, Darian joked that it was a message for her.

"What message, Darian?"

"What do you think? Watch your step."

Askara groaned and walked over to study the mural's colorful images of Buddha and the bodhisattvas. "None of these best the one we saw in Cave One," she said. "Wow, Bodhisattva Padmapani, fantastic. Remember that one?"

"Of course, I've seen it many times. You stood there and practically drifted away looking at it. Padmapani is the most famous bodhisattva here. Didn't you hear the guide explain that?"

Askara shook her head *no.*

"You can tell if the image is Buddha or a bodhisattva because the bodhisattva wears princely garb and jewels, even a crown of pearls."

"But Buddha was a rich prince before he became enlightened. He would have worn those too."

"True, but the bodhisattva is a being who is still in the process of becoming enlightened and who helps others in the world to obtain liberation. Depictions of Buddha, with a raised dot at his third eye, a serene face, and only a loincloth, signify he didn't need or want jewels anymore."

"That face of the Padmapani Bodhisattva was like looking at an angel; it reminded me of Leonardo's depiction of the angel in his painting *Virgin of the Rocks.* Do you know it?"

"No."

"There's the same serenity, like feminine energy, in them. I'd like to know what *they* see, to feel peaceful like that."

"Hey, we've been walking for hours. We've covered the major caves. Let's return to the hotel. Tomorrow, Ellora. You'll have plenty of time to ponder those caves too."

THE FOLLOWING DAY AT THE ELLORA CAVES, ASKARA
realized the power of the human effort to depict the divine
affected her in a way she would not have anticipated. The
brochure termed them "the epitome of rock-cut archi-
tecture," a phrase that didn't register until she saw the
Ellora site—"the largest single monolithic excavation in
the world."

Thirty-four caves cut out of the Charanandri Hills, of
the one hundred total, belied the feat of excavation using
simple hand tools. The entire vertical face of the hill had been
altered. The cap, the remaining basalt rock face—dark gray,
almost black—seemed to trickle down to touch the excavated
yellow-ochre stone-like paint dripping down a canvas. The
Ellora caves, the guide emphasized, served as temples and
lodging for Hindu, Jain, and Buddhist adepts and pilgrims
from the fifth to the tenth centuries. All were welcome. Some
idols had been damaged over time, others even destroyed, but
the paintings and carvings remained intact. Yet none of the
murals impressed Askara like those at Ajanta.

From where she and Darian stood at the top of the
temple complex, monsoon rain dripped down the hills
to refresh grass on the ledge above their heads. Far below,
women in bright saris and men in white pajama suits
looked like colorful ants scurrying among the massive
free-standing elephant sculptures. The tourists occasionally
looked up at the decorative pillars towering above them to
where rolling dark clouds gathered in the hills. They laced
through the temples, staring at niches of full-figured stone
women balanced on a raised hip as if they had paused in
the dance of creation. In front of a temple platform, where

the frieze of elephants stampeded from the stone, pigeons pecked for bits of food before flying high to roost in nooks and crannies.

Darian and Askara walked along the upper edge to descend the stone steps to the ground level. She broke from her thoughts abruptly when she hit a bump in the path. She grabbed Darian's hand to steady herself.

"Thank you for bringing me here, Sweetie. I need to tell you something strange that happened back there."

"What?"

"This place blows me away...sculpture on such a huge scale, built by hand. I mean it dwarfs humans, makes them ants. I was thinking about what inspires people to work so hard, what drives them to create. You know, when a sculptor works in stone, it's tough, like Michelangelo with marble. He said he saw figures in the stone and carved it to set them free. Imagine seeing Mother Mary holding Jesus in her lap and chipping away to release them. Ellora—well, this entire hill—was chipped away to create these temples and freestanding sculptures. That would be like Michelangelo chipping away the Vatican to free the Virgin Mary. That's not a Western way of thinking. It's more like deconstructing to create something. The more you take away, the more you emphasize what's left. Know what I mean?"

"I think so. But didn't Michelangelo do the same, just on a smaller scale? In our Eastern philosophy, creation and destruction cycles show the illusion of physical life. You work hard to honor your deities while you can, and you do it with whatever you have at hand because your spiritual life depends on it. In this case, the Charanandri Hills. Michelangelo had fine marble; we have rough hills."

"But you remove everything to create something entirely different. That's my point. You arrive at the 'no-thing,' empty space, and turn it into a grand 'some-thing.'"

"Right. That's one way of looking at it, I suppose."

"Darian, okay, what blows me away is I feel this in me. A lot has been removed from me, taken away, yet I don't know why or when. It left less of me. I don't feel grander like an artwork. I feel diminished. And I don't even know what that rest is. Does that make sense?"

"Not exactly, Askara, but I feel some of what you mean. When Minoo died, I felt like much of me had been taken away. I was left with little of me. Meeting you, Askara, and loving you changed all that. I feel more solid, more real now. But I'm talking about life after trauma. You haven't gone through that sort of trauma, luckily."

"I don't know what I've gone through. An odd feeling never leaves me…like something is misplaced inside me but not lost. When I looked at that mural of the Padmapani Bodhisattva, I felt something. It made me sad but also glad. Darian, I know this sounds weird, but I think I have to do something, but I don't know what and when. Then I will finally feel solid again. That fortune-teller said I will learn something about me that I don't know here. He said I have a guru who tells me things I don't remember. He said something in a cave would speak to me. I think that Padmapani Bodhisattva did. I think Ellora did."

"I once was lost but now am found. Like that? Is that what you're thinking, Askara? You are expanding who you are. You're living in a new country, doing things you've never done—things that show you new aspects of yourself that you didn't know earlier. It's natural. Life is about growing."

"It's more physical than that. I think there is something I have to do in actual time to understand something that came before. And by doing it, I chip away at the stone. I can come closer to the peace I saw in the bodhisattva's face."

"I'm sure you'll solve your spiritual puzzle. It's good to be inspired. That's the point of so much human effort—to reach for the divine. Meanwhile, though, why don't you write an article about Ajanta and Ellora, you know, a view of the East from a Western perspective? In India, we take these sites for granted; we've known about them for so many centuries. You could have a niche market. Send it out to travel magazines that specialize in holy sites of the world. If that exists."

———————— ⚭ ————————

WEDGED UNDER THE CAR BAY'S NARROW OVERHANG TO avoid the downpour, Askara waited for Darian to return from work. She saw the guard swing the gate back when Darian's driver pulled up. She rushed toward the car.

"Askara, what's wrong. Has something happened?"

"Great news, that's what. I got it. I got the Madagascar job!"

"Fantastic! Let us park. Quick, take cover. The sky's splitting."

Askara looked up to see a black cloud directly overhead. The bottom shifted and looked as if it would dent the ground at her feet if it dropped. It burst. Heavy rain pummeled her, knocking her sideways. She bolted for cover, surprised rain could hurt that much. She rubbed her arms held tight to her chest and sprinted through the soggy grass to the parking garage. The sound of thunder reverberated inside the building, bounced off the cement, and amplified. She blocked her ears with her palms.

Darian rushed over, grabbed her hand, and sprinted up the stairway to their flat. He pulled her in and slammed the heavy wood door. He tossed her a tea towel from the kitchen while she stood at the door in a pool, looking bedraggled.

"No way to wring the Ganges from my hair. I'll take a quick shower."

"I'll make tea."

When Askara returned to the kitchen, Darian greeted her with chai and biscuits. "Thank you, Sweetie. It's odd. Even when it's hot, a downpour makes you cold."

"Ha, wait. In a month, when the rain hits you, you'll feel like you're in a steam bath. But today, it actually cooled off a bit. Now, tell me your news."

Askara pulled out the letter and waved it in front of Darian. When he reached for it, she said, "Nope. I'm going to read it to you."

Dear Ms. Timlen, on behalf of the Christian Coalition of Catholic Churches, I am pleased to inform you that you have been chosen to report on the Walking the Dead ceremony practiced by the Malagasy people of the Catholic faith in Madagascar. The stipend will cover your flight and compensation at three thousand US dollars for the article. Unfortunately, we are not able to compensate for food and lodging whilst in Madagascar. We will retain rights to the article and send you copies of the magazine publication. This is a wonderful opportunity for you as we mail to dioceses all over the world. The priest in Antananarivo, Monsignor Devereaux, will serve as your contact in Madagascar. You will find him at the Church of the

Immaculate Conception. We will issue your com-
pensation check upon verification of the article by
Monsignor Devereaux.

"You have to foot the bills until it's published? They don't give you an advance? You're lucky we can handle it. Think of someone without funds. They're out of the running."

"Darian, it says at the bottom, the payment is split in two. Monsignor Devereaux will authorize a partial payment after the ceremony takes place. Look at the bright side. I got the job! It's the beginning of my new career. The article will bring me other jobs, ones that allow me to live here and work wherever. Perfect!"

Darian hugged Askara. "Yes, you're right. I am very happy for you. For us. We'll get to see a new place, visit my friend in South Africa, and possibly set up a Dalal enterprise there."

"Always the businessman, huh? Even when the news is mine."

"We have to make a living, don't we? Might as well look at opportunities. You're no different from me. Your business is more on the art side rather than commerce; that's all."

"Touché! Hey, I should restudy French. Too bad I dropped it in high school. I know a little Creole, enough to get us taxis."

"That's an advantage. Did the Coalition–of what–Catholic Churches? Did they tell you when the assignment starts?"

Askara reread the letter and noticed an additional fact she had overlooked stating the ceremonies occurred from August to October every year. Included was information about contacting Monsignor Devereaux, who would procure a family's permission. The family had to approve of the reporter writing an article on the ceremony and taking photographs. Many families refused. There should be no charge for attending the ceremony, although some families appreciated financial help to host the ceremony and welcomed a contribution. In that event, Monsignor would take care of the contribution on behalf of the church. The letter warned Askara she must not make a personal donation if asked, as that would set a bad precedent.

"So, you said August is miserable here. Want to go then?"

"Yes, that gives me time to pull some things together. Did you tell me this is done in other countries, or just in Madagascar?"

"Practiced in Madagascar but came from Indonesia. The Malagasy people believe the deceased is a bridge between this world and the world of spirit. Honoring them influences the luck of the living."

"Catholics worship ancestors?"

"Madagascar was a French colony. Maybe Catholic missionaries felt okay about the practice, so now the Church incorporates it? I don't know."

"I'll quiz you on the plane ride to Madagascar. Do your research. How's that?"

"Sounds good. I'll have answers by then. Hey, I just thought of something. Madagascar isn't so far from Lesotho—not really; well, it's a lot closer than India. Do you think I could ask Sara to meet us there? She's always wanted to meet you. She's fun; maybe we can tack on some lemur tour or an environmental tour or something after my job ends. What do you think?"

"Ask her. I would like to meet her, but it may be more convenient for her to meet us in South Africa."

"True. Okay, I'll run it past Sara and see what she can manage and where."

A LONG LINE OF PEOPLE EDGED FORWARD SLOWLY TO THE departure gate. Outside, a small airplane choked and sputtered before settling into a constant whine that leaked through the opened lounge door to assault the passengers. Askara, growing more irritated, chewed her lower lip.

She wondered how so many people could cram into that plane. From where she stood it looked like a red-and-white toy hardly large enough for a pilot and copilot. She fumbled and twisted the braided metal band of her watch. 3:33. She grimaced, always the same weird time. She watched the thick Bombay dawn lift over high-rise buildings. A uniformed man snapped her attention back to the room when he smacked his palm with a wooden ruler and motioned her to step forward. She could see over the wagging heads of passengers halted at the next checkpoint. One traveler nervously withdrew his passport and emptied his pockets. Coins clanked on the countertop and rolled on the polished linoleum floor.

When her turn came to approach, she said, "What is this? You're checking our belongings here?"

The guard, indignant and disgusted, stared at her. "Your papers must be in order."

"I realize that, but we already went through immigration and customs back there. We're departing, not landing."

The man gritted his teeth and spat the answer. "This, madame, is to make sure you are who you say you are, you've been where you say you've been, and you deserve to go on."

"Deserve to go on? To leave a country, or to arrive? What nonsense!"

"See that man over there? He thought he could exit, but he was wrong."

Askara watched a demure, middle-aged man in a brown suit cover his face with his hands as two guards led him through a metal door.

"What did he do?"

"He didn't settle his account. He still owes."

Askara reached into her pocket to finger the wad of traveler's checks, wondering how much this exit would cost, but she stopped short when the guard burst out laughing.

"That won't help you now. Once, yes, but not now. Save your silly paper money."

Perplexed, Askara replied in a tempered voice. "What is it? How much to get out of here?"

The guard exploded with loud, raucous laughter, gripped his sides, and slammed into the nearby wall. Others in line faded. Only Askara stood in the dimly lit room to face the convulsive guard. She stepped backward to rush for the door. She grabbed the knob, jerked it, and landed face-flat on a brick wall. The guard howled with laughter. Cold sweat bubbled on Askara's forehead. Her stomach lurched. She felt along the wall for a seam, an opening. The guard closed in like a lion after an antelope, circling. Askara swallowed hard; she tried to scream. No sound came.

The guard slapped the ruler across his palm and shouted into her face. "What's the measure of *your* life? I'll wager you have little to recommend you, not enough for an exit visa. But don't worry–that's the point. We don't issue visas. We all work to keep you here. We don't want you to leave."

The man spun around, dropped on all fours, and sunk his canine teeth into Askara's Achilles' tendon. Pain shot through her leg like a surge of white-hot lava. Her extremities turned into ash and blew away.

Askara sat up, gasped like a drowned person sucking for air and convulsed into the fetal position, pulling her knees to her chest. She slammed into Darian's back. He bolted upright in bed.

"Askara, what is it? Are you ill?" He grabbed her clammy hand. What's wrong?"

Askara looked at Darian, and, for a minute, she didn't know him. Wiping her blurry eyes, she whispered. "Where are we?"

"Home, Bombay."

She saw large luminescent green threes on the clock face. "God, three thirty-three? Why is it always three thirty-three?" She dropped into the soft folds of the sheets, breathing like she had run a marathon. "I thought we were in Madagascar at the airport, but it was in Bombay. The airport guard was hassling us."

"Just a dream, Askara. Compose yourself. You're safe with me, at home, here in Bombay."

Askara realized she had dreamed this same scenario ever since the Madagascar acceptance letter had come. Sometimes the guard was a serpent, lion, or hyena, but on the worst nights, he was a human who ripped and tore at her flesh until she woke in terror. Regardless of his form, he attacked, and she woke at 3:33 a.m. every time, in the darkness before dawn. But this time was different. She couldn't tell it was a dream.

CHAPTER THREE

Bone Turning Ceremony

B ombay's terminal, crisscrossed by passengers, reminded Askara of the last time she was in the airport with Darian. Although calmer this day, one thing seemed odd. Their driver and guide, a worker from Darian's Bombay factory, looked appallingly like the man standing four people ahead in line for their same Madagascar flight. He was so similar that Askara waved to him, which caused the man to face forward promptly.

Askara's visual memory, typically acute, baffled her. She never forgot a face. Simple logic told her this was impossible; he could not be the same person. Yet the perception jogged her memory of an earlier incident in the Khartoum airport in Sudan when she thought she had recognized someone in line. She found it peculiar that a pattern would repeat two misperceptions, both in airport passenger lines. She suddenly felt highly agitated and vulnerable. She asked herself: *What's going on?*

A deep-down feeling of dread surfaced again. Askara looked around, trying to spot anything out of order—a person, an action, anything. Nothing. She felt a wave, a transparent warp in her field of vision, flit past—a fast-moving series of images too quick to decipher that evaporated before she could focus on one. She hoped she wasn't getting sick. The ripple unnerved her. Maybe an ocular migraine? She blinked and looked away.

Askara didn't mention the sensation to Darian. Her nightmares had revived old anxiety in him that she knew too well. He must think she was falling into that weird desperation she had in California, that paranoia of someone tracking her, someone trying to find an item they thought she had. She looked at Darian and forced a smile. He smiled back. The faint crinkles at his eyes touched by softness made her sigh and relax. *Darian's such a kind man,* she thought. *I don't want him to go through any pain again, especially pain caused by me.*

Askara took a deep breath and recalled the naturopathic doctor had told her she was severely deficient in B vitamins, which could lead to fuzzy thinking. That's it, she decided. Taking vitamins daily had made her feel much better for the last several months. But she had slacked off recently. *That's the answer: I will buy them in Madagascar, start again. That will make everything okay,* she assured herself.

Their flight passed without incident until it encountered a storm over the Indian Ocean near Seychelles. The night flashed white in staccato patterns. The plane took a rough downward drop and lurched to the right, causing drowsy passengers to wake rapidly, grip their armrests, and whimper. Children screamed. Flight attendants' call lights illuminated the seats and aisle.

Just when everyone calmed, another hard knock jostled the plane. The pilot pulled up sharply, pressing passengers into their seatbacks. Nervous chatter in the cabin gave way to tense silence pierced by wailing babies. The plane climbed through massive clouds illuminated by bursts of jagged lightning.

Askara dug her nails into the armrest. Darian pressed his hand over hers. A scratchy voice over the intercom said, "Please remain calm and seated. Unexpected turbulence due to storm…." A loud hiss drowned the pilot's voice when the intercom popped and crackled and a less audible, urgent voice came on: "The captain requests staff take their seats immediately."

The plane began leveling, but a shallow hard drop like swatting a fly against a window caused the cabin to jerk, creak, and moan. Askara heard someone behind them retch. Her stomach lurched. When the plane nosed downward and leveled out several minutes later, she lifted her window shade. Reflected *fasten seat belt* messages flickered white against the glass. The captain came on the intercom, apologized for the inconvenience, and assured the passengers they had cleared the storm. He promised clear sailing from there on out.

Two hours later, when the plane touched the runway without a jarring bump, the passengers cheered and clapped, elated to be on the ground. Darian collected their bags from the overhead compartment while Askara grabbed her camera bag and pack from under the seat. Stepping off the plane into a warm, sticky environment made her breathe deeply like a swimmer gulping for air. Keeping up with Darian, who trotted across the tarmac runway, she followed but bumped into his back in the dimly lit terminal entrance where passengers clogged a small aisle and filed through like cattle on a precipice.

Military men with guns lined the airport terminal, standing erect like dark sentries guarding Fort Knox. Askara smiled as she passed but stepped out of line a bit as she approached a guard who raised his rifle and motioned her back in line. Seconds later, she saw the man she thought she had recognized earlier at the airport, but he no longer looked familiar to her. He took a different turnstile and disappeared from view.

Darian noticed Askara staring at him and asked, "Did you want to speak to that man?"

"Not really. I thought I had seen him in Bombay, maybe at your factory."

"I didn't recognize him. I think we need to be careful. He noticed you staring at him. The guards noticed you staring. Seems people are jumpy here...and armed."

A faded, almost illegible sign in English and French read: *Present passports and customs declarations here.* Although three turnstiles were available, only one was manned. An hour passed before she reached the passport agent, who ordered her to open her camera case and display everything on a table.

After a ten-minute inspection, he checked her passport and waved her to another station where she had to show her declared jewelry—a wedding ring, gold earrings, and a watch. Askara had forgotten about her amethyst pendant under her blouse. But remembering it, she had decided not to bother since they would lose their place in line, and all she wanted was to be out of the airport. When the agent read her declaration page, he asked if that was all her jewelry. She paused.

"Why?"

The agent said stiffly, "You want to leave with jewelry?"

"Yes."

"Register it, or guards will take it back when you leave our country, say it was not yours. You keep records of all you bring into the country and all sales receipts for what you buy in Madagascar. No exit without ownership records, sales records, bank exchange vouchers, hotel receipts."

"Just jewelry?"

"Everything—camera, film, trinkets, stones, vanilla, all purchases."

"Clothes?"

"Only expensive: silk, leather, fur. Keep all records, or you go to police station for permission to leave Madagascar. Takes much time. You will miss return flight."

"Okay, okay," Askara said with annoyance, noticing a long line had processed through while she and Darian remained, to the apparent irritation of tourists waiting behind them.

When Darian stepped forward, saying, "Thank you for your help, sir," he nudged Askara forward before she spoke again. The man shoved Askara's paperwork forward, dismissing them with "Go. Taxis leave."

They gathered their things and rushed to baggage claim, fearing their luggage would be missing but found it under the watchful eye of a man in an olive-green work suit.

"Thank you," Askara said, grabbing her luggage handle. Darian pressed a tip into the old man's hand and lifted his bag. The man smiled a toothless grin and covertly turned his palm up to Askara, who rolled her eyes, pressed two crumpled dollar bills into his creased hand, and watched him grimace. He didn't release his grip on her bag.

She wondered, *too little for him? Greedy guy.* His gaze fell on the Cross pen in the outer mesh pocket of her pack. Irritated, she went for her backpack. When a guard approached, Askara yanked the pen from its holder and surreptitiously handed it to the man, whose mouth expanded into a wide cavernous smile. He tucked the bills away, carefully placed the pen into his shirt pocket, released her pack, and backed away before the guard questioned them.

Darian and Askara stepped onto the curb outside of baggage claim, and a taxi stopped immediately. A man jumped from the passenger's side to load their bags, asking, *Qu'est-ce que votre hôtel?*

"*Prendez-moi a l'Hôtel du Parc, s'il vous plait,*" Askara replied.

"*Oui,*" he replied and threw their bags into the trunk.

Darian grinned at her. "Well done! That French review helped. You'll be my guide."

ON THE TWENTY-MINUTE DRIVE FROM THE AIRPORT into the capital city of Antananarivo, people barely discernible in the dark and visible only from the glow of their cigarettes crowded the edge of the unlit road, making the drive on the rutted road unnerving. The driver wove in and out, around and through groups of walkers.

"Seems the entire country are night walkers," Darian said to Askara. "With few lights, it's a dangerous proposition, but look, hundreds are on the move out here."

"Wonder where they're going?"

Askara noticed the man seated on the passenger's side, the taxi driver's assistant, laid a gun across his lap with its shiny metal clearly visible in the dashboard lights. The fine hairs on her neck felt like stinging electric currents pricking her skin. She wanted to lean into Darian and whisper something, but she dared not move. She watched the gun. The pre-morning haze had lifted when the driver pointed to the city lights in the distance and said, "Tana."

Crossing the city, watching it come into view like a creature evolving from a phantom, spooked Askara. Shop owners rolled up the metal security gates from their shop facades to reveal windows and front doors, lifeless dark eyes peeking out through a hazy film to a new day. Women swept the narrow, raised walkways in front, tossing water from small buckets to scrub away muck with brooms made of sticks. Butchers, preparing for another day, suspended whole animal carcasses head-down from hooks outside their shops and arranged cages of noisy chickens for shoppers. Flies buzzed with excitement. The smell of blood and dust made Askara roll up her window and cover her mouth with her hands.

When the taxi driver pulled up to the hotel's entrance, armed hotel guards greeted them, opening the door for Askara and Darian and ushering them in rapidly while porters collected their bags. Darian exchanged US traveler's checks for francs at the front desk and returned to pay the taxi driver and his assistant gunman. They saluted military-style, saying, "*Merci. Au revoir,*" but remained at attention while the hotel guards followed Darian back through the entrance door.

Darian joined Askara, whispering, "Well, that was a first."

"Better first than last. So intense. That's really riding shotgun."

After registering, a valet led them upstairs and opened the door to their room. A mildly stale odor of perfume, cigarettes, and mosquito coil wafted out into the hall. Next to the four-poster double bed, an air conditioner groaned and spat out chilled air in seizures. Darian placed a tip in the boy's hand and nodded toward the door. The boy left quickly, shutting the door with a firm click.

"Did you know Madagascar would be like this, Askara?"

"Wild? No. The travel brochures never mentioned it. It's like the Old Wild West days in America or something."

"I have a feeling no cavalry will rush in to help us if there's a shootout."

"This is a grand adventure, I guess, although I'm so glad I'm not on this trip alone, Darian. Remind me not to do business in Madagascar. I'm no match for it."

"Agreed. I don't think there's much money in vanilla anyway. If the cab driver needs a guard, well, we'd better stick together and preferably be indoors before dark."

Askara smiled at Darian and opened the sliding glass door to the small balcony where Tana's downtown glowed golden yellow from electric streetlights set against the gray morning sky from their vantage point. "It's kind of overpowering, Darian. I wonder if I won the contest because no one else applied? Maybe the subtitle should have read: 'those faint of heart need not apply. Fools gladly accepted.'"

"This hotel is fine, Sweetie. They even have a restaurant downstairs. We're just tired. Things will look better with a shower and breakfast. Coffee will help. I'm sure this city, Antananarivo, is fascinating, not to mention that bone-turning ceremony you've come to witness."

Askara smiled and stretched out on the bed. The last words she mumbled, "glad it's not my bones," drowned in her pillow. A knock twenty minutes later startled her. She sat up abruptly when a voice called out, "Madame, monsieur, *petit dejeuner.*

Darian, dripping wet, grabbed the white cotton robe from the bathroom and walked to the front door. Askara rubbed her eyes. A thin, young man carrying a silver metal tray filled with covered dishes and a small vase of brightly colored zinnias said, "Bonjour, madame, monsieur."

He set the tray on the glass-top table near the balcony door and lifted the silver cover of the serving dishes to display a blood-red papaya filled with purple berries, a plate of croissants, soft cheese wedges wrapped in silver foil, and saucers of jam and butter. Pouring coffee from a silver pot, he nodded toward a small creamer and sugar bowl placed on top of an envelope with words scrawled across it in a large, loopy script.

He spoke timidly in English. "My envelope says I am your guide, Imboule. I am studying English, please. Welcome to Tana. Complimentary breakfast by hotel owner for you."

"Thank you, *merci*, Imboule. *Je parle une petite francais.* My name is Askara. My husband is Darian. You are our guide for what? Did the Monsignor send you?"

"I return for you later in the morning."

"For what?"

"To take you where you go. *L'hôtel* gives me to you. Mr. Ed told me to show you Tana."

Askara liked this timid young man dressed in a red plaid shirt and brown polyester slacks. "Okay, you show us Tana today, but do you know the Monsignor?" she said and tipped him.

"I know Mr. Ed," he said.

"I don't," Askara replied.

"Imboule, how many francs is your fee for today?"

"Only ten thousand Malagasy francs, madame."

Askara made a quick mental calculation while Darian's eyes flared. She realized it was about five dollars. She nodded in agreement. "You have a car, or do we rent one?"

His surprised look made Askara smile, "No, madame. I hire one for you."

"How much is the car for a day?"

"Twenty thousand francs, madame."

"Okay. Come back for us in two hours."

After Imboule left the room, Darian said, "Nice kid, I didn't hear any mention of this when we signed in, did you?"

"No. Maybe foreigners can't roam around by themselves? It seems the tourist industry wants to protect its clients. I guess Mr. Ed is the concierge or something."

"Hmm…an Englishman at a French hotel?"

"Maybe. Or Monsignor could have assigned him to us?"

Askara spotted a wedge of folded paper sticking to the jam dish. She pulled it out and read: "Greetings, Askara. I am Ed Healy, project manager for a San Francisco film crew on location to shoot documentaries about lemurs. A friend of mine is your friend in Frisco, Jack, your photography prof at SF State. He told me you'd be here on assignment and asked me to look out for you. This is a wild country. I thought you might need Imboule. He's an honest guy, very helpful and intelligent. He'll you get around and keep you safe. Me and my crew are staying here at the hotel, too. Look us up. I'd love to hear about your project. I've wanted to film the ceremony myself, but they don't like entire camera crews disturbing the ancestors, so no family has accepted my offer. Maybe they don't like me. How'd you get permission?"

He signed the note: Ed Healy, project manager for Lemurs Alive Documentary, Antananarivo, Madagascar.

Askara handed the note to Darian. "Read this. So, on this large, strange island, we already have a contact, an American from San Francisco." Askara put the note down and smiled. "But I don't have full permission for this assignment until I meet Monsignor Devereaux."

Drawing back the musty burgundy curtain for a full view, Darian said, "Let's eat on the balcony. The city is awake."

They watched Tana bustle with people bringing their goods to the bazaar. Small, black taxis darted in and out of nearby hotels, and in the distance, the large outdoor market came alive with vendors' white umbrellas springing up like flowers after a rain.

Askara sipped strong black coffee tinted with vanilla-scented cream. Her fatigue evaporated. She smiled, realizing this was the first day of her new career as a photojournalist on a dream-come-true assignment in Madagascar.

—————— ✂ ——————

LATER THAT MORNING, THEY MET ED HEALY, A SHORT, balding man who thrust his rigid, square palm out and vigorously shook their hands like he was priming a pump.

"Glad to meet you, been waiting down here in the lobby to see you," he said and reached into his bag to withdraw a small tape recorder. "Just clips onto your waist. Jack knew you'd have trouble with customs, so he sent a few things for your shoot along with me. We had a helluva time getting our Velvia film through customs, though. They wanted to inspect every damn canister, would have exposed it. They couldn't figure film being in a cooler. Had more trouble with that than all the other supplies put together."

"Thank you. I'm surprised Jack made all these arrangements. He must have known before me that I got the assignment."

"He went to bat for you, that's for sure. Good guy; known him since we were kids."

"And thank you for Imboule. I met him earlier this morning. His English is pretty good. My French is pretty bad, Darian's pretty nonexistent, but I know we'll manage. How do I handle the more complicated interviews? Do you come with us? Or Imboule?"

"No, I'm not invited, and sorry to say neither is your husband. It's a big deal that you can go. Imboule is your driver. I booked a Malagasy woman on your behalf to translate for you. People accept her at their ceremonies. She's fluent, a local girl who lives in London mostly. Very intelligent. We've used her before, fluent in English, French, and Malagasy."

Ed Healy looked past the front desk and started walking. "Great, there she is now. Come on."

Askara saw a skinny woman talking to a European man. From an A-line skirt, her legs hung like strings that disappeared into stacked black heels. When Askara approached, the woman turned to smile in recognition.

"Hello, I'm Askara Timlen," Askara said, extending her hand, "and this is my husband, Darian Dalal. You must be the translator?"

"Yes, hello, pleased to meet you both. I am your translator, Meamoni. Mea for short, and this is my husband, Alistair."

"Nice to meet you. Are you going on location with us, Alistair?" Askara said.

"No, but I will accompany Mea on some errands for you," he replied. "I have things to take care of before we push off for London."

Mea broke in. "As soon as this job is complete, we are moving back. We've been here for two years; it's time to go now."

Alistair brushed his straw-colored hair back from his high sunburned forehead, saying, "How many days do you need Mea's services?"

"I'm not sure yet. I haven't met Monsignor Devereaux, but I imagine no more than a couple of weeks."

"Right," he said, casting a concerned look at Mea, who averted his gaze.

"Madagascar is a fascinating place, an ancient land with many exotic plants and animals, not to mention people. I hope," Mea said, pausing with upturned hands, "that you capture the feeling of its beauty and people and customs, not just the scar of poverty."

"I don't know how much latitude I have in this report yet. But I agree with you that a comprehensive picture is far more interesting than one with a narrow scope, although my focus is the Walking the Dead custom."

"But a custom out of context is only an exercise. Respect for the meaning goes beyond the ceremony, far beyond."

Askara liked how forthright Mea was but hoped her personal views wouldn't spill over into her translation of the event. Askara wanted facts—undistorted, unflavored.

"Mea, I intend to show respect in this process as, I am sure, you do." Alistair smiled slightly at Askara's handling of the situation. She continued, "We have a driver, Imboule, whom Ed Healy arranged for us. I assume we will not have to fly anywhere, but this is a large island."

Mea winced at those words. "You don't like to fly, Mea? Madagascar is too large an island to cross overland in a short time if that's required," Askara added quickly.

"I do not object to large jets, but the domestic planes we have here…they are small. Sometimes you wait for one or two weeks for them. Our air service is very poor."

"Oh, well, we may not need to fly at all. How about trains?"

"The train service is more reliable, not like in the UK but reliable enough. Also, we have bush taxis."

"Bush taxies? Perfect. I love them; use them often on trips."

Alistair broke in. "Here they're like small lorries that seat ten or twelve, with great Mercedes diesel engines. They go anywhere."

Dyan Dubois

"We'll wait and see what we need. So, Mea, when do we meet the family hosting the ceremony? Do you know them?"

"I could take you over this afternoon. It's on the northern edge of Tana, well, just beyond it, actually. But I am not sure if the monsignor has arranged a meeting with the family yet. We need his permission. I could call his secretary and ask. Monsignor Devereaux is a very busy man, as you might imagine. He may not even meet you in person. His secretary assistant handles much of the monsignor's business so that he can attend to sacred matters. His assistant's name is Father Gestang. Can we sit here in the hotel café, and I will explain some things over coffee?"

"Yes, just let me run upstairs for my notebook. I'll be back down in a few minutes. Darian and I will meet you in the café."

Walking back to their room, Askara asked Darian how he felt about Mea being the contact and translator. His reply surprised her. "I feel something is off, but I can't figure what. Can you?"

"Unfortunately, I don't think Mea is well. Her husband keeps staring at her like he wants to prop her up if she teeters on her high heels. She's a very nice woman; they are both nice, but she is hiding something. What? I have no idea."

"I think you need to contact the monsignor yourself, Askara. Don't rely on Ed Healy or Mea. They may not speak for him—should not, it seems to me. This could be a more delicate matter than you think."

"I'm so glad you're here with me. You always make things—well, clearer, not black-and-white rigid but easier to focus on. I love you, Sweetie."

"That has to be the strangest compliment you've ever given me. Thanks. You know I'm here for you…always. Let's get this project done and see the island. I especially want to visit the lemur reserve. Plus, we owe Sara a fun time when she joins us. I feel indebted to her for the way she supported you in East Africa."

When they joined Mea and Alistair, it appeared as if they interrupted an intense exchange. Mea looked on the verge of tears. Alistair's face, with tiny beads of sweat above his lip, was mottled crimson. Mea stammered at first but began by telling Askara she needed to understand the ceremony's importance and gravity, what it meant to the family hosting it, and what Askara could and could not do at the ceremony.

"You see," she began, "our country is not rich like America. Most of us survive on agriculture in one way or another. But we are a proud people, and we respect our ancestors above all else. To us, the dead are our link to our Creator, *Zanahary*. Most of us are Christians, Catholics, and Protestants in equal amounts. But we have a long history of traditional beliefs we combine with what the Christian missionaries taught. We have no problem with that. Outsiders might, but we don't. The dead are our way, our go-between, to contact our supreme god. Ancestors protect us; they heal us; they have the power to change our fortunes, for good or evil. We look at them as gods, our contact with the beyond.

People consider their ancestors more important than the living family, more deserving of respect, more needed. They make our daily lives better. We must show them honor to avoid great hardship," she said and teared up. "They can save a pregnancy, make a bountiful harvest, spare us from calamity, and protect us from disease. Our *razana*, our ancestors, determine our customs and ways of living with respect for our Supreme God. We all bow down to them. We honor them above all else."

Mea paused. "Does this make sense to you, Askara? Do you understand what I am saying?"

"Yes, you're very clear and direct. I intend to show absolute respect. But I am curious how your traditional beliefs blended with, say, Catholicism. In other parts of the world, the Catholic Church stamped out local beliefs."

"I am not sure. I know the first missionaries were Catholic since the French occupied the island, but later our queen turned against the Catholic Church, and many followed her and became Protestant. Initially, church missionaries wanted to bring us to the Christian god; they ignored our traditional beliefs, but at some point, the two flowed together."

Mea explained that the ceremony to honor the dead is also called the Bone Turning Ceremony or Walking the Dead, but the Malagasy word is *famadihana*. The tradition links the living to the dead in respectful remembrance, so every family who possibly can afford one must host a famadihana, even if it's thirty years or more since the relative died.

"Unfortunately, these ceremonies are expensive because the host has to feed the crowd of family and friends and buy new silk shrouds for rewrapping the remains. Silk material is costly in Madagascar. It's imported. A family avoids guilt and blame from others by hosting a famadihana, but here in the highlands, especially among the Merina and Betsileo people, this ceremony is the most important thing a family can ever do because it strengthens the link between the living family and the deceased relatives who reside in the world of spirit."

"What are you, Mea?" Askara asked.

"I'm Merina," she said. "My family has hosted one, and I have attended several. I know well how these go. I can guide you, so you do not make mistakes that could disgrace the family."

"Mea, why would anyone want an outsider to come to a sacred event like this and photograph it?"

"Many would not…ever. I imagine there is more to it in this case."

"What?"

"Money. You see, it is sometimes necessary for a family to seek help with the financial part, but they would not want others to know. Have you been asked to contribute?"

"No, but I haven't met with anyone here aside from you. The organization that hired me advised me not to contribute personally."

"Would paying money to the family change your mind?"

"No, not if I could afford it. But when would that come up? How much would they want?"

"When we visit the family, if they like you and approve of you, then they will ask for something. I imagine they will request a contribution for the silk shroud or for something. The food is ceremony food, and aside from the meat stew, it is not so expensive since many family members grow their vegetables. But they could ask for a contribution for food also. For you, it would not be more than one hundred US dollars. Would you agree to that?"

"Yes."

"I will let the family know. They will ask you to visit soon. The family's astrologer will set our meeting time and date since the ceremony's fate is ordained by the moon, sun, and stars. There is one thing I feel I should tell you now. The relative, in this case, died unhappily."

"Oh, I'm sorry to hear that."

"Because of that, the family would *not* want you to take a picture of his face. People would see his tears frozen for all time. They would know he carried sorrow. This ceremony is to make him happy. Then his tears will dry up and disappear. You can take pictures of the ceremony, but remember, do not photograph the deceased's head."

Askara didn't know what to say. She wondered, *Would a thirty-year-old corpse have a head? A skull, yes, but flesh? Do they embalm and preserve the skin?* She thought it better not to ask Mea specific questions. As it was, Mea looked very frail.

"Of course, I will do as they say. I will act with absolute respect. I want to ask the family if Darian and my friend Sara, who is coming to visit us, could attend. Can you find out for me?"

"I am sure they can come as your guests, but they will have to stand at a distance, out of respect for the family and friends who want to crowd close to the shroud. You can sit in the yard at the ceremonial dinner but not at reserved tables. Guests sit on grass mats on the ground. You three can do the same but sit beyond the local guests out of respect. They believe the closer they sit to the ancestor's family, the more benefit they derive. The guests will be happy to ask you questions. Do any of you speak French?"

"Not really."

Mea smiled. "Pantomime," she said and glanced at Alistair, who tipped his head toward the door. "We must go. I will come for you tomorrow. This afternoon, you secure church permission. The Monsignor will give his okay. He is only a formality. The family decides the rest. Oh, wear a long skirt and loose blouse; dress like we do in Western clothes when we visit them. The family will appreciate that respect. No jeans and T-shirt."

"Of course. Thank you for telling me. See you here at what time?"

"Be ready at ten. I'll come to the foyer for you. And bring Malagasy francs, not dollars. This first time, come alone," Mea said and made a weak smile in Darian's direction. "If the astrologer specifies another day, I will leave a message for you at the front desk, and we will reschedule, but I think they planned on this."

Mea emphasized that the family must feel comfortable with Askara; otherwise, Askara would have to look for another family, which might prove difficult. Mea told her to bring presents for the first meeting as a sign of respect: soaps, toothbrushes, matches, chocolates for the children, and maybe a bottle of rum for the adults. She stressed the family was giving Askara a chance few foreigners get—and they knew it. Askara must show respect. Mea acknowledged that the famadihana must seem an odd custom, but the goal was to honor the deceased's lifetime and spirit.

"Honoring the dead in this ceremonial way bestows great blessings on the family, ensures the ancestors will help the family from the other side, and elevates their prestige in the community. The greatest honor of life is respect for the dead," she said, her tired voice barely a whisper by the time she finished.

Askara paused before replying. "Is it respect for the process of death, Mea, or for the dead?"

"The dead never die. They take spirit form as ancestors. The act of death dies with every passing, but the ancestor lives on. It's ultimately respect for our Creator, Zanahary."

"But is death something that takes a perceptible form, other than the remains? Is there something I will see at the ceremony, like a ghost or something?"

"Only the dead know, or their loved ones to whom the relative speaks or maybe appears. You won't see anything.

Every Malagasy who *walks* at the ceremony wants to know: What do the ancestors know? What do they say? Possibly one of them will see his ghost."

"If someone gets an answer, do they tell?"

"No. Death loves silence. A flapping mouth is hushed before the words can leave."

Alistair, looking both bored and nervous, chimed in. "It's better to view this rubbish as an anthropological element, a custom of a culture that hasn't entered the twentieth century. Many claim to have spoken with death, but they can't repeat what was said. I figure there isn't a sane one amongst 'em."

"Alistair!" Mea said with hurt surprise. "Don't say such things; you'll anger the ancestors and bring ruin on our heads."

Alistair patted Mea on her bony shoulder. "Sorry, Love, this is the part of your people I can't stick. You know I am very fond of them, but this...." Mea recoiled from his touch, avoiding his eyes.

"Why?" Askara said. "This is a respected custom, isn't it, Alistair?"

"Oh, yes, very much, probably the strongest one, but the mix of Christianity and paganism—I just don't get."

Mea quickly added, "It has developed over time, but possibly you need to be more open to it. You see, Alistair converted to Islam, Askara, and the small Muslim population here does not observe this."

Alistair's face reddened, making his light hair blanch in comparison to his face's splotchy crimson. "Muslims nowhere would observe this. But I *was* more open to it, remember, until your uncle asked me to help pay for his father's exhumation— not contribute, but pay for the entire thing."

"We'll talk about this later," Mea said with a disgruntled look, thin furrows rippling her brow.

They nodded, stood up, said goodbye, and quickly walked away. After paying the bill, Askara and Darian remained seated. They heard Mea and Alistair arguing in the foyer before they exited the hotel. When they walked past the front desk, Askara paused to decipher the French newspaper headline of the morning paper. A slight European man with a pencil-line mustache and wearing a black beret approached her.

"Pardon, *parlez vous francais*?"

"No, English," Askara said with a smile.

"I would like to invite you and your husband to enjoy breakfast with me. I love to practice speaking English. I am a French local. Jean-Paul is my name."

Darian introduced himself and shook hands. "Here?" Darian said and pointed to the café.

"No, a few doors down the avenue. A boutique restaurant, *très bon*, if you please."

"Yes. My wife Askara and I would be happy to join you."

WHEN THEY ENTERED THE BISTRO, THE STAFF PERKED up upon seeing the elderly man and gave them the best table by the front window. Askara wondered if he owned the restaurant or if Jean-Paul was a local favorite with the French-speaking downtown set.

"Ah, well," the elderly man said as he took his seat, shook out the white linen napkin with a snap, and draped it across his dark suit, tucking a corner into his shirt collar to secure it.

"I am Jean-Paul, as I said, very pleased to speak with you."

"I'm Askara Timlen, and this is my husband, Darian Dalal. Thank you for inviting us."

"What brought you to our faraway island? I think you are Canadian from your accent. Yes?"

"No. American. My husband is East Indian, from Bombay. I'm a photojournalist. I've come here on a work assignment."

Jean-Paul sloshed his coffee into the saucer and took tiny sips, careful not to spill a drop. "The lemur project? The world is fascinated by these creatures."

"Yes, I might work with a crew on that project too, but my main reason for coming is to write about the Walking the Dead ceremony."

Jean-Paul lowered the saucer from his mouth to study Askara, his deep-set brown eyes shaded by bushy gray eyebrows. "Strange custom, one of the strangest."

"Have you attended one?"

"Oui, years back. I would not do it again."

"Why?"

Jean-Paul leaned forward to speak in a throaty whisper, "More gets exhumed than bones! Nasty business."

"What do you mean?"

"I cannot say exactly, but I was glad when the bones were laid to rest. For weeks after, however, I had terrifying dreams."

"About what?" Askara said, goosebumps rising on her arms.

"Strange things, ghosts, I imagine is how you would describe them. Swirling, cold vapors that made my stomach lurch. One touched me; a bony finger pushed into my chest. The coldness burned a scar in my flesh. I still have it."

Askara, overcome by curiosity, said, "Can I see?"

"Askara!" Darian said, shocked.

"Madame, please. Leave this old man some dignity."

"I'm so sorry. That was rude, but would you describe it to me?"

"It is here," he said, pointing to the center of his chest, just below the sternum bone, "like a hot-iron brand, a circular shape with a crescent halo. The chest hairs were singed and never grew back. I feel like a branded sheep." Jean-Paul blinked and lowered his voice further. "This may sound strange to you, but sometimes the mark aches, and it always happens on the same day of the month that I attended the ceremony, a Tuesday—not every month but the same day nonetheless."

Askara began to view her tablemate differently—he was not just an old man but also an adept spinner of tales. She wondered at his talent for entertainment, assuming his next gesture would be to sign on as her guide, with no small number of francs as compensation.

"Jean-Paul, few foreigners are admitted to view the ceremony, right?"

"Oui."

"The family still has to approve of me when I meet them. If they do, then they let the Monsignor know. If he approves, then I'm good to go. But I have to do as my translator, a Malagasy woman, says—exactly as she says. When we get there, if the family decides I cannot go, I have to leave the gifts for them, then walk away with no complaint, even though I have come so far to do this, and not bother the Monsignor by trying to beg for the assignment. Is that usual? How did you go to one, Jean-Paul?"

"I had to go. I was part of the family. I paid for the exhumation silks. The deceased was my wife's grandfather. I had no choice, you see, but I told my dear Pauly—Paulette was her full name—my dear Malagasy wife, when she lay

Dyan Dubois

dying some ten years back, that I would never exhume her or permit anyone else to. She cried and cried, begging me to reconsider. I said, 'no,' and that was that."

"Even though she wanted it so badly? Even though it's an honor to do it?"

"I don't think she knew her mind. She had seen the torment I went through. How could she want that for me again? As to the honor, I guess I don't believe in that. My French Catholic blood runs too thick in my veins. That is one custom here that I do not sanction."

A young waiter with a tray of croissants, butter, and jam came to refill their cups. Askara smiled and thanked him, but he remained, staring at his feet for an awkward second until Jean-Paul dismissed him.

"What torment?" Askara leaned forward and asked in a hushed voice.

The Frenchman's saggy eyelids welled with tears. He dabbed them with a clean corner of the cloth napkin draped on his chest. "After that ceremony, I was never the same, mentally. I suffered a breakdown some four months later that haunts me even today. I worked in government service, and the breakdown nearly cost me my job; I had to go on leave for a year," he said, wincing as the sun broke through the stained-glass peacock window and cast blue-green streaks on his parchment skin.

Darian sighed audibly to get Askara's attention and knitted his brows at her. He made a subtle motion for them to leave. She ignored it.

"I'm so sorry. Losing a loved one is terrible, especially after an entire life together."

"Jean-Paul dabbed his mustache and said, "You don't know."

"What? Why that scared you so much? Or what loss is?"

"Her grandfather…his spirit rose out of a swirling white mist. It was he who burned his cold, searing finger in my chest, telling me I had angered the ancestors because my people—the French settlers, he meant—had murdered innocents, and I would have to pay for their sins."

"How?"

"He did not say. I worried for my wife and children until I broke down. Nothing of a drastic nature happened to them. As time passed, I reconciled to the ceremony. My doctor dismissed it as a flutter of the heart that cut off blood to my brain, but I will never go to that ceremony again, much less participate in any way. Now I am old. I never thought I would see this old age, but here I am. I have grown children, and they have grown children. My Pauly lived long enough to enjoy a few of them. All my family, but one, lives here in Madagascar. The stray sheep moved to London and married, yet she is dearest to my heart."

"Possibly you misunderstood the ceremony, monsieur?" Darian asked.

"No, I comprehended what I saw, what I felt. God's mercy on my poor soul brought me back. It is not right to retrieve a soul from its resting place. I know that now. I had been born a chaste Catholic in France, and I shall die a chaste Catholic in Madagascar. If I fell into a wayward life with Malagasy Christianity, I have atoned."

"But Catholics here, don't they blend the old beliefs with their own?" Askara asked, remembering Mea's words.

"Why yes, more than most, but is it correct to do so? Where else in the world do Christians exhume their dead to parade them around the village, showing them new huts, plowed fields, children, and the like to gain the favor of ancestors and bring blessings to the living family?"

"Nowhere that I know of."

"Exactly. Only in Indonesia, but certainly not in any civilized European country."

Jean-Paul pulled the napkin from his collar, dabbed along his pencil line mustache, and rose from the table. "I would like to stay and dine with you, but I must go. Please, enjoy yourselves as my guests. I will inform the staff. You may want to reconsider the ceremony, madame, for your own best interest. If you continue, I wish you and your husband well. *Au revoir*," he said, bowing slightly before rattling off in French to the maître d'. With silver-tipped cane in hand, Jean-Paul exited the small bistro.

"Well, that was odd," Darian said, looking at Askara's hand trembling on the handle of her coffee cup. "Don't take him seriously. I believe he told us the truth, but he's had a stroke and has some brain damage. Nice old guy, just a bit off in the head."

"Darian, really? How could he make that up?'

"He must have heard us in the hotel café or heard Mea and Alistair arguing in the foyer. Clever guy. He even mentioned someone that fit Mea's description. I'm sure everyone here knows everyone else, even though Tana has—what, seven million people? The downtown set with French connections is much smaller, probably still a colonial club."

Darian's rational appraisal made Askara feel better, but she wondered why anyone would bother to share a story like that. He even teared up about his deceased wife, Pauly. Askara decided to verify something. She called over the maître d'.

"Bonjour, monsieur. Are we to eat here, like the man said, as his guest? Do you know him well?"

"Oui, madame. His family used to own this bistro. His wife Paulette was the first chef many years back. She trained the chef we have now. Let me bring the menu. Everything is excellent, you will see. Jean-Paul often treats foreigners to meals here, his way of honoring his wife and building goodwill. I believe, madame, Monsieur Jean-Paul desired a word with you outside," he said and nodded to the entrance. "The waiter will return to take your order shortly. We are at your service. *Bon appetit!*"

Askara saw Jean-Paul slumped against the entrance wall to the restaurant, relaxing in the shade, balanced on his cane. She told Darian to order for her and that she would be right back. When Askara approached Jean-Paul, he pressed a small worn bottle into her hand as if he were only greeting her. She glanced at it and started to ask what it was, assuming it was an old perfume bottle he had picked up at a thrift store when he placed his splotchy hand over hers and closed her fingers tightly around the little bottle.

"Keep this safe. It means very much to me, and someday it may mean very much to you. Do not talk of it to others, only to the younger priest, Gestang. Contact him."

"Okay," Askara answered, finding his hand cold, his demeanor awkward, and his request oblique.

"I go to close the door. *Le Pierre est très important. Le temple est guarded.* Look to the house of Anjou. Like a phoenix, I rise." He paused and followed his gray mustache with a finger as if it could take him on a journey. "I tell you this to protect my granddaughter's unborn child, the one closest to the door."

With those words, he patted her hand and turned to walk away. Askara started to follow him to ask questions but halted. She stuffed the little bottle into her dress pocket and returned to Darian.

CHAPTER FOUR

Seeking Permission

⁂

Askara prepared for her visit to the family of the deceased. She arranged silver foil-wrapped chocolates, brightly colored toothbrushes, small Crest tubes, Bic pens, and little soaps in a gift box. She thought they seemed odd items to ingratiate herself, a foreigner, to capture the family's most sacred ceremony. For the family's matriarch, she included a sizeable contribution of money, by Malagasy standards, from Ed Healy, who hoped to film a documentary of the ceremony while Askara took still photos.

Askara didn't want to mix her opportunity with his, but she felt she owed him something since he and her professor were friends from San Francisco. Ed told Askara she would be his best chance, a great opener, with her tawny skin. Askara had looked at him, taken a deep breath, and let it go.

A knock at the door signaled time to leave. Askara glanced at the clock, precisely 2:00 p.m. Thinking *Mea's punctual*, Askara opened the door to find her looking even thinner in her dark-colored, A-line skirt and white blouse.

"Ready, Askara?"

"Yes," Askara said, lifting the gift box. I have everything."

"Oh, could you leave your necklace and rings here?"

"Why?"

"You don't want to look like a rich foreigner. Let me check the gifts." Mea looked over the items and said, "Good. This will help; you will see."

"Doesn't the family want the ceremony documented?"

"No, not really. They may agree, but not without reservation. Some members are afraid."

"Of what?"

"Offending the ancestors, especially by bringing foreigners. For that reason, for today, your husband could not join us. We must ask their permission for him and your friend to attend—that is, once they approve of you."

"Okay. I get it…sort of."

"I explained to them that you are all Christians, like us, but still they worry. People are superstitious. But it would be terrible if the ancestors got upset. A family I know on the north end of Tana suffered greatly after a ceremony. Apparently, the ancestor was very displeased because the family put on an elaborate feast to show off, hoping to discover where the deceased had hidden his valuables—not out of respect for him but out of greed."

"How would anyone know that?"

"From the series of mishaps. The granddaughter broke her foot, the rain came in torrents that evening although the astrologer had picked the day to be sunny and bright, the newly planted seeds washed away, and worst of all, a snake slithered into the house and bit the deceased's sister."

"All that during the ceremony?"

"No, over the next three years."

"But things like that could happen and be a normal part of life."

"Almost everyone knew it was the old man, the ancestor. There was an argument. Half the village said it was the old man; the other half said *no*. The local priest said *no*; the family's astrologer said *yes*. People lined up behind one or the other. It caused many conflicts in the village."

Askara considered her words carefully. "Well, some things should be forgotten since you can't go back and change what has happened. You have to move on, go forward in life."

"Westerners think like that. You go from A to B to C, or from past to present to future. But the Malagasy believe you can go from future to present to past, back again, and even jump around in time. Life works backward, forward, and sideways."

"I agree, time is fluid to some degree. But in a specific event like the ceremony, how can you go from future to past to future again?"

"Well, look at that family. They planned for the future, for years, to have the ceremony. Now the ceremony is in the past, but it affects the family's future, possibly for generations, because of how it went. So, if they can host another one and do it to that ancestor's satisfaction, it will erase the past, correct the present, and change the future. It could bring them good luck."

"So, Malagasy people feel what the family does in the Bone Turning Ceremony can affect the family for generations?"

"Yes. That is why it is so important that we do this right and make the family happy, for everyone's sake. Let's go. It will take a while to get there. I saw Imboule parked at the front, but he can't be the one to drive us to their house today. Imboule isn't Christian. I hired someone else, my friend who is Christian."

"I never thought of that," Askara replied, wondering if she would fit the family's definition of Christian. She didn't want to mention Darian being Parsi. How could she explain that? *At least Sara is Catholic*, she thought. "I'll pay you back for the driver."

"I will add it to my bill."

———————— ❧ ————————

THE RIDE ACROSS TANA TOOK FORTY MINUTES ON CON-gested boulevards. They drove past French-style houses with tile roofs that looked like a child's game of blocks strewn across the undulating hills. The main road gave way to narrow lanes in shanty dwellings that became rutted dirt pathways, hardly wide enough for the small taxi. By the time they reached the family's house, a brick-and-mortar building set in a compound of three homes joined by a communal tin roof, Askara began to worry that she might not make an appropriate impression.

Children played in the red dirt, kicking pebbles, cre-ating an orange haze until they spotted the taxi at the gate. A small boy darted off, shouting. A gray-haired man who emerged to greet the taxi spoke to Mea in Malagasy, ignoring Askara. The children giggled and encircled the guests until one sharp word from the man scattered them like sparrows. They gathered again near the compound wall to watch silently while Mea and Askara walked into the house.

Askara sat quietly in the front room, listening. The man chattered away to Mea, stopping periodically to look in Askara's direction with a stern expression, his brow cracked like a dry riverbed. Askara made mental notes, too afraid to pull out her notebook in case that displeased the man.

He spoke to Mea in an increasingly emphatic tone. Askara assumed things were not going well.

"He wants to know if you are French," Mea said, facing Askara. The man gesticulated with sharp hand movements, spitting his words rapidly. "He doesn't like the French."

"No, tell him I am East Indian and American."

The venom drained from the man's face when Mea translated. At the end of their conversation, Mea turned to Askara. "He likes you, but he wants to see your hands and your camera. He noticed it in your bag. You weren't supposed to bring it today."

Askara reached into her bag and pulled out her Canon F-1. "I forgot to unload it. Sorry."

The man held the camera up in his large hands, turning it on every axis, but he never popped the cap to look through the viewfinder. Solemnly, he handed it back to Mea with a nod. Then he motioned for Askara's hands. He didn't touch them. He looked at her upturned palms while he spoke to Mea.

"He says you have a kind heart. That's good. He approves of you."

Realizing the small tape recorder might be difficult, Askara, explained to Mea why she would use it. Mea translated. A conversation between her and the man sounded like an argument, so Askara withdrew the small black rectangle with its dangling microphone and handed it to the man.

"Tell him I'll use this to record the ceremony, the singing, the music."

Mea translated. The man's brow wrinkled into multiple grooves; his voice thundered against the wall. "He wants to see it work."

"Tell him to sing something."

The man grinned and belted out a *hiragasy* song. He rattled on, gesticulating dramatically in front of the small recorder, while he stared at the little red light on the machine. When he stopped a few minutes later, he sat like a marionette abandoned by the puppet master, all legs and arms folded upon themselves, his face frozen but expectant.

Askara said, "Now tell him I will play it back. It captured his voice, and I will use it to capture the music and words of the ceremony just like this." She started the tape.

The man flew from his stool, eyes wide, grinning, dancing to his voice, and whirling around and around. He grabbed the recorder from Askara's hand to hold it up close to his ear. He laughed. He cradled the little black box in his large, calloused hand when he spoke to Mea.

"He likes it. He wants you to give it to him."

"I will, after the ceremony. Before I leave, I'd love to."

Happy with the translated reply, the man patted the box and handed it back to Askara with a smile.

"He likes you. He says the ancestor will be pleased. No one in the village has done this. He asks that you give it only to him, not to anyone else, especially not to his brother."

"Agreed," Askara said and handed him the box of gifts. "Thank you." She started to tell Mea of Ed Healy's offer, but Mea hushed Askara immediately.

Askara felt confident that she would write an exciting story but felt less sure about the photographs. When Mea explained photography to the man, he demanded that Askara take no pictures of his deceased grandfather. The living should not capture the face of the dead, he insisted. Askara knew the Christian Coalition of Catholic Churches expected her to do a photo essay.

"Please assure him I will not photograph the deceased's head, only the outer shroud, and that will be from a distance. I must have at least a few shots of the procession holding up the shroud. The others can be of the participants, the ceremonial meal, the dancing, and singing. Can I photograph the tomb?"

"Yes, that is allowed. He wants you to swear on the Bible."

The man walked away and returned with what appeared to be a King James version in Malagasy. He motioned for her to place her hand on it. He mumbled something. Askara replied in English that she swore not to photograph the ancestor, only the shroud. Mea translated her pledge, so the man smiled and placed the book down on the table to shake Askara's hand. Mea nodded, implying time to leave to Askara, who smiled, thanked him, and followed Mea to the taxi waiting at the gate. She watched the man hand out silver-wrapped chocolates to the children, who began leaping up and down like frogs to get the candy.

Pensive on the drive back to the hotel, Askara realized she had not thought about how she would react to the actual exhumation...until now. Would it be creepy? The man's grandfather had died years back. What would the condition of the corpse be? Would there be a corpse or only a skeleton? Would it stink? She knew that even if it did, she had to ignore the smell. She had once seen a corpse two days old, and that was horrifying, as much for the makeup as for the supine pose, hands crossed on the chest as if he would rest comfortably for eternity in that satin-lined box. The image had never left her.

She figured this family must be wealthy by Malagasy standards—rich enough to host a ceremony. Some families struggled for years to save the money for the mandatory silk shroud—but this man was clever also. He had figured a way to get a foreign contribution to make the ceremony possible.

Ed Healy had informed her a missionary associated with the Catholic coalition had met the family years back when the deceased helped build a church on the island. When the family appealed to them for help, the coalition decided a story on this oddest of Christian practices would interest and alarm the many thousands of subscribers to the *Catholic Coalition News Magazine*.

The coalition granted permission for the article, terming the investment "compensation for previous labor," a face-saving gesture for the family in the eyes of Tana society, and a way for the coalition to eliminate jealousy and prevent others from requesting help. Askara realized the family didn't need Ed Healy's money. That would only muddy their intent in the eyes of the village. Askara was surprised Ed had even tried.

Two days later, when Mea received notice that the family submitted the final approval to Monsignor Devereaux, who had signed it immediately, they announced the ceremony would take place on the second Saturday of the month, as required by the family astrologer. Askara felt relieved everything was a go. Since there was a time lag, she asked Darian if, after Sara arrived, he wanted to leave Tana to see more of the island before the ceremony.

"We have a free week. How about visiting the coast and a lemur reserve, take an environmental tour—you know, be tourists?"

"When does Sara arrive today?"

"Her plane is due in at four this afternoon. Imboule will drive us to the airport."

Darian agreed the coast was a good idea, but first, they should show Sara a bit of Tana. "We've seen little of the city ourselves," he remarked.

At the airport, Askara spotted Sara from a distance, recognizing her swagger immediately. Askara smiled and waved from the lounge window. In return, Sara made large loops in the air like she was flagging down a truck.

Darian smiled, "Very animated, as you said."

"Very, you'll see."

When Sara stepped through the lounge door, Askara grabbed her and gave her a big hug.

"Bloody hell, you've gotten stronger, Askara. Must be working out. Ah, here he is—Darian, the man I heard about often while escaping our lynching, listening to hyenas, and crossing no man's land, being thwacked by acacia limbs. Thought you were a figment, maybe a full-on hallucination. Good to meet ya, Darian. I'm Sara."

Darian leaned in and gave Sara a polite hug. "No need to say your name; it's emblazoned in my mind by your most loyal fan. Very pleased to meet you. I am so glad you have come."

Sara beamed. "Well, Askara, hope you don't have crazy adventures set up. Don't think I can make it through a rerun of Africa."

"Nope, all's quiet. We're so glad you've come to join us in Madagascar. What a place. We haven't seen much, but now that you're here—well, we're planning some outings. First, let's get you settled at our hotel and plan where to go for dinner. I'll explain the rest."

Later, when discussing dinner, Sara insisted on eating local food. "It's one of the best ways to meet the people. Eat what they like where they like it; works every time." The concierge tried to influence them to choose fine French restaurants, probably because he would get a kickback, Sara said, but she pushed for Malagasy food.

"We're close to the Zoma Market, walking distance if you're not too tired," Darian said. "There are many eating establishments that feature local favorites in that area."

"Hmm…eating establishments? Darian, are you worried I want to eat off grass mats on the ground? Relax, that's tomorrow, not tonight. I just want local cuisine. I'm ready for a good nosh."

They walked the noisy streets to the enormous market. The hills above the market, packed with French colonial-style houses and commercial buildings stacked one on top of another, reached the city's highest point where the Queen's Palace, with its corner towers and church spire, gleamed in the late afternoon light.

They chose a restaurant, realizing there was no need for a reservation, plus it was too early for dinner, so they walked into the market. They crisscrossed from the central plaza to adjoining alleys and looped back, so they wouldn't get lost in the maze of stalls. Many of the vendors were closing shop, but a few smiled and waved the tourists over to see their produce: tomatoes as large as grapefruits, cabbage the size of soccer balls, mounds of finger-long red or green chilis, thick clumps of gnarled ginger root, and squawking chickens and turkeys crammed into woven baskets.

Sara admired the produce, complimented the vendors on their crops, especially the golden-red squash and purple eggplants, but explained she had no way to cook, so she couldn't purchase anything. The vendors didn't understand her, but that didn't stop them from bargaining until the three foreigners drifted away.

As the setting sun faded to dusty rose, they found the handicraft section of embroidered woven fabrics, leather goods, wood carvings, and polished gemstones. Askara walked around several stalls looking at stones while Sara gravitated to the leather goods, studying the crocodile handbags, belts, and satchels. When Askara stopped at a kiosk of board games, Darian joined her.

"Look at these. Rosewood boards and rounds of polished stones—quartz, petrified wood, marble, feldspar, pyrite, opaline—and this one is guinea fowl jasper. See, the surface looks like interlocked feathers. The vendor beamed and spoke in a mixture of Creole and rudimentary English, which Askara didn't understand. He slipped behind a burlap curtain and brought out a game board twenty-four inches across with polished balls of amethyst, citrine, rose, smoky, and crystal quartz resting in shallow wells.

"For you, madame, special, only two hundred thousand francs, pleased to you."

Darian whispered but stopped when an American man stepped up to them and said in a booming voice, "I bought one like that yesterday for one hundred fifty thousand francs."

Askara and Darian turned. The large man stood beside a smiling woman who reprimanded him, "Oh, John, hush. You're gonna ruin it. Let her haggle."

Hearing that, Sara approached but drifted away again when a snakeskin satchel caught her eye.

"Hell no, I'm not. I'm just tellin' her where she'll do better."

The vendor grimaced, seeing Askara put the amethyst ball down, and countered, "Madame, one hundred eighty thousand francs Malagasy, special to you."

Askara asked the American man, "What do you think?"

"Not worth it. There are better sets."

Askara thanked the vendor and asked the American couple, "Have you been all through the market?"

The woman's short, curly hair reflected rosy sunlight when she shook her head to reply. "No, not all the way. It's huge. We spent the entire afternoon yesterday and only saw one-third of the Zoma."

"Is it good?"

"Good? Amazing. Things from all over Africa: carvings, fabrics, jewelry, utensils, musical instruments, art, everything. Would you like to walk with us? We've been warned—*safety in numbers.*" Elaine smiled, looking up at her companion, "Not that I worry much with John towering over me, but since it's late, please join us."

"Sure." Askara motioned Sara over from the kiosk, where she was haggling over a leather wallet.

The tall man thrust out his massive hand. "John Stevens and this is my better half, Elaine."

"I'm Askara Timlen Dalal, my husband Darian Dalal, and our friend from Australia, Sara Sanford."

"That fella's not very happy; lost a sale," John said, looking at the vendor.

"Maybe not," Askara said, "I might make him an offer after looking around. He'll be ready to compromise. I knew it was too expensive."

"Guess I shouldn't have busted in. I thought you didn't know."

"No, that was great. Totally unscripted. Now when I return, he'll be easy to deal with."

The group walked on with John in the lead. He turned to Sara and said, "Australia, that's great. I'm from Texas. I think we both like open space. This market's too crowded for me."

"Got that right, and the wildlife here is either flayed or stuffed. Did you see the croc back there?"

"Nope. Alive or boots?"

"Boots with teeth."

"You're kidding," John replied and broke into a boisterous laugh.

"Fair dinkum," Sara said with a grin.

The vendors' large white canvas umbrellas, like gigantic flowers, started folding in the dimming light. Whitewashed colonial houses above them faded in the last rays of the sun.

John glanced at Darian. "Got your money and passports hidden?"

"Yes."

"Good thing. The guide yesterday warned us this market is a den of thieves."

"They always say that…and then did the man offer you a discounted rate for him to guide you safely through the market?"

"No, he wanted to go home. He said if you come back to the market, don't wear jewelry or a watch or carry important things. And don't stay late."

"Oh," Askara said, turning her diamond ring to the inside. "Good advice."

"John wears a necklace his best friend Gary made for him—see," Elaine said, pulling the chain out from his collar. "Gary teaches at the industrial arts school in Detroit, where John teaches. It's a sign of lasting friendship, commemorates their scuba dives. Gary soldered it closed—no clasp—you know, for divers. We do a lot of scuba diving. I left my jewelry in the hotel safe."

John pulled the gold link chain from his shirt to show the design—two leaping porpoises nose to nose. "My buddy went on sixteen dives with us in the Caymans."

"Do you still dive?" Sara asked.

"Every chance we get. Elaine and I joined the dive club in Mauritius…went out last week on the southern end of the island, had to leave though. American Marines were conducting a drill. Clearing sea urchins, they said."

Sara burst out laughing. "That's what your military does?"

Elaine butted in. "John, it's a goodwill project. They clear the beach of sea urchins to help promote tourism."

"Yeah," John replied, "that's what the boat captain said. They were too far out, beyond the reef, when I saw them."

Askara's interest piqued. "You think it's a military operation? Do you know much about the Diego Garcia Island near Mauritius?"

"The military post?" John said. "Not much. I do know the locals don't like Americans being there."

"Is it for nuclear testing?"

"No," John said with a laugh. "It's convenient for keeping an eye on the Indian Ocean, for whatever that's worth, but it's too far from the Middle East to be a good base of operation, in my opinion. Unless they're spying on sea urchins."

Elaine sped up the group, navigating quickly past caged chickens, stinking fish, and piles of eels to an interior pathway where she spotted more leather goods—belts, purses, wallets, and satchels. Turning to Askara, she held up a bag, "Not bad. A knockoff of Prada for a few bucks."

They rounded a cluster of umbrellas for the exit to the boulevard when a dark figure sailed by them in mid-air. John stumbled forward and groaned. A second man rushed from the left, leaped high, and yanked John's necklace off his neck. Elaine screamed.

"Bastard!" John shouted, reaching for his throat. "He got my necklace." Elaine touched the burn mark on his neck that

Dyan Dubois

oozed droplets of blood. "I didn't see them coming; they were so fast. Shit-eating bastards! They broke my necklace."

"Look at the horrified faces on the vendors," Elaine said, motioning at the staring crowd rattling away in Malagasy.

An elderly woman hobbled forward from her umbrella, abandoning her quacking ducks crammed in wicker cages, to speak to them in Malagasy. When they answered in English, she retreated to her blanket and whispered to a young boy seated beside her who darted off at a dead run.

Elaine and John led the group to look for an exit, with Askara, Darian, and Sara walking close behind. They had gone only a short distance before a man in a black beret cocked sideways on his Jimi Hendrix Afro, in faded blue jeans and a blue jean jacket, accosted them. He flashed a broad smile and produced a badge from his jacket pocket.

"I am Antananarivo Police Officer Ejema, here to serve you," he said in English with a Creole patois. "Someone attacked you?"

"Yes," John replied. "How'd you get here so fast?"

"We will catch this thief. My men follow them now. No worries. What was stolen?"

"My gold necklace."

"You are with this group, yes? You must all come with me to the police station. We make a report. You declared the necklace when you landed in Madagascar?"

"No."

"No?" Ejema said with horrified surprise. "Why not?"

"I didn't think about it. I always wear it. I declared everything else." Askara looked at John and fingered the undeclared amethyst necklace under her T-shirt.

"This will make the case difficult. We need proof the thief stole something of value."

"Ask the vendors; they saw it, about twenty of them."

"They will not say. They are scared of market thieves too."

"Let's forget it!" John said. He turned to Elaine and whispered, "Let's go. This is a lost cause." He politely said to Officer Ejema, "I don't want to go to the police station and file a report, but thanks for coming so quickly to check on us."

"My men were following you. We saw the thieves track you. They disappeared from our sight just before the attack."

From the way Ejema paced around John and the others, it was clear he took his job seriously, creating a human shield to protect the foreigners, although no threat was apparent. The duck vendor approached, rattling away, her gummed lips smacking in excitement.

Ejema continued, "You see, not everyone is afraid. This old woman identified the man who robbed you. She sent her grandson to bring us. We must file the report. You will now need an authorized police signature on the customs form to leave the country, with or without your necklace. You failed to register it. In the eyes of the law, you brought it in illegally. Either way, my pleasure is to help. Let's go, all of you."

Ejema and four plainclothes policemen escorted them through the market to the locals' rapt attention since they immediately recognized the undercover policeman Ejema. They fired questions at him as the group passed. Ejema nodded and smiled.

Darian advised Askara and Sara to say nothing unless asked, reminding them this was John's problem and that they should have dinner and return to the hotel as fast as possible.

When Ejema burst through the station door, head held high, the milling crowd in the hall stared at John, Elaine, Askara, and Sara—John's height alone a cause for wonder. Ejema ordered the gawkers to hush their mumbling.

"What do you think they're saying?" Sara whispered to Askara. "It's times like these that I wish I knew the language. Remember what happened to us last time, the Blue Nile nightmare."

"Shh, I get part of it," Askara said, "something in Creole about the foreigner easy to spot like a tree."

"Great, they see us as easy targets! It should be fun getting back to the hotel intact," Sara whispered.

Ejema escorted them to a raised platform where John stood level with the seated police captain on a dais to explain the events. Ejema, in a suppliant posture, removed his beret. The banter went back and forth between him and the captain for half an hour, marked by bold gestures and tonal peaks and valleys before Ejema turned and told the others to sit behind him while he continued his report.

Askara leaned over to Darian. "Somehow, I think the story is becoming much more involved. We should walk out."

John attempted to break in, but Ejema waved him down. The conversation raged on. Finally, after twenty minutes, Ejema turned to them. "Now we prepare the release papers. Follow me."

Walking down the crowded hall, they turned to enter a small office where two men sat at a square black wooden table, with blisters of paint rising like patterns on a tortoiseshell. Ejema spoke rapidly as the younger of the two typed at great speed on an ancient manual typewriter that filled the room with reverberating key strikes and grating, aggressive carriage returns. After several minutes, the clerk wrenched the paper free of the machine and handed it to the man next to him for a signature, who in turn passed it to Ejema for his signature. Ejema then gave it to John.

"What's this?"

"A request to amend your customs declaration to include the missing necklace. Without that, we cannot continue. You must show you owned it before you can report it stolen."

"Okay," John said, signing the form. "What's next?"

"The police report."

"Sorry about all this," Askara said, rising. "I hope you get this sorted out, but we have to go."

"Madame, you are witnesses to a crime. You cannot leave."

"John's wife is the witness. She saw it."

"Sit!" Ejema ordered. With a quick eye movement, he directed them to the left.

Askara slumped into the rickety chair and grimaced at Elaine, who seemed increasingly concerned about what was coming next. Policeman Ejema continued to fill out a report, stopping to question John more often, the women and Darian less. Askara checked her watch, wondering if they should return to the hotel to eat.

"Thank you for your patience, monsieur," the captain said to John. "I hope the remainder of your stay is pleasant. We will contact you at your hotel tomorrow with your copy of the customs papers, and I hope to return your necklace at that time. This gang works in the Zoma market. Their luck has run out. We will find where they hide like rats and surprise them."

Before Askara could speak, Ejema walked out the door to a corridor full of people clamoring for his attention like he was a rock star; in fact, his cool swagger again reminded Askara of Jimi Hendrix. His assistant escorted John, Elaine, Askara, Darian, and Sara to the glass double door exit.

"Sorry, the afternoon turned out like this," John said to Darian, folding the documents and stuffing them into his shirt pocket. "Meeting us took up your evening too. You should take a taxi directly to your hotel. It's not safe at night here. We enjoyed meeting you."

"Don't apologize. It wasn't your fault," Askara said. "Sometimes bad things happen to good people." With raised eyebrows, she looked at Sara.

"But I feel bad we wasted your time and all. Look, Elaine and I are planning a trip to Toamasina on the coast. If you'd like to come along, we'd love to have you. We'd like to treat you to dinner there. I think, from what we've seen, there's safety in numbers, and you are enjoyable company, all of you."

"When are you going?" Darian asked.

"We bought tickets for the Wednesday eight a.m. train," Elaine said.

"You're not flying? I thought the coast was pretty far."

"Only about one hundred and forty miles." John laughed. "Plus, domestic flights are a joke. A friend told us they might have return bookings every two weeks or so from certain towns, if at all. We want to see more of the island than the capital city. Well, what do you say?"

"Sounds good," Sara said. "The more the merrier."

"I have an appointment at the Catholic church tomorrow, so Wednesday works great for us," Askara said.

"Settled then," Darian said, shaking John's hand. "We'll book tickets for the eight a.m. train and see you at the station Wednesday. Good night."

———— ✿ ————

THE FOLLOWING MORNING, ASKARA ASKED DARIAN IF he would mind if she and Sara slipped out to the Bijou Café for early coffee. He smiled and replied he would think it odd if they didn't catch up on each other's lives in private.

They weren't due at the church until ten, so they would have plenty of time to chat before the meeting with Monsignor Deveraux.

Askara could feel Darian and Sara were shy of one another. She knew it was her fault. Too much building up by Askara had made each feel they wouldn't measure up. Askara knew, with a little bit more time, they would click.

Askara struggled with a flood of confusing memories that cascaded in her brain when Sara arrived: disjointed images and bits of remembered or maybe imagined conversations. An ominous feeling crept around her, and for some reason, Sara's presence exacerbated it. Things didn't add up. She couldn't bridge the gaps. She wasn't sure what lay in the crevices that separated what she clearly recalled and the darkness that clung to those thoughts.

She sensed Darian felt her confusion. She wished she were soldered together like the porpoises of John's stolen necklace. But even John's chain had broken. Her intangible recollections could as well. She wondered, *What would be left?*

Sitting down at the café, Askara and Sara both ordered a robust French roast. After a couple of sips, Sara's eyes brightened. "I like your bloke, nice guy. I can see why you married him."

"I'm so glad. I noticed you two have hardly spoken to one another. I worried my two favorite people in the world... well, maybe wouldn't jive. And, Sara, we're not legally married yet. Something went wrong with the paperwork in California. We had no time to correct it."

"It's not that, Askara. No worries on that score. But I've wanted to talk to you in private about...about our African trek. Looking back on it, that was the hardest traveling I've ever done —the most dangerous for sure—but some segments make no sense. It's like I forgot chunks and have only shadowy recollections. Makes me feel kind of crazy. Guess I haven't felt free to talk around Darian. How much does he know?"

"Wow, me too! He knows everything I know, but even Darian said something similar about Sudan. Things don't make sense. He has gaps too. Recently, Darian took me to see some amazing caves outside of Bombay called Ellora. Something fell into place for me in that place. Spiritual adepts like Buddhists, Jains, and Hindus made pilgrimages there. You gotta see them when you visit us in Bombay. They're only a day's drive from the city. Anyway, at Ellora, they cut away so much rock from the hillside that freestanding sculptures of elephants and even temples look like they were built from the ground up, not carved from the top down. That made me realize something."

"What? You want to be a sculptor?"

"No, something about me, about us, all of us—you, me, Darian, maybe even your friend Impho in Uganda. We were all carved out from the top down...by Nagali."

"Whoa, what the hell does that mean?"

"We all lost memories because of that hypnotic crazy guy Nagali. He took away chunks of who we are. That's why things don't make sense. Sara, he cursed us."

"Okay, that's too far out for me. Remember, I'm a farmer from Australia, not a hippie from Haight-Ashbury. You sound nuts!"

"Let me explain." Askara began. "That night, at the dinner in Mombasa I'd told you about—the one when I was to make a contact to purchase heirloom jewelry from Mr. Nagali, the creep who was Ugandan President Idi Amin's personal soothsayer, well, he showed me an amulet and hypnotized me—everything, all my problems, started there. He wanted to control my mind for some reason. Darian broke in and disrupted him, almost hit him. Nagali drove away, super pissed off. That started all the troubles that spilled over to when you and I traveled together. I don't know how or why, but I know it did. Somehow, Nagali cursed me. When you wrote me about the trouble you and your co-worker Impho had in Kampala at the agricultural conference when you ran into Nagali, I figured he put a curse on poor Impho that made her pass out. Same thing he wanted to do to me that night in Mombasa. No accident. How is Impho now? How are you? Heart-of-hearts talk now. How are you, Sara?"

"Weird. I feel responsible for what happened to Impho. She still suffers. Her tribal shaman has her doing rituals and fasts to cleanse herself of that guy. He told her Nagali wanted something from her. She keeps herbs tacked on her door, so his spirit can't enter and hover over her bed…so he can't reach into her dreams. She's not the confident woman, the head of the collective she used to be. Recently, she stepped down to let a younger, more aggressive woman become president. The shaman said Nagali searches for something and that I know about it, and so does my friend. He meant you. I don't; I have no clue. Now Impho doesn't like or trust me. We work together, but the way she looks at me, it's like I'm a poisonous snake she wants to keep at bay. The guy who liked her at that conference…well, he never recovered after he challenged Nagali. He went back home to work on his family farm. He told Impho she was cursed, and now he was too."

"I'm so sorry, Sara. That's horrible. But how do you feel… in your head, in your mind?"

"Like a chunk is missing. I can almost see something. I know it has a lot of meaning, but it's hazy and stays out of reach. Some days, I'm fine. Some days, I feel like a dark cloud is ready to break over my head, but instead of rain, blood will pour down on me. Makes my stomach turn."

Askara sat back and nibbled her croissant, feeling guilty for her role in exposing innocent people to Nagali, but she realized she had no control over that. She really didn't. She wondered if anyone did. She was innocent too. But she hoped to make this trip a rejuvenating one for Sara, Darian, and herself.

"Well, I wish I could wave a magic wand and make everything right. That was a drag, the whole Nagali thing. We each have to find our way beyond it. I went to a few meditation sessions in San Francisco led by a neat guy. He told me that your mind is your best friend or your worst enemy. Make it your friend. I've been working on that. When Nagali pops into my mind, I visualize something I enjoy, like a beautiful sunset, a rose, or ocean waves. It helps."

"Good idea. I'll practice that, too. Think I'll imagine healthy plants, or newborn foals, maybe a new Range Rover. Just kidding!"

"Good idea, except the Rover. Don't put in specific people, he warned me. Darian told me he repeats prayers; he's a Parsi, and that helps him. So, Sara, let's make a pact. We will enjoy ourselves on this trip, and when you decide to tour America, I will too. We'll do a road trip all over the West and get the leather chaps and native jewelry you've wanted."

"Fair dinkum, that's a deal! But for now, are we running late for your church appointment?"

Askara checked her watch. "We should get Darian. I'd love your help with Catholic protocol. I know nothing. Oops, can't say that too loud. They'll jerk my assignment."

"Can't tell you how many Hail Marys I've said…enough for an eternity, I'm sure. I've got this!"

"I need official written permission from Monsignor Devereaux to report on the Walking the Dead ceremony, my first journalism assignment. My translator Mea said he's given an informal green light. That means the church is okay with the project. Such a weird blend of Catholicism and traditional Malagasy beliefs, seeing their ancestors as links to the divine. Many families cover their bases by also having a priest come."

"Not so weird. I've heard of something like that…maybe in Bali? The monsignor comes?"

"Possibly. It's not necessary. Here in Madagascar, the ceremony's called 'turning the bones,' or 'walking the dead.' Famadihana is the Malagasy name. I wanted you and Darian to be up close with me, but at least I got permission for you to attend. You need to stay back, out of the way of the procession, though. People will sing and dance as they carry the shrouded remains around the streets. Then there's a ceremonial feast for the deceased. Should be interesting."

"Yep, a new twist on Catholicism. Something to tell my family."

"It's next week. That's why we're doing tourist things now. Then home to Bombay."

"How does life work for you, Askara? Do you like living in India?"

"I haven't done Bombay for very long. It's an adjustment for sure. Hey, living with a man is an adjustment, acting married. Add to that a new country, foreign in-laws, and trying to find work in a new profession. Overwhelming. But I can't say that to Darian. We're committed, and his family is wonderful. That's the good news. Can't quite picture growing old in India, but hell, I can't picture growing old!"

IMBOULE WENDED PAST THE FAR REACHES OF THE market on narrow lanes that followed the base of the hills, taking a hard right on a tree-lined boulevard to accelerate uphill to the church. The church's stone portico, freshly washed by a woman wringing out a wad of crumpled rags, dried quickly in the sun. Askara had started up the steps when the woman motioned to the heavy wooden door at the far left. Askara, Darian, and Sara stepped inside to the calm of the dimly lit church. The stagnant warm air carried the aroma of pungent incense and old prayers.

"Hello? Bonjour," she called to the emptiness. From the front, she heard a faint "Bonjour." Padded feet drew closer. The chapel door swung open when a priest entered, his black robes stirring the dead air as he approached.

"Bonjour. I am looking for Monsignor Devereaux."

With a heavy French accent, the man said, "I am Priest Gestang, Monsignor Devereaux's assistant. How may I help you?"

"I am here on a journalism assignment to report on the Bone Turning ceremony. Monsignor Devereaux was to give me written permission, and I need help understanding the local culture for the article."

The priest smiled. "We all need help with that, but I will assist if I am able. I believe I have your permit on my desk. Wait one moment, please. I will get it for you."

When he returned, Askara asked, "The walking the dead custom—do you believe in it, sir?"

"I have witnessed several. I know the practice. I respect that the Malagasy people, good Catholics, believe in it."

"Has anything odd ever happened during one?"

"Please, madame, I am very busy this morning."

Exit Visa   75

"Well, I heard of one that went badly. A French gentleman said the ancestors were upset because of something that went wrong. Is that possible?"

"Umm," the priest said as he straightened the folds of his black cassock. "I heard about this assertion. I believe you refer to Monsieur Jean-Paul?"

Askara lowered her voice to a barely audible whisper. "Jean-Paul told me in confidence that I should contact you. It is his granddaughter Meamoni who will translate the ceremony for me. She is pregnant, and Jean-Paul fears her baby will die if she does because the baby would be *the one closest to the door.*"

The priest audibly sucked in his breath and clucked. "Tsk, tsk. That will not happen. Foolishness only. Idle words."

"People seem to believe there is power released in the ceremony."

"Oui, they do. Her unborn child is fine. Sadly, her grandfather Jean-Paul…. I received word this very hour: Jean-Paul passed into God's hands this morning. The service is scheduled for Thursday."

"He's…dead?"

"Oui."

"From what?"

"Old age. Jean-Paul has been in fragile health. I am sorry to deliver this news in such an abrupt manner, madame."

Askara looked at Darian and Sara. "Can I have a minute alone, please?" They nodded and walked up the aisle. When they pushed the front door open, light flooded into the silent church again, but Askara felt a dark, cold knife pierce her stomach.

"Monsignor, Jean-Paul said I could talk to you. I hope he was right. The deceased man in the ceremony was Monsignor Devereaux's personal servant, wasn't he?"

Hearing this, Priest Gestang blanched, his round face mottled like a full moon. "I am not a monsignor, madame. Say no more. *Vous partez*! Go!" He escorted her quickly from the chapel, rushing past a parishioner lighting a prayer candle. On the outside steps, he whispered, "Go back to your country. Forget this ceremony. What is done is done. Do not contact me again."

He turned like a dark cyclone, rushed up the stone steps, and slammed the heavy door behind him. Askara remained at the curb, stupefied. She looked around for Darian and Sara but didn't see them in the adjoining garden. Such little time had passed since she, Darian, and Jean-Paul had coffee that morning, and now he was dead?

Askara wanted to offer her condolence to Mea. As she walked across the street toward Darian and Sara, she had a sinking feeling that the street scene—the trees, buildings, people—were false like a diorama. She felt shaken to her core.

Darian patted her back. "I see you got the permission. Good. The news of that gentleman's death really affected you. Are you dehydrated? Hungry? You look so pale, Sweetie."

"Um, yes. I think I drank too much coffee this morning. Let's go back to the hotel for a bit. I need to lie down. I'm not sick. I'll be okay with a little rest, just shocked."

Darian spotted Imboule smoking a cigarette under the shade of a large fig tree and waved him over. Darian and Sara chatted about the Zoma Market robbery on the drive back to the Hotel du Parc while Askara silently stared out the window. When she stopped to ask the front desk if she had any messages, the receptionist handed her a note. Askara opened it quickly.

Mea had sent word: a family death would prevent their meeting before Askara goes to the coast, but she would be in touch. Holding the note in her shaking hand, Askara realized her concern for Mea was misplaced. The closing door meant Jean-Paul's death, possibly a message from beyond from his loving Pauly. Askara sighed and felt a little better. At least Jean-Paul's loneliness would be over. But what an odd thing that he knew of the warning but thought it applied to Mea.

As the three of them rounded the corner of the second-floor hallway to go to their rooms, Askara saw something at her door. She approached slowly, looking ahead and behind for anyone who might have left it. The hallway was empty.

Darian reached first to lift the package. "Has your name on it, madame," he said and handed it to her.

Sara passed them, saying, "Knock on my door when you're going out," and walked on.

Askara eased the box from its fabric cover. Shaking it, she heard a rattle. Beads, or small stones, hit a hard surface. Darian unlocked their door. Not looking, Askara set the box on the table edge, but it fell onto the tile floor and opened. She touched a damp piece of folded paper secured by a string of shark's teeth. The English scribble read: *You are drowning, madame. Go home. There are dangerous things in these waters!* A reddish-brown color, the shade of dried blood, stained the lining of the box.

"Yuck! That's blood!"

Feeling queasy, Askara rushed to the bathroom to wash her hands. She stood at the basin and gripped the edge to try to stop shaking. Her spine tightened. She jerked upright and looked behind her. The faint image of a man stared out from the shower curtain, but when she wheeled around, the shower stall was empty. Her guts turned on a skewer. She grabbed her stomach and writhed in pain. Bending over, she tried to reach the basin but collapsed and hit her head on the floor. The sound of drip, drip, drip came into her awareness. She focused.

Darian hovered above her. Calling "Askara, Askara," he gently rubbed her face.

The painful lump on her head pulsated. Darian pulled her into his lap and cradled her in his arms. Two feet away, the box lay upside down.

"Look at that!" she said and pointed. "Get it away!"

Darian reached over to flip the box upright. Triangular bits of paper had scattered on the floor beside the handwritten note. No dark stain tarnished the bottom of the box. Darian hoisted Askara up to hold onto the basin's edge. An image in the bathroom mirror made her cringe. She saw across her forehead a brownish smudge like the mark of a bloody thumb drawn quickly. She touched the spot that burned cold.

"See that?" she cried, grabbing the soap. Askara scrubbed and scrubbed until the mark disappeared into her abraded red flesh.

"What? Askara, what's going on?" Darian carried her to the bed. She squirmed, whimpering like a child.

"I feel sick."

A loud knock at the door made Darian jump. "Yes?"

"Madame, I am Imboule. I have a message for you."

Darian covered Askara with the bedcover and cracked the door to see the young man standing with an envelope in his narrow-extended palm. "What do you want, Imboule? Madame isn't feeling well."

"Please to give me English-French dictionary. Then I study and become a government guide."

"Okay, Imboule, yes. But for now, madame must rest. See you tomorrow for the ride to the train station."

Darian started to close the door when Imboule pulled a piece of paper written in carefully executed letters from his brown polyester slacks. *Imboule Francis Tarcicius, Cite Valpinson, Lot 266, Tana, Madagascar.* He placed the note in the envelope and handed it to Darian, thanked him, and retreated. Darian slammed the door and rushed back to Askara.

CHAPTER FIVE

The Coast

I mboule arrived early to drive Askara, Darian, and Sara to Gare Soamieryma Station for their 8:00 a.m. departure to the coastal town of Toamasina. They assumed the train journey would be the best way to see the countryside, as Elaine had suggested, to enjoy the people at the stops along the way and meet locals traveling to the seaport. Plus, they could all be together. The alternative, traveling by *taxi brousse*, didn't win anyone's vote.

As the train pulled away from the Antananarivo station, platform vendors shrunk to dots obscured by the heavy cloud of smoke the engine belched. People in the crowded car settled down with the side-to-side rocking of the train on iron rails. Screaming babies fell asleep, along with their tired mothers, and in time the whole of the train lulled into oblivion.

Screeching brakes roused the travelers when the train slowed to forty mph approaching the first station. Passengers stirred; some prepared to get off. The blur of green vegetation that had demarcated fertile land from dusty villages opened out to idyllic vistas of hills terraced with young rice plants. Vendors rushed toward the train as it slowed for the station. Running alongside, young men shouted and held up baskets of apples, fried foods, cups of water, and roasted nuts to the open glass-pane windows.

"Yum, that looks good," Elaine said, surveying a tray of fried pastries stuffed with vegetables.

"If you don't mind ptomaine poisoning." John laughed. "No, Elaine, you'd better stick with the sandwich you made, or you might spend the trip in the bathroom."

"Horrible thought! I saw the train bathroom—a hole cut into the bottom of the car with some kind of basin below it. Stopped me cold; couldn't go if I wanted to. You're right; I'll stick with my food."

"Look over there at that pretty girl carrying a basket of flowers on her head," Askara said, admiring the anthurium stalks with their thick, waxy red hearts and the orange-and-purple stalks of birds of paradise placed next to them. "Wow! I love the vegetation here."

"Back home right now, there's snow on the ground and ice on the lake. I don't miss it," Elaine said and took a photograph of the young girl standing regally in her brightly colored clothing.

"Where are you from in Michigan?" Askara asked.

"Just north of Detroit." The young girl floated over to raise the flower basket for Elaine's inspection. "Oh, I can't refuse. Look at those dark eyes; the girl's a beauty."

"Elaine, is that how you shop? If the salesperson is good-looking, you buy?" John said.

"Well…."

The girl handed an anthurium to Elaine, then another, then four more. Before Elaine could stop her, the girl had placed six of the large, red flowers in her hand and three birds of paradise. The other flower vendors, seeing this, rushed over to hoist their baskets up to the window. The girl hissed and waved them off. Elaine smiled, deep dimples defining her tanned cheeks.

"Now see what you've done, Elaine? They all have nice eyes, don't they? Makes you want to buy from all of them! What are you gonna do?" John said, exasperated with the onslaught of vendors as Elaine paid the girl the eight hundred Malagasy francs she requested. "Not even going to bargain? You're a tough customer," John said.

Elaine pulled the large bunch of flowers in through the window, dripping water across Askara's jeans, and sheepishly smiled.

"Oops, sorry, Askara."

"Better watch out for her, Askara. Elaine attracts 'em like flies."

"Well, she's great for the local economy. Bees to honey."

"Hey, I'm no pushover. These will brighten our room. Here's a tissue, John; wrap it around the stems."

"You mean so I can hold them the rest of the way?"

"No, so we can prop them up in this crevice between the seats. Askara, don't mind John. All this jiggling makes his back sore. He's cranky!"

"I think we should have flown," John said, trying to stretch his long legs in the cramped space between their seat and the one in front.

"But John, we'd miss all the scenery and...Askara's company. She didn't want to fly."

"How come?" John asked, turning to look at Askara.

"Well, the return flight's in a week. I have things to do, plus it's not a sure bet."

"Yeah, that's what I've heard. I'm not complaining, really. I like to give Elaine a hard time. She calls the shots.

She's good with money, and this is much cheaper than flying."

"Finally, he admits it: I call the shots."

"Some shots, Elaine, only some."

Askara settled back as the train lunged ahead. Everyone seemed lost in their private worlds. Sara read *Riders of the Purple Sage*. Darian worked on a crossword puzzle, and Askara thought about Jean-Paul. He had whispered something to her, something that made no sense: "I go to close the door. *Le Pierre est très important. Le temple est guarded.* Look to the house of Anjou. Like a phoenix, I rise." She thought his words the rambling of age, something from his past since he talked of his deceased wife Pauly as if she were standing next to him. Askara paid little attention, assuming the door was to the house of someone named Anjou, whoever he was. But Jean-Paul's death made her wonder. What was he saying?

"Cheer up, Askara," Elaine said, looking at her. "It's not so bad. The train's on time so far. Hey, did John tell you we met Ejema again?"

"No, when?"

"He showed up at our hotel last night, kinda surprised us. We were in the restaurant having dinner. He joined us."

"I'm surprised he could afford it on a policeman's salary."

"He had popped in to talk. In fact, we had to beg him to have dinner, our treat. John's very fond of him. Who'd figure this big white guy from Texas and this small Black man from Madagascar would hit it off so well? I guess it's the artist thing; artists always seem to find each other and get along. They understand each other immediately somehow."

Askara smiled. "Don't you understand John, Elaine?"

"I love his art, but I don't think the way John does.

I'm a jock. I've been a high school PE teacher for twenty-three years. Sports, I understand. Art, I appreciate it. But I wouldn't say I *understand* it—not at all, and definitely not the artistic personality. Nothing fazes me. But John—he gets hot under the collar pretty fast, the temperamental artist thing, I guess."

"My husband's like you. He's a businessman—pragmatic. In some ways, I wish I were more like him. Things don't affect him like they do me. I'm high-strung, more like John, I guess."

"High strung? You seem pretty calm to me. Anyway, Ejema gave John a copy of his band's tape. Ejema's a singer. He said he and his group, also called Ejema, went to South Africa to try out to be a Paul Simon backup group on some album."

"Wow, that's great. I knew there was something unique about him."

"You mean besides the seventies Afro, bell-bottom jeans, and the faded jean jacket for a cop?"

"Yeah, that undercover thing was funny. I haven't seen any Malagasy people dressed like that. He must have watched a lot of American movies or something."

"He asked John to design an album cover for the group. He also said he wanted to see you again; said he had questions to ask you. Looking at the grimace on Askara's face, she said, "No, it's not like that. He has a wife and two kids, and anyway, John told him you're married. Ejema was embarrassed that John thought he was interested in that way."

"What kind of questions?"

"Like who you work for, stuff like that. Things John couldn't answer."

"What did John say?" Askara asked, looking over to see John slumped against the window asleep.

"That we hardly know you and that he should ask you himself. Did he come to your hotel?"

"No, not that I know of. I may have been out, though."

"He'll probably catch up with you when we return to Tana. We have to complete more papers—can you believe that?—to go with our passports. By the way, save the stubs for this train fare and all your receipts; they have to equal your cashed traveler's checks."

"Why?" Askara said.

"I think it's some black-market thing, a way of checking on people."

"I've never done so much accounting on a trip in my life. What a hassle."

The train chugged uphill to a broad, green valley flanked by rice-terraced hills on the right before it descended to the lowlands. Mist colored the paddies in soft blue light. The engine faltered with a sharp jolt that woke John abruptly and made Darian drop his magazine. Askara grabbed her camera from its bag and popped on the telephoto lens to lean out the window, clicking successive shots of women with their skirts hiked up above their knees, standing in calf-high water to tend delicate green rice shoots. The other passengers looked at her with blank expressions. She jerked back into the cabin.

"Wow! There's a tunnel ahead. Pull the window up, quick. There's a waterfall before the opening."

John grabbed the latches on the glass panel to close the window when a tangle of wet vines and flowers punched through the opening. Water hit the train's metal roof and sprayed the seats and the passengers. No one spoke. No child cried. The train plunged into darkness, but after several minutes, daylight resumed. The train leveled out and chugged through the tropical forest, where monkeys jumped in the trees, screeching. The steep embankment on the train's left side amplified the railway sounds. Passengers found it impossible to talk in anything less than a shout. After leveling out, the train pulled into the station.

"We're on schedule," Elaine said, checking her watch. "We're about one-third of the way there. It's supposed to be a long trip."

"It's only about one hundred forty miles, I think," Askara said, unwrapping a piece of bread and butter leftover from her hotel breakfast. "Shouldn't take long."

"No, but when you're going forty mph on the straights, time and distance don't equate."

John stood up to stretch. "Our concierge told us to take a *taxi brousse;* said it would take about six hours. But the cost of petrol, the availability of a taxi to take us there, wait on us, and return, which he said was the only way to do it, and the danger of ambush by bandits made it a bad choice. Before sitting on this damned uncomfortable seat with no place for my legs for hours, I would have agreed. But now I have to use a bathroom Elaine said is disgusting."

"Better wait. You won't like what you see. The station's got to have a bathroom," Elaine said. Standing beside John, Elaine gripped the seat when the train jolted to a halt, throwing her sideways into him. Thin outstretched arms punched through the raised windows to offer lichees, pastries, and sticky rice balls.

Askara said to Darian and Sara, "Hey, this is our chance. Let's go!"

They rushed to the pale-yellow station, where they found crude but enclosed toilets. Askara purchased a bottled lime drink from a boy resting in the shade of a large tree alive with the chatter of small green parrots when she spotted

Darian standing alone on the pavement and joined him. John approached, wiping the sweat from his reddened face, and they lumbered back toward their car.

"Do y'all want to try for a taxi now? I'm really tired of this. It's killing my back."

Sara started to answer, but seeing the train accelerate, she said, "Let's go."

Askara and Darian entered the nearest car to walk the length inside, but the others trotted alongside the train, unable to recognize their compartment in the line of identical green and yellow railcars. John waved toward one and hopped onto the car's metal steps, yanking Elaine up behind him. He reached for Sara's hand, but the train accelerated. They yelled for her to catch the next car back. When Askara looked out her window, she saw Sara pacing the train, sprinting to the rear door. Askara rushed to the top step of the platform to see Sara grab the handle, leap from a hard run, and land on the lowest step like an Old West movie bandit.

"Fair dinkum," Sara gasped, "always wanted to do that! Zorro's got nothing on me!"

Askara gave her a playful cuff on the arm. "Sara, nobody's got nothing on you! Trust me."

"How many hours to Toamasina?" Darian asked the conductor when Askara and Sara settled in their seats while the man punched their tickets.

The conductor replied in Malagasy, pointed to his watch, tapped his finger, and walked away. He opened the car door, stepped across the hitch to open the next compartment's sliding door, and disappeared before Darian could catch him for clarification.

John leaned forward and whispered, "So, Darian, what's the word?"

"Do you honestly want to know? We have hours left, like six of them."

"Holy shit. How long is this damn ride, Elaine?"

"I told you in Tana, it could take twelve hours. You agreed."

"I didn't hear that. I would have never agreed to that."

"Calm down, John. Get out your deck; entertain yourself."

Sara looked at John with a wry smile. "Poker?" Her bright blue eyes widened when she said, "I love Texas Hold'em."

"No kidding? An Aussie knows my game? Hard to believe. I gotta see this. Okay, what's the pot—real money or francs?"

"We're here. Malagasy francs are fine by me."

Elaine rolled her eyes at Askara and Darian and whispered, "This should keep him quiet. He loves to win. Guess Sara's our sacrificial lamb for the rest of the journey."

Askara exchanged places to give John and Elaine more room, moving to a window seat behind the open row. She leaned up against the partially closed window and dozed off with the rocking of the train.

Three dark forms—cutout silhouettes—darted across her closed eyes. Askara heard a small voice whisper: *Do not forget what you came to do.* When Askara looked over at Darian, he was making chapatis over a small coal fire with desert sand rushing past him like a river, sucking a belt of stars to the distant horizon. Orange sparks illuminated his face. "I'm so glad you're here, Darian," she said. "Odd things are happening. I want to go home."

Darian stared in her direction and said nonchalantly, "You have no home, not until you secure your exit visa. You cannot join me for dinner."

Askara surveyed his position on the opposite side of the swiftly moving river of stars, realizing she dared not cross the gulf that separated them. It sucked everything in its wake.

"But I'm hungry...and tired."

"I know you must be. I long to share my dinner with you, nourish you, care for you, but first, you must answer your calling."

A dark form approached Darian at the charcoal fire. Dull orange flickers defined the intruder's broad features. The shadow man said, "Welcome to our world, where we of the earth dwell with respect, where ancestors light our way to understanding, where spirits serve the One Who Sings the Eternal Song. Welcome, sister; we sing in praise of your assistance."

Askara pondered the shadow's words. "Am I dead? Did I die? Is that why I see both of you?" As the words skipped from her mouth, the vista opened out to encompass scores of dark shadows—men, women, children—who encircled a small fire on the opposite side of the river of stars.

"No, sister, your body exists in earth time. Your spirit is here with us where dreams guide our days, where endless time unaware of passing is the music of our sphere."

"And Darian? Where does he dwell?"

"He is here because you wished it. His home is elsewhere for now."

"Am I here because I wished it?"

"No, you are here because *we* wished it. The open door must be closed. The ceremony, walking the dead, is an ancient initiation ceremony handed down from the Mother and Father of us all. It was used as a way station between worlds in our ancient days of wisdom, a place to cleanse, before stepping into NoTime. It became corrupted. It lost its vital essence. The ceremony became a mundane ritual, a transition from the world of matter to the rarefied world, with no respect for purification. Thus, our world has suffered from a thick, unfeeling—an unknowing that caused those on earth to forget to honor their ancestors.

A sharp jolt threw Askara forward; she hit her head on the seat in front of her. Dazed, she heard Sara's voice yell: What the hell was that? Askara opened her eyes and felt something wet dribbling down her forehead.

"Askara, you're hurt," Darian said and grabbed his handkerchief to hold to her forehead.

"What happened? Where are we?"

The train's brakes screeched to a loud, grating, metallic stop when John answered. "Don't know, but I think we hit something on the track."

Sara picked up the scattered cards and handed them to John. "Guess the game's over. Damn, never been beaten by a woman, much less a non-Texan, at *my* game. Glad I don't have to tell the boys back home about this disgrace. And, Elaine, you say nothing." John counted the pile of cash. "Looks like twenty thousand francs. Well, that's a train wreck on top of a train wreck!"

The passengers chattered in Malagasy as they picked up their displaced bags, boxes, and caged chickens. Darian and John stepped off the train and stretched in the afternoon's oblique sunlight filtered through the tall, green sugar cane fields lining the rail line. A slight breeze made the plants dance in the humid heat. Passengers began pouring from cars that stretched down the track for a quarter mile. After asking several people what had happened and getting replies in Malagasy, John marched down the line, searching for a conductor.

Elaine, Askara, and Sara joined Darian to escape the stuffy, metal car, now a stationary oven. "Any luck?" Elaine asked, swatting mosquitoes from her face.

"No. I didn't see any officials, but John walked down the line to find someone who speaks English." Darian looked at Askara's small cut. "Good, it stopped bleeding. Keep pressure on it a bit longer. I have antiseptic in my dock kit. How do you feel?"

"Okay. I'd fallen asleep and was having the craziest dream. I still feel foggy." Askara spotted a gentleman nearby and approached him. "*Qu'est-ce que le problème?*"

"I do not know, madame," he replied.

"Where are we, do you think?" she continued.

"Near Ranomafana."

"How much longer to the coast?"

"On this train? I do not know. By auto, two-plus hours."

"Do you know this area?"

"No, madame, not well. I stay in Antananarivo. I visit friends here. Excuse me," he said and hurriedly walked away to join a pregnant woman returning from the field where the passengers were relieving themselves.

John returned to join the others. "By train, we're maybe four hours away, I think. We better get going before sunset. See those insects hovering over the sugarcane...those mosquitoes as large as monkeys? They'll eat us alive."

"You take malaria medicine, don't you?" Elaine asked, looking at Darian, Sara, and Askara. "It's rampant here, you know."

Sara spoke up first. "I hate taking that stuff."

Askara chimed in, "I've traveled in Africa and India, and I've never taken it. I'm not sure it works. The mosquitoes become resistant to the medications, and you have to take stronger and stronger meds," she said, slapping a mosquito from her face. "But I never planned to be stuck in a sugarcane field. I don't think I can stay here much longer.

I don't have topical repellent either. I brought mosquito coils in case we stayed in a hotel without air conditioning. Fat-lot-of-good they will do out here! I'm going to find out what's happening."

Askara walked the length of fifteen cars, asking people what the problem was as the setting sun touched the sugar cane and the slight breeze failed. She found a railroad conductor who spoke broken English. He explained that a train down the line had engine trouble, so his train's engine had to pull that train to the next station, some eighteen miles away.

"When our engine returns, we will leave promptly," he promised.

Askara's face fell when he said he expected to reach Toamasina by midnight. She battled the swarming mosquitoes and picked her way around passengers who had pulled their luggage out to the flat area to sit on. She noticed a few passengers, bags in hand, walking to the small village. She ran back to the others.

"Look, we've got to go. This train may be stuck here for hours. Our engine went to pull another train. If we hurry, we might be able to get a *taxi brousse*. Come on, I doubt there are many taxis."

"If any," Elaine said, checking her wristwatch.

They navigated the lounging bodies by the train and made for the only tarmac they saw. Looking down the road, Askara spotted an Indian family—women in sarees, men in cotton pajamas—standing by the road, listening for the sound of a motor. Fifteen minutes became thirty, and no vehicle appeared going in either direction. Askara walked over to speak to the Indians.

"Hello. Are there taxis here?"

The taller of the two men replied, "If we are being lucky. No taxis in this village, but the road is going to the coast. A car must be coming this way. We are waiting."

"You mean a private car? Someone is coming to pick you up?"

"No, a ride with *taxi brousse*—bush taxi—we are hoping."

"How much do they cost?"

"One person—as much as twenty-eight thousand francs Malagasy—too much. But better than getting attacked by dacoits in the night. This train, it will not be going for days."

As he spoke, Askara heard the sound of an approaching car and turned to see scores of people waving frantically. The three Indian women unfurled their scarves and waved large arcs in the air. The man Askara was speaking to rushed to join them. He withdrew a wallet from his pajama pants and waved it high in the air. The taxi swerved to avoid people flooding onto the road and screeched to a halt in front of the Indians. They jumped into the small van. A woman's braceleted arm appeared from the van, signaling for Askara to come. When she motioned for the others to join her, the taxi door slammed. The vehicle lurched away in the dwindling evening light.

Breathless from running with their bags, Askara reassured the group, "Okay, good, now we're first in line. Don't let anyone get in front."

"Or last…depending on how you look at it," Elaine said, looking at the desperate people down the road from them.

"There should be…." Askara's voice trailed off. The raucous engine of a microbus roared in the distance.

People began surging toward the sound. When it came into sight, Askara jumped up and down, withdrew a thick wad of francs from her pack, and waved them madly in the air. The microbus sped up, halting several yards short of their group. They rushed to the sliding door. Askara, Darian, Sara, John, and Elaine pushed and shoved their bodies and bags into the back two rows behind the eight people already squeezed on top of one another. The driver shouted, the door slammed, and off they drove. A disgruntled person left in the road kicked the bus's rear fender in anger as it crept past.

A few minutes down the road, out of sight of the train, the driver pulled over to collect fares—a whopping sixteen US dollars each for the Americans. The driver attempted to make John pay for the equivalent of two seats since he was a large man, but he backed down when John reached over to grab his collar to speak to him directly. The driver took the wheel without another word.

The microbus careened along lonely, dark roads to the coast. At one point, Askara wondered what amazing sights she was missing before she dozed off again, slumped against Darian's chest. Later, when the driver called out, "Which hotel?" the sleepy passengers woke. The excitement of seeing city lights thrilled them. The first stop, Hotel Etoile, a modest, clean-looking place, seemed appealing, but the valet informed the driver there were no vacancies. A couple grabbed their bags, climbed out, and disappeared into the hotel garden. Having no idea of where to stay, Darian asked the driver to choose a hotel for them. Les Flamboyants, he answered. Air-conditioned rooms. Good food. Out from town.

When the driver pulled up in front, the French proprietress of Les Flamboyants met the microbus at the gate and greeted the tired group as if it were the middle of the day, and she had expected them. Askara observed the hotel must have seen better days. What once must have been a grand establishment now craved repair, as much as the proprietress craved cosmopolitan company, Askara learned. She looked delighted to see the foreigners and introduced herself with a flourish of her hand.

Madame Tison checked them in and made sure the porter turned up their air conditioners, saying the hot, humid nights outside were preferable until the rooms chill. She delighted in showing them the outdoor pool surrounded by a garden grown wild with aromatic jasmine, its tiny white flowers weaving around the other plants in a sinister way, filling the moist air with an overwhelming scent. The only swimmers in the pool were the large-eyed, webbed-foot sort that croaked. After chilled beers, the guests said goodnight and retired to their rooms for simple in-room dinners of cheese, crackers, fruit, and wine.

Askara stretched out on the firm bed while Darian showered, wondering at her odd dream on the train, one she attributed to fatigue. She wanted to tell Darian about it but decided not to. She didn't want to stir up old memories of her mind being muddled like it had been during the Nagali fiasco. They fell asleep to the loud hum of the air conditioner and the choking odor of mosquito coil.

CHAPTER SIX

Baobabs and Pirates

When they roused in the morning and walked down for *petit déjeuner*, the staff laid a buffet table with baguettes, butter, jam, croissants, oranges, bananas, and small glasses of orange juice. The aromatic smell of black coffee wafted throughout the ground floor.

John walked over to inspect the breakfast and turned to Elaine to whisper in a loud voice. "So, what's the main course?"

"You're looking at it. French eat like this. You're not in Texas anymore, John, no pork chops and potatoes, not even scrambled eggs."

"Good God, no wonder they're small people. Who could survive on this?"

"Shh, we'll go into town and find a breakfast house."

"Damn right, we will."

Askara grinned at Elaine when Sara walked over to John to say, "I'm with you; I'll even treat you with your own money," she said with a smile, grabbing the coffee pot.

"You're on! And tonight, it's Texas Hold'em. You won't best me again. Be warned, I'm raising the stakes."

Over breakfast, they talked about sightseeing around Toamasina. John had picked the lighthouse trip to the Isle of Prunes, nine miles out from the harbor, when Madame Tison entered the dining room with a flourish of her crimson skirt.

"Bonjour! I heard you deciding what to do. May I suggest I contact my dear friend to give you a special treat? He has a wildlife collection, which he hopes will become a wildlife park one day. It's small but fascinating." Madame Tison assured them that people would come from their countries expressly to visit his park someday.

"But today," she added, "you will see lemurs, tortoises, chameleons, two boas, and many wild birds that have made their homes around the small lake. Be aware, you will find no restaurant," she said, looking John's way. "Eat well before you go, and I will prepare flasks of drinking water for you to carry. A donation to his project is requested, which you can pay me. I will hire a fluent taxi brousse driver for the day to take you wherever you choose. I would also suggest our lovely church, Notre Dame de Lourdes, then the local bazaar in Toamasina, and the park of banyan trees next to our French colonial mansion, a relic of former days, part of my family's history. You can no longer so inside, but it is a *faritra atsinanana*, a point of interest for tourists and a fond memory for us French settlers."

The group agreed and began discussing among themselves what to include. The fact that they wanted to do it all, plus have a local meal, resulted in seeing the city and the harbor first and the wildlife refuge the following day.

SUN GLINTING ON THE SAND OF THE HARBOR MADE their eyes smart. Shipping crates lined the docks, private fishing boats and commercial boats bobbed in the water, and humidity sucked the life out of the group. They located the ticket agent for the boat ride to the Nosy Alañaña Lighthouse and boarded within minutes of paying. The ride, bobbing on gentle waves under the blaring morning sun, lulled the group into a trance. When the small boat pulled up to the dock, the captain wished them a happy visit and said he would return in an hour and wait for them.

Sara led the charge to the lighthouse, moving quickly over the hot sand. When they reached the 197-foot tower, the highest in Africa, Sara read aloud from the plaque. They realized it was closed to visitors, so no one could climb the steps up the octagonal tower. A strong metal fence protected it.

Darian walked to a large tree to sit on a bench, fanning himself with his hat. "This is very much like Bombay at this season, minus the monsoons. Hot, humid, and assaulting light bouncing off the water. I'll look out for the boat taxi, right here in the shade of this tree."

Sara grinned. "Hot, humid?" Feels good to me. Wish I could swim in that turquoise water."

"Go ahead. You'd be dry by the time we reach port again."

"Askara, if you will, I will," Sara said. "Remember, we started that way. You thought I was a swim coach at the Hilton in Nairobi."

"Okay, coach, let's do it!" Askara said and kicked off her sandals and took off her sunhat. Sara removed her hiking shoes, socks, hat, and her travel vest with bulging pockets.

"Guess my jeans and safari shirt will dry almost as fast as your skirt and T-shirt. Who cares? Let's go. Race you to that buoy."

John and Elaine joined Darian in the shade and watched the women run into the water and dive through the waves.

Sara and Askara kept swimming farther out toward the white buoy that bobbed up and down on gentle waves.

"So, Sara, are you having a good time? Kinda tame compared to the last time, isn't it?"

"Great time! Nice company. Tame is okay. It took me months to recalibrate after that trip with you and that Nagali incident in Kampala. This is a vacation. That was a survival challenge. Maybe once is enough for that kind of travel."

Askara smiled. "Maybe once is too much. This water is so clear; look down. Thirty feet of clarity, at least. Perfect. Warmer than I thought it would be, though."

Sara looked back at the shore to the tree where the other three were resting. "Why are they waving? We'd see the boat from here. What are they yelling?"

Askara turned around to see a fin in the water about fifty feet from them. "Oh, shit! Shark."

"Bloody hell! I hate those things. Askara, fight if it comes at us. Stay close. Punch the nose."

The women swam fast toward the shore, slowing to turn and look. The shark appeared on their right, made a wide turn, and circled them. Askara power kicked, whipped the water to white froth when she dropped back to come alongside Sara, who struggled to keep up.

Suddenly the shark curved and veered off to the side. They saw John swimming at them. He chased the shark farther out, turned, and swam with Sara and Askara to shore. John stood and dragged the women by hand when they reached shallow water, one on each side until they reached the sandy beach.

Breathing hard from fear and exertion, Sara quipped, "Whoa, John, nice boxers. And no, I won't forgive your gambling debt; don't even try to tempt me. But I will buy you dinner."

"Hell, what good are you two? That bastard was tracking you; he'd swung wide to come in fast. I was ready to slam him."

Askara, trembling, looked at John. "I hate sharks. He almost got us. Thank you, John."

Elaine and Darian rushed up. Elaine laughed nervously and held her sun umbrella in front of John. "John's a great swimmer, a diver. He knows sharks, and no, he's not the streaker type." She turned to her husband and whispered, "Pull your boxers up."

Sara laughed. "That's a relief. Thank God, he's not a swimsuit model either or else he'd starve."

"See if I save you again. In fact, I'm gonna bet the hell out of you in Texas Hold 'em tonight just out of spite, after I eat a huge dinner paid for by you."

"You're on. We could have handled that fish," Sara said with a sheepish grin.

"Speak for yourself. I'm glad our swimsuit model swam out. John, I hope you win the game. That'll teach Sara," Askara said and leaned into Darian's chest. "That was freaky."

"That was horrible to see," Darian said, stroking Askara's hair. I wish I could swim." He extended his hand and shook John's vigorously. "You're impressive. And streak if you like. You deserve to do whatever you want."

"Eat. That'll suit me," John said. "A good shark steak, or maybe beef, if they have it."

———————— ❧ ————————

IN TOAMASINA, THEY TOOK A WALKING TOUR ON THE *Avenue Poincaré,* in the commercial hub, and drifted past the *Notre Dame de Lourdes* Church, its white spire and palm trees, the only point of interest on *Rue de Farafaty*. They walked streets choked with bicycles and rickshaws, stumbled on the broken sidewalks, and looked at buildings' cracked cement facades until they found the "old town district" consisting of Creole houses built on stilts. Hot and tired, they hailed motorized rickshaws to take them to the *Place Bien Aimé* to sit in the large park with ample shade from baobab trees where a French colonial mansion crumbled in decay.

The immense baobab trees cooled sections of the park, a welcome relief from the afternoon's oppressive heat and humidity. Elaine wandered in and out of the shade, admiring the trees, craning her neck to look up one hundred feet to the thick-limbed branches covered with green leaves that shimmered in the onshore breeze. The others joined her at a plaque where she read aloud to the group.

"The Malagasy call it *reniala,* mother of the forest. There are eight species of baobab, but six of them are found only here on this island. Look at that trunk, like a fat kid slumping. I'd never allow my PE students to sit like that. The trunk holds lots of water, so the tree can handle extreme climates. No wonder people call them bottle trees. Wow, thirty feet in diameter. That's wider than our house in Detroit!"

"This tree is saving my life right now," John said. "I can't stick this heat anymore. I wanna eat lunch in town, go back to the hotel, and take a long, chilled beer-induced nap in our air-conditioned room. Anyone interested?"

Everyone nodded in agreement.

IN A DROWSY FOG, ASKARA HEARD SOMEONE OUTSIDE their room say, *Banquet est server dans le restaurant à sept heure, s'il vous plaît.* The woman's voice paused, then resumed, as she walked down the hall, repeating the message at every door.

Askara pulled back the heavy curtain and looked out at the coastal town's narrow but orderly boulevards edged by shade trees and modest houses choked by tangled vegetation. When she opened the sliding glass door to the balcony, the moist salt air, tinged with rank fish, invaded their air-conditioned room. Leaning out, she caught a glimpse of the pale sand beach where gray waves swelled, frothed white, and melted without a sound.

"Let's go down, Sweetie. I'm hungry. Skipping lunch wasn't a good idea, but my nerves were shot."

Elaine accosted Askara and Darian, who were entering the restaurant for dinner. "Hi, sleep okay?"

"Yes, thanks. The drone of the air conditioner put us out."

"I wanted to chloroform John; he snored so loudly. He's coming down soon. Sara's in the front, talking to the concierge."

When they entered the dining area, a young man escorted them to a table and poured black coffee. "The smell is enough to wake you," Askara said and reached for her cup. "Whew! Strong, yummy."

"We may never sleep tonight," Darian said, taking a sip. "We may never sleep again, but this is worth it. I can't remember ever having such wonderful coffee."

"Has to be to wake you when the air's this heavy," John said, catching up with them. "It's worse than the Texas coast."

Sara strode in like she had been out surveying the property to purchase it. "This place is great! I saw a huge chameleon by the pool; he turned orange to match the bricks. Let me at that coffee. Umm, love the aroma."

"What's that ?" Askara said, watching John hold a small plate and saw back and forth on a dark slab of meat he had gotten from the buffet table.

Sara looked at the serving boy and smiled. "Don't mind him. He's American. Yep, you don't see service like this in Australia. Holding the chair, wow. But I never know if I'll hit it right. I mean, it's not as easy as climbing on a horse. You miss your seat, and bam, there you are, floundering on the floor like a beached whale."

"Don't worry, Sara; I'd pick you up. IF you cancel my debt."

"Hell no, gotcha now, John. Never back down; that's my motto."

Darian leaned in to whisper in Askara's ear. She smiled. He nodded to the entrance. Everyone turned to see Madame Tison walk in, her chiffon dress a sail catching the AC's breeze.

"Very grand old girl, I must say."

Askara buttered a baguette and glanced around the formal dining room—twenty orderly circular tables draped with white linens and only five tables full. "Interesting place. I'm glad we're here. That driver could have suggested a shack somewhere for all we knew when he dropped us off."

"Have you talked to Madame Tison, the owner?" Elaine asked and motioned for her water glass to be refilled by the waiter. "She's full of stories. I came down to escape John's snoring and hung out in the foyer, reading a magazine. Highly entertaining woman."

Elaine recounted what she had understood. Madame Tison looped through French, English, and what Elaine assumed must be Creole like she was weaving a net. In the foyer, Madame went fishing with her stories. She caught plenty; the front lounge swelled, listening to her. Elaine commented, it seemed like people come just to hear her, guests and locals too. She's a regular attraction.

Madame Tison had come out from France with her husband forty years ago to settle in Toamasina, which she clarified they called *Tamatave* then. She had lived in Madagascar as a child before her parents returned to France. Madame Tison had explained that her hotel used to be *très grand*. They hosted fancy dress balls, traveling plays from Europe, torchlight singers from Paris, even Black jazz musicians from America. The good old days, as madame phrased it, were *magnifique*. When her husband died, she almost sold the place to return to France, but things had changed so much that she didn't like France anymore when she looked at properties. Plus, it was much more expensive. The France she loved had become a dream. The Tamatave she loved from her childhood also had changed, but she chose to stay where she and her husband had lived for all those years.

"Her family ties in Madagascar go way back, which she emphasized several times," Elaine said.

John laughed, "And that was all in the ten minutes while you waited to ask her about the lemur park, right?"

"I should interview her," Askara said, "and do a travel article for the *San Francisco Chronicle*. People enjoy reading about characters like Madame Tison. Personal history makes good reads."

"Hush!" Elaine said and raised her eyebrows in the direction of the madame approaching.

"Bonjour, *mes amis*. And how are we enjoying?" Madame Tison raised her metallic blue specs to her nose, untangling a crimp in the rhinestone chain.

"Very well," Elaine replied. "Thank you."

"And this, Madame Elaine, is your friend, *n'est-ce pas*? The journalist?"

"Bonjour, Madame Tison," Askara said, smiling up at the woman standing over her.

"Is this the latest fashion in your country, madame? Bathing suit under sundress for dinner?"

Askara blushed when she realized her blue suit was visible under her pastel yellow cotton sundress. "I plan to swim after dinner, madame."

"Here?" she said, pointing a jeweled hand towards the far window that faced the sea. "*Chérie*, you are far too beautiful for that sea, especially at night. The sharks will take you away. No one swims on this side of the island, not this far north. It is *très dangereux*!"

"We saw one out at the lighthouse. I didn't think they'd come so close to shore."

"Fishermen die every year here from shark bite. I would not wish my guest to feed those brutes. *Mon Dieu*, I despise them! Unfortunately, our pool is, as you see, a lotus water garden now. It was too costly to keep up. You must go to the north end of the island for good swimming. I am sorry."

"I love to walk along the sea. That's good enough, especially in the moonlight."

"You may walk to your heart's content, *chérie*, as long as you go in a group. This is a wild country. The coast is much safer than Antananarivo, but it is better to be safe than sorry, *n'est-ce pas*?"

"Oui, madame, merci."

"Your name?"

"Askara Timlen Dalal."

"Oh, yes, I saw it in the registry. Are you of French descent? You look Mediterranean."

"A bit French plus English, from my mother's side, East Indian on my father's."

"Ah, I can always spot even a droplet of *sang français* in one's breeding. It imparts a specialness. Have you been to France?"

"Yes, a couple of times."

"Have you family there?"

"No."

"Well," Madame Tison said, removing her specs, "I must attend to my other guests. *Bon appétit!* Call at the desk with any questions or to hire a driver. See you after dinner. *Au revoir.*"

"Good-bye," the group said in unison.

John grumbled. "The French. They're the only ones I know who'd spot a drop of French blood. Hey, I'm German. Do you think anyone ever asks me about that? No! It's like a bad word unless you're talking about precision instruments or something. The Nazis made being German a disgrace!"

Elaine smiled, "What? John, you don't think you're a precision instrument?"

John turned scarlet. Sara, Elaine, and Askara couldn't stifle their laughter, although Darian didn't laugh, trying to show solidarity with the other male at the table.

LATER THAT EVENING, AFTER AN EXCELLENT MEAL, THEY discussed their next outing while sipping French liqueur.

"Walking Toamasina, haggling with street vendors, resting under massive baobab trees, riding in cramped rickshaws, outswimming a shark at the lighthouse, and watching the riptide slice waves into gray-green ribbons. Been there, done that," John said. "But this hotel garden is good."

Lulled into a comfortable daze, they enjoyed the ribbit of croaking frogs and the scent of jasmine in the humid air stirred by outdoor fans that dispelled mosquitoes. All agreed it was delightful to share this trip, a good memory. They noticed quite a few new faces had joined them in the garden. Elaine told them weary guests from other hotels in the city center would come to Madame Tison's place to relax in the garden at night, enjoy good liquor that was hard to find in the city, and, at times, even live entertainment, as the waiter had informed her earlier.

A pleasant-looking young man in his mid-twenties approached their group. "Bonjour, I am Philippe, nephew of Madame Tison. She requested me to visit you."

"Hello, sit down and join us," John said, pointing to a chair. "We're from the United States, here on holiday. I'm John, my wife Elaine, and our friends from India, Askara and Darian, and this crazy Aussie, Sara, is a real card shark. Watch out for her."

"I, too, lived in the United States, in Pennsylvania."

"God help you!" John joked. The young man didn't laugh. Repressing a grin, John continued, "What took you there?"

"I went to university for graduate studies."

"Which one?"

"Pennsylvania State University—engineering."

"Now what?" Askara asked.

He looked at her as if she had asked a difficult question. "I returned to Madagascar to start a telecommunications company."

"Were you born here?" Sara said.

"No, in France, but I lived here from age two to seventeen when I left to attend the Sorbonne Université in Paris."

"Which do you prefer?" Elaine asked as she neatly folded the napkin she had used and placed it on the table.

"Childhood here was good. Université was great. Graduate school was difficult. But here, many French do not mix with non-French. I miss the American melting pot. My Aunt Clarisse, Madame Tison, always insisted I should embrace everyone. She is part Malagasy, you see. Of my family, I am the only one, besides my aunt, who feels at home in Madagascar. My brothers and sisters prefer Paris."

Philippe turned his head quickly, hearing his name called. "I must go. Please enjoy your stay. We are at your service."

When he walked toward the foyer, Askara thought she saw a dark silhouette clinging to his back, like a cutout of black paper glued to his shirt. She jerked involuntarily; the image faded. She wondered at the liqueur's strength…and her level of fatigue. At the sound of a gong, everyone moved inside, where Philippe waved them into the Red Velvet Lounge, which Sara whispered was named for its red velvet overstuffed chairs, chaise lounges, and red brocade wallpaper.

"Fair dinkum, the perfect image of a Parisian brothel, I reckon."

Madame Tison joined her guests, the perfect hostess for a captive audience. She began by telling amusing stories of past hotel guests—some famous, some notorious—but she quickly moved to her favorite.

"My favorite person, from the history of Madagascar, is one whom I might say is infamous yet beloved by me, Captain Misson of Provence."

Madame Tison made a broad sweep with her gold-braceleted arm to point at the wall behind her where a large oil painting hung. Its heavy varnish glistened in the ambient light. A uniformed young man, his chest broad to the stiff wind that swirled around his unruly black hair like a dark halo, stood with one boot securely balanced on a rock in the foreground and smiled with confidence. His finely chiseled, weathered face and wry smile echoed the smugness of his companion several steps behind him, a priest dressed in a black cassock, his round, ruddy face looking directly at the viewer. He also gathered the dark folds of his mantle around him against the stiff wind. In the background, a ship sat anchored on a placid pale green sea. A plaque, front-and-center on the ornate gilt frame read: *His High Excellency the Conservator.*

Madame Tison explained that the young man in the portrait loved adventure. After receiving a good education that had prepared him for a distinguished career in finance, Misson left his home in France to travel the world by sea as an adventurer. On one of his many travels, he befriended a certain Dominican priest, the one pictured beside him, Father Caraccioli from Rome.

"The time," she emphasized, "was at the beginning of the French Revolution in 1790 when the philosophy of Jean Jacques Rousseau fired the flames of discontent…and the quest for liberty. The Dominican and the captain shared a common dream of utopia. They aided the revolutionaries until they decided to honor God and Liberty by crossing the seas to establish a new equalitarian society.

"They chose the little-known island of Madagascar where they established a small base in the well-protected bay we now call *Baie des Français.* They named the colony the International Republic of Libertalia. But those dreamers had a practical side—how to fund their adventure-loving natures? Finding the answer in pirate trade, they raided ships as far away as the Mediterranean Sea, acting, of course, in the name of God and Liberty, for the salvation of souls, even if that meant sending them prematurely to heaven." A broad grin stretched Madame Tison's crimson painted lips.

"Their republic consisted of three ships and three hundred Comorian workers lent them by the Queen of Anjouan. They had aided her in local conflicts between the kings and queens of the four islands in the Comoro Archipelago by raiding passing ships and disabling them. She was indebted to them, you see. Gangs of sailors—English, Dutch, and Portuguese—enlisted, seeing the good captain's victories at sea. Some African Negroes joined in.

"Thus, the colony started. The pirates had seized the first women of Libertalia as slaves, but Father Caraccioli assigned them husbands and performed a group wedding ceremony immediately since no great country can prosper without children, and no marriage is legal if not justified in the eyes of God. Local Malagasy women also married the new settlers voluntarily, as did my kinswoman, my great-great-grandmother, who married Captain Misson for love.

"The colony grew rich from pirated booty. True to their ideals, the good captain and the priest devised a new international language, freed the slaves, disarmed the war prisoners who had been taken at sea, offering them the freedom to leave—minus their guns—or to stay and settle. They introduced an elected parliament to make laws, with one member representing every ten voters, and they kept detailed paperwork as indeed any good, modern state should. Hence, we know their story. And with the latest printing press, they published a republican code of conduct and an official gazette.

"Captain Misson became 'His High Excellency the Conservator' and served the people well...so well that the word of their prosperity spread. Thus, the Malagasy natives grew jealous of the new settlement's wealth, not quite converted to these two prophets' humanitarian ideals. One night they made a surprise attack, slaughtering Europeans. My kinswoman was spared, like others, because of their Malagasy blood, but poor Father Caraccioli was the first to be murdered. The good captain, Misson, however, escaped with a handful of French sailors. Unfortunately, they had difficulty near North Africa when a cyclone overturned Le Grande Serpent; some survived, but the captain disappeared. No one knew his fate.

"Years later, two Frenchmen—survivors of that shipwreck—returned to La Rochelle with a manuscript they had saved, written by the good captain himself. It was a record of his Republic of Libertalia. We kept it in our family until modern times when we gifted it to the library sponsored by the French Embassy in Antananarivo."

Madame Tison, holding her rapt audience in an upturned hand, smiled and tipped her head. No one stirred. She concluded: "This lovely painting was created in 1800 by a French artist who had visited the Republic of Libertalia after leaving the Congo, a Monsieur Simon Marchand. He worked from sketches he had drawn while here in Madagascar. My family, glad to have a record of their prodigal son, purchased the painting some fifteen years later when Monsieur Marchand appeared at their door in Paris with a canvas roll under his arm."

Madame Tison bowed. "And that ends the story of the famous Captain Misson." The hotel guests clapped and whistled enthusiastically. Blushing slightly, she clasped her braceleted hands together at her chest and said, "Please, enjoy your stay in Madagascar, and come back to see us often."

A man seated near the door shouted, "Madame, what became of the treasure? They say the captain was a famous pirate."

"Ah," she said with a twinkle in her eye, "we do not know. The good captain's records make it clear that much in the way of gold coins and jewels had been seized in raids. He mentions the 'treasure of all treasures' that he himself guarded 'would astound the world and make the Pope cry.' One can only dream how ornate an object that must have been considering the wealth of the Vatican. But alas, we have nothing but his written word—all else vanished."

Madame raised her cognac to salute her guests. "*Bonsoir*," she said, and turning, she left with a swish of satin in her wake.

John laughed. "The grand dame should have been an actress. She's got it down."

"Don't you like her?" Elaine asked. "I do."

"Like her? She's superb; pulled the audience right in, held 'em, a class act. Great for business too. You know, if you ever come back to this part of the world, you'll come back to see her. Right?"

"I sure would," Elaine agreed, "because I like her."

"Yeah, she's very entertaining. I'm not saying I don't like her; I do. She leaves you no room not to."

John looked at Askara, lost in thought. "What about you, Askara?"

She roused from her faraway stare. "Oh, she's great, a born storyteller."

"You see, just the response she hopes for—and gets. She's shrewd, that old girl; very shrewd."

"John, you're always suspecting people."

"No, Elaine, you misjudge me. I am always reading them. That's all. Like Askara here—her mind is a thousand miles away."

Askara grinned. "Kind of. I'm pretty tired. Think I'll go up now. See you all in the morning."

Darian took Askara's cue and wished the others good-night. Walking up the stairs, he said, "What's bothering you, Sweetie? Do you feel well?"

"I need to get back. This has been fun, but I came here to work, my first journalism assignment, and all I'm doing is tourist stuff. Can we head back to Tana in the morning... rent a private car?"

"Yes. That suits me. Sara has plenty of things to do in Tana if she chooses to go back with us. Who knows, she may want to sightsee with John and Elaine some more. You're right. You came to work; sightseeing comes second."

CHAPTER SEVEN

The Famadihana Ceremony

O n the morning of the ceremony, Mea seemed agitated when she arrived at the hotel to speak to Askara. Wondering if she were ill, Askara asked Mea when she stepped out of the taxi, "What's the matter?"

Mea fumbled with the tissue clutched in her palm. She remained silent for several seconds before replying that Alistair was to accompany her, but they had a disagreement. They argued, she confided, because he did not want her to take this job, so he stayed home.

"Alistair thinks the ceremony is rubbish, and it might strain me. You see, I am pregnant."

The declaration shocked Askara because Mea was so thin. "How many months?"

"Six."

"I would not have guessed. Any complications? Is that why he's worried?"

Mea winced. "It hasn't been an easy pregnancy. I haven't put on weight. I have miscarried before." Tears glazed Mea's eyes. "I want to get this ceremony done so that we can fly back to the UK for medical care and the birth. Our baby must be a UK citizen, born at a hospital, in case there is a problem."

A feeling of dread washed over Askara. The last thing she wanted was to strain Mea or jeopardize her pregnancy. "You don't have to do this. You've done enough. The family has met me and approved. I can handle the famadihana. You can translate my tape right after and fly to England. No need to attend the ceremony yourself."

Mea looked at her with sad, droopy eyes as if she had not heard Askara's words. "You see…I am older than I look. I outnumber Alistair by twelve years."

Askara took this admission as one in a list of intriguing revelations about Mea. Years earlier, when Alistair—a white Christian Britisher—met Mea, he had already converted to Islam. Mea remained a Christian, which, as she pointed out, most Muslim men wouldn't allow. Mea, of Black-African and French heritage, married a white man from a rural, conservative farming family in Holsworthy, in the west of England. Now they were expecting a mixed-race child, which neither family wanted to accept, but who, if born on English soil, would be a citizen of Britain when his mother was not.

"Mea, how old are you?"

"Thirty-seven. My age, plus previous miscarriages—one at six months—is why we are so worried. That and this job."

Askara put her arm around Mea's shoulders and gave her a soft caress. "Don't worry, Mea; I can handle this. Thank you for all you have done."

Mea looked at Askara's dark, probing eyes, dropped her entwined hands into the pockets of her brown A-line skirt, and said in a low voice, "We need the money."

"Yes. Absolutely, I can pay you today. You should have mentioned this earlier."

For a second, Askara entertained the thought she was being set up. Mea didn't look pregnant, but she did look distressed. "What about this ceremony bothers Alistair so much? Why doesn't he want you to go?"

Mea fixed Askara with a hard stare. "Sometimes things go badly if the spirit of the deceased is upset. A restless spirit can cause problems for the living."

"Like what?"

"They can frighten you to death, curse you, even curse your unborn child!"

Mea elaborated, trembling as she did, saying if the deceased had enemies when living, they would be jealous when the ancestor is exhumed, whether they are in body or spirit themselves. They band together, and at the moment of the deceased's triumph in the Bone Turning Ceremony, they bring him down. It can be vicious. If the deceased himself had a malicious nature, he might delight in tormenting the living.

Often the dead resent being dead. It depends on how that person passed over, if spirit guardians ushered him over, or if the Bringer of Death ridiculed and tortured him, especially in front of other ancestor spirits. In some cases, the deceased takes revenge when the rewrapping of the shroud empowers his spirit.

Askara found this mumbo jumbo challenging to believe, although she could see Mea thought it was real. She attributed her own anxiousness to Mea's fears for her unborn child and her strained marriage. Anyone would be nervous.

"Look, Mea, I appreciate all you've done. You got me the family's permission to attend. If you will translate my tape recording after the ceremony, that's all I need. There is no need for you to go with me. Could you do that within two days after the ceremony?"

"Yes."

"Well, that settles it. You'll receive full pay as we agreed today, but you will not attend. Okay?"

"If that is how you want it," Mea replied with an audible sigh of relief.

Askara waved for Imboule, who sat slumped in the Fiat rental car by the valet parking lot. He pulled up to join them. Askara told Mea to instruct Imboule about the change, that he would drive them and make sure he understood the directions. Mea explained in Malagasy where the family's tomb was on the city's outskirts to the north and the time he should pick up Askara, her husband, and their friend at the hotel. She emphasized he should not park nearby but wait for them, watch the crowd from a respectful distance, and not anger the family in any way.

Askara pulled out an envelope from her pack, placed Mea's fee inside, and hugged her goodbye. Mea climbed into the taxi with Imbloule, and they started to pull away.

"Thank you, Askara. God bless you. Stay alert! The worst thing is to run!"

ON THE DRIVE TO THE FAMADIHANA, IMBOULE HEADED north while Askara settled back, squeezed between Darian and Sara, with her feet resting on her camera bag, pondering Mea's warning. What did she mean by "the worst thing is to run"? She noticed Imboule studying her in the car's rearview mirror.

"Imboule, do you understand the ceremony?"

"No, madame. I am a Muslim. We do not keep this ceremony."

"Have you heard of it being dangerous?"

"No, madame."

Darian looked at Askara, slumped on the sticky plastic seat, and asked, "Why did you say that?"

"No reason."

Sara snickered. "They say dead men don't lie. Maybe that only applies to pirates, but I doubt an old skeleton face will say much. No worries, friend. Get your story and photos, and afterward, let's go out for a good dinner. I've heard the locals love a dish called *smalona,* smoked eels stuffed with olives, mushrooms, and apples. I'd like to try that before I go."

"Wow, Sara, that sounds terrible, but you get what you want. I'd like to try the dish called *nem,* small crepes with a veggie filling, potatoes, cabbage, and onions, deep-fried. What do you want, Darian?"

"*Rabimbomanga sy patsamona.* Not sure how to say it, but it's sweet potato leaves stuffed with dried shrimp in a tomato sauce, served over rice, a local favorite."

"Okay, when we get back, we'll ask the concierge for the best locals' favorite restaurant in Tana. We'll celebrate. Too bad our holiday is almost over. I like this place."

Imboule slowed, turning from Tana's main boulevard onto a rutted, narrow road that followed garden plots, little green rectangles of paper strung along a dirt rope. The morning light illuminated the hilltops above. A slight breeze came up. Imboule pulled over at a crossroads, pointed to the right, and said, "Over there, walk that path. I wait here for you."

"You aren't parking closer, Imboule?" Darian asked.

"No, monsieur. Mea said no. I am Muslim."

Darian shook his head and looked at Askara. She was busy gathering her camera bag, checking her film, and testing the cassette recorder when she mumbled something about it not being allowed.

"Don't leave for any reason," Askara ordered Imboule when they stepped out.

"Madame. I wait here."

They followed the footpath through weathered tombs until Askara caught sight of the man and his family. He waved her over to where two men were digging a hole within the walls of a weathered stone structure.

"This must be it." She motioned to Darian and Sara to stay back.

She clipped the recorder to her belt when a group of jubilant people in bright-colored Western clothes gathered near the tomb to watch, laugh, and sing. Askara whispered into her microphone: "Turning the bones ceremony, August twentieth, 1975, north side of Antananarivo, Madagascar."

A wave of nausea tickled Askara's stomach when the acrid smell of the unearthed grave reached her. She coughed into the microphone. Guests continued to join the group. Several played lively music on a flute, while others strummed an instrument like a banjo, and drums got the people to dance with their hands waving overhead, smiling. A crowd of forty people gathered at the tomb to sing as the grandson and another man lifted the corpse from the earth, removed the old shroud, now brown with age and dirt, and rewrapped the corpse in the new silk shroud. The man Askara had met—the relative hosting the famadihana, the deceased's grandson—cinched the lengths of pure white silk in a woven grass mat to secure the bundle. They hoisted the lumpy sack overhead and danced, lifting the remains high and low, showing it off. Some people prayed; others cried in remembrance; others laughed with joy.

Askara whispered into her mic: "The grandson is parading the deceased in the sun and air, so the ancestor can feel the sensation of life again."

The grandson supported the head part of the shroud for all to see. People waved hello and danced. The joyous crowd followed the shroud parade around the tomb and beyond.

Askara spoke into the mic: "This is when they show the ancestor new changes in the village and inform him of births, deaths, crops, and marriages while people in the entourage dance to the music."

She raised her Canon F-1 camera and clicked away, its high-speed motor drive shooting nine frames per second. She followed the shroud at a respectful distance, using the telephoto lens to zoom in. The crowd pushed and shoved in the wake of the ancestor's mantle, each jockeying for a better position to receive a spiritual advantage. Askara climbed a low rise of earth to elevate herself above their heads. She saw Sara and Darian off to her far right, watching the procession from another small hill.

The host held his grandfather's remains high as they cruised the village. He shouted and pointed. Askara figured he pointed out where pivotal events had taken place since his grandfather had gone to spirit: children born, huts built, fields plowed, crops harvested, animals raised and sold, friends and relatives born and died. The crowd appeared entranced by the singing and dancing.

When they rounded an animal pen next to a thatched hut, Mea appeared as if from thin air. The guests didn't notice her, but Askara waved. She stepped down from the mound to approach Mea, her camera snapping photos as she walked. She didn't perceive her position relative to the shroud until she was directly in line with the corpse as if she were family. The grandson looked her way and stopped abruptly. The singing carried on. He shot her a fiery look, waved her away, and shouted something. The camera's motor drive kept clicking.

Mea yelled, "Askara! Stop! Back up! Don't turn. Back up now. Lower your camera. Bow your head! STOP!"

Askara followed Mea's directions immediately. She felt a gust of icy wind blast her face, chilling her flushed cheeks, turning her gut to mush. She wanted to lift her head, but she couldn't. She felt frozen in place.

A menacing shriek ripped through the crowd, a howl like a wild animal caught in a trap, crying for its life. The crowd whimpered. An immense pressure pushed down on Askara's shoulders, crushing the blades into her spine. A pain shot through her chest, making it difficult to breathe. She panted and waited, eyes closed, scared she was dying.

The family astrologer, howling like a wolf, circled the corpse, shaking his fist at the sky, babbling frantically.

Mea edged through the crowd toward Askara. In a strained voice, she said, "Askara, you angered the ancestor. You took pictures of his face. He woke with fury. Now he cannot look at his village with pleasure because a mortal dared to look him in the eye. Mortals and spirits should not exchange direct glances. This disobedience disgraces the family and brings ruin. The astrologer is telling the guests this."

Trembling, Askara cried, "I did *not* look. I didn't see anything! Tell them."

Mea offered Askara's words to the angry crowd, but the astrologer wailed in rebuke. He bolstered his proclamation, saying he had seen a warning earlier, on June thirtieth, when an earthquake hit Madagascar. He had cast this day for the famadihana, but the stars, shaken when the earth roared, fell out of alignment that morning. When the foreigner stepped into the crevice between earth and spirit, the astrologer realized there would be a problem. The disrespectful woman angered the ancestor. Now he could not rest. His family would receive no blessing from this ceremony.

The crowd gasped, hearing his dire prediction. Soft gray dusk descended rapidly. Over the hilltops, the sky, streaked with heat lightning, flashed with a staccato rumble. The guests pointed to the sky and huddled close, wailing. A family elder screamed and dropped to the earth, flailing like a beetle on his back trying to right himself. In a deep intonation, he bellowed words that made women shriek and children cry.

Mea's voice trembled when she whispered, "Askara, you are responsible for this, he says. For the ancestor to rest, the astrologer says you must save his spirit from this torment."

The grandson rose and, with bowed head, solemnly took his place near the litter. The family pulled the silk tightly around the remains and walked silently to the tomb, where they lowered the bundle and covered it with loose earth.

When Askara looked for Darian, she saw two men holding him and Sara in place. Darian's face looked contorted with concern. Askara wanted to run to him, but she dared not move. Eyes pinned her feet to the ground.

The deceased's grandson turned from the tomb, wiping tears from his face, and thanked the guests for attending but demanded they leave quickly. The astrologer assured the worried guests no harm would come to their village.

The grandson walked away, leaving other family members to finish the reburial, his wife and children quaking in tow. Askara and Mea stood alone in the dim light to let the crowd disperse.

"What will happen now, Mea? What should I do?"

"I don't know. We must leave this place. It is not safe," Mea said and headed downhill, waving for Darian and Sara to follow.

"Mea, I don't think I photographed the ancestor's head. I'm sure I didn't."

"They think you did. That is what matters. We will know from your photos."

"What will they do to me?"

"The family will not physically harm you if that is what you are thinking. But they will ask for the money for another ceremony, although," Mea said and trotted ahead, "a second ceremony is never performed for the same ancestor. They may say they want money to honor another family member and appease their ancestors in that way, but do not give it to them. That would prove your guilt."

"I feel terrible about this."

"Askara, do you remember that Alistair was going to come to the ceremony in the beginning?"

"Yes. I thought so."

"He did not come for a reason. When our landlord heard I was your translator, he told Alistair that the family had abandoned the grandfather to die when he was ill. They never waited on him, never got him herbs, never had the shaman come. Our landlord, a respected village elder, predicted evil would come from this ceremony. The grandfather would get his revenge on the family. The family would blame you for the ancestor's displeasure to keep the sympathy of their relatives and neighbors, pocket the money for this ceremony, and even get more for another. He said it was a trap. You weren't in the correct position to photograph the deceased's head. I am sure of it. The litter was above you. I was opposite you, in front of the remains. I saw you."

"When did you come back? Why did you?"

"Once Alistair explained, I didn't feel it fair to leave you out here. I got a taxi and arrived after the exhumation had begun. Alistair wanted to come with me to ensure I was safe, but many know he is a Muslim. And sometimes, an Englishman is not seen with clear eyes here."

"Are you sure the ancestor is angry with us? Do you trust the words of that man?"

"No, I am sure he is correct. The astrologer made a mistake and is trying to cover it up. But, yes, the ancestor spirits are upset. You saw the sky. They were lured to the famadihana out of the family's greed, not honor, so they felt tricked. The gate between worlds opens for only a short time. The ancestor spirit must leave before it closes or risk getting stuck at the new moon. If that happens, he cannot return to the ancestral world. He will roam the earth, possibly torment others out of anger. Who knows what misfortune will take place in the next few days? But I do know this— the family will attribute it to you for photographing the ancestor's face."

"I missed my chance for a great cover story, my first assignment."

"You have an interesting story for a foreign audience. You got photos, except for the reburial. Yes?"

"My camera clicked away as they lowered the corpse. I heard it. I was too afraid to move and stop it."

"End your article there. Do not include the closing remarks. You will have the cassette recording, yes?"

"Yes," Askara said, inspecting the microphone. "It's been running the entire time." She turned it off.

"I expect something will go wrong now. You will lose your film, or it won't turn out, or the sound recording didn't work, or…."

"Or what?"

"Or you won't make it back to submit your article."

"What do you mean by that?"

"It is only days until the new moon. Much can happen in that time. Be very careful, Askara."

"Mea, do you mean my life might be in danger?"

"Yes—if the deceased believes you are responsible. If this was all a hoax to get money, then the family is in danger. Spirit ancestors will avenge themselves on the culprit, not you. I am not so worried about you, but someone will pay."

"Won't they take revenge on the ancestor's grandson? It's his fault."

"He may truly believe it is your fault. Possibly he didn't know the others had not attended to his grandfather. By the way, he and his family left in silence. I think they believe it is your fault, although it worked out well for him in ways, which, of course, he will not tell anyone."

"I should expose the family as frauds. That would capture the readers' interest."

Mea got a pained expression; her thin skin taut across her high cheekbones formed delicate ripples. "Please, show respect for our customs. The ceremony is a great honor—and no one takes it lightly. The ancestor will take revenge in some way."

Askara saw Darian and Sara reach Imboule at the car. When Mea and Askara approached, Imboule spoke rapidly to Mea in Malagasy. She urged them to jump in.

"What's going on?" Darian asked, grabbing Askara's cold hand.

"Something went wrong. What did Imboule say, Mea?"

"He saw a dark, swirling cloud rise from the tomb hill, an evil sign, so he decided to drive closer to fetch us. We must leave immediately."

In a tone one would use with a child, Mea explained to Imboule that it was fire smoke, nothing more, knowing Mohammedans had forgotten the ancestors' ways. When she asked how he could see what he didn't believe in, Imboule apologized, realizing his breach of faith, and replied he saw only fire smoke from the banquet.

Darian and Sara remained silent, listening to Askara and Mea, but everyone dropped into silence on the bumpy drive back to the hotel. Wild thoughts raced through Askara's head. Unsure of what had, or had not, taken place, she did know the pain in her gut. Now, a cold-hot knife cut deeply.

When they dropped Mea at her compound, Askara saw Alistair peer out from the second-floor window and rush downstairs, his heavy footfalls on the cement as audible as his heavy panting. Mea jumped out of the car to meet him.

"I'll contact you at the hotel tomorrow," she said and hurried toward Alistair, teetering on her stacked heels. Alistair threw his arms around his wife and led her in without acknowledging the others.

Askara sat on the back seat, digging her fingernails into the vinyl upholstery as they jostled along the backroads to Hotel du Parc. When Imboule pulled into the circular drive in the front, two guards, standing on the oil-stained red carpet, opened the door to escort the guests into the building.

"No Woman, No Cry" sung by Bob Marley poured into the foyer from the nightclub. Askara raced upstairs to their room. When she opened the door, the smell of smoldering mosquito coils made her sick. Turning to Darian and Sara lagging behind her, she said, "I need a drink. Wanna go down to the bar for a glass of wine?"

"Doubt they have it, but, yes, good idea," Darian said. "We want to hear what happened back there."

"Fair dinkum, weirdest thing I've seen. If that was an honor, why the hell were people freaked out?"

"That's what I need to talk about with you. Let's go down."

The bar was relatively empty. Only two couples circled each other on the small dance floor, and a few singles sat at the bar. Askara looked over to see Ed Healy, slumped forward on the bar, straighten up quickly, unwrapping his short feet entwined in the stool's metal legs. When he called out for them to join him, he motioned to the bartender for service.

"What would you like?" Ed laughed. "Let me guess, wine? The French are alive and well on this island, so, of course, there's wine. Bordeaux for all?"

"Fine," Askara replied, taking the barstool next to Ed. Darian sat next to her, and Sara took the stool on the other side of Ed, to his obvious delight.

"I called on you earlier…thought we might eat together. The desk said you were out."

Askara forced a slight chuckle that faded. "I was on that ceremony assignment today."

"Oh? How did it go? Got the shots for that article? I wanted to go, but the family didn't consent. I was busy anyway with the lemur documentary. Did Meamoni translate for you?"

"Yes, she will."

"Is turning the old bones amusing? What do you say, Darian, worthy of a documentary?"

"Possibly. However, I didn't understand much of what was going on."

"It didn't go all that well," Askara said, taking a swig of red wine.

"How come?"

Darian looked at Askara and shook his head *no*, but she continued. "The family says I photographed the deceased's head, a major faux pas."

"Let me guess...and now the ancestors are pissed off, and you need to pay up to appease them. Right?"

"Yep, you got it. The ancestors are pissed off," Askara replied, seeing Ed's pulpy face widen to a grin. "I didn't, at least I'm pretty sure I didn't, do anything wrong."

"You're a reporter. We do things to get a good story, even piss off spooks."

"It stopped the ceremony. The family left."

"Their loss," he said, gulping down a beer. "Actually, it'll be yours when they ask you for money. That comes next. Don't do it. I've been there. Rabbit hole."

"The ancestors cursed us saying that for the gate to the spirit realm to close— I think the one closest to the door at the new moon—someone will have to pay so the ancestor can rest."

"Who the hell is closest to the door at the new moon? And what the hell does that mean anyway? What and where is that freaking door? Askara, it's a load of bullshit. Forget it."

Askara shrugged and moaned audibly...offering no formal reply.

"Hey, Darian, tell your wife this is a load of crap! Askara, you're not falling for that stuff, are you? I'd heard the Christian mag that hired you had been looking for two years to find the right family to buy. The Malagasy typically don't let outsiders go to the walking-the-dead-bone-turning thing. Yeah, the family's gonna come back at you, Askara, for more—that's how they'll settle the curse. I suppose a local holy man, probably the family's astrologer, explained what went wrong. Right?"

Askara, feeling sheepish, whispered, "Yes."

"Sorry, honey," Ed said with a raucous laugh. "You've done been had. Too bad you missed the opportunity for the article."

"But I didn't, Ed. I mean, I got the shots, and I recorded it. Mea's going to translate the tape for me."

"Well, no worries, eh? You got your story. Go home, publish it, and leave the family to fight over their misfortune—or fortune—I should say."

Darian joined in, "Good point, Ed."

"One thing I've learned," Ed said, leaning in, "is never show your backside. Never show you're vulnerable, not to anyone, not for anything. If I've learned anything since I left Ohio, it's that."

Ed drained his glass, tapping it with his index finger for another. "Just today, when we were filming the lemurs, damned if one of those critters didn't swoop down and hit the camera lens while we were filming a mother giving birth. It would have damaged the lens if I hadn't had a filter on. It did ruin the shot. That's just an animal. Think of the havoc people wreak. Whaddya say, Miss Sara Aussie? Am I right?"

"Right. In Australia, we say never turn your back on a croc…odile. Same shit applies here."

Ed turned dark, laughing, and made a loud whoop. "I like you, girl. Move closer to me. I wanna get to know you better."

Sara smiled, "Not on your life, bloke. I've got my reputation to think of."

CHAPTER EIGHT

The Translation

After a fitful sleep, dreaming an airport official refused her exit visa, Askara woke with a start when someone knocked. She walked to the door and stood listening. Imboule's voice made her jump.

"Madame, le petit déjeuner."

When Askara opened the door to see the young man holding a silver tray of covered dishes and a small yellow-and-white vase full of daisies, she said, "Bonjour, Imboule. I didn't order this." He tipped his head and walked in to set the tray on the table by the sliding glass door.

"Bonjour, madame, bon appétit. Monsieur ordered. Meamoni will come to you this morning at eleven. Do I drive for sightseeing today?"

"I'm not sure. Check back after Meamoni arrives. *Merci*, Imboule," she said, ushering him out the door, handing him a tip.

Askara eagerly awaited Mea's arrival with the cassette tape translation. She figured Darian had gone out for a walk since she had slept in. She felt anxious, wondering what the village elder had said at the ceremony when he blamed her, and every-

one had stared at her with repulsion or what she thought was repulsion. She had received no word from the deceased's family, neither a request for money nor any form of condemnation. In fact, they had been silent since the ceremony.

Askara had taken time to write down some notes of her perception of the event. If Mea asked her about specific instances, Askara hoped they could compare notes that would clear her of accusations. When she reviewed the event calmly and slowly, she realized the guests had departed rapidly after the elder's decree and had left without jeering or overt anger. How could that be? The most crucial event in a family's life had gone array, yet no family member had as much as insulted the person supposedly responsible. That made no sense to Askara.

By the time Mea knocked on the door, Askara hardly waited for her to sit before she began a rapid volley of questions. The fatigue evident in Mea's constricted expression made her stop.

"Mea, are you unwell?"

Mea raised her heavy lids with effort and rolled her eyes. "Not very well—exhausted. Do we talk here? Where is your husband?"

"Out, not sure where. Should we go to a café to talk?"

"No, this is better; no one will hear us."

"I'm sorry this has been so hard on you, Mea. But it's over. Just give me the translation, and we're finished."

"You may find this translation incredible. And you may find you are not finished."

"What do you mean?"

"Do you recall the ceremony well?"

"Fairly well. I was jotting down notes before you came. I have it all except for the few lines spoken by the elder."

"I also thought I had recalled it...until I listened to the tape. More happened there than I heard at the time. I don't know how to tell you this. The ceremony was a small part of what took place. It was like a window or a door, a view to another realm. The deceased ancestor, or some spirit, used the gap between our physical world and the spirit world to send a message, a request, to you."

Mea shifted uncomfortably in her chair and held up a stack of papers. "All this!"

"But Mea, the spoken ceremony lasted only a few minutes, remember?"

"I do. But all this," Mea said, flipping through the papers, "must have happened. I didn't make it up. Your microphone recorded it."

"No, I trust you, but how is that possible?"

Mea shrugged her bony shoulders. "I don't know. Let me explain the main points first. The ancestor knew the family was dishonest. After discovering they could get more money if someone wrote a news article about it, they agreed to the ceremony. That angered the grandfather and his relatives in spirit. The ancestor said his grandson did not care for him when he was alive or dead. But the man did not die because of their neglect. He cries he was poisoned."

"Oh, God, his family murdered him?"

"No, Askara, not his family." Mea started to shake, clutching her stomach. She blurted out, "The ancestor felt you were responsible because of something you did."

"Work for the Christian Coalition of Catholic Churches? That's crazy. I don't believe it."

"The deceased explained the injustice started a long time ago, in a distant time and place, but it must end now. The speaker said an innocent soul will be exchanged at the new moon for balance." Tears rolled down the sunken hollows of Mea's cheek. "I think this innocent soul is my baby!" She grasped her belly, "My baby, Askara. You must help me."

Askara exhaled rapidly. "What have I done? Nothing." She threw her arms around Mea, crying, "I am so sorry, Mea. I never wanted to harm anyone. This makes no sense. Your baby is fine; no harm will come to him. I think there's a misunderstanding. Earlier, it seemed the innocent was Jean-Paul." Askara took a deep breath and tried to think calmly. "Could you tell who was speaking?"

"The voice on the tape said that you would speak those exact words. The reply was: 'Think about your dream, the exit visa. Remember, you once held a vessel of power. Obtain your exit visa; do your duty by helping the servant in a time gone past, in a lifetime you shared. Then you will understand and move forward.'"

Askara pressed her finger to Mea's lips. "Shh. I don't want to hear anymore. I'll read it myself." Mea handed the cassette tape and the transcription pages to Askara. "Don't worry, Mea. I'll work this out. Your baby will not suffer. Trust me." Askara, disturbed but hoping for more, looked at Mea's dark, murky eyes that blinked like a lake slapped by a gust of wind. She said curtly, "Mea, go home and rest. I will meet you tomorrow at the hotel café at four. Do not speak of this to anyone, not even to Alistair."

"Askara, we have little time. The ancestor said by the new moon."

"I'll come up with something—somehow. I promise. Go now. Rest."

Askara couldn't get Mea out of her room fast enough. She popped the cassette into the player with shaking hands and collapsed on the chair to listen to the famadihana ceremony. Seconds passed, becoming scratchy minutes. The tape rolled on wordlessly. Askara flipped the cassette to the other side and rewound to the beginning. Poised like an ice sculpture, she waited, chewing her nails. Nothing. She fast-forwarded, rewound, and flipped the tape from side to side, trying again and again. Lifting it from the machine, she checked the label: "Walking the Dead report by Askara Timlen, Madagascar, August 1975."

Frustrated, she threw the cassette on the bed and grabbed the typed transcript. Scanning it, she stumbled on a passage. She trembled, reading these words:

Daughter, I feared this would come to you, a hurdle you must clear to resume your journey home. When the worlds aligned in this ceremony, I took the opportunity to reach out to you. Earlier, when you chose not to cross the Chinvat Bridge into the world of spirit to join me, you extended your earthly duties. Such is the ensnarement of the physical. Having spiritual wealth at your feet, you rushed back to the material world. Now you must make right something from a previous life to gain your exit visa in this one, thus paying a debt.

Askara felt the blood drain from her face. She leaned back in the chair. Her heart raced, cold sweat beaded on her forehead, and numbness crept up from her feet. She cried out, "I don't know how to. Who are you? The Respected One? I do vaguely remember. But I've lost my ability to see the way I did when you were my teacher. I put you out of my mind. It was easier, less painful."

Askara heard a reply as clearly as if the Respected One, her adoptive father from ages past, were in the hotel room with her. "The question is, daughter, are you willing?"

"Yes."

"So be it. Stand ready; your vision will become clear."

Askara flipped through the remaining papers in the stack to see typed letters fade as fast as she turned the pages. She blinked. Only white stared back at her. She whimpered.

How? What does Mea know? Did the pages contain information Mea could summarize? If the cassette had been wiped clean, was Mea's memory of the message deleted simultaneously?

Askara longed to talk to Darian, to relax in his arms, but he and Sara must have gone down for breakfast. She threw on her olive-green skirt and jacket and ran downstairs to the café.

When she crossed the polished tiles of the foyer, she heard a familiar voice, a raspy whisper. "Bonjour, madame." Turning, she saw a thin, humped-shouldered man silhouetted against the light pouring in from the street window.

"Bonjour, Jean-Paul," she replied, noticing he clutched a black umbrella. "Rain today?"

"Sun. Will you join me for a café au lait?"

"Odd, I was thinking of you, and you appeared. But you're dead, Jean-Paul. So, I must be dreaming or crazy."

"Not dead to you—am I, madame?"

"That's the scary part; you look just as you were." Askara shook her head. A starched-uniform waiter, uncomfortable in his brittle suit, approached and melted through Jean-Paul on his way into the café.

"This is one thing I object to," Jean-Paul whispered. "The *garçon* should escort us to the table and pull out your chair." Jean-Paul motioned her in and pointed to a table. When seated, he unfurled the table linen. "A good *garçon* can make you feel happy to sit and relax with a café au lait. But how can you relax when the poor boy's suit crucifies him, and he can't bend to pull out your chair?"

Askara smiled. "One of the deficits of colonialism, I guess."

"Madame? Yes? You want le petit-déjeuner?" the waiter asked.

"I'll watch you enjoy," Jean-Paul said, crunching his bushy eyebrows. "One of the many travesties I must endure."

"Non, merci, café au lait," Askara said, attempting to act normal.

"You appear *très fatigue*. Did the ceremony alarm you, Madame Askara?"

Askara welcomed his initiating the topic, even if Jean-Paul were a figment of her imagination. Someone cared, even if that someone wasn't alive. "It was a failure," she whispered into her coffee cup. "People blamed me for photographing the deceased's face, a terrible transgression."

Jean-Paul nodded. "I know. I attended."

Askara eagerly listened to his perspective and quickly realized the ceremony snafu had nothing to do with her camera shots. It began long ago. The family had let the grandfather, a good and decent man, languish unaided for selfish reasons. They didn't want to pay for the medicine. That was their crime, one heinous enough to guarantee the anger of the ancestors.

Jean-Paul agreed that negligence caused the current rift in the family. But he continued, explaining the man of the recent famadihana had died in a previous time, and that circumstance was the crux of the problem. He had been the personal servant to the archbishop of Avignon in France during the French Revolution. His life then precipitated the current situation, and both events, then and now, relate to Askara.

"That entanglement is what called you here to Madagascar at this time. Your opposition appears greater than you can imagine, madame. A certain family on this island will do anything to protect their heritage."

Askara held her napkin over her mouth, pretending to brush croissant crumbs away. "Can you help me from your side? I know nothing of this. How would I know about life in France at that time? Much less what people want of me this time. I'm being framed, and I don't know for what."

"No. Neither can my granddaughter Meamoni help you. This is your journey, madame. When I look back at my sadness, wondering if my line is cursed, I fear for dear Meamoni. She is not a robust woman; childbearing is *très difficile* for her. You will never see her again, not even to say goodbye. She and her husband Alistair are driving to the airport as you sip your café au lait."

Askara's eyes widened. She leaned over the table, lowered her voice, hung her head, and said, "The ceremony opened some sort of door between the spirit world and this one. Correct? If the door isn't closed before the new moon, the ancestor won't rest peacefully. Is that it? The one closest to the door at the new moon will be sacrificed to close the door, an innocent soul. That innocent soul could be your granddaughter's unborn child. I had thought it was you, Jean-Paul. Guess I was wrong."

"*Mon Dieu.* You understand little. I shall leave you with this. Look to Brother Gestang for help and to the Kalanoro. Contact the priest. He was a young man assigned to Monsignor Devereaux. In church command, he is second to Devereaux, and he, like Devereaux, belongs to a society. Everyone knows Priest Gestang and the monsignor disagree. Possibly, this friction will loosen Gestang's tongue. You have little time before the new moon. Act quickly. Do not overlook the secrets held by many."

With those words, Jean-Paul faded into the chair's upholstery. Askara stood and swiped her hand above the chair but felt nothing.

"Yes, madame, you waved? More café au lait?" the waiter said.

"No. I'll sign for the bill now."

Askara tried to piece together the information but came up with little that made sense, aside from that permission to cover the ceremony originated with the Christian Coalition of Catholic Churches, and Devereaux must sign off on it. And it was the monsignor who chose the family and arranged her permission to attend. Priest Gestang was only a go-between. Ed Healy had suggested Mea as the translator, but that meant nothing. None of the facts elicited any pertinent information. She wondered, *what do I do now?*

When Askara left the hotel café, she looked up and down the street for Darian and Sara. A young boy spotted her and ran up with a basket of red apples. "*Mademoiselle, très* sweet." He forced an apple up to her mouth, but she waved him down. He stepped back. "*Trois por deux francs.*" The boy looked at his basket, picked out three medium-sized apples, and dropped them into her bag. Exasperated, Askara withdrew the francs from her pocket to pay. The boy flashed a large smile, saying "Merci, mademoiselle," and accosted the next person who exited the hotel.

Askara returned to her room, where she heard the shower running. She tapped on the door and asked Darian where he had been. He replied that he and Sara had taken an early morning walk around Lake Alarobia, the freshwater lake in the city, to see the birds listed in the hotel brochure. He asked Askara to go, but she had not replied, so he let her sleep.

Darian stepped out from the bathroom to greet Askara and describe the lush forest surrounding the lake and the birds—black herons, the Madagascar grebe, red-billed teals, and many others he had never heard of that only thrive in Madagascar.

"I'll take you there. It's fantastic."

"Did Sara like the walk? I'm glad you two have bonded. I knew you would. But don't leave me out."

"I would never. I also want you to rest. You've been very edgy lately. Yes, Sara's quite knowledgeable about the natural world, more than I am." Darian stepped back into the bathroom to finish shaving. "I'll be out in a minute. Sara's getting ready too. Thought we could all go out for *mofogasy*, those fried rice flour pancakes everyone loves."

"Great idea, and strong coffee," Askara answered, her mind drifting. *Time is running out, and the new moon comes in a few days. Jean-Paul is not the one closest to the door at the new moon. Mea's baby may not be either. It could be anyone, even me.*

She realized she must discover the answer to this riddle. The cassette tape translation, according to Mea, warned for the deceased to rest, the door between the ancestral world of spirit and the living world would have to be closed. Something had to be resolved to make that happen. But what exactly, she didn't know. Askara did know it related to something or someone in the past in France.

"What the hell," she grumbled. Askara felt Father Gestang possibly held the answer. Her mind swam in circles, growing muddier and muddier, so she focused on Darian, who always comforted her. Pragmatic Darian had answers when she had only questions, but now was not the time to ask.

Askara laid down on the bed. She thought she saw a dark form slip between the curtain folds like a lengthening shadow in the corner of the room. Her body stiffened.

The room turned cold. More dark forms seeped in from crevices in the walls, from under the front door, through the balcony's closed glass door. A purple-gray mist hovered over her prone body. She felt words imprinted on her mind: *Come with us.*

She asked the room, "Am I dying?" She thought she heard a soft reply: "No one dies in transit. What greets you, we cannot say. Your actions, past and present, will determine that. We are conveyors. We are not answers. We are Kalanoro."

The shadowy forms lifted her body upright. Askara stood among them, watching her body become the substance of silvery vapor. All sensation left her. She weighed nothing; she felt nothing. Thoughts remained, spread thin like a blanket on rough ground, conforming to uneven terrain. What seconds earlier had looked like knots in muddy water expanded to distinct, perfect circles—orderly arrangements, clear and calm—organized patterns that shifted with the group movement. She traveled with the other forms like a volvox, a spherical ocean organism, an aggregate connected by silver impulses of thought. Images rushed past, too blurred to decipher. The unit hurtled along at tremendous speed, unaffected by outside pressure, held firm by inside cords of shimmering light. Askara, with no thoughts of her own, pulsed with the group, unified by a distant sound that pulled the volvox along. The dark forms receded into vapor; warmth returned to her feet, to her chest. A surge of molten lava exploded up her spine to her head.

Her eyes flew open. A figure approached and stood like a dark sentinel, beckoning her on. His eyes, like a television screen, projected visions from another time and place. He spoke slowly as if to not disturb the images that rushed like water from a breached dam. Askara swam in and through the visions with no resistance. She understood these words: *Be silent, watch, listen.*

Askara saw a man slumped on a stone floor. The voice spoke:

"The servant died wrongfully in the distant past. In the current famadihana ceremony, his spirit awakened to the crime in France many years ago. In the present, earthly curses from his unloving family, who tried to impress society with false respect, made him wail with anguish. From far away, you answered his cry. His lament that he was wronged again by the man he served and loved in France must be resolved now in Madagascar while he wedges open the portal between the worlds."

Askara gasped. "A Christian group hired me to write an article about the famadihana ceremony. That was all! I don't know about this other stuff."

"Your world works that way. You believe yourselves to be directors of fate when you are receivers. You must return to that distant time when you and the deceased ancestor were companions. Witness for him. Do not be afraid. We Kalanoro are your silver cord. We draw you back like pulling a fish from the stream. Learn from your journey. We think; you perceive. Look to Brother Gestang for information."

"What about Darian?"

"It will be but a blink of the eye in his world before you return."

CHAPTER NINE

The King's Treasure

ale yellow light pushed by muffled footsteps on polished floors broke into bits, falling on Askara's head like glitter. She felt her body race through a tunnel, its walls covered in moving images like a film on fast-forward. The light and pressure made her head throb. She shut her eyes. Her stomach lurched from the twisting and turning.

When the force abated, her head stopped vibrating like a colossal bell coming to rest. She opened her eyes to discover she was stuck on a high ceiling, clinging like a fly to ornate plaster molding. Below, a king sat on a velvet throne, lost in thought, his plumed hat and walking stick placed on the table by his side. A hard rap on the door roused him. Askara watched in stunned silence.

A small, portly man motioned a *valet de chambre* to bring his silk jacket on which the servant carefully affixed the blue-ribbon Star of the Holy Spirit. The king smiled confidently at the emblem, France's highest order, worn only by the *noblesse de court*.

"Come, come, we want our hair curled and powdered!

Petit lever begins at eight o'clock, and we must have our garden walk now."

The servant hurriedly tied a silk ribbon to the finished coiffure and bowed low as he left the chamber. Outside, the king inhaled deeply and looked out at the sun shining on the Versailles gardens, bouncing off the water that flowed from the mouths of marble nymphs. The king smelled a rose and inspected a caged bird, enjoying the summer morning warmth before walking to the Hall of Mirrors.

He waited to receive clergy and nobility, joined by his two brothers who stood on either side of the throne. The large double doors swung open. In walked the Archbishop of Vienne.

"Bonjour, Your Majesty," he said, bowing. "May I speak plainly?"

"You usually do," King Louis XVI said, squinting his eyes to bring the man's image into sharper view.

The archbishop began. "Many fear the Third Estate's dislike of the clergy."

"Yes, we are aware," the king replied, straightening his vest.

The archbishop continued his plea for King Louis XVI to bring a concord for public welfare, explaining the Third Estate had pressed the clergy to join the Commons. And Abbé Sieyès had compounded the already tense situation by stating that the clergy and the nobility who would not join must forfeit their rights as representatives. The archbishop warned the king that the rabble, who now called themselves the National Assembly, posed a severe threat to the church.

"And to your reign," he added. "Many of the clergy, mostly the poorer parish priests, have pressed hard to join them," he whispered with horror, "but even some priests and canonries have as well."

"This will pass. Have no worry. The people love their king," the king replied.

The Archbishop of Vienne warned the king such a schism could bring them all down. "The people are malcontent. The price of bread steadily rises, peasants balk at the noble landowner's taxes, and the church tithe has come under attack. How can the church survive without tithes, sire?" he asked in disbelief.

He reminded the king that the church had schools to run, land and property to manage, and that the priests must attend to the needs of the souls God entrusted to their guardianship.

"The king must act decisively to stop this anticlerical spirit that has come upon the people. Even now, the discontents gather in Masonic lodges and discuss the theories and writings of the heretic Rousseau." He stressed, "There is no longer respect for the contemplative life, and surely *they*, the people, cannot be trusted to lead. No! An ill wind blows that will bring destruction in its path, sire."

"You," the king said in a wavering voice, "tell me to bring about a concord? How?" The king's advisers had informed him the incendiary pamphlets promoted new ideas, a declaration of rights, national sovereignty, and even the call for a constitution.

King Louis XVI fired back at the archbishop. "And where has the church been in all this? The role of censorship belongs to you. Do your duty for the crown. How can I bring reconciliation when illiterate peasants, inflamed by bourgeois lawyers, call for greater privileges? They should be listening to the church instead of to lawyers. The clergy have failed, not the king."

He reminded the archbishop that the provinces' conservative nobility had turned against their own class and supported these changes. Yet, they wanted to retain their social rank and feudal dues and be exempt from taxes.

"And what had the church said to that?" he asked.

Chagrined, the archbishop admitted, "This issue is not an easy one, sire. The clergy need your help."

"Royal sovereignty will prevail at all costs. Let the people say what they will; it cannot amount to much—a few concessions. That should appease them. This general restlessness and the exaggerated desire for change is a passing thing. We are greeted with '*Vive le Roi!*' when we go out. The people will continue their devotion to the crown. But, Archbishop of Vienne, you must quell the disturbance in your ranks. Control your priests, particularly that troublemaker, Abbé Sieyès. We have been generous with the Church, not out of obligation but respect. The clergy's numbers are not grand, yet the Church owns one-tenth of France. Be content! Teach your clergy the same humility. That is how you can best serve your king…and how you can survive. My people love their king."

"Your Majesty, possibly I listened to gossip, but if conditions should worsen…the Church can rely on your protection. Royal troops will come to our aid, n'est-ce pas?"

"Do not fear; this small discord will not come to that. We assure you. We rule with God's blessing and the Church's support. That will not change."

"Merci, Your Majesty," the archbishop said, bowing low before he departed the Hall of Mirrors.

"Your Majesty," called the guard's voice, "the Archbishop of Avignon wishes an audience with you."

"Show him in," King Louis XVI replied softly.

The archbishop, a thin, hawk-faced man with pinched features, entered and bowed low. "Thank you for coming so quickly, old friend," the King said, grimacing and heavy-jowled, his bright blue eyes surrounded by blood-shot vessels. "Come, sit. I haven't the strength, nor the wish, to speak loudly, nor to use my honorific *we* at this time. I am distraught. The people and the king are not united. This palace is full of spies. My trusted manservant Jean-Baptiste Cléry recently brought me disturbing news that Paris is awash with fear."

The archbishop quickly agreed. "Yes, everyone turns on everyone, sire. The streets are dangerous, even for commoners. So many factions. Mon Dieu! Stealing is rampant. Commoners attack bakeries because half their wages go for bread. A loaf costing eight sous now goes for twelve. No one can afford the exorbitant price. What does that leave for wine, fuel, and candles? Nothing. People are desperate, sire, and afraid. Fights break out on the avenues. People look to you, their king, for help."

Askara shook her head, wondering why she was in revolutionary France, clinging to the ceiling like an insect. Looking at herself, dirt clotted on her worn leather boots, touching the rough-weave of her peasant shirt, feeling the ache of hunger in her empty stomach, she ran calloused fingers along her rough, angular face. She was not the woman she knew. She was a man, a commoner, a voyeur. But why?

"When I approved the decree," King Louis continued, "requiring clergy to take the civic oath of loyalty to the republic, it was by force, as you must know, archbishop. I had no heart for it. When I stood and said, 'I, King of the *French*'—how onerous that sounded to my ears. I am the King of *France*. France is my country by divine provenance. Their title belittles me. They made me swear to employ the power delegated to me to maintain the constitution decreed by the National Assembly, one they forced me to accept. What humiliation! Yet, I had no choice. I had to take that oath. The queen and the Dauphin joined me. We attempted to make a convincing display of national unity. What else could we do? The filthy *san-culottes* in the streets would love to see us slaughtered. I must do everything I can to preserve my throne and family."

"Your account grieves me, sire," the Archbishop of Avignon said and bowed slightly.

"The pope condemns me. The Church turns on me. Archbishop, you pretend you do not know? Don't insult me further. The pope's second letter suspended all priests who took the National Assembly oath, and in no uncertain terms, he fervently objected to the clause that specified the clergy's election must be by the people. Appointment by the Church, the letter stated, remains the only sanctioned way. The pope is sorely vexed with me. I fear he will not come to my aid since he believes I have let him down."

"Say no more about the pope. I know this situation grieves him as deeply as it does you, *Majesté*."

"But I am surrounded. The pope is free! He must understand my plight. In loyalty to the Church, I could not take Holy Communion from a constitutional priest; such a sacrilege is too great, so I dismissed my confessor. That ignited the rabble. They attacked nunneries, set effigies of the pope afire, and robbed churches in many provinces. I grieve for these blasphemies against the Church. You in Avignon have been spared much. Paris is full of malcontents who cry for freedom, yet they so quickly and brutally murder their own when the wind changes course."

"Majesté, you must send an envoy to the pope to explain to him in detail…."

"Explain? If only there was a reasonable explanation. All sense has left the people! Just days ago, when the queen, children, and I rode from this royal prison-palace, the Tuileries, to take Holy Communion at Saint-Cloud, an angry mob surrounded the carriage at the gate as we left. They shouted obscenities at Queen Marie Antoinette, jeered at the Dauphin, even shook their fists at me. We remained trapped for two hours like that. I kept my composure, as did the queen, but I could see her hands, clasped around the boy's, shaking with fear. After much distress, they forced us to return to the palace without celebrating Holy Mass. That evening the queen broke down in tears, begging me to flee. I feel I must take action for the sake of our family. I must protect our sacred heritage, perform the duty of royal blood, preserve our lives and those objects entrusted to me that signify our royal lineage."

"Of what do you speak, Majesté?"

"We may need to escape with our valuables that belong to my Bourbon line."

The archbishop gazed at the king, who was washed pale by sleepless nights, his thinning fair hair clumsily swept into a powdered wig, gray shadows dulling the once lively spark in his eyes. The archbishop knew the queen sought her brother, the emperor's help, so they could flee to safety in Austria. He had promised to help quell the revolutionary spirit in France and yet had done nothing.

The king's aunts had already moved to Rome for protection. His ministers advised the king to flee, the right course of action in times like these, saying royal blood, *sang royal*, must be preserved at all costs. The archbishop offered to act as a negotiator between the National Assembly and the foreign powers gathered at France's borders, ready to invade to save King Louis XVI and reinstate him, should it come to that.

"What, old friend, do you advise since the Vatican will not come to my aid?"

"Majesté, I agree that you and the royal family should escape, but it will not be easy. I applied for permission to visit you. They kept me waiting for days. Even as I entered the grounds today, angry people shouted at me. Citizen soldiers patrol the streets by the hundreds. Sentinels stand at each garden gate, all along the river, and at every entrance to the city. The National Committee issued a stamped pass that I was required to show every step of the way. As we speak, the guards stand ready to rush in. Escape will be most difficult to achieve, but I will assist you in whatever manner I am able."

"I must escape and take my family, our precious *sang royal,* and the Bourbon inheritance to safety."

ASKARA FELT SMALL HANDS PULLING HER FINGERS AWAY from the plaster molding of the high ceiling. She gasped and plummeted through darkness to land with a plunk on the soft hotel bed, air knocked out of her. She wheezed.

"What's the matter, Sweetie?"

"Darian?"

"Who else would you find in your bedroom?" Darian said and laughed. "You passed out. I came out to ask you a question. You didn't even hear me. You must be exhausted to sleep like that."

Askara thought, *I must be crazy.* She smelled a strong odor around her, part barnyard, part fear. "I stink."

"Shower. I'm finished. Then let's get Sara and go out to the small lemur park in the city. Imboule can drive us."

"Good idea. How late is it? Should we get dinner too?"

"You must be hungry. It's ten in the morning. You only slept a few minutes. You probably had crazy dreams, too. Short sleep is like that. You mumbled."

"Yes, you're right. I dreamt I was in the French Revolution."

"Let me guess. Were you the amazing pirate Captain Mission?"

"No, but I was a man, a smelly one."

Darian laughed and held Askara in his arms. "You feel like a woman to me, although you're correct. You smell like badly cured leather. Must be the Tana marketplace on your clothes. Shower fast so that we can have some fun."

Askara looked at Darian, relieved he was so glib, so happy, more like the Darian she had met in Greece at the Oracle of Delphi. But she seemed more the Askara she had been at the Oracle of Delphi, mystified and confused. She pondered how authentic the vision in France had felt...even smelled. She shook her head to dispel the cotton.

"Lemurs, perfect. I'd love to see them. Let's go for a big dinner tonight, one with good French wine."

"Red or white?"

"How about red, white, and blue, the colors of the revolution? And we can tour Tana in a Berlin—dark green with yellow woodwork, pale yellow wheels, white velvet upholstery—pulled by six horses."

"Hmm, I'll try to find a carriage like that, but it's unlikely. Would you settle for a donkey, madame?"

Askara gave a quick head jerk, wondering why she had said that. She felt like she was slipping. She didn't know where she would land, but Askara knew she would hit hard. Smiling at Darian, she grabbed her fresh clothes and went in for a shower.

In the medicine cabinet mirror, she caught the faint outline of small dark forms around her. She heard whispers like dry leaves in the wind say, "Kalanoro keep promises. Seek Priest Gestang." Askara wheeled around to survey the empty room.

———————— ✢ ————————

Sara's face lit up when she saw Askara coming down the hall to fetch her, but Askara read her friend's countenance, full of fear and confusion, and that alarmed her.

"What's up, Askara?"

"The lemur park. Darian wants to go. Since you are best buddies now, guess you bonded over nature while I've been...."

"Temperamental and hard to take." Sara threw it at her. "Darian and I are enjoying this country, but you're sulking. What the hell is it with you, Askara?"

Askara stood still, her face boiling hot, her eyes blurring from tears.

"No you don't, Askara, no crying. That's an easy out."

"Sorry, Sara, can we go into your room for a few minutes? I need to talk."

"Sure. Your husband can wait on his mistress. Right?"

"I don't think that. Really. I'm glad you two get along. I haven't talked to Darian much. I've been worried I'd scare him. That's why I need to talk to you."

They walked into Sara's room and shut the heavy door. Sara pointed to the chair at the small table and said, "Talk away but don't cry. You Yanks cry too much."

Askara blurted out the dream, explaining that she had never felt the same after the Nagali fiasco in Kenya when he tried to hypnotize her, and somehow, it just kept going. At first, she was a total mess, said weird things, acted paranoid and suspicious, but in time, she got over that…until recently. Darian stood by her, but she could see the pain in his eyes.

When she joined him in Bombay, life became better and worse for her, better because the paranoia washed away, worse because she felt like she was in a fine prison in Bombay. She no longer had the freedom she enjoyed—hiking, visiting with her friend Anna, doing whatever she wanted to do when she wanted to do it. But now, here in Madagascar, weird dreams and odd interactions, like the one with Jean-Paul, haunted her as if something Nagali started clung to her—something she didn't understand, something she feared. The old feelings of losing her sanity had returned, but she didn't want to tell Darian.

"I've put him through so much stress, but I need to confide in someone who can understand."

Sara softened, seeing Askara's distress. "Okay, Askara, I can see you're stressed. I've seen it before. You drop down into a hole, but you don't need to. You've got a great bloke who adores you. Don't take things out on him. I agree there is something strange going on. I wonder if dear old Jean-Paul had dementia. My grandmother had it. Wow, rips you up when someone you love doesn't even recognize you—not that you were close to Jean-Paul, but you did develop a friendship with his granddaughter Mea.

"Sometimes, Askara, you're a sponge. You absorb too much. When you try to wring out the excess, you get tangled up. I think that's where you're at right now, twisted up inside. Let go of what Jean-Paul said, that body turning ceremony, all of it. You had a stressful dream, for sure. Dreams that are like movies really mess with your head. An alternative doc in Melbourne told me they're usually related to a person's diet. Well, we've been eating new food, even street-stall food, so let's attribute the dream to that. Okay? Hey friend, hang in there."

"Okay, makes sense. But, Sara, do you think, deep down, I'm crazy?"

"Hell, yeah, bloody batshit crazy. Who isn't?"

Askara laughed. "You fit the category too."

"Whaddya think we're friends? And why do you figure neither of us has regular nine-to-five desk jobs? Can't stick to it. So, relax. Let's go with Darian to the lemur park—he really likes nature—take in a good dinner and enjoy my last days here with you two. All right?"

Askara gave Sara a big hug. "So, if I get worse, you'll let me know. I mean, like give me a kick, so I don't hurt Darian inadvertently?"

"I'll whip your ass if you're mean to that bloke. He's a really good guy, and there aren't many of them out there. I looked around a bit, didn't like what I saw. I'll tell you something amusing. I had a flash that you were a French bloke. Gotta say you weren't a looker. You smelled like sweaty riding leathers. And that was your highlight. Your looks? Well, let's just say a baboon's butt would of put you to shame."

"God, I hope it was just a flash."

The comment stunned Askara. She changed the subject with, "Hey, I need a favor. After the park, I need to drop by the church to speak to the priest Gestang. Guess he handles my paperwork for Devereaux. I dread what he's going to say about the ceremony. Will you come with me? Darian's not into it. Do your Catholic duty, please."

"Relax, sure. Never hurts to light a prayer candle. The priest won't say anything. Nothing about that ceremony was your fault. Let's end our stay with fun—maybe one more quick tour, like to the west coast to see the Avenue of the Baobabs in Morondava?"

Askara smiled. "Sounds good. Lemurs first. And the people here—I love 'em. They're fun, welcoming, and that Ejema guy—wow, funny. He could be a Hollywood actor, maybe a comedian. Malagasy people are so friendly, except the guards at the airport. But lemurs, they're the best."

CHAPTER TEN

Rosary Beads

C linking rosary beads caught Askara's attention when she and Sara entered the Immaculate Conception Cathedral. Sara veered from the aisle to sit where she pretended to pray with eyes closed. Askara doubted she prayed, realizing Sara only wanted to avoid the priest. A strong whiff of incense, myrrh, and frankincense lingered on the wooden pews. Two women had entered, crossing themselves at the altar, while a nun disappeared down the nave's left side.

Askara gazed at the pointed reddish-wood Gothic ribs overhead that arched from stone pillars like whale ribs to support the high ceiling. She saw no priests in the nave, so she knocked on the chapel door while admiring the hall's stained glass window depiction of Jesus as a herder of lambs. The sharp sound of heels clipping across the stone floor drew closer. When the wooden door slowly opened, a man leaned around the edge to peek out.

"Priest Gestang, I am Askara Timlen Dalal. We spoke earlier about the famadihana ceremony and Jean-Paul."

"Yes, yes, I remember you. What can I do for you, madame? I thought you had left Madagascar."

"No, sir. I took a trip to the coast. Can we speak in private? I have questions."

Priest Gestang glanced around and whispered, "Meet me in the confessional." He pointed to the wooden structure.

Askara entered through the door and soon heard him sit in the cubicle adjoining hers. She waited for him to speak. After several minutes, the priest said, "What is it you want? Are you confessing?"

"No, sir, I'm not Catholic. I want to ask about Jean-Paul and the ceremony."

"Yes? As to Jean-Paul, he was a wonderful man. God called him home. As for the ceremony, the family hosted it for their grandfather but interrupted his eternal rest in doing so. I do not condone the practice. I daily pray for his soul, and I suggest, madame, you leave Madagascar. Publish your article if you wish, be kind to Madagascar's people if you desire the coalition to publish it and be done. Go home."

"Can I meet with Monsignor Devereaux? I have questions for him."

"He is not available to you, madame. What is it you want to know? Let's resolve this and send you on your way," the priest answered, his beads clattering against one another. Askara tried to read his expression through the wooden screen that distorted his face, but she couldn't.

"I feel something is wrong...I mean with the deceased ancestor. He wants help."

"He is at rest in the hands of God. He does not need, nor care, for anything now."

"You just said to me his eternal rest was interrupted. That's similar to what the Kalanoro told me."

The confessional became quiet; only the priest's sigh disturbed the air. "Madame—Kalanoro? They are fictional little people, like the leprechauns of Ireland. Surely you do not believe they exist. Child's folly. If Jean-Paul mentioned them, it was in jest, or possibly old age had overtaken his mind."

Words floated back to Askara like goose down on a soft wind: "we think, you perceive." She gathered her courage and began speaking rapidly, recounting to Father Gestang what the Kalanoro had impressed on her.

"The ceremony is an ancient initiation ceremony handed down eon to eon from the Divine Mother and Father. The ceremony offers the deceased a waystation between worlds, a place to cleanse, to release the earthly world before stepping into NoTime. The dead grandfather in the famadihana ceremony cannot move on until someone exposes his death for what it was in a previous lifetime, a murder."

Askara, hearing the priest groan, snapped. "His family had not loved him during his illness or before, according to what people say. They hosted his famadihana to gain money. Jean-Paul implied the same to me. What should I do?"

Father Gestang's voice became taut like a bowstring ready to snap. "Madame, do not listen to gossip. If I did, I would think you are the problem. The family says you caused the grandfather great harm. Daily, they come to say prayers for him. They told me you photographed his face and caused him to become stuck, neither finding peace nor moving on, a severe offense. You are to blame. I personally do not believe this. I know you are innocent, but for your safety, return to your country now. Monsignor Devereaux is not your ally."

"Sir, please, help me. The Kalanoro told me to come to you. They said you would help me because you know the truth. They said the ancestor did not die an innocent death. The Kalanoro said you know why."

The priest rose and knocked into their shared wall. Askara felt the wood tremble. "Go now. Speak of this to no one. We will meet again. Come alone to the graveyard behind the church this day, at dusk. Alone!" His compartment door creaked and slammed shut.

Askara walked out to the nave expecting to see Sara, but she was gone. The place was empty, except for the smell of incense. Askara walked out the front door into the light of late morning to see Sara sitting on the stone steps, talking to a young vendor boy.

"Let's go. Darian's waiting."

"Okay, that was fun." Sara chuckled. "A journal entry for sure—my first formal visit to a church in five years—said a prayer and everything."

She paid the boy for five oranges while Askara motioned for Imboule, who had waited under shade trees across the road, to pick them up. On the way back to the Hotel du Parc, Askara thought about how she could get away by herself.

"Sara, I know I can trust you. And you can trust me. I need a favor. What I'm going to ask you to do is on the up and up, but you need to be okay with a white lie."

"White, black, red, green, you know me. I'm here when you need me. What is it?"

"I have to lie to Darian. I don't want to, but getting my story published depends on it. Otherwise, I've wasted his time and money and not made anything for all the effort, except for seeing you, always a great joy."

"A great joy BUT. So, what's the deal? I hope you're not having an affair...with a priest. That's not on. Can't cover for you, sorry."

"God no, nothing like that, but I do have to meet with the priest tonight. Evidently, the monsignor is against me.

He feels I blew the famadihana, and he doesn't want me to get my story published. He's jealous because he's never been invited to one. The locals do not like him. Priest Gestang said if I could meet with him, we could figure a way out, but no one should see us. Top secret stuff, or else Devereaux could get rid of him. He would transfer Gestang to Tasmania or somewhere."

"Will you go to dinner with Darian, to a fancy place that serves several courses and wine? You know, the kind of dinner that takes a long time. That will give me the chance to meet the priest. I'll get back an hour or so later. Enjoy a long dinner, drag your feet for dessert, or something. But say you're starving, and you want to eat early, at dusk. And you want fancy food. Okay?"

"Askara, Darian won't go to dinner just with me. He's too proper. If you don't go, he won't go. The only way he would if it's bad manners not to. So, what's your excuse?"

"I have a migraine. I've gotten them before. He's seen me. I have to stay still in a dark room for hours. He won't stay and sit in a dark hotel room with me and leave you to do nothing. He'll feel bad about leaving our guest Sara alone. He's a gentleman. He will want to take you to dinner. But you pick a place that's more formal, leisurely. Insist on a nice French restaurant, preferably with music and a good wine list. He won't refuse your request. That's not how he rolls. It's not a terrible lie, maybe not white—pewter gray, let's call it."

"Okay. But if Darian somehow finds out, it's on you. Tell him you forced me into it."

"Sure. You're a lifesaver, Sara, a real friend. Not just that, a sister."

ASKARA WAITED IN BED WITH A WET WASHCLOTH ON her forehead in the dark room while Darian showered and got ready to take Sara to dinner. When he leaned over to kiss her face, she mumbled, groaned, and sighed. Darian eased out the door without a word.

Askara lay still, listening. When the hall was quiet, she dressed, pulled a long scarf over her head, and calmly walked down the hallway, and slipped into the WC next to the massage room until the coast was clear. She exited past the dormer window onto the iron grillwork balcony stairs that led down to the hotel's rear garden, which was alive with throaty bullfrog chants. Padding across the soft grass to the far side, beyond the parrots, whose cages were covered for the night, Askara walked the narrow lane they had taken earlier to the Zoma Market in the daytime. Streetlights of the hotel district glowed a dull orange. She walked uphill for several blocks, passing the Church of Immaculate Conception's entrance, where the stained-glass windows threw a burst of color onto the polished stones.

She kept to the shadows, heading for the rear of the graveyard where a familiar feeling engulfed her. She followed the stone tombs to the farthest, massive, gated sarcophagus with stone angels perched on all corners. She didn't know where Priest Gestang meant to meet, but here in the shadows seemed the best place to wait.

She stopped short. Hidden in the cement fold of an angel's robe, she saw a man huddled, his head down. Askara started to bolt.

"Good evening. I am glad you understood the Kalanoro's message," he whispered.

"Message? I didn't get one. You had told me to meet you here."

"To come here is what I said. Ah, yes, that is the way. Kalanoro impress with thought. So natural, *n'est-ce pas?* But you understood where to look. Good. The Kalanoro tell me you serve."

"Serve what?"

"Our goal. My life may be in jeopardy. His Grace Monsignor Devereaux suspects I have divulged a great secret. But, you see, he is mistaken. My mission is to protect the innocent. I failed once, for which I suffer daily."

"I don't understand."

"You see, the poor man, the grandfather you woke in the famadihana, happened upon something by accident, something precious to the monsignor. The poor servant had no idea of its significance. His poor soul cannot rest because he may have been killed for what he saw. You must have heard him moan and cry, n'est-ce pas? He suffers greatly. Did you hear him at the ceremony?"

Askara thought back about the cassette recording. There was a sound she couldn't recognize—a mumbling cry, whimpering. She assumed it was a distortion caused by the recorder being in her pocket. When she relistened later, the sound had vanished, so she forgot about it.

"No. Do you mean someone cursed the grandfather?"

"Not only His Grace but an entire family dedicated to protecting certain things." The priest's voice fell to a sullen, flat tone.

"I don't understand what you're telling me. Jean-Paul said some things, but…."

"Ah, yes, God rest his soul. Jean-Paul, I assumed he was the weak link in the chain, not from lack of strength but from strength of conviction. He witnessed much in his years, too much. With time his eyes became clearer, as mine have. You see where that took him."

"What do you mean?"

"He is dead—is he not, madame?"

"From old age."

"Think what you will. It is better that way, safer."

"Look, Father Gestang, Jean-Paul left me a note. I don't know what it means."

"Convenient. Do you think many who die a sudden, natural death are so thoughtful?"

Askara, losing patience, said in an exasperated whisper: "I go to close the door. *Le Pierre est très important. Le temple est guarded.* Look to the house of Anjou. Like a phoenix, I rise. What does that mean?"

"You know already. The Kalanoro have visited you. They must have impressed the meaning on you. Think."

Askara felt the Kalanoro had much to lose, but what door did they refer to? The reply floated into her thoughts:

The spirit door, the bridge between the living and the spirit world of the ancestors. We Kalanoro believe if the door remains ajar, our kind will disappear from this realm. The grandfather falsely honored in the famadihana stands as a wedge between the worlds. His was a wrongful death because he died with anger and anguish. Understand, the Kalanoro are Keepers of NoTime, yes, but more importantly, we are keepers of the earth. We nourish and protect this land. If we leave this grand island—home to animal and vegetable life unknown elsewhere in the world—it will die. Invaders will plunder the resources, cut the trees, harvest the foliage, trap the animals. This ancient land, heir to an era far grander than you can imagine, is key to balance in the world. There are medicinal plants here, known only to the Kalanoro, that cure any disease. Preserving this island means saving life on Earth if, and only if, this land remains under the protection of the Kalanoro, who are guided by NoTime wisdom. You see, we, as the first humans of the land, have everything to lose. The portal must be closed.

Gestang said, "Now you know. The fact that we are involved is no accident. The fact that Jean-Paul died is no accident. The fact that I am compelled to help you, and the fact that you came to witness the famadihana of an innocent man murdered for what he discovered is no accident, madame."

Askara sat numb on the stone steps of the tomb for a few minutes. "What could be so powerful?"

"That I cannot say. The secret is heavily guarded for a good reason. I hope you never find out. It would surely mean your death."

"Is something in a temple? What is *Le Pierre*?"

"You might call Le Pierre guardian forces, a French lineage noted for loyalty and military skill. One especially celebrated member started as a king's page before becoming Captain of the King's Dragoons, then a commander, and by 1788 he was Brigadier of King Louis the Sixteenth's armies."

"Okay, so? That man must have guarded a temple. '*Le temple est guarded*,' Jean-Paul said. Look to the house of Anjou. Who's Anjou?"

Brother Gestang sat very still with his head tilted to one side as if listening to unheard words. "Ah, I see. Anjou seems·to be a discrepancy. It could appear as another word. This part eludes me. You see, I am not privy to all the information. I have no idea how many members are involved, although I know Monsignor Devereaux is. Yet oddly, Monsignor Devereaux knows nothing of the Kala-noro. They deny their presence to him."

"Members of what?"

"A society. You only need to know that it stands for honor."

"Okay, what about 'Like a phoenix, I rise?'"

Father Gestang smiled. "The phoenix is a bird that rises from the ashes to live again."

"I know that Greek myth. Why would Jean-Paul say he's like that bird?"

Gestang explained that the phoenix was a symbol for the ascension of spirit, but more than that—birth, death, and rebirth. The society Jean-Paul referred to with that symbol had been, for many lifetimes, involved in protecting the sacred. In ancient times, more distant than our paltry, written human record, the phoenix lived and walked this land of Madagascar when it was not an island but part of a vast landmass, and the bird was not a myth. The phoenix was real, not unlike the DoDo bird in Mauritius, to which it was probably related, yet the DoDo could not fly. The phoenix could. Greek mythology didn't include the DoDo. Evidently, the DoDo had been cursed for something it neglected to do, so its wings could not support its weight for flying. But the phoenix was a favorite of the Kalanoro, not for eating but for divination. The bird spoke for the wind and told the Kalanoro of changes the world over. It brought them news from the aboriginal peoples of the world. They said the great bird was a nimble flight bird whose favorite resting spot was in the warm ashes of an extinguished fire.

"You see, madame, ancient peoples mastered fire long before European records prove it. Thus, the legend came into being, yet the bird's significance has always been misunderstood. Jean-Paul's message meant ascent of his soul. He knew his death transition was imminent."

Askara slumped over, resting her chin in the crevice of her knees. "I don't know what to do! This doesn't make sense to me."

"You do know. You must clear the ancestor's agony, which will put his soul to rest, and he will move on, thus closing the portal. To do that, it appears you must reveal who murdered him."

The Kalanoro closed in like a sea fog around them. Askara and Brother Gestang froze. From the far end of the cemetery came the sound of the metal gate creaking open. Muffled voices disturbed the mist. A faint lamplight along the perimeter of the graveyard swung to and fro with footsteps. Father Gestang pressed his hand on Askara's shoulder. A voice called out, ordering the others to inspect the headstones. Gestang held Askara in place.

Lights swung along the rows of tombs. Excited voices called out. Two men approached the sarcophagus where Askara huddled with Priest Gestang. One almost grazed Askara's leg.

"Nothing here," the man called and rejoined the others to search along the far wall. Eternal minutes passed before the cemetery gate creaked shut, leaving the graves in darkness.

"Monsignor Devereaux doesn't know who he looks for. That is to your advantage. The Kalanoro work to keep your identity secret. You have little time. The new moon is less than forty-eight hours away. When the Kalanoro took you to the hotel in Toamasina...."

"What? They took me?"

"Oui, that is their way. There you met a woman, a Madame Tison, and heard her story about a Captain Misson and a Father Caraccioli, pirates during the time of the French Revolution who settled here in Madagascar."

"Yes."

"You must know more, the Kalanoro say, to be of help now."

The priest continued to explain that the Kalanoro feared the invaders for what they did to the people—taking the local women and forcing them to marry foreigners, enslaving men they captured here and upon the seas, abusing sacred rites in the name of their religion, killing animals of the forest for pleasure. The Kalanoro feared a source of power these miscreants had stumbled upon when they attacked *Le Grande Serpent* out at sea. Misson, a pirate, raided the ship that had sailed from the Marseilles dock carrying a precious package, brought by a courier, for the ship's captain en route to a holy city in Ethiopia.

The Vatican searched for the goods, but the pope abandoned the pursuit, assuming a great secret remained hidden by the sea. But forty years ago, a zealous priest came from war-torn Europe to minister to a small flock of devout Roman Catholics on this remote island of Madagascar. Monsignor Devereaux's interest in history stoked the search again and kindled the Kalanoro's fears.

Father Devereaux served the church and the people well for many years, but he was a man of formidable dedication and focus. So, when his attention shifted to what the Vatican termed a treasure hunt after he learned of Captain Misson and Father Caraccioli's colony on Madagascar, he became obsessed. He discovered the Vatican did not provide any information about Father Caraccioli, because the man's pirating life caused him to be expunged from Rome's records. He was discounted as an errant sheep only mentioned by an entry in a paper on Libertalia, the village he helped establish on the island.

But the monsignor methodically gathered every scrap of folklore about Libertalia, the utopian colony created during the French Revolution. That research led him to Madame Tison, a local French-Malagasy beauty, a descendant of the captain and his native island wife. Madame Tison was born here but educated in France, returning at age eighteen to Madagascar. She became Monsignor Devereaux's friend, who turned arch enemy.

"You must understand, Madame Tison's story of the infamous Captain Mission, her great-great-*grand-père*, spurred on Monsignor Devereaux with a devotion the pope would have admired had it been for the love of God, not treasure. I am sure the answer to this riddle lies with that woman. And with you as Anton."

Askara laughed. "That's quite a tale."

"I would have also laughed," Priest Gestang said, "had I not met the Kalanoro."

"You people believe this crap?" Askara said, growing irate.

Gestang recoiled but explained he believed in the island's little people since they had saved him from death when he contracted typhoid fever after a heavy rain season and lay near death, wracked by chills that made his teeth chatter and burned by a high fever that made his mind roam unchecked. That was when he heard a resonant voice call his name. He thought the voice of God was calling him home.

But when he opened his eyes, he saw a small, dark man standing naked at the foot of his cot. The man said with great kindness that he was a friend and would make the fever stop on one condition. The priest asked the condition, fearing the apparition desired his soul. The small man asked him to be a voice for his people, the Kalanoro, to speak their hearts and talk to the invader world represented by the Catholic priest Devereaux so that the Kalanoro people could live in peace.

Gestang relayed his thought: Simple! He nodded in agreement, aware of the absurdity of his delirium. The small man waved a bird feather fan that streaked colored light across the priest's chest and head while he chanted. Many black figures appeared from a vapor. They ran nimble fingers over his body, pulling the fever out. When he woke two days later, it was as if he had never been ill. He assumed the vision had been a fever-induced delirium, nothing more.

He thought little of that experience until one day, when teaching catechism to the village children in the southern end of the island, a small boy handed him a worn glass vial that he had uncovered while playing. The priest marveled at the surface embossed with a little fleur-de-lis below a crown. Assuming it had washed ashore long ago, he wondered if it had belonged to the revolutionary colony upon whose ruins the village sat.

When he returned some months later to the diocese in Tana, he showed the vial to his superior, Father Devereaux, who said nothing for several minutes. He then thanked Gestang, and, clutching the vial in his bony hand, the monsignor dismissed the priest. He admonished Father Gestang to hold silence on the matter as the colony was a stain on the French record—not to mention the church's—in Madagascar. Priest Gestang respected his superior and agreed.

Late that afternoon, the priest again saw the small dark man, but this time in full daylight in his chamber. The apparition spoke just as he had before, with great kindness, and said: *Ça a commencé*. It has begun.

Priest Gestang looked at Askara and said, "That was the beginning of my friendship with the Kalanoro and my understanding of certain things. I did not know the deceased from the Walking the Dead ceremony, other than he was the monsignor's servant, but I do know he was poisoned."

Father Gestang reached into his robe and pulled out a small vial of the same description. Holding it in his palm, illuminated by the silver Kalanoro glow, he said, "The Kalanoro say this is how you will release the ancestor's spirit from his torment, with this vial."

Askara instinctively reached to take it from the priest's hand, but he closed his fingers around it. She pulled back, saying, "Do I have a choice in this, Father Gestang?"

"Choice is a luxury, n'est-ce pas? No, you do not. I do not understand your role or why you were chosen, but I wish you luck. Remember, the Kalanoro watch over you."

"I'm stunned. I have no idea what to do."

"His Grace is an early riser. I meet him at eight a.m. to discuss the day's business. You must arrive at seven. I shall leave the chapel door unlocked. Tell him you know of the vial. Let him take it from there. Time is running out."

"Thank you, I guess. Please, ask the Kalanoro to protect me and my husband and Sara."

"If at any point my communication with you is broken, wait for the Kalanoro to contact you. Do not come to me for any reason," Priest Gestang said.

"Broken?"

"This is *très sérieux*, madame," Brother Gestang said and rose from his crouched position with a rustle of his cassock, made the sign of the cross, and vanished into the mist.

Askara started back to the hotel, keeping to the shadows, furtive as an alley cat until she reached the main road. She sprinted past tourists and locals strolling in the humid night air to arrive at the hotel, where she attempted to rush past the hotel security guards at the door.

"*C'est très tard,* mademoiselle," the guard said, hurrying to open the door for her.

"Oui, merci," Askara said and leaped into the foyer entrance, tripping on the welcome mat. When a familiar, husky voice called her name, she looked up to see Ed Healy approaching.

"Askara, you okay? You look like the devil's after you. Thought you'd left the country without saying good-bye to me."

"No, we went on a side trip with some friends to the coast. That's all."

"Let's have a drink. I'm pushing off tomorrow. Filming's done."

Ed opened the wooden door to the bar, sliding his meaty hand across the sandblasted glass cursive letters, *Easy Lounge*. He glanced behind to see security questioning two men at the door. He rushed in, pulling Askara with him. They sat at a small table in the back, as far from the scratchy speakers as possible, Ed's eyes glued on the entrance.

"So what's up, Ed? I don't have much time. Darian's waiting."

"I got my footage. I'm ready to leave. This trip's been a hassle from first to last. You'd think I was stealing the crown jewels or something the way me and my crew have been treated. Turned me off to the whole project. And the accounting! Can you believe you have to verify every film canister, shirt, shoe, toothbrush—you name it—to get out of here without paying an arm and a leg in fines. It's crazy, much worse than it used to be—all that just to get an exit visa."

"Yeah, I'm not looking forward to leaving. Well, I am, but not to the paperwork."

"Did you declare everything when you landed?"

"Almost. I forgot my necklace. I never take off my amethyst necklace," Askara said, pulling out a thumb-size faceted stone dangling on a gold chain.

"That'll be a headache. You wore it but didn't declare it? If I were you, I'd stick it in my underwear to pass customs. It'd be a lot simpler."

"Do they frisk women?"

"I wish! I'd sign up for the job. No, they are not like that unless they suspect drugs."

Askara checked her watch. She realized she had a little time to spare when Ed shouted to the bartender. A skinny waiter floated over from his barstool, where he had been chatting with the bartender in a conspiratorial manner. Ed ordered a couple of beers. The waiter served them and retreated to resume his delicate egret pose at the bar to flirt.

"Askara, you know that old guy who died, Jean-Paul, nice old guy? He left a weird note for you, told me to give it to you." Ed's mouth pulled side to side in an involuntary twitch like he was chewing cud.

"Yes, I liked him." She took the folded note and stuffed it in her pocket. "Thanks."

"Some people gossip he was murdered, you know."

"What?"

"My guys, you know, my 'special friends' here in Madagascar," Ed said, nodding to the far left where three men sat in a dark corner. "I use the word *friends* tongue-in-cheek. They're why I'm leaving. They told me that the note, something about a house of Anjou and closing a guarded door—old man babble—riled them up. They're watching you. Be careful. I know these guys. You don't want to tangle with them, trust me."

Askara's body turned cold. Chill bumps popped up along her arms. Hearing Jean-Paul's name made her heart pound. Her mind raced like a desert wind. Realizing she hadn't heard Ed's last few words, she said, "Sorry, the music's loud. What was the last thing you said?"

"You look exhausted, Askara. The song stopped a minute ago. Anyway, my ex-special friends over there—he tipped his head discretely to the side—have made my life a misery. They think I introduced you to a guy they don't like."

"What does that mean?"

Ed looked down at his beer. "Well, you're smart enough to catch the drift."

Askara patted Ed's square, fat hand, felt the clamminess, and whispered, "No, I'm not."

"They asked me lots about you."

"What did you tell them? We hardly know each other."

"I've done some stuff here…well, not on the up-and-up, nothing real bad…a couple of black market wildlife purchases they know about. Don't give anyone a reason to snag you—not your necklace, nothing. They know your room number."

"What do you mean?" Askara said in dismay. "The sharks' teeth thing?"

"It's an old voodoo trick from the African slaves the French brought here meant to scare you into leaving. Guess you're stronger than they thought. Didn't stop you."

"Ed, do you know what they want and why?"

"Nope, near as I can figure, they think you know some-one or something they've been paid to find out about."

"What?"

"Hell if I know, but I do know these guys don't work cheap. They searched Jean-Paul's house. That freaked Meamoni. She and her husband left for England right afterward. When's your flight, Askara?"

"A couple of days."

"Askara," Ed said, standing to block her from the mercenaries' view, "take the necklace off. I'll mail it to you in America. I can hide it in a film canister. I have hundreds."

Askara looked up at Ed's bloated face, unsure of his motive, and said, "No!" Her sharp reply traveled through the near-empty club.

Ed lowered his hand, rolled his eyes, and turned away, saying, "Good luck, lady. Tell your cute girlfriend that I said goodbye."

Askara remained seated, watching the men in the corner watch her. When a group of tourists entered the bar, she bolted. Running up the stairway from the foyer, gripping the teak banister to balance, she landed on the mezzanine to check behind her. She saw Ed walk out the front door, with his 'special friends' marching behind him. Askara rushed to her room.

Darian wasn't back yet. Her sigh of relief turned to panic. Askara didn't want to be alone if those men came knocking at her door, nor did she want Darian to bump into them. Askara had no idea what they knew. She wasn't sure what she knew, but she understood the high stakes. They must leave the country as soon as possible and return to their apartment in Bombay. Once a prison, Bombay now glowed like paradise. She took a quick shower and climbed into bed. She did yoga breathing. Her body relaxed on the cool, crisp sheets. Her mind drifted. A small dark hand lifted her and carried her to another time and place.

CHAPTER ELEVEN

Failed Attempt

The king slumped over, burying his wigless head in his hand. He knew he must flee to save his family. He didn't know who he could trust; even his palace crawled with libertine spies. Never a man to rush into the face of danger, he had no recourse. His wife and children, his reign, and the sovereignty of France dangled in the balance. He couldn't understand his subjects. Why would they revolt? He ruled fairly. He enjoyed hunting, making objects of beaten copper, eating fine food, all innocent acts.

He knew the commoners despised his wife, an Austrian. They didn't look beyond her love of frivolity, a little gambling, a little theater, a love of clothes, things all women enjoy if they can. He knew her to be a good mother, a loving, kind mother. She performed her wifely duties if he showed an interest, which he rarely did now that they had children. He had fulfilled his duty successfully...after a small operation.

The attraction of an elegant food spread, now that was something to lust after. Still, Marie's kindness to him as her king and husband never wavered. They were friends.

They had grown up together. After all, he was fifteen when they married, and she, a fourteen-year-old princess of Austria. He was aware as she matured that she found certain pleasures with others; he couldn't begrudge her that. He appreciated her decorum in the matter, which ensured he never had to face the schism between his moral and his religious life.

His grandfather King Louis XV's debauched lifestyle with many mistresses loomed as an example not to repeat. His father drilled into his son Louis, "A life like that brings many dangers to the soul. Your mother, God bless her, was a pious, kind woman. Follow her example and choose the same for yourself, and do not stumble in your grandfather's missteps." He reminded his son to hunt and ride, eat and drink to his heart's desire, and when he needed an outlet for carnal pleasure, to look to his queen only.

But now, King Louis XVI faced a threat he never could have imagined—his people. The economic stress of long wars hung over his head. Never a good manager, he faced increased debt because of costly battles, primarily loans to the American colonies during the American Revolution. The call for fiscal, social, and governmental change, fired by pamphlets expressing ideas of the Enlightenment, circulated in France and inspired the commoners to petition for equality with the clergy and nobility in the Estates General Assembly. But these sectors of society could not agree enough to bridge their antagonisms.

King Louis watched as the National Assembly meetings degraded into defiance of his royal government. The queen pressured him to enlist several foreign regiments loyal to the king to come to their aid in both Paris and at Versailles. The Parisian outburst against the royals stunned

Louis. When the people stormed the old royal prison, the Bastille, and captured it, a symbol of the Bourbon despotic rule—King Louis XVI's lineage—he didn't need anyone to tell him what their message meant. He must act now to save his children, his queen, and himself. But he needed help.

They had survived many insults and accusations, but the royal family now feared for its future. The Constituent Assembly brought up the discontent of the starving Parisians and rumors that Royalists were conspiring against the people who supported the notion of liberty expressed in the "Declaration of the Rights of Man and the Citizen," in short, *Liberte, Egalite, Fraternite.*

Rebellious thoughts threatened the stability of King Louis XVI. A march on Versailles by hundreds, primarily women, resulted in a siege on the royal palace. When the Marquis de la Fayette—*Lafayette*, the French aristocrat and military officer who had fought in the American Revolution against the English—heard of the march, he rushed to rescue the royal family. He escorted them to Paris.

There the king submitted to signing a constitution that disallowed hereditary titles, broke up the country into departments, imposed restrictions on the king's powers, allowed for the confiscation of church lands, provided for the election of priests by voters instead of the Church, and dissolved most of the monastic orders. So many problems stymied the king into disbelief. He tried to ignore them... until he no longer could.

King Louis XVI knew the rabble would next call for him to be deposed. When he discussed the situation with Queen Marie Antoinette, she contacted her brother, the Holy Roman Emperor Leopold II, to request sanctuary for her family and aid to combat the revolution in France. She feared for their lives. She told her husband she knew one person would come to their aid: Hans Axel, Count von Fersen. King Louis realized her plan's wisdom, but to ask his queen's lover for help brought a bitter taste to his mouth, although he liked the man.

King Louis XVI shouted to his attendant priest, "Contact the Swede, Hans Axel, Count von Fersen. He resides here in Paris. Tell him we request his help."

"Where does he live, Majesté?"

"You can find him with his lover, an Italian woman, Eleonore Sullivan, who's married to a man of great wealth, an Anglo-American. She now lives a disreputable life in Paris as the mistress of a wealthy Scotsman plus Count von Fersen, who is often at her house. We cannot be fastidious now; we need help."

"Majesté, this is unseemly! Can you not think of another?"

"No. In times such as these, the unseemly becomes necessary. As for Axel von Fersen, he is a good man in most regards. Yes, he enjoys worldly pleasures, but we trust him nonetheless. We have no money we can raise without suspicion since my queen cannot sell her jewels. Von Fersen has offered financial help, which I intend to repay.

"I will not send you, an archbishop, to find the count. That would arouse attention. So, you must go in disguise. Dress like a common priest. If you enter the Italian woman's house, that would be reasonable to an onlooker. The woman would call upon a common priest to say prayers for her soul. Everyone knows she is Catholic. They will assume she repents."

"I will do as you command."

"The second thing depends on the first. Secure Fersen. Then I may send you to the Archbishop of Avignon with a package intended only for my family if I cannot deliver it myself. These items are sacred to our Bourbon lineage and must be protected at all costs. Instruct the archbishop to keep them securely and safely hidden. I will ask for their return, or the Dauphin's guardian will, or possibly Count von Fersen on the Dauphin's behalf. No one else will I send, not even one of my brothers. Keep the package within the walls of the Papal Palace in Avignon until my emissary comes to retrieve it. This is my command to heed if I am unable to take them myself."

"Yes, Majesté, I do as you command."

"Someone approaches. Here, take this copy of the 'Civic Constitution of the Clergy.' It was our topic of discussion today."

When the archbishop stood to leave, the doors swung wide open. An angry palace guard shouted at the priest to leave immediately. The archbishop bowed to the King of France and said, "I shall post this notice at the Papal Palace as you instructed, Majesté, and I shall make haste to speak to those concerned about this matter."

As the cleric walked past the revolutionary guard, the man grabbed the pages from his hand to read the title. The guard smiled approval and waved the priest down the hall with a dismissive hand gesture. Once outside, the archbishop walked quickly to his carriage and ordered the driver to make haste before the irate-looking mob could charge his carriage.

The next afternoon, arriving at Eleonore Sullivan's home disguised as a novice priest, the archbishop knocked on the door. A servant answered and escorted the priest to a sunny room where he sat quietly in a carved mahogany chair, looking out at the garden. He admired the soft white calla lilies, "like angels reaching to heaven," he remarked to Madame Sullivan, who surprised him with an invitation to supper.

He accepted and dined with a handsome gentleman, Count von Fersen, and Mr. Sullivan, an older, gruff-mannered, ruddy-faced man whose odd American twang abused his dismal French. During the meal, the archbishop mentioned he had visited King Louis XVI, who passed along his regards, especially to the count. Von Fersen nodded, understanding the inference, and excused himself directly after the meal, saying he had promised to visit an old friend who wasn't feeling well, the Baroness von Korff.

"Well, Frederik, it is unkind of you to leave so soon," Eleanore Sullivan said as she escorted him to the front door.

"Madame, you must understand. As King Gustavus III's special representative to the French Court and aide-de-camp to General Rochambeau in America, I should travel in style, n'est ce pas? Unfortunately, the *sans-culottes* have momentarily interrupted the transfer of my monetary compensation. You see, I have no proper conveyance. Baroness von Korff kindly offered the use of her carriage, which I must return this evening. Thank you for the lovely meal," he said, bowing to kiss her hand. Mrs. Sullivan smiled with her lips curled in a pout only he could see, turned away, and bid him good-bye.

When she saw the archbishop approach in the hall, she said, "I see you are on your way also?"

Relieved to leave the indolent company, the archbishop replied, "Merci, madame, for an enjoyable evening. But I must be on my way. The streets are not safe for clergy at night. Au revoir."

The priest quickly hurried down the steps to avoid being seen and walked down the street, slowing under the trees' black shadows. After Madame Sullivan shut her door, he circled back to speak to Count von Fersen, who waited unseen in the darkness. The archbishop whispered as they walked to the waiting carriage.

The count gave the archbishop an affirmative nod and murmured, "I shall make the preparations. No one should see us together. *Excusez-moi*, but I cannot offer you a ride. Au revoir."

When von Fersen arrived at the courtyard of his quarters, citizens milling on the street stared at the baroness's fine carriage, a Berlin. With dark green and yellow bodywork, pale yellow wheels, and white velvet upholstery, this carriage, as fine as any an aristocrat could own, enraged the citizens milling around on the roads. Yet this nobleman—neither a French citizen nor the Berlin's owner—was a decorated soldier of Sweden and a lady's man of note. The citizens excused his outings night after night when the count drove the dappled gray Percherons to the countryside, obviously for a lover's rendezvous.

But on the seventh night of outings, the short-legged, thick-necked horses snorted and stamped while the livery harnessed them. Trotting willingly at the slack in their reins, they hurried from the courtyard for a midsummer night's ride.

Several miles down the road, the count reined in the Percherons when he spotted two men standing in the tree shadows beside the road. Count von Fersen jumped down from the carriage, handed the reins to one of the men, and mounted a waiting horse.

"Take the Berlin to Madame Sullivan's house. Make sure you are seen. Wait there in the courtyard. After one hour, drive the Berlin to meet me at the spot I showed you, beyond the customs post, on the road from Porte Saint-Martin.

There you will find three of my soldiers dressed in yellow livery. I will take the Berlin from you. You will return to Paris in a hired carriage. *Comprenez-vous?*"

⁂

"WAKE UP, *MES CHÉRIS*. IT IS TIME TO DRESS," THE QUEEN said as she quietly pulled the Dauphin from his bed. Gathering a dress in her hands, she lowered it over the boy's mop of flaxen hair. The boy fell back into her arms, limp with sleep. She pulled white stockings up his thin legs and placed slippers on his feet.

His sister walked over to ask, "Why do you dress him like a girl, *ma Mère?*"

The queen propped the boy up against a bed poster to place the wide-brimmed bonnet low over his eyes. "It is better this way. Go, *Mignon*. We must hurry. The Duchesse de Tourzel waits for you downstairs. Make no noise and help your brother. I will join you later." The queen gathered her children in her arms and kissed them before leading them downstairs to the king's First Gentleman's unoccupied room. Carefully she unlocked the door.

"Good, you are here, Duchesse. Take the children to the carriage. Von Fersen will meet you there."

Count von Fersen, dressed as a hired hackney-coachman, sat laughing with passers-by, but he put away his snuffbox when he spotted motion in the darkness by the palace door. Checking that no one was near, he whisked the Duchesse and the children through the shadows to the carriage, where the children slumped and fell asleep. The Duchesse sat rigid, fidgeting with her lace, waiting.

Queen Marie Antoinette checked the clock. More than an hour had passed. All was calm outside. She rose from her bed, put on a simple brown dress and a black hat with a heavy veil that concealed her face, and sat on the bedside chair waiting for the king. The sound of soft padded feet made her stiffen. "Louis?"

"Yes, madame," the King said, entering the queen's chamber. "Help me with these horrid clothes." He handed her a brown suit, a dark green overcoat, and a gray wig. "An accomplice, Chevalier de Coigny, has worn these same clothes for twelve nights, traveling from the Tuileries at this very time. Pray the sentry finds me to be him. And pray I survive the man's stench."

"When we reach the northeast frontier and have an army escort into my brother's empire, you may wear whatever you please, Louis. Now, let me tuck your hair under this wig."

The king and his queen, dressed in plain dark clothes, crept along the black corridors until they could see the line of carriages in the courtyard. The king kissed his wife tenderly before he crept through the shadows to Fersen's carriage, where the children and their governess hid. With a subtle flick of his whip, Fersen signaled Marie Antoinette to come.

When she slipped aboard, von Fersen slapped the reins urging the horses to a fast trot, leaving the Tuileries Palace on the bank of the river Seine to grow smaller in the distance. As they passed, citizens on the streets of Paris glanced casually at the hired carriage's nightly outing of no importance.

At Porte Saint-Martin, von Fersen slowed the team when he saw Baroness von Korff's Berlin. The road, consumed by shadow, appeared deserted as he pulled up along the fancy carriage. He spoke quietly to the men in yellow livery, bodyguards of the king.

"*Bonsoir.* How do you keep in this warm evening, *messieurs?*"

"*Bon, merci.* A quiet night for travel," they replied, acknowledging the code.

"*C'est bon.* I will drive the baroness, her children, and their governess, and their steward to Bondy in the Berlin. From there, I am off to Belgium. You take this hired carriage back," Fersen said, handing the leather reins to a livery. "You two, ride on with me."

When he jumped down, he nodded for the passengers to climb into the larger carriage. And surveying the road, he climbed to the driver's seat and snapped the reins, sending the six-horse team cantering down the deserted road. When the horses tired, Fersen slowed to a steady trot.

Inside the Berlin, King Louis checked his watch and smiled. "It is nearing three. All is well!"

At Bondy, the Berlin pulled into the post-house where the tired Percherons were traded for a team of fresh horses. While the livery tightened the harnesses, Fersen walked to the carriage door.

"No one pursues us. There should be no problem from here. Outside of Chalons, we will find the first of our troops. After that, there is nothing to fear. The Marquis de Bouillé has dispatched the Duc de Choiseul and forty hussars to meet you after Chalons, in the village of Pont de Sommeville. And I shall call on you two weeks later at the court of Emperor Leopold II, my dearest queen," Fersen said with immodest affection, "where we will play a game of cards and laugh at the fools who thought themselves smarter than we."

Marie Antoinette extended her hand with a loving smile. Fersen gripped it tenderly as she spoke. "We are in your debt, sir, and look forward to the opportunity to repay your kindness."

Leaning forward to address Fersen, King Louis XVI caused the count to relinquish the queen's hand when he checked his Bréguet watch. "I would love to see Lafayette's embarrassment when he wakes to find us gone. I hope the sans-culottes throttle him while his guardsmen jeer! What delight I would take in that!"

"Yes, *Votre Majesté*. His career will not be worth a sou. So much for the French hero of the American Revolution! Possibly he should have stayed on since General Washington valued him so much."

The king added solemnly, "I was impressed with him too. Such a pity, a good soldier gone to waste."

"The team is ready. I am away now. *Bon voyage!*" Count von Fersen said, saluting King Louis XVI before climbing onto a fresh horse. "I shall see you at court, Votre Majesté."

As Fersen galloped away, the heavily laden Berlin clattered west toward Pont de Sommeville. The passengers fell asleep with the carriage's rocking until a sharp clang jolted them awake. The wheel had struck a narrow bridge's stone wall, causing the carriage to lurch from side to side as the driver struggled to rein in the frightened horses. The impact snapped the traces. The second horse on the right stumbled, making the team lunge, dislodging the passengers from their seats. The king shouted.

When the liveries jumped down to free the horse tangled in his leathers, the animal shied and hit the stone wall, cutting its leg on a jutting stone. The driver shouted to the passengers to dismount. The queen gathered the Dauphin in her arms and climbed out, followed by the others, to walk where morning light sparkled on the dew-covered ground. The queen and the Duchesse de Tourzel escorted the children to the small river bank to relieve themselves while the king watched his men free the horses from the tangled harness and push the carriage back from the stone wall.

"What is the damage?" King Louis said, his voice constricted with fear.

"He's lame, Your Majesté. The cut is deep. I can bandage it, but he can't go fast. The wheel is bent. The driver led the limping horse across the bridge and tied him to a tree. He washed the cut, packed mud over the wound, and tore a horse blanket into strips to wrap the wounded leg from hoof to knee. He reinforced the bandage by cinching it with a strip of leather.

King Louis grew more agitated, checking his watch repeatedly. "We must hurry. We're losing time!" He called his wife and children to board the carriage, but the guard asked the king to wait. The king snapped. "No one must see us. It is full morning now. How much longer?"

"Your Majesté, this may take some time, possibly an hour, even longer."

"Well, pull the carriage yourselves to the other side of the road, behind those trees. We shall sit in it to wait. We shall stand down for the harnessing only. Make haste!"

The royal family sat quietly in the carriage's shadowy cab, the king checking his watch continually, the queen stifling tears under her black veil. She whimpered. "Louis, I'm scared."

"We must reach Pont de Sommeville by two-thirty this afternoon, at the latest. We are still hours away. We must not come to ruin now!" the king said, wincing.

Queen Marie Antionette rallied composure to calm her husband. "Mon chéri, Count von Fersen told us the troops would be there, and so they will. Do not worry. Even if we are a little late, they will be there. We shall dine with my

Dyan Dubois

brother in Austria to plan our triumphant return to France before you know it. Take heart, for all our sakes."

The king caught the edge in the queen's last sentence and straightened his back, thrusting his rotund midriff forward. "You are correct," he said before he fell into a heavy silence.

The royal family disembarked while the men attached the straps and riggings to the carriage. The men aligned the team to the damaged carriage with much maneuvering as the day's heat grew. The powerful, broad-backed horses set to work, at the slow pace dictated by the injured animal, two miles an hour. The governess, the Duchesse de Tourzel, did her best to entertain the children as the carriage lumbered along. She unwrapped biscuits, cold cuts of pork, cheese, apples, and pastries from her bag—a welcome feast to the children—although the adults had no desire to eat.

The day passed slowly. Other carriages and horseback riders took no particular notice of the Berlin or its passengers. But when they arrived at Pont de Sommeville, dusk settled with no sign of the Duc de Choiseul or his men, so the royal family stayed within the carriage at the post-house when the driver changed the horses for a fresh team. Unescorted, the Berlin continued on the road to Sainte-Ménéhould, expecting to meet the troops promised to them, but when the carriage pulled into the village, the king's jaw fell slack.

"Where are the hussars? A detachment should meet us here. I see no one!" He hissed with anger.

"Calm yourself; they must be hiding to avoid being seen," the queen said, attempting to sound confident.

As the carriage slowly crept through the village, peasants stared but could not see inside the fine carriage. Recognizing the Berlin, a soldier ran up, quickly saluted, and spoke in a low voice. "Majesté, at last, you have come. The villagers, suspicious all day, have wondered why the men came here. Choiseul withdrew. He sent us a message that you would not arrive today as planned since you did not meet him at Pont de Sommeville, so now his men sit drinking wine at the local wine shop. Only I have paced the street, keeping watch for you."

The king growled. "I did not meet him because he was not there!"

"No, Majesté, he is, even now, taking cover in a nearby forest, waiting for you. The irate villagers drove the Duc de Choiseul and his men off with pitchforks, fearing soldiers had come to collect overdue rents on behalf of the local landowner. I let my men dismount since I thought you would not arrive tonight. We must not be seen talking. The villagers suspect...."

The commander broke off and walked briskly into the darkness, away from the carriage. The king saw two men point at the carriage. He tapped the cab for the driver to move on. They continued to the outskirts of town, but when the king looked behind for any sign of a promised escort, his silence and fear blanketed the carriage; even the children who had talked and played games became quiet.

The carriage ambled along for miles before stopping at Clermont en Argonne for fresh horses. By midnight, the Berlin rode down the hill and through the cobbled streets of Varennes. The town appeared quiet until someone near the church shouted, "Halt!"

King Louis slammed a strong fist on the carriage wall, shouting for the driver to continue. Slapping the horses with the reins, the man hurried the team to a gallop when national guardsmen jumped from behind the stone archway that spanned the street, bayonets raised.

"Halt! Halt! One more step, and we fire!"

The driver reined to a stop. A soldier approached and knocked on the carriage door. "Show your travel papers!"

The Duchesse de Tourzel handed him the travel papers that verified they were the Baroness von Korff family with travel attendants.

"Get down. I want to see you!"

In the dim lantern light, the soldier, unsure of who they were, sent for a local judge who had lived at Versailles to come to identify the passengers. The soldier and a local shop owner escorted the group to a small shop that sold candles and pots of brown sugar. Upon entering, the passengers remained silent as the soldier stood guard outside the door. The shop owner allowed the fatigued children to lay on the straw bed and the apprehended women to sit frozen on rickety, straw-bottom chairs while the unidentified male traveler paced the short length of the room.

When the elderly judge, roused from his slumber at home, walked into the shop with the national guardsmen, he entered, unaware of what they wanted of him. Seeing King Louis XVI, he immediately lowered on a knee and bowed his head in respect, saying, "Votre Majesté!"

The king, touched by the old man's devotion, acknowledged him with an inadvertent smile. The shopkeeper and the judge sat stunned while the guardsman turned on his heel and rushed from the shop.

The shopkeeper gathered his wits. "Your Majesté, forgive my humble accommodations." Turning to his wife, he barked, "Fetch wine and food; you can see how fatigued they are!"

The elderly judge, rising with the help of his cane, said, "Majesté, in the morning, I will provide you with an escort from here. I am sorry for this delay. Let us make you as comfortable as possible until you continue your trip. Forgive this intrusion. I am sure there is some mistake."

"My dear man, it is good to see you once again. I would be most grateful for your help. I expect my soldiers to arrive soon. When things are calmer, you must come and stay at Versailles as my guest. The queen and I would be most happy to host you and your family."

The king shot an encouraging look at his wife, who remained stiff and pale, unable to speak. She reached into the folds of her cloak to withdraw a small bottle and doused her neck and wrists with her favorite perfume of orange, jasmine, iris, and rose flowers from her garden. She appeared to revive somewhat but remained stiff with horrified silence.

"Majesté, what an honor you give to this old man. I shall look forward to it."

The royal family passed five hours in the shopkeeper's quarters before a hard knock on the door roused them.

"Ah, Captain Bayon," King Louis said in a melancholy voice, "you have come."

"Majesté, I have here," he said, crumpling a paper in his fist, "I have here a decree from the assembly confirming Commander Lafayette's order for the royal family to return to Tuileries." The captain looked down, unable to face the king. "Majesté, you know all the people of Paris are…well, the interests of state demand, you must understand." When the queen glared at the fumbling soldier, he averted his eyes and fell silent.

The king snatched the decree from his hand and read it. "According to this, there is no longer a King of France!"

He growled, handing the order to his wife to read. In an attempt to stall, he said, "Can you wait until eleven in the morning? The children must rest. This has been very difficult for them." Hearing the jeering crowd outside shout, "To Paris! To Paris," his voice collapsed under the weight of theirs; the king realized he had no alternative.

When the door flung open, and the Duc de Choiseul, a small, sturdily built man of thirty-two, walked in, the king's face lit up. The duke took the king aside and whispered, "We can dash for it. We can reach the frontier. I have fresh horses in the street, as well as hussars."

King Louis considered the idea. He walked to a window. Outside he saw hundreds of armed villagers shouting as they waved sticks, pitchforks, and knives.

"We would never make it," the king sighed. "If the crowd does not slaughter us here, the national guardsmen will apprehend us down the road. We have no option but to return to Paris. The plan should have worked. Contact von Fersen and let him know what has happened."

"But Majesté, think...."

"I believe we can weather this. These are, after all, my people. I am still their king! I shall work out an equitable solution."

The queen looked at her husband with a wild, furtive stare. "But they detest me! You hear how they call me the Austrian bitch. *Madame Déficit!* Your advisors told you the sickening things they accuse me of in their pamphlets. I fear for our lives."

King Louis XVI took Queen Marie Antoinette by the shoulders and looked directly into her clear, light eyes. "My dearest, those people, they are...they are not true Frenchmen. They are troublemakers—bourgeois lawyers clamoring for attention, that is all. They do not speak for the heart of the French people, our people. They are malcontents. Their anger will soon fade. All this trouble is more to do with a bad harvest than anything else. Naturally, the blame must fall somewhere, but it will cease. I have decided I will modify the tax system and punish the grain hoarders. That will please the people; the cost of grain will drop, and they will again be happy. The French are a most agreeable people. This difficulty will pass. You will see."

The duc glanced at the queen, whose eyes had welled with tears. She pulled her black veil down, stifled her sobs, and looked at her children as they slept on the cot. "Sir, what about our children?"

The king looked lovingly at his thin, small boy in a girl's dress, sprawled next to his older sister. "They will be fine. The Dauphin can go to your family in Austria for a while, learn to hunt and ride properly. God knows hunting has been my only true enjoyment. I would be most distressed if he did not enjoy it also."

The queen slumped on the rickety straw chair and put her head in her hands. When she looked up, the Duc de Choiseul and the king were whispering but broke off when Marie Antoinette cleared her throat in warning. The stairs up to the shopkeeper's bedroom groaned with the weight of someone's descent. Madame Sauce entered and curtsied to the people gathered there.

"I will make le petit déjeuner. Monsieur Sauce has come." She made another clumsy curtsey, tripping on the stained apron of her dress, and whispered in a low voice. "Majesté, I…I just wants to say, well, don't give up being king. There's many who loves you and the boy. It would be a shame…."

"Merci, madame. I am your king, as always."

"And, Majesté, you should stay put in that big palace with all them nice things. God wants you to. You was born to rule France. Those Austrians…they won't treat you so well as your own people."

The queen lifted her head to look at the shopkeeper's wife, who was oblivious to the insult she had voiced.

"Thank you, madame. We would indeed enjoy some food before we set out for Paris. And madame, I would be in your debt for one small favor."

"Yes, Majesté?"

"Kindly call your husband. I must speak to him for a moment. I believe he and the judge are out on the street in front."

"Yes, Majesté, I sees him talking to villagers. They are plenty upset. Maybe you should go out and speaks with them. That would calm 'em down."

Her words were drowned by a new round of chanting, "*Vive la Nation!*" causing the king's soft, pale face to splotch red. "I do not think so," he said grimly.

When Monsieur Sauce returned, he spoke to his king in private and dismissed Madame Sauce to fetch a loaf of bread, pressing twelve sous into her palm. She wiped her hands on her cotton apron and said to the king, "You see, Majesté, there's the problem. Many can't afford bread. It's what we live on—four pounds a day. I used to buy a four-pound loaf for eight sous. Now it's twelve sous. That's more than half a day's wages, just to eat bread. That don't say nothing about a few vegetables, a small piece of meat once in a while, oil, wine, wood for our fires, candles to light our table. The bread queues—that's what this anger is all about. Them people outside, they don't hate you, not the queen neither. They're hungry. Give 'em bread for eight sous, and them mischief-makers will be quiet."

"Shut up, woman, you've said enough!" Sauce shouted at his wife. "Go about your business; fetch the food. The king leaves for Paris soon."

Without another word, the shopkeeper's wife finished wiping her hands, took the coins the duc held out and walked through the front door to the street where an angry mob jostled for position to see inside and catch a glimpse of the royals.

"Look, Monsieur Sauce," King Louis XVI said in a voice full of forced good humor. "I must attend to my family business, a personal matter, but I need you to bring me the box from my carriage. The wall between the driver's side and the cabin has a false panel. Reach below the upholstery until you feel a latch that releases the pressure on the wood panel. You will find an iron box. Bring it to me without anyone noticing."

Seeing Sauce hesitate, the king continued. "It is not a weapon. I am no fool. It is something for my boy, something to remember me...."

At these words, Queen Marie Antoinette broke down in tears. Sauce went rigid. "Oui, Majesté. I return shortly. Your carriage is at the livery. Do not attempt to step out of my shop! The national guardsmen have muskets aimed at the door; peasants have pitchforks. The sooner you leave, the better. I don't know what would happen if...."

The king nodded. Sauce opened the door and stepped out into the pastel morning light while King Louis XVI turned to the Duc de Choiseul.

"You must—at all costs—help us in this. We carry with us extremely important items that must not be lost or destroyed. Our royal lineage depends on it. As soon as they take us, you and the hussars ride toward Belgium to catch up with Count von Fersen. Tell him I trust him to deliver my box to the Archbishop at the Papal Palace in Avignon. The archbishop will keep it for me. Do not open the box. This is gravely important!"

"*Oui, Majesté*, I will do everything you request."

"Do not fail me!"

"I will find Fersen and deliver the package and the message as soon as possible."

The queen approached the duc, saying, "And please convey our thanks to Fersen and ask him to visit us in Paris. Give him our heartfelt prayers for his safety and success in helping us with this."

The king raised an eyebrow at the evident passion in his wife's voice, saying, "None other than the Archbishop. Remember that. Only he should receive this package."

"Yes, *Majesté!*" the duc said with a bow.

The door swung open. Madame Sauce hobbled in with a burlap bag and a jug of wine. When the crowd glimpsed Queen Marie Antoinette inside, a new round of obscenities flowed as the crowd convulsed with anger. Madame Sauce slammed the door quickly. A national guardsman fired his musket into the air, swearing to take better aim if the rabble didn't move back. The duc braced his body against the door and told the others to move back.

Madame Sauce cried, "You'd better go soon before them storm my house. Them out there is getting worse, threw mud at my skirt for housing you." She shook the mud off, stamped her feet, and removed three loaves of bread, a roll of sausage, and four eggs from the burlap wrapping.

"I'll make food. Then you go! One person's dead, an old man from the next village. He heard you was here, rode to see you, had the cross of St. Louis on his uniform. The crowd waved him to get off the main street. He kept coming on his horse, said he had to salute his king. They shot him dead, those guards."

"Who shot him?" Louis XVI asked in horror.

"A national guard soldier from Paris shot him in the back, they said."

The king looked stricken. Renewed shouts outside woke the Dauphin, who, frightened and disoriented, screamed. His mother rushed to him, cradling him in her arms to wipe the tears from his ivory cheeks. Handing him to his sister, the queen stood to speak to her husband in the corner of the small room.

"Do you trust him to bring it to us?"

"What choice do I have?" the king said, taking her hand in his.

The duc started to speak but stopped short when Monsieur Sauce fell through the door, almost knocking the queen down. The duc steadied her and slammed the door to onlookers.

"Pardon, Madame, someone shoved me and tried to wrestle me," he said as he pulled the box out from under a sweaty saddle blanket.

"Monsieur," the king said with respect, "this is a family matter. Kindly retire to the kitchen with your wife for a few moments. Leave us to pray together. You," he said to Madame de Tourzel, "kindly step into the kitchen and prevent any interruption."

The king, queen, and the duke huddled in the middle of the small room, the children watching with interest. The king pulled an ornate metal filigree key from his coat pocket and opened the lock. Carefully he removed a lumpy, gold silk bag.

Dyan Dubois

"This is our future, monsieur. Do not fail us. You must entrust it to von Fersen to deliver to the Archbishop of Avignon. No one must open it by order of the king! It is for the archbishop's eyes alone."

When the king placed the bag in the duc's hands, its weight made his hands drop. Unbuttoning his vest, the duc stuffed the awkward bundle next to his stomach and straightened his jacket over it. "I go now, Majesté, before they come for you. It will be easier."

The Duc de Choiseul saluted King Louis XVI and Queen Marie Antoinette and made a low bow before stepping out onto the main street of Varennes to an uproar of "*Vive la Republique!*" and "*Tu vas en prison, Madame Déficit!*"

Sauce bolted the door as soon as the duc walked out, urging the royal family to eat hurriedly and depart for everyone's safety. Fifteen minutes later, surrounded by armed guardsmen, the king and his family stepped out of Sauce's shop to the main street to climb into the Berlin. The jeering crowd, held at a distance by the guardsmen's bayonets, chanted so riotously that the National Guard threatened to shoot them. Guardsmen flanked the carriage to form a barrier between the royals and France's people while escorting the king back to Paris.

After a hard ride, the duc and his hussars found Count von Fersen at Stenay. Hearing the National Guard from Paris had been sent to retrieve King Louis XVI, von Fersen turned back to help the royals. The duc explained what had happened and handed von Fersen the lumpy silk bag from the king, admonishing him. "No one but the Archbishop of Avignon must receive this. No one must open it, by orders from the king! You, von Fersen, must deliver it to his hand."

"I shall do as you say," Count von Fersen replied with a slight bow, "And the queen…how was she when last you saw her?"

"She conveyed heartfelt prayers for your safety and requested you visit the palace soon. She looked composed, I think, for the children's sakes."

Dyan Dubois

CHAPTER TWELVE

The Archbishop's Secret

Looking down, Askara saw her dirty leather boots. The dank smell of urine and body odor made her stomach lurch. She raised a muscular arm, covered her mouth with a callused hand, and rubbed dense stubble along her angular jaw. Askara faded quickly, becoming the foul-smelling man who whispered in raspy French.

"Michel, did you get it out?"

"No, Anton. I found the quartz vein, but I couldn't pry the stone loose. I struggled, rocking it back and forth until my fingertips bled. My blade made only a shallow crevice. I inched up and down the crack repeatedly until finally, the block tipped forward a little, but I replaced the stone when I heard a noise coming from the archbishop's quarters. Someone argued with His Grace. You get the bundle. I must go to His Grace. Ride to Marseilles. Deliver it as I told you, and I will see you back at my house in a couple of days.

"Anton, no one must suspect us. Hurry, there's no time to waste! Remember, Anton, the man paying requires absolute secrecy, or else we die," Michel whispered, pretending to slice his neck with an imaginary knife."

"Oui, *je comprends.*"

"Do not cast your eyes upon the contents of the leather bundle. I do not question what it holds, and neither should you. That is an order, Anton."

"*Au revoir.* Marseilles by daylight," Anton replied, his raspy voice fading as the two men separated, Anton toward the tunnel vault and Michel toward a dark passageway that dripped with foul water.

--------------------- ❧ ---------------------

WHEN MICHEL RETURNED WITH TWO GLASSES OF WARM cognac, a man shouted from the archbishop's bedchamber. "Who is outside?"

Michel didn't recognize the voice. He heard the scuffling of heavy boots. "Your Grace, it is I, Michel." Soldiers rushed the door, ordering him to stand back. Michel obeyed, saying, "Is His Grace ill?"

"His Grace is dead!"

The servant lunged forward between the soldiers to see the archbishop's fallen body on the stone floor, his eyes milk-white, rolled back, mouth contorted into an anguished grimace.

Michel fell to his knees, clasping a length of his father's robe, and cried, "Mon Dieu, Mon Dieu," pulling the fabric through his fingers as if he could reel back the soul of its owner.

"When did you last see him?" the captain bellowed.

"He stopped by the kitchen at dinner, as he often does, to bless us."

"Did he say anything to you?"

"No, *monsieur le capitaine*, nothing other than to bring two cognacs this night."

"Where does that tunnel go?" the officer said, pointing in the distance.

"I do not know, monsieur le capitaine," Michel said, quivering.

The captain clenched his jaw and shouted, "Go, there! Stand by the entrance."

When the archbishop's servant approached the opening cautiously, making a wide arc to avoid the priest's dead body, the soldier followed him with sword drawn.

"You stink this place! You are no archbishop's servant. You're a sewer rat!" he said and pointed at the stains on the hem of Michel's robe.

"No!" the servant cried to the captain towering over him. "I work in the kitchen; ask the others. They know me."

"The Archbishop of Avignon would never let a kitchen servant stinking of sewage serve him cognac. Where were you? In the tunnel—for what?"

"Outside at the night soil pit, sir. Forgive me."

"Call the kitchen staff," he commanded his soldier. "We will see about your story. Shackle him in the courtyard below."

The soldier led the trembling servant to the large stone column in the archbishop's private garden. Michel saw the other kitchen servants marching through the trees at saber point to climb the stairway to the archbishop's chamber. When they reached the portico and were told the archbishop was dead, they cried, made the sign of the cross, and muttered prayers.

"That man there," the captain said, pointing down at the servant lashed to the tree, "does he serve the Archbishop of Avignon?"

The fearful group answered: "Oui, *commandant*."

"Would he bring the good priest nightly cognac?"

"Oui, commandant."

The captain bellowed, "Was that man," he said, pointing at Michel, "in his sleeping quarters this night?"

"Non, monsieur. After supper duty, he left," one monk answered. "He lives in the village by the creek. He is a farmer. The archbishop raised him as a son, but he was not suited for priesthood."

The captain ordered his soldiers to escort the monks downstairs when one shouted as he passed the column where the archbishop's servant stood roped to the tree.

"God will make you repent. Murderer!"

Michel struggled against his ropes like a wild animal. The captain approached with his sword raised, pressed its thin silver tip into the servant's soft, fleshy throat, and said, "Sewer rat, where is it?"

"What?" Michel gasped, trying to breathe without moving.

"What was in that vault? Give it to me, and I will spare your worthless life."

"I have nothing, as you can see."

The saber dug in, warm droplets of blood dripped onto Michel's robe. The captain leaned in closer, pressed harder. "Give it to me, and you go free; otherwise, I kill you here, now."

The pressure on his throat made it difficult for Michel to reply. In an anguished whisper, he said, "Monsieur le capitaine, a man visited His Grace yesterday. I overheard him say he would deliver a satchel in four days to the dock at Marseilles."

"What satchel?"

"I do not know. His Grace seemed disturbed today and called for early cognac."

"Was the man a nobleman?"

"He rode a fine white horse. Please, sir, have mercy. The archbishop was a father to me. He found me on the church steps, only hours old. His Grace saved me. He raised me here in the monastery as a child. I was his most devoted servant and son. I would never hurt him," he said and sobbed. "He allowed me to live as a farmer, a householder in the village by the creek."

The soldier unleashed Michel from the tree. "You will ride with us to Marseilles tonight. We will watch the dock day and night for you to identify the courier you saw. Then I will consider releasing you. But first, come into the archbishop's chamber with me."

Michel wanted to refuse, but the captain's sword told him to resist was useless. The captain ordered him to sip the warmed cognac he had brought to the chamber. He waited. Nothing happened. The captain snorted. He ordered him to take gulps of the second cognac. Still, nothing happened. When Michel's nose twitched, and his body swayed, a sly smile spread across the captain's face as he watched and waited. Michel's face flushed red; he stumbled but remained erect. Irate, the captain shoved the servant into his guardsman's grip and rattled off commands for his men.

———— ✄ ————

ANTON GALLOPED ON THE ROAD SOUTH, GROWING MORE confident with increasing distance. No sound other than his horse's heavy breathing cut the black night. The unevenness of the road caused him to slow as he approached the ancient Roman bridge.

His horse tripped. A front hoof struck a rock obliquely, sending it over the low wall to the river below. Anton lunged forward in the saddle. He straightened up, pulling the reins with a quick yank, causing the exhausted animal to stumble to a walk.

Anton knew no fool would ride as he did, galloping at night without moonlight, pushing his horse so hard. He took comfort in that. An owl hooted in a nearby tree, and the night shone with cold starlight, making specters appear in laced tree branches. Anton reached for the flask of wine secured to his saddle. Taking a long swig, he relaxed into the rhythm of the horse's relaxed sway.

From the pattern of the stars, he figured it was nearly three in the morning. His wine-induced good humor swelled with the vision of gold coins he would be paid, the feast he would bring home to his pregnant wife and small son, and his sister's joy, learning of money to free her husband from prison. He imagined entering his house with a side of cured beef balanced on his shoulder, baguettes, and bottles of wine. He saw his son run up to greet him, grab a loaf, and suck on it until the crust turned gummy. A smile spread across Anton's face. The vision whisked away the hollowness in his stomach.

When he took another drink before tying the flask to the saddle leathers, his hand knocked into the leather bundle. A metal object struck his knuckles. He remembered his friend's demand—do not look upon the contents—but Anton had not promised he wouldn't feel them. He loosened the leather pouch and placed his thick hand on the silk bag within, careful to avoid the wax seal. Groping carefully, his fingers slid across an object of smooth metal that was cool in the night air. He traced a cross shape with a flared base and felt the gentle rise of a human form, arms extended, feet overlapped, a crucifix.

His fingers fumbled over a stiff paper roll secured by a soft leather strip, a key, several small vials with swelled embossed bellies, and a shallow metal cup with a rough surface. Anton took another gulp of wine and wondered at the objects' value—more than the coins he would receive as payment, he figured, but hardly worth the effort to steal.

But Anton had sworn to his friend to perform his duty. He withdrew his hand carefully and tightened the leather bundle. Whatever the objects, they paled before his vision of coming home with food for his hungry family and his sister's joy.

The distant screech of a night cat roused Anton from his thoughts. Seeing dawn approach, he spurred his weary horse to canter, keeping to the cover of dappled trees that skirted the road like looming hands in the rising mist. When he approached the Marseilles harbor in first light, life began to stir. Fisherman untangled their nets along the dock and prepared for their day at sea. Fish market vendors mulled around.

Anton wended his way along narrow lanes, making for the harbor's north end, where he could see a tall ship's mast above tile rooftops. He approached through the shadows, keeping back from the walkway. Anton spotted the ship's captain walking his deck in the cool gray light, barking orders while sailors hoisted sails and secured heavy ropes. Anton dismounted and tied his horse in an empty lane of unopened shops and watched.

The thunder of hooves running on cobblestone unnerved him. Anton crouched low to watch a carriage approach, its Belgian horses blowing hard from the exertion. The carriage halted with a loud clatter. Anton knew the person in the carriage, undoubtedly not a citizen of the republic but a member of the aristocracy, if not royalty, could jeopardize him. His part in this plot could cost his life. He wondered if he were a traitor to the revolution, a traitor to the crown, or a traitor to the church? Possibly all three? Whichever, his neck would roll from the guillotine if someone caught him.

A mustached man in a silk vest and breeches emerged from the carriage to look around. His guards dismounted to speak to him, but Anton couldn't hear their words. Someone called out to the ship's mate securing the mainsail and motioned. The captain waved a small white flag with a green fleur-de-lis emblem.

Anton rushed from the shadows with the bundle, saying, "Here is your delivery, monsieur." The guards drew their swords and surrounded him. Anton tossed the bundle at the nobleman, who caught it mid-air.

The man opened the leather satchel without withdrawing the objects and carefully felt the silk bag's contents, inspecting the intact fleur-de-lis wax seal. After several minutes of study, he said, *"Merci."*

"The reward, monsieur?"

"Oui," he said with little expression. "Do not cross us. No mention of this, or we will hunt you down like an animal. You and your friend."

Anton spat. "Pay me, and I will be gone forever!"

The man withdrew a small pouch of coins from his jacket and dropped it to the ground. Anton scrambled to pick up the purse, quickly examined the coins, and shoved it into his shirt.

"Tell your friend what I have said. Inform him to tell no one if he wants to see his son home again to your sister."

Anton nodded, yes, and bolted into the alley shadows, where he crouched to watch the ship's captain row to the dock to receive the bundle from the mustached aristocrat. The captain took the bag, saluted the nobleman, and rowed back to his ship, shouting orders. Sailors hoisted anchor. The ship, *Le Grande Serpent*, eased out of the harbor to catch the morning breeze, but the nobleman didn't stay to watch. He jumped into his carriage; the driver snapped the whip; and the Belgians felt the sting. Leaping to a gallop, the horses ran past fishmongers who were too busy hauling boxes of fish to give a second look.

Anton smiled, feeling the gold coins' weight in the pouch hidden under his waist belt, and walked toward the lane where his tethered horse stood. When he approached the exhausted animal, he heard the sound of many horses' hooves striking the cobblestones, men shouting, and irate geese honking alarm. Soldiers in red vests spread like ants on the dock.

Anton spotted his friend Michel riding a republican army horse, surrounded by soldiers, held at sword point, his hands tied to the saddle horn. Anton dropped his horse's reins and slipped behind a stone wall to watch. Soldiers accosted a fisherman straightening his nets. The old man pointed to where the carriage had been. Soldiers fanned out along the dock.

Anton ran through back alleys toward the bustling city center, his chest heaving for air, his legs cramped from exertion. When he saw a brothel, he rushed in.

ANTON SLEPT THE DAYLIGHT HOURS IN A SMALL ROOM upstairs in the brothel. When he woke, he walked from his room down a narrow hall towards the privy. Encountering a young brunette with quick black eyes, he moved aside to let her pass, trying to avoid her intense gaze.

"Finally, you wake, monsieur. We thought you dead. A sleeping man in a brothel is as good as dead, don't you agree?"

"Pardon, I was très fatigué."

"I, too, am très fatigué, but that does not mean I get to sleep all day. Sleep is a luxury for those who can afford it. Men like you do not help us. Go somewhere else!"

"I am going as soon as possible."

"Why do you wait? Is it because soldiers have come to the city? Is that why you run so hard that you sleep an entire day away?"

"I work hard on my farm."

The young woman looked at Anton's haggard but ruggedly handsome face. "Possibly you sleep until night's safety to escape our city?"

"I paid for the room. You will have it for business soon."

"You could be that business, monsieur. That would help me. I would not go out if I were you. Soldiers are here, now, visiting the women. You may be spotted." Anton looked at the soft outline of her childlike face and started to reply when she continued, "The soldiers are hunting for a spy for an aristo, the one at the dock this morning before *Le Grand Serpent* set sail. They offer a reward for him. I could use money. I wonder how much that award would be? Do you wonder, monsieur?"

Anton, growing suspicious of the young woman, said, "Why do you tell me?"

"It would be a shame for that man to lose his horse and his life in one short day, don't you think?"

"Who tells you these things?"

"My last sailor," the woman said, tossing her head back, so the dark curls fell away from her pale moon face. "There is a reward. Shall I be rewarded by a highwayman or a soldier, I wonder?"

"Mademoiselle, a man can travel and not be a highwayman."

"I am not a rich woman, monsieur; you see, I must support my ailing mother. Medicine is costly," she said with a mischievous smile. "Would you like to help me buy her medicine? It would be good for you. I could then forget the sailor's description of the man your height and weight with worn knee boots such as yours who fled the harbor, abandoning his poor horse—a horse my cousin took to the livery. A man," she said with a twinkle in her eye, "who fled on foot. That would be very tiring, correct?"

Anton grimaced.

"How can a woman trust such a man, you might ask. Yet, a woman could trust such a man if he helped her. I am a simple girl, monsieur, with simple wants and a short memory. I have no desire to be involved with the likes of Robespierre's men. However, I could help return his horse if such a man would take me north to my village to see my mother and deliver her medicine. It is not much to ask, to buy medicine for an ailing woman and deliver it. Leaving this city with someone posing as a wife would help that man. Soldiers would not suspect. Do you agree?"

Considering her proposal, Anton said, "If you secure my horse, I will buy your mother's medicine, cover your lost wages, and take you to deliver it, but only on back roads, and you will return on your own."

"Easily done. My cousin, a stable boy at the livery, will fetch your horse, the bay gelding with a white scar that he found in an alley. I will tell him to meet us at a rendezvous point on the north road where it splits by the river. From there we will travel the hills to my village. You will pay him and me for our labor, oui?"

"Oui. Tell your cousin we leave after dusk."

"Mais oui!" the young woman said smiling, her dark eyes alive with excitement. "Until then, stay in your room. I will bring food up to you. There is a domicile of my friend we can reach in the dark. She will put us up. Monsieur, what is your name?"

"Anton."

"I will call you Maurice. *C'est bon ça, Maurice.* You will pay for me for this entire day and night."

ON THEIR WALK NORTH TO MEET HER COUSIN IN THE evening gray-purple light, Anton learned the girl was eighteen years old, several years younger than himself. When he asked why she worked at the brothel, the girl smiled and told him it was good pay being a *belle de nuit,* and her *madam* was fair, mostly. Besides, she couldn't find work in her home village—high-paying work that would not shame her mother.

"Ma mère is all I have. My father died of a fever when I was eleven. Four years later, my mother grew ill with terrible pains in her body. My mother needed medicine, she said, because her bones were breaking. She cried all the time. I was fifteen, yet I had to feed us, so I went to a nobleman's house as a kitchen maid's assistant, but he took me to bed. After several months his wife found out and ordered me to leave. I had no place to live, no money to live on, so I came to the city for work. Madam at the Rue St. Claire Brothel took me in. Now I have food, shelter, and enough money to buy my mother's pain medicine that arrives by ship at the Marseilles port. Then I take it home to her. She thinks I have a dock job. That gives her pride. The medicine gives her relief."

"But you're still a child."

"No one is a child with a woman's working body, monsieur. That time passed. Madam is good to us. She never lets men beat us, and I can go home every two weeks to stay with my mother for a night. I dislike large sailors reeking of drink who press me into the mattress until I can't breathe. They handle women like ropes—yanking here, pulling there with rough, short fingers, scratching with hard, callused hands, but this is my life."

"You should find other work while you're still young, get married, have a family."

"Would you marry me?"

"No!" Anton said curtly. "I don't even know your real name."

"You see, no one else will either. Men think like you. I am a nobody, but my name is Germaine."

"I meant 'no' because I am married."

"So that's why you don't touch me?"

"Oui…and you are a child."

The girl's pleasant smile faded; her mouth turned down so severely that the lower lids of her eyes followed. She turned away from Anton's stare. He sat on the fallen log where they waited for his horse, picking matted green moss from reddish bark before he spoke again.

"I am almost nineteen!"

"Germaine, I have a cousin who owns a bakery in village Lafayette. I can speak to him about you. I know he needs help. He and his wife cannot handle all the work, especially in these days of baking bread day and night."

The girl's eyes lit up. "I would work hard, monsieur. You will see. But I have to make enough for my mother."

"You will have to talk to my cousin. I don't know how much he can pay. What do you make at the brothel?"

"*Monsieur*, sometimes I make very much money, but madam takes it and gives me just enough for my mother's medicine and at times new clothes for me—she says we must look good—and for perfumes."

"That is all?"

"*Oui*, madam says I am an apprentice. When I am older, I can have more."

"Well, the bakery job will match that. With a respectable job, you have the possibility of marriage."

"Someone like me?"

Anton winced. "You are a child. You could hide your past. With a new start, oui."

In the dim light, the girl's face reddened to a deep pomegranate color. The heavy black liner around her eyes ran and smudged her cheeks. She wiped her eyes. Anton thought of his pregnant wife and the baby she carried, possibly a girl. What would her life hold if her father went to prison—or worse?

"I will do everything I can to help you, Germaine, if you help me now."

Anton snapped to attention, hearing hoofbeats on the road. They jumped into the scrub brush. A birdcall pierced the evening that Germaine answered with an identical sound, motioning Anton to crouch low and stay out of sight. Through the bushes, Anton saw the silhouette of a horse and rider approach at a gallop. He recognized his horse. The rider raised his hand in the air. Germaine rose from the ferns to wave her headscarf, making pale swirls over her head for the boy, who abruptly reined the horse and dismounted at a trot.

"*Comment ça va?*" he said, eyeing the man in the bushes. When Germaine nodded permission, the boy continued.

"Men watch the livery. When they find this horse missing, they will search. Stay off the main road. Take the path along the stream, the shepherd's trail home. *Cousine*, I hope your friend is worth so much. I heard a soldier say he works for the royals."

Hearing this, Anton stood up. "Do I look like a fool? Someone paid me to deliver a package…that is all I know. That is all I want to know. Like you, I was for hire!" he said as he pressed a few coins into the boy's palm. *"Merci* for delivering my horse! Now go."

The boy kissed his cousin on both cheeks, whispering something to her quickly. He called out, *"Au revoir,"* and trotted through the bushes to take a footpath back to Marseilles. Anton and Germaine mounted the horse, reined sharply to the right, and followed the stream bed north. They rode at a slow pace in silence for half an hour.

"We must leave this trail now," Germaine said.

"Why?"

"My cousin whispered there is a trap for you not far from here, where the stream curves left to a village. Soldiers wait there. They paid my cousin to direct you this way."

"Why tell me now?"

"I cannot let you fall into a trap like a rabbit. You seem a good man. The shame would be my haunting. And my cousin did what he was told, so he was paid."

"Where do we go from here?"

The girl grabbed the reins to stop the horse. "You go there," she said, pointing through the dark trees to a distant valley. I ride your horse to my village…alone."

"No! When the soldiers spot my horse, they will shoot."

"They will not. My cousin says they want you alive. They have no plan to kill you until after they speak to you."

"It is too dangerous. Come with me, Germaine. I will take you home to your mother, and then I will disappear."

"They will expect that. Monsieur, if you disappear, who will offer me the hope of decent work and marriage? I would die, worn out and discarded when my beauty fades, sentenced to sweep slop from the streets. No, I take my chance with you, Monsieur Anton, Maurice. Destiny brought you to me. You, too, are caught in a spider web—no different from me. This escape is a chance for us both. I will ride into the village where the soldiers wait. I will say we struggled, and I escaped on your horse."

Taking both hands, she ripped the seam of her cotton bodice and scratched deep gouges in her neck and bosom with her fingernails. Blood pricked along the narrow lines.

"Quick! Hand me that stick," she said, pointing to a moss-covered limb on a fallen tree stump.

Without asking, Anton jumped down from the horse. He struggled to snap the limb but called to his back. "I don't want to leave you. They may shoot. They may not wait to question…."

The girl gave the horse a vicious jab in the sides with her sharp-heeled boots, making the frightened animal lunge sideways. Anton rushed to grab the reins, but his horse jumped out of reach. The girl reigned him hard and charged into the darkness at a full run. Anton started to yell to Germaine but swallowed his words. He stood still and strained to hear the animal's heavy breathing as the sound of snapping twigs grew fainter with distance, leaving him alone in the dark.

Abandoning the path quickly, Anton stumbled over forest floor debris for hours until exhaustion overtook him. When he stopped, he buried himself in a thick patch of ferns and slept.

Raucous bird chatter roused him in the heat of the overhead sun. Stiff and hungry, he searched for water, wondering at the bravery—or stupidity?—of the girl who risked so much to help him without giving him time to pay her.

Anton reached a small village by mid-afternoon and stopped at the inn for a meal. The innkeeper's wife, a portly, pock-faced woman, informed him she had a full house of soldiers the previous night, "a wild group" searching for a bandit. When Anton asked what kind of bandit would be in the area, the woman described him with great emphasis as an aristocrat who drank fine wine and ate pastries and roast chicken, one who rode the finest white stallion in the land, a man who should visit *madame la guillotine*.

Anton sighed in relief, thankful for the imagination of the dim-witted. One piece of information she told him gave him ease—the soldiers then rode to search the province east of the river where the bandit had ravaged a young girl who, by pure cunning, had escaped on the man's horse and was safely delivered back to her ailing mother. After a hearty meal of mutton and bread, Anton departed to follow the road northwest to his home near Avignon.

When Anton greeted his pregnant wife, his arms loaded with a side of cured beef, loaves of bread, cheese, and bottles of wine, she marveled at his good fortune. He lied, explaining that he had aided someone on the road who had paid him generously for saving him from bandits. Anton's family dined merrily, enjoying their feast.

After their son went to bed, his wife informed him of the latest news: many in Paris had died at the guillotine, a baby had been born in their village, and she had harvested the herbs in their garden. She said she had heard a man of wealth, an aristocrat who lived on the Rue de Mont Blanc, a friend of the Archbishop of Avignon, had been found dead by a local farmer on the road to Marseilles, his carriage abandoned on the roadway, his horses stolen.

She informed her husband in a whisper that people said he was a spy for the Austrians. "They say the Austrians are invading France." Hearing this, Anton grew quiet.

ASKARA FELT ANTON'S WARM TEARS FADE ON HER cheeks. Dark forms melded together to lift her silver essence out of Anton's body. Linked in thought, the Kalanoro carried Askara like a gossamer web wafting in a breeze to gently lay her down on the hotel bed. Her eyes jerked open when she felt the cool bedspread on her back. The shadows retreated like a mist, leaving Askara alone in the room with the weight of Anton's grief pressing down on her.

CHAPTER THIRTEEN

The Legacy

W hen Askara and Darian stepped out of their room to meet Sara downstairs for a café au lait, the sight of a crumpled note taped to the door made Askara's skin crawl. Carefully she unwrapped the folds while she held her breath. *Hi, where are you? We leave this afternoon and want to say goodbye. Get in touch. Elaine and John.* Sighing in relief, Askara crammed the note into her pocket and ran down the stairs two at a time.

"That note woke you up, didn't it, Askara?" Darian said when he caught up with her in the foyer. "I think it's good our vacation is almost over. I see the kind of stress in you I saw after Nagali tried to hypnotize you in Kenya. I don't like it, Sweetie. Sometimes I worry about you—actually, often. I wish we could roll back time to Greece when I spotted you at the Oracle of Delhi. You looked so relaxed and happy."

"Thanks, Darian, that's a mixed message for sure. Life happens; shit happens. I can't help it if I feel things acutely. Besides, for all your cool demeanor, you get rattled too. You don't show it like I do, but it's there. You think I don't know? I can practically hear you at times thinking: 'Is Askara all right in the head?' Well, Darian, that hurts."

"Sweetie, it's not like that. I do worry, yes, but for your safety. I don't like some interactions we've had here. Something feels off to me."

"Ha, there you go. Something feels off. See what I mean? You pick up on things too. But you stuff it."

"Hey, you over here," Sara called out in a loud voice that made everyone in the café turn to look. "Come sit down."

Askara snickered. "They were expecting rock stars or something. See their disappointed faces."

"I hope Sara has had a good time," Darian said softly. "I think I've spent more time with her than with you."

"G'day. What's on?"

Askara motioned for service. The Malagasy waitress studied Askara's face intently when she ordered coffee, so much that Askara wondered if she had a toothpaste smear or something. She rubbed her hand quickly across her mouth and watched the girl walk back to the cook, a heavy-set Frenchman. The waitress whispered something to him that made the chef turn to stare at them.

"I win friends wherever I go," Askara said sarcastically, watching the chef approach.

"Madame, I am Chef Pierre," he said.

"Bonjour, monsieur," she said nervously.

"I am a friend of Jean-Paul," he said, leaning close to her. He whispered something in her ear as if no one else was at her table or in the café. After the waitress disappeared like a vapor, sliding through the kitchen's wooden double doors, he announced to the table in a hushed tone, "I am here to help you."

Askara looked up and studied his weathered face—more a field peasant's than a fancy chef's—and said, "In what way, monsieur?"

Dyan Dubois

"Jean-Paul was a member, as I am."

"Of what?"

The look of dismay on the chef's face would have been comical at any other time: knitted brow, furrowed forehead, eyes squeezed to small brown dots, and jowls slack with blue beard stubble. With a visible twitch, his face straightened like an unfurled flag.

"Do not presume I am an idiot, madame."

"Do not presume I am not!" Askara snapped back and stood quickly.

Darian wedged himself between the chef and Askara. "Sir, step away. You're upsetting my wife."

Stunned, the chef whispered, "*Pardon*, monsieur, I only want to say, we are ready to serve."

"Serve then. Pastries and coffee, please. Now!"

Confused, the chef replied, "*Oui, monsieur.* Contact me here if we can be of service."

When he walked away, Sara leaned over the table. "Bloody hell, what did that bloke mean?"

"I have no idea, Sara, but I don't think it's food service. Poor old Jean-Paul mentioned something about being a member of a group he called Le Pierre, probably a colonialist social club. Maybe the chef is too. I think all the French here are related in some way. Forget him. Let's eat. I'm starving. Just look at the dessert tray over there—yummy napoleons. They remind me of having tea in the garden at Jubilee Palace in Ethiopia. You loved them. Remember?"

"What an experience that was, seeing Emperor Haile Selassie in person. Wonder if the emperor's still in prison?"

"I haven't read that he's not," Darian said. "He's eighty-three now. They should set the old man free, let him live out his remaining years in peace."

When they left, Askara slammed the café door harder than she had intended, making the glass panels rattle. The chef looked up. A strange thought came to her: The chef could have easily killed Jean-Paul, slipped a little poison into the old man's dinner. What could be simpler? She recalled an offhanded statement Priest Gestang had said: "Le Pierre is a guardian force."

Of what? she wondered. *How far would they go to 'guard' something or someone?*

"Darian, do you think they have secret police here?"

"No. Why? Are you worried about getting permission to leave Madagascar? That incident with John was just a common market theft. You should see Morocco's bazaar."

Checking her watch, she realized she had little time to reach the chapel to speak to Father Devereaux before he began his daily duties. "I don't see Imboule. I forgot to tell him I needed him this morning. Okay if it's a fast uphill walk to the church?"

Before Darian and Sara could answer, Askara loped down the lane on the market's north end. They zigzagged along dirt paths in front of small butcher shops where goats hung upside down with their necks slit, blood draining into buckets. Backing away from the shops, Askara nearly knocked into the cigarette vendor loading his bicycle basket with neat lines of hand-rolled cigarettes.

Sara grimaced. "That was like Sudan…remember those butcher shops? I thought you were gonna puke."

"Yep, almost did. Then and now."

They rushed past crying babies waiting for their mothers to feed them morning mush and street vendors cooking pancakes over charcoal fires. When they turned toward the wide, tree-lined boulevard that led to the Church of

Immaculate Conception, Askara told them she needed to run, and she would see them after her meeting.

Askara entered the chapel, breathing hard, just as Father Devereaux crossed himself at the altar. He was startled when he saw her. "Sorry, Father Devereaux," she said, catching her breath. "I would like to talk to you a moment, please."

"Madame, if it is not an emergency, I will speak to you after I complete my rounds in thirty minutes."

"Sir, I have a message for you. I was told to tell you the vial you lost has been found and is in safekeeping."

Askara watched the tall, gaunt man stiffen. He turned his back on the crucifix. "And what vial, may I ask, madame?"

"A small glass vial, one of three."

The priest walked closer, studying Askara's exertion-flushed face. "Who conveyed such a message to you? Can you verify your words?"

"I saw the vial with my own eyes."

"Where?"

"Here, in Tana."

"Who has it?"

"I don't know now." Not intending to implicate Brother Gestang, Askara added, "The man who showed me the vial has since died, an elderly Frenchman named Jean-Paul. The glass vial, worn and old-looking, I guess was yours, sir?"

"Oui. Jean-Paul du Lac. I was his friend. He should have come to me, unless, of course, he was the thief. You see, the vial belongs to me. It was stolen. Why would a foreigner be involved in a local theft?"

"I am not involved. Jean-Paul asked me to deliver this message when we had coffee together. Sadly, he passed soon after. Maybe he knew he was going to die and wanted to make sure you knew about the vial. Now I have delivered the message. Good-bye."

"But why didn't he come to me as his friend? We could have worked this out, even if he had stolen the vial for personal use," the monsignor said, trying to appear calm. "Did he mention where I can find it? I can reclaim it without ceremony and put an end to this misunderstanding."

"That I do not know. Jean-Paul showed me the vial once only and told me to deliver the message if he couldn't. He was a sweet man. But I gotta go now."

"Wait, wait. Is there no more to the message?"

"No, sir."

Father Devereaux motioned for Askara to sit in the front pew. He gazed at her with penetrating eyes like he was peeling away her skin to look within. He said in a soft, modulated tone, "Thank you for this message. I do not know what to make of it. Jean-Paul was dear to me. Daily I say prayers for his soul, as I will now say prayers for yours." Devereaux made Askara feel like a rabbit in a trap. She dared not open her mouth for fear she might set her tombstone. After a couple of minutes, the priest said, "You are quiet, yet you do not seem relaxed. Why is that, madame?"

"Well, monsignor," Askara said in an apologetic voice, "I am not Catholic."

"And does it make you nervous, being in God's house? It should calm you, no matter your sect."

"Well, Father, you see, I grew up afraid of the Catholic Church."

Her words caught Monsignor Devereaux off guard. He composed himself and told Askara, "Remember, *we* are all Christians." He elaborated on his association with the Christian Coalition of Catholic Churches, whose goal was to break down barriers between Protestant sects and barriers between Catholics to increase world unity. He stated that the Coalition hired her to write an unbiased article about Madagascar's famadihana ceremony to bridge understanding and to demonstrate Catholicism works in Madagascar as an encompassing, tolerant world religion.

Askara listened, wondering what reply her Sikh father would give the monsignor, whose face became gaunter by the second. Large dark hollows swallowed his cheeks.

Askara said, "I didn't come to take sides in religious practice, only to report on an unusual burial tradition. And, sir, *we* are not all Christians."

"Well, I am very busy. I must attend to my duties. Thank you for your message, Madame Askara. I hope you enjoy the remainder of your stay. And that ends when?"

"Saturday."

"So soon? Well, bon voyage," the monsignor said and quickly walked to the church door to escort Askara out. Before she could say goodbye, he pulled the front door closed. Askara heard sharp footsteps rush down the inside corridor and a door slam in the distance.

Askara waved to Darian and Sara, who emerged from the shade trees across the street to walk back to the hotel.

"How was it?" Darian said, seeing Askara's disgruntled expression.

"Weird. I don't like that man."

Sara grinned, "It's amazing; he looks so much like the Grim Reaper. Guess all the lost souls weigh him down."

"I wouldn't want to meet him on Halloween. He could scare the shit out of a saint!" Askara replied, smirking. "Just think what he could do to a sinner." She snickered and dropped the subject.

"Hey," Sara said, "let's swing past that gemstone vendor in the market on the way back. I wanna see if he has amethyst paperweights. Soothes the nerves."

"Paperweights?"

"No! Amethyst, a healing stone."

Sara looked at Askara and said, "You could use some. You're wound tight. Ready to pounce. A good thwack with an amethyst paperweight could be just the thing."

Entering Hotel du Parc, they heard Elaine's voice ping across the foyer. "I hoped we'd see you before we left. I left a note on your door."

"You were up and out early," John said. "This is the second time we've stopped by."

"Let's get coffee," Elaine said, "so we can talk. Plus, I need a table to spread out these bills and receipts to get them in order before we go to the airport."

When they entered the café again, Askara noticed Chef Pierre lit up like a candle. Askara ignored him and walked to a window table before the waitress could seat them. "This should do, Elaine. We'll pull another table over, so we can spread out."

Elaine checked her watch. "We've got time for breakfast, John. We'd better eat here rather than risk airport food."

"How about it, y'all, hungry?" John said. "Seems like they have a real menu here."

They ate under the scrutiny of Chef Pierre, who came over to inquire if the omelets with hollandaise sauce were to their liking. Askara avoided his penetrating stare and let John reply, but the chef remained, towering over their annexed tables.

"Madame, I am most interested in your good opinion of our dishes. My dear friend Jean-Paul had told me you respect our local cuisine and French culture. I have a secret recipe I would like to share with you, as a present, Jean-Paul's favorite dish."

Askara looked up at the chef, smiled, and put him off. "Maybe later. Thanks."

"We'll miss you all," Elaine said, cutting off the interchange with the chef. "Come visit us when we return to the states in July. John'll teach you to fish—you too, Sara. Come to America. Spending time with all of you in Toamasina was a blast."

"Guess who checked in here?" John said with a wry smile.

"Who?" they asked in unison.

"The grand dame herself, Madame Tison. I couldn't believe it when I saw her in the lobby. She recognized us right off and asked about you, Askara. When I told her we were leaving today, she asked if you were too. She wants to see you, said she'd leave a note at the desk."

Elaine chuckled. "She acts like she owns this place too."

"Maybe she does, Elaine," John said in her defense. "You should have seen the way she dressed…had one of those stoles on, the 1940's type with the mink head clasp. Haven't seen that in ages, except in old movies. Who'd want to wear a dead animal in this climate?"

The young waitress walked over to refill their cups from a steaming silver pot of coffee and placed a carousel of sweets on the table, compliments of the chef. Sara smiled at Askara and raised her eyebrows at the napoleons, then grabbed three.

Chef Pierre straightened the linen napkins at the adjoining table. With a slight wave of his index finger, he beckoned

Askara over. She turned away. After breakfast, when Askara hugged Elaine and John good-bye in the lobby, wishing them a safe flight back to Mauritius, she started upstairs to join Darian and Sara on the mezzanine when Madame Tison accosted her.

"Bonjour, mon amie!" Madame Tison said, kissing Askara on both cheeks, her braceleted hands jingling. Such a wonderful surprise to see you again! I shall order coffee to my suite for us. Come. We must visit. All of you. Please, be my guests."

Darian and Sara declined, telling Askara if she wanted to go out sightseeing with them for the afternoon, she had better get ready. Askara started to refuse Madame Tison's invitation but decided she should go. *Maybe*, she thought, *Madame Tison could solve the riddle of the vials.*

In madame's suite, the view of Tana's Zoma Market with white umbrellas against a cloudless lapis lazuli sky took up an entire wall. Madame motioned for Askara to sit in the tapestry wing chair at the glass table by the balcony door. Madame's nephew Philippe entered from an adjoining suite and took a seat next to Askara. Madame sat across from Askara in an ornately carved claw-foot Louis XVI chair to study her.

After minutes of silence, Askara said, "Quite a room."

"Yes, thank you, I decorated it," Madame Tison said, looking around. "My brother owns—rather, owned—this hotel before he died. Now it is mine and my nephew Philippe's by inheritance."

Philippe looked down at his folded hands, saying nothing. "Lucky you, Philippe. It's a great place."

Madame Tison cut in. "Someday, God willing, he will understand that. What is important now," she said, "is you, Madame Askara."

"Me?"

"Oui, madame. It seems you play cat and mouse with us. You are in a dangerous position. One in such a position needs friends—powerful friends."

"Are you my friends?"

"*Bien sûr.* But of course! Why else would we have come to you?"

"You tell me," Askara said. "I'm not part of this game, whatever it is."

"Our mission is no game, madame. We will help you expose Monsignor Devereaux for what he is—a murderer!"

"Of whom?" Askara said, confused and irritated by the accusation.

"His servant, some whisper, and of course, Jean-Paul." Madame Tison unsnapped a tortoiseshell hairpin securing her bun, loosened the knot, and snapped it without looking at Askara. "I want something, which I believe you have, an object that belongs to my family: a tiny, glass vial."

"You are mistaken, madame. I do not have it. It isn't worth much, even as an antique; it's worn, even slightly cracked."

"You have seen it! The beauty is not in the form but in its presence and sentimental value for me."

A knock on the door interrupted them. Madame held her index finger to her lips for silence. "*Oui, qu'est-ce c'est?*"

"*Votre café, s'il vous plait*, madame."

Madame Tison looked through the glass view hole. When she opened the door, Chef Pierre walked in carrying a tray of pastries and coffee. Askara froze. Setting the tray on the table, he stood in silence as madame bolted the door.

"Madame Askara, my cousin Pierre. I believe you have met. He told me you were less than cordial. It is good, your defense, but you need help. Time is running out. Your visit this morning to the church stirred the hornet's nest. We wish to keep you alive and send you safely home, but first, you must be honest with us."

"Who is 'we'?" Askara asked, staring at the three of them.

"The society for the preservation of, well, of French artifacts, one of which is the vial. Ours is a family organization."

"Look, this is absurd! I don't know about any artifacts, just that silly vial, and I don't have it!"

Chef Pierre broke in and spoke rapidly in French to Madame Tison. She stood abruptly, her heel catching on the carpet. They walked into the adjoining room, madame last, and slammed the door. Madame Tison spit angry French phrases at Chef Pierre before they returned to join Askara and Philippe.

"Why are you here in Madagascar, Madame Askara?" she asked in a sharp tone.

"To report on the Walking the Dead ceremony."

"For whom?"

"The Christian Coalition of Catholic Churches."

"Do you know Father Devereaux is a member of that organization?"

"Yes, he told me. Why?"

Madame Tison spoke gingerly. *"Ma chère,* this is a family matter. That vial and a few other things have been in my family, well, for a very, very long time. They are special to us, a link to our French past. Unfortunately, many years back, when I was eighteen and Monsignor Devereaux was my family confessor, I made a blunder. He blackmailed me for something I said in confession. Mon Dieu, what a corrupt heart he has!

"I was young and very in love with a man my parents considered beneath our family station. Let me say anyone

Dyan Dubois

desirous of my hand would have been found wanting in their eyes. You see…the blood of French royalty flows in our veins from Captain Misson.

"Yes, the man I spoke of in the painting—the family's black sheep, a revolutionary, a pirate—was a distant relative of King Louis XVI. Some of our family escaped the bloody scourge, the French Revolution, waiting out the Reign of Terror in hiding, but the young braggart Captain Misson fled by sea. He landed here in Madagascar, desirous of creating a utopian settlement, and avoiding the revolution, so he wouldn't be guillotined.

"Ma chère, I know you may find this a trivial point—you Americans are so proud of your democracy—but aristocratic lineage is *très important!*"

Askara bristled at the condescension. "Captain Misson's story is real? I figured it was a ploy to pull guests in."

"He was the black sheep. You might say he was overly educated. He read too much of Jean Jacques Rousseau's philosophy, and being young and impressionable, he fancied himself some sort of savior. He was my great-great-*grandpère*. He set sail to establish a utopian society based on liberal ideals to atone for his aristocratic blood, I suppose. He became a pirate to support his flamboyant lifestyle, but in time he regretted that decision. He died in a storm off the coast of Morocco.

"Well, let me be totally honest. That is the story I tell when I explain his portrait. *En vérité*, Le Grande Serpent was attacked off the coast of Morocco by a French military ship, and Captain Misson died at sea, leaving his Malagasy wife, my kinswoman, and their children to live here in poverty.

"But in the end, he did not discredit the family. He stored with his wife relics of our French heritage. Indeed, he saved them. He had taken only one, his favorite drinking cup, on that fateful voyage back to Paris. He never traveled without it. Our family relics have cemented our family bond ever since."

Askara fought to remain impassive. The mention of the ship's name plunged her back to the vision of her as the man Anton when he greeted the mustached aristocrat at the dock, handed him an important bundle and then watched from the shadows as the aristocrat passed it to the ship's captain who boarded a sailing ship, Le Grande Serpent, and left the harbor.

"What were they—the possessions?"

"Sentimental objects, evidence of our royal blood."

"And the little vial—you say it's been in your family—so what does monsignor have to do with it?"

"He discovered one by accident. No, no, ma chère, I must speak plainly. He tricked a young, innocent girl—me—into handing him one from our family legacy. He stole our heritage, our history as a family! He knew nothing of it before that day when I made a confession. He is no holy father—no, no, just a thief—who blackmailed me for certain information."

"Askara," Chef Pierre said, "Give us the vial, and we will deal with Monsignor Devereaux. We will show him the evidence of his betrayal. You and your husband should leave on your scheduled flight, and all will be well."

"If I had the vial, I would, but I do not."

"We thought he had shown you the vial. We thought you had it."

Askara dumped the contents of her purse on the table. "Check for yourself." They carefully picked through the contents: makeup, passport, sales receipts, travelers' checks, coin purse, book, notepad, pens. "I never had it. I saw it, though. Jean-Paul showed it to me. He asked me to tell Father Devereaux I had seen it. Then Jean-Paul died. That's what I did this morning at the church. I told Devereaux I had seen it. That's all I know about the vial. I'd promised Jean-Paul. I kept my promise. That's it."

"Jean-Paul?" Madame Tison said in surprise. "If he had it, that is, well…."

"What?" Askara asked.

Madame stopped abruptly and clasped the silver-blue eyeglasses dangling from a gold chain around her neck. She torpedoed Chef Pierre in rapid French for a couple of minutes.

She began. "I believe you are in grave danger. "You have been fooled, no less than me in my youth. Someone uses you. My family will strive to protect you. We will continue to search for our hereditary possessions.

"Devereaux is not to be trusted! Nor is Brother Gestang! They watch and follow you. On our side, we will also watch and follow them. You can trust us three, no one else. You should be safe here in the hotel but take no chances. We will see to it that you depart on your Saturday flight. You have our word."

With moist eyes, Madame Tison stood to embrace Askara. "May God go with you, *ma chère*! Philippe, escort Madame Askara to her room. Stand guard. No one is to enter, and no one is to leave! We will bring dinner to your chamber, madame. This is safer for you."

"I am a prisoner, then? And my husband?" Askara said with indignation. "What about our friend Sara?"

"She, too. We guard all of you for your own safety."

Chapter Fourteen

Ejema

When Monsignor Devereaux's voice rang out along the slate corridor, frantically calling for Brother Gestang, the priest straightened his cassock and rushed to his superior.

"Convene a meeting—immediately! Make the arrangements."

The monsignor waved him into his room and shut the heavy door. In a low whisper, he continued that there was a grave matter to discuss. Brother Gestang straightened his back, looked at Devereaux, and tried to minimize his response. He whispered back that there was little reason to convene a society meeting, what with Jean-Paul's demise and Renee Guise residing in Arles, only they two were left. He suggested they handle the problem, whatever it was, between them.

The monsignor paced the austere room several times, stopping to gaze out the window at the rectory's burnt-orange tile roof. Turning on his heel, he faced the priest and spoke in a clipped whisper.

"I was visited this morning by that American woman. She spoke...." He stopped to inhale deeply, attempting to swallow his anger and calm his voice. "Madame Askara says Jean-Paul showed her a vial."

"Preposterous, Your Grace! How could that be? Do you not have the only one?"

"She assured me that the vial is in safekeeping, whatever that means. I did not pursue it. Rather, I acted like I didn't know what she was talking about."

The monsignor looked perplexed—his face red with heat, eyes wild. He stared at Gestang, mumbling that she must be misguided, duped by Jean-Paul...and that, of course, he had sent it to the Vatican, the one vial given to him by Gestang, the very one the village boy had dug up from the sand...and that he had received permission to display it at the French Embassy Museum once he completed his research on the early French settlement Libertalia.

"Of course, Your Reverence," Gestang said, emphasizing his higher status, "at the Vatican for cataloging, I believe you had said earlier."

Gestang reminded the monsignor, attempting to defuse the situation, that he had seen the communiqué from Rome permitting Monsignor Devereaux to host a historical display in the French Embassy Museum. Gestang sought to allay the monsignor's suspicions by saying the American woman had stumbled onto something—who knows what—to spread confusion. She had listened to poor old Jean-Paul ramble in disjointed sentences. The American must have been confused, but Jean-Paul had piqued her interest, nonetheless.

After all, Gestang concluded, "The American is a reporter. She looks for a story. She didn't ask you for money, I hope? Or for a favor, with her difficulty related to the famadihana—did she?"

"No. I would be happier if she had. No, Gestang, she stunned me by repeating that Jean-Paul warned her I would not listen. What do you think that means? What could she be getting at? Why did Jean-Paul assume I would not listen to her?"

"I do not know, Your Reverence." Gestang suggested that Madame Tison instigated something by telling the American a fancy tale of Libertalia and her beloved Captain Misson, the scoundrel, who the American probably wanted to incorporate in her magazine article.

"No, Monsignor Devereaux, this must be some black-mail scheme. Madame Askara is clearly a gold digger. Jean-Paul confided something, threw her a tidbit from his twisted mind, and she seized the opportunity to embellish. I am quite sure she will contact you again with a request in dollars. Ignore her."

The monsignor said he felt less confident of that, but he assured Brother Gestang he could make it very diffi-cult for her to get her exit visa paperwork processed. "She attempted to do what? Blackmail him? Lure him into a deal to purchase a vial, perhaps? And for whom?" He mused aloud. "She could have no use for a worn, pathetic little vial related to French history on the island, especially since Americans cannot see beyond their own country...if she really is American."

"We'll see if detainment suits her. I'm sure she will be more than ready to leave Madagascar with her husband and friend and forget her time here when she realizes whom she tampers with. After all, it is I who signs off—or not—on her article on the famadihana, an event she botched anyway. If it were up to me, I wouldn't pay her. But the Catholic Coalition has to make that determination."

"Excellent! Yes, Your Reverence, turn her over to the police. Have that Ejema fellow take her in. Make her regret this blackmail attempt."

"Brother Gestang, you quickly jump to blackmail. Find out where the woman stays. Report to me as soon as possible. I will teach her to respect the laws of Madagascar and my prominent position."

"Yes, Your Grace. I have a contact at the market. Sooner or later, all foreigners go there. I will find out for you and report back."

Monsignor Devereaux cast a wary eye on his diminutive brother. "I do not want to see her again. I shall let the police deal with her. You also stay away from her. She is trouble. Have the police handle this."

Brother Gestang bowed in compliance as Monsignor Devereaux swept from the room like an impending storm sucking away years of silent prayer. The chamber flooded with peace again once he left to pursue his hospital rounds.

———— ⚜ ————

At the Zoma market, Gestang found his friend Kandreho, the elderly man who had carved the church's statue of the Virgin Mary. Hunched over a block of stone, the stonemason methodically rasped a sharp corner with his metal file. Trying to straighten up to greet the priest, he contented himself with a sideways twist to greet him.

"Bonjour, Priest Gestang, another commission? You must order quickly. The stone becomes stronger as I grow weaker. Soon I carve my gravestone."

"Old friend, you will still be here when I am long gone. I am sure of it. No, I have come to speak to your grandson, the policeman. Where would I find him?"

"My Ejema? Father Gestang, pray for his soul. The life of a policeman *est très difficile*. I wanted him to be a stonecutter. But no. He chases bandits in the market." The old man smiled broadly, seeing Ejema strut toward them.

"Bonjour, *grand-père*, comment ça va?" Ejema said with a slight tip of his head. "Bonjour, Father Gestang."

"I want to speak to you," Father Gestang said, tilting his head to indicate in private. "*Excusez nous*, Kandreho."

Ejema walked over to the clearing while he scanned the market scene and listened to the priest request his help with a foreigner he felt was in danger, an American who came to report on the famadihana ceremony.

"I know the very one, Madame Askara. I believe she is safe. Who would want to harm her? The family has gotten over their upset. Only a few still grumble, but no one means her harm, I am sure."

"I want you to watch out for her, Ejema. Let me know where she is. We can't risk an international incident."

"Her full married name?" Gestang asked.

"Madame Askara. I do not know her husband's family name," he lied.

Ejema looked up from his note writing. "I know her personally. What is madame's problem?"

"She fears someone follows her, a person who is angry about something related to the famadihana for monsignor's servant. The family accused her of photographing the deceased grandfather's face. I believe it is a money issue, blackmail of a foreigner, but she confided she thinks it is something more," Priest Gestang said in a low voice.

"Oui. I heard. All Tana heard. Many gossip that a curse will fall on the family, even the village, all of Tana. They say she stole his spirit with her camera. The deceased ancestor is very angry. People hear him moaning and wailing all night. But people love to complain."

"Nonsense. Do you suspect a family member?" Gestang said.

"No. But if the American is scared, I will offer my services as her protector."

Father Gestang leaned in close to Ejema and whispered, "Tell her that she need not fear for her soul. Tell her my exact words. And make sure she understands that I have sent you to her, to protect her, but that she should not tell anyone about it. They might misunderstand my interest. This is purely ecumenical, a priest's concern for a member of God's flock. Do you understand, Ejema?"

"Oui," Ejema said, filled with the pride of responsibility. "I go to her now. She stays at the Hotel du Parc."

"You know that?"

"Yes, she and her friends spent time at the police station after her friend, the American named John, was robbed here in the market. We are friends now."

"Oh. Tell Madame Askara **not** to come to the church. Make sure she understands that part of the city is too dangerous for a woman alone, the cemetery and woods too open, especially just before dawn. No one should be there, much less a foreign woman on her own."

"Yes, Father. Shall I walk you back to the church? I was not aware of trouble in that area."

"No, no, merci, it is full daylight. I will sit and talk of old times with my friend Kandreho. He tells me he will not be here for long."

Ejema turned and smiled at his grandfather. "Oh, yes, he has certainly grown weak. Now he lifts the weight of only one man in stone!"

EJEMA TIPPED HIS HEAD IN RESPECT FOR THE PRIEST AND sprinted from the market stalls, smiling at the girls seated on their mats under wide umbrellas who were fanning flies away from their vegetables and spices. When he reached the Hotel du Parc and swaggered up to the reception desk to request Madame Askara's room number, he emphasized it was a police matter. The clerk ran his tapered finger along the guest roster until he found Darian Dalal and Askara Timlen. The clerk started to speak to the policeman, but a tall Frenchman stepped in quickly and edged him aside.

"Monsieur, we do not give out our guests' room numbers. You may leave a message here at the desk. We will deliver it to her door. The guest can then meet you in the foyer if she pleases."

Ejema seemed to not recognize the arrogant young Frenchman who acted like he owned the hotel, although he knew all the other arrogant hotel managers in Tana. Pulling his badge out from the inner pocket of his jean jacket, he said in a surly voice: "This is a police matter. I must speak to this lady. What, monsieur, is your name?" He pulled a pencil and pad from his jacket, making sure to brush aside the hem to reveal the gun holstered at his waist.

"I am Philippe Legrand, owner of this hotel. Monsieur, you are….?"

"Police Officer Ejema. Please escort me to the ladies' room immediately. This is official business."

Philippe stepped out from the dark wood counter and silently led Ejema upstairs to the second floor. As Philippe rounded the corner, he coughed three times in rapid succession, which caused a man stationed at the far end of the hallway to jump up and disappear down the exit stairs. Philippe stood behind the police officer when they reached the room, deferring to his authority and able to look over his head at the door.

Ejema knocked. "Bonjour, madame. I am the policeman Ejema. Please open the door."

For a moment, nothing happened. He repeated the command with emphasis: "Madame, Officer Ejema to see you. Kindly open the door."

Philippe reached around Ejema to jiggle the doorknob three times, saying it often sticks in the humidity. Askara opened the door with a quick jerk. Seeing Ejema, she smiled. Looking beyond him, she saw Philippe with his finger pressed to his lips, signaling her. Ejema walked in and slammed the door quickly, leaving Philippe in the hall. After whispered pleasantries, Ejema walked back and opened the door brusquely to see Philippe still standing there.

"Thank you. You may go, sir!"

"Madame, what is the problem?" Philippe said with urgency. "Shall I get help?"

"No. We have mutual friends, that is all. Merci," Askara said and shut the door.

They listened as Philippe walked away.

Ejema relayed his message to madame. "Brother Gestang worries for you. He sends this message: 'Do not fear for your soul.' He asked me to look after you."

"That's his message?"

"Oui, and he urges you **not** to come to the church because the city is too dangerous for a woman alone, and the church cemetery and woods are also, especially just before dawn when no one is patrolling. Is someone following you, madame?"

Throwing her hands palm up, Askara said, "How would I know? Silly thought. Who would follow me?"

"Has the family of the deceased threatened you?"

"No…well, sort of."

"They are silly people, not modern. They only talk. That is all," Ejema said with a knowing look.

"Look, Ejema, I was a little scared of them. They think I ruined the ceremony, but they…well, I can't blame them. They don't know about cameras. I think I got a little worried, but I feel better now. Why don't we go out, take a walk? My husband's asleep in the bedroom."

"Oui, madame. Excusez moi. But first, we must submit a request at the station, so the inspector will assign me for your protection until you leave."

———— ✃ ————

AFTER AN HOUR AT THE POLICE STATION, ASKARA'S CASE was documented and stamped with four different signatures, and she was free to depart the station, but not the city, until her flight. She and Ejema walked past the market, going toward the Immaculate Conception Cathedral.

"Can we see the stained glass at the church? I love the light when it hits the colors. Surely I can go there with you as my protector?"

"Yes. Priest Gestang did not want you to come this way alone, but he would be happy to see I protect you, my assigned duty."

"True. It would be good for Monsignor Devereaux to see us also. That will reassure him Father Gestang is doing his job, caring for the safety of foreign women. Don't you think?"

Ejema swelled with pride, realizing—yes, he could show the monsignor that he took his duty seriously as a policeman, especially as it related to foreigners' safety also. When Askara suggested Ejema speak to the monsignor and tell him about watching her by the police inspector's order, she emphasized how that would impress him. She advised Ejema not to mention Father Gestang. Monsignor Devereaux should understand that he works by command of his superior, the police inspector. She stressed that being told to do something was never as impressive as in the line of duty.

When they entered the church, Askara spotted the monsignor readying for the afternoon service. She walked down the central aisle to greet him.

"Hello, Father!" she said in a cheery voice.

Devereaux wheeled around, his face ashen, seeing her there with the Antananarivo policeman who stepped forward with a confident swagger and broad smile to say, "Father, have no worries. The police are here to protect madame." He flipped open his badge.

Monsignor Devereaux glanced at the photo identification and said, "Excellent!" but turned quickly to walk away. He called back over his shoulder. "I give communion in forty minutes. I have duties; excuse me."

"He was impressed with you, Ejema; I could tell," Askara said as they descended the stone steps to the street.

"For a holy man, he seems jumpy."

"For any kind of man. Can I treat you to coffee," she said, "at that European café on the hill? I've wanted to go there. The view is supposed to be excellent."

Ejema explained he had been there on assignment but never to eat. When she questioned if it was to watch for thieves, Ejema smiled and replied, "No, but the Café is known for mercenary soldiers; it's their rendezvous point in southern Africa before going to Botswana and Namibia.

He laughed. "Thieves stay away. They are scared of mercenaries. But three years ago, I posed as a waiter to intercept a shipment of guns."

Askara raised her hand for a taxi. One swerved across the lanes to stop for them. "So, what happened?"

"I cannot say. Top secret. But I can say I earned my revolver that day." Ejema grinned. "Not every policeman has one; few do."

Askara glanced down at his holster. "Keep that hidden, please."

———————— ⚭ ————————

ASKARA RELAXED AT THE CAFÉ WHEN SHE SAW NONE OF Ed's special friends, only tourists, primarily French-speaking. She finished her salad quickly and waited for Ejema to finish his burger and fries. But she grew restless with the afternoon sun dropping and regretted leaving Darian and Sara behind with no word. Neither understood her lately, she knew, but she only wanted to protect them. She expected them to be offended, knowing she would be upset if the tables were turned. Time was running out, and she couldn't see how to expose Devereaux.

Would Ejema be capable of opposing the church? She wondered. *Would the police inspector?* She knew she must speak to Brother Gestang and the Kalanoro, but the Kalanoro had to contact her, not her them.

She shredded the paper napkin in her lap. A man three tables away watched her like a hawk watching a rabbit. She shifted in her chair and turned to Ejema. "You and John hit it off. Correct?"

"Yes, John is a great man. I was fortunate to meet him. He has many music contacts in Detroit. I gave him several of my band's cassette tapes. He has promised to take them to Motown Studio and others."

"That's your thing? You're a singer with a band?" Askara said, feigning surprise because John had mentioned that to her earlier.

"Yes. Didn't John tell you? I hope to make that my life. My band's music is popular in Madagascar. A Frenchman visiting here promised to air it on the radio in France. He didn't. But now, meeting John, I feel we will get airtime in America. He and his wife Elaine enjoy helping artists. They promised me."

"So, when you're famous, then what?"

"I will travel the world. I will come visit you in America."

"No more police duty?"

"No, no. Police work is *très dangereux*. I do not like this gun. Well, I do for now because I have never wounded a person. I use it for target practice only and to scare criminals. I think it looks good, like in your American films."

Askara glanced over and saw a man, very much the look of a mercenary soldier, staring at her. "Let's go." She signaled the garçon. "*Billet, s'il vous plaît*." The boy scribbled a ticket, walked to the cash register where a woman tallied the bill in francs, and returned. Askara pressed money in his hand, saying, "*Pour vous*, merci."

The boy's eyes brightened. He surreptitiously stuffed the tip into his trouser pocket and took the remainder to the woman.

As they walked away, Ejema said, "Madame, you gave the boy too much!"

EJEMA ESCORTED ASKARA BEYOND THE FRONT DESK TO her hotel room door, telling her not to worry—he would not be far. She knocked, and Darian opened the door. She was happy to see that Darian and Sara had been sitting at the balcony table having tea.

"You've been gone a long time. You worried us," Darian said in a gruff voice. "You should have said something."

"I'm sorry. You were napping. I took Ejema for lunch as a thank-you after he escorted me to the church." She thanked Ejema and dismissed him in a perfunctory manner. He took the meaning and left abruptly. When she stepped inside, Askara whispered, "Something bad is going on. I didn't want to involve you, but I can't hold back now. I am really scared. I think I've gotten us into real trouble by photographing that famadihana ceremony."

Sara gave her an affectionate cuff on the shoulder. "Yeah, we were talking about it. Askara, we're here for you. Darian and I think we should all leave early, rebook our flights for tomorrow morning if possible."

Darian hugged Askara. "Sweetie, you did a great job. You got that article, you had an amazing experience, but something is wrong here. It's not safe."

They stopped talking when they heard a commotion in the hall, the sound of running and doors slamming. Darian tried to unbolt their door from the inside, but someone had locked it from the other side. Askara pressed her ear against the heavy, wooden door, straining to catch the garbled French. She could make no sense of the words. Footsteps along the hall slowed to silence.

Darian rechecked their door. He heard a male voice outside say, "Everything okay here—just a precaution. Keep your door bolted." Darian checked his watch. "It's less than forty-eight hours before our scheduled departure. Should we try for an earlier flight? Can the desk help us?"

"Fair dinkum, time to get home to Lesotho. Can't wait. This trip's been fun, but duty calls," Sara said in a fake upbeat voice. "What do you think, Askara?'

Askara looked at Sara but made no reply. Immense fatigue overcame Askara. She swayed and slumped into a chair, sinking like a rock to the river bottom. Darkness flooded into her feet and rushed up to her legs. Water black as ink spread into her chest and arms, turning her mind to mud. Askara's head lolled to the side, eyes shut.

"Wow, she's exhausted," Sara said. "Never seen someone fall asleep so fast; it's like she passed out."

Darian walked over to nudge Askara. Feeling her pulse, he carried her to bed and laid her down, saying, "She's exhausted, Sara. Let me call for room service. Seems we are locked in. It's safer in here, anyway. We'll dine early, if that suits you, since we skipped lunch. Maybe play some cards."

"Good idea. We should all stay together—well, here I mean, in this hotel. Safety in numbers. Besides, you asked about my brother Timmy. I'll tell you about him, great bloke. He loves his racehorses—that's his passion—and Ayers Rock, a place sacred to Aboriginals and to my brother. A huge rock. Turns blood-red at sunset. Has some interesting folklore, I'll tell you. Yep, plenty to keep us busy while Askara catches some zed's. She needs it."

CHAPTER FIFTEEN

Kalanoro Forest

B rother Gestang crouched in an alcove listening intently for any noise from the adjoining chamber. It had been over forty-five minutes, by his calculation, since Monsignor Devereaux stormed out of his quarters. The rapid pacing and scraping (wooden furniture?) across the stone floor and the room's haphazard rearrangement of papers meant the monsignor had worked, not prayed. But to what end?

Brother Gestang chastised himself for his *naïveté*. Devereaux had become increasingly ill-tempered and testy the last few years, which he attributed to his arthritic condition. When the monsignor spoke of the swelling in his joints, Gestang said prayers for his relief. When he complained of the weight of his duties, Gestang sought to lighten his load. When Monsignor Devereaux asked Brother Gestang to pray for his soul, Gestang was stunned—surely his eminence did not need what little intercession his own inferior could offer—yet he prayed for him, nevertheless.

But now, it seemed a reasonable request. The monsignor had made a great effort to hide something, the very item that Priest Gestang now wore under his cassock, a small glass vial—the one the village boy had gifted to him years back, the one Monsignor made Gestang hand over, which Gestang retrieved surreptitiously with Antivo's help—the one both the monsignor and Madame Tison presently sought. He recalled the monsignor once mentioned to him, in a moment of church mission comradery, that early in his career at the Church of Immaculate Conception, a young woman had given him a present that she had said was fit for a king, but it would ruin her family if she were discovered to have given it away.

Gestang had watched Devereaux's face stretch into a subtle smile when he asked why someone would give such a gift to the monsignor. What could it mean?

The monsignor replied serenely that the woman respected his wise counsel and wanted to acknowledge his assistance by gifting the monsignor something he could include in his dream project, a French Madagascar artifacts exhibition. Gestang, now realizing the small vial's value, understood Monsignor Devereaux would do anything to keep it secret when his precious vial went missing. The monsignor had lost his treasure.

Priest Gestang walked a tightrope. The small vial hung from his neck like a ship's anchor. But the only way to keep him from drowning was to contact Madame Tison to discover why she maneuvered to hold the foreigner Askara captive at her family's hotel. But first, he felt he owed it to Monsignor Devereaux to ask him plainly and honestly to explain the vial that Gestang had at one time given him, thinking it a village relic.

Eventually, Gestang knew he would have to appear before the church tribunal in Rome to explain. With a

clear conscience, he wanted to say he had done everything possible to help his superior when temptation
hung on his shoulders like a heavy cloak. Gestang had
known Devereaux to be responsible and chaste, but the
years had eaten away at him. He had grown increasingly
inward, sulking, and bitter. Brother Gestang knew he
owed his monsignor the opportunity for confession and
absolution.

Clasping the small vial in his hand, Brother Gestang
eased out of the alcove into the church proper to search for
Devereaux. He ran through the corridors, surprised to see
no one, the other brothers being at the annex for supper.
When he burst in at food blessing, he saw the alarmed faces
and knew the monks thought him a madman.

"Where is His Grace?"

"Is something wrong, Brother Gestang?"

"No! But I must speak to the monsignor. Have you
seen him?"

"He has not come this way. Please sit with us for dinner."

Without replying, Gestang spun from the door opening and sprinted down the hallway. When he rounded
the corner at the far end, he ran directly into Monsignor
Devereaux, who looked wild himself, his hawk-like eyes
contracted, the prominent vein on his forehead casting a
shadow down to his temple.

Monsignor's deep voice quaked. "Brother, why are you
running?"

"I was looking for you, Your Grace. We must speak
privately."

As the two priests walked down the corridor, their
robes rustled along the smooth floor like the frantic fluttering wings of doves. The monsignor entered the door

to his chamber and waved Gestang to a chair. He bolted the door.

Before Devereaux could speak, Gestang reached into his robe and offered up the small vial dangling in a hemp rope cradle. Monsignor Devereaux's eyes widened. He snatched the vial from Gestang's open palm, clasped it to his chest, smothering it with his knotty fingers, and sighed audibly. "Thank God. *Très bien*, Brother Gestang. Where did you find it? Have you seen others?"

"Others? I believe this is what I gave you years ago, a relic from the village built on the site of that revolutionary colony, Libertalia. Is it not the same? Is it not singular?"

Monsignor Devereaux's elation faded. "Yes, yes. I had misplaced it. Thank you."

"No. It is not the same." Gestang fired back. "This vial was given to me by an old man who confessed before he died."

"Who?"

"Your servant, Antivo."

Monsignor Devereaux couldn't hide his surprise. "The man's been dead for years!"

"Shortly before he died, that very day, poor Antivo handed it to me for safe keeping."

"For years, you have kept this from me?"

"Your Grace, I did not keep it from you. He gave it to me, I assumed, as a memento of sorts. I did not hide it, nor did I realize you sought it...until recently."

"Yet you confront me with it now. Why?"

"I am not confronting you, Your Grace. I merely want to know what is the significance?"

"That is my business and mine alone—historical research. I should like to have it. Did Antivo speak of something more?" Devereaux asked, fidgeting with his robe.

"No, Your Grace. But I fear this vial has something to do with Madame Tison and others. It appears the American woman, Madame Askara, her husband, and their Australian friend are being held in house arrest at the Hotel du Parc by Madame Tison. Possibly Madame Askara knows something?"

"Held forcibly? By Madame Tison?"

"Yes, a policeman, Ejema, stands guard. The government must be involved also. Your Grace, you know the American well, do you not?"

"Only slightly," he replied, head turned as he spoke, looking behind him. "She came here to write an article on the famadihana ceremony, the one that honored my old servant Antivo."

"I was told, Your Grace, she was with that policeman Ejema in a taxi and seen openly at a public café with him. He showed her his gun and made her sit while he ate. The police must be trying to frame her for that ceremony's failure. She was responsible, after all, for what the native Malagasy consider a curse, a failed famadihana."

Monsignor's great height snapped upright. "What do you mean, a *curse*?"

"She foiled the ceremony, they say. The spirit of your dear servant Antivo cannot rest."

"Yes, yes, I heard of that silly affair—such paganism, that ceremony! The pope has sent countless communiqués regarding the church's position—'Educate the people, so they turn from these pagan ways'—but that is not an easy matter. They desire the blessings of their ancestors more, I believe, than the blessings of the pope!

"Brother Gestang, do you think you could contact her? Would you go to the hotel and bring her here to me?

Madame Tison cannot hold her by force! We can offer the American a haven here at our church. No one would dare search here, but you must do this in secrecy. I do not want the church implicated. Would Madame Tison and her family recognize you?"

"Your Grace, I am a local priest. They know me but not well. They rarely come to church."

"Good! Go then. I shall keep that vial in safety here. I fear Madame Tison may be looking for this very thing. As the legend goes, it came on a ship about two hundred years ago and was found at the revolutionary colony on the island's south end. It is of historical interest for that reason only, an artifact of French settlement. I have studied its history. The vial found by that village boy and given to you, which you entrusted to me since I am the church historian…the cardinal has requested I keep it in safety until the French Embassy in Antananarivo can mount a proper historical exhibit. Unfortunately, there were other relics, but they went missing years back.

"Now, this vial has turned up. Give it to me. Thank you. I long suspected my manservant, Antivo, might have stolen it, but his death prevented my asking. Well, you see, you have brought great news, Brother Gestang. I am hopeful once again that the remaining historical items from Libertalia can be found, and I can initiate that display soon. Bring the American to me."

Brother Gestang bowed and kissed the monsignor's ring before hurrying to his quarters to change clothes.

———————— ✧ ————————

ARRIVING AT THE HOTEL DU PARC, GESTANG LOOKED A mess in a crumpled shirt and overly long trousers that caught at his heels. When he approached the smooth, dark wood reception counter, Philippe stared.

"Brother Gestang, is that you? You are red in the face. Are you ill?"

"No. I must speak to the American woman, Madame Askara."

"Why?" Philippe said, waving a hand below the counter to catch someone's attention from the adjoining office.

Madame Tison walked out to greet Brother Gestang coolly. "Bonsoir, Father. Madame Tison, proprietress of this hotel. How may I help you?"

"Oui, madame. I remember you. I must speak to Madame Askara immediately."

Madame Tison leaned forward over the counter to whisper, "I believe she is being held in detention in her room by order of the Antananarivo police. As we speak, they watch her door; even I am forbidden. This young woman may be more than she appears. I feel this matter is better left to the police."

"My matter, madame, is of no great consequence. Just convey the message when you are able that Monsignor Devereaux wishes to speak to her. That is all."

Madame Tison held out her hand to cradle the gold bauble hanging from her chain link necklace. Gestang shook his head in confusion. With a red-painted nail, she flipped open the cabochon to reveal a clock face.

"It is nearing eight. Don't priests retire early to prepare for tomorrow morning's prayers? Philippe," she said in a curt tone, "accompany Father Gestang up to the room, although I am sure the police guard will not let him pass."

When they topped the last step to the second floor, Philippe looked down the hallway, confident he would see

Ejema and the guard posted at the door, as they had been, but no one was there. Philippe and Priest Gestang trotted toward Askara's door. Both stopped short, seeing it ajar. They entered. Bedding, clothes, pillows, and papers were tossed everywhere, but there was no sign of Askara, her husband, her friend, or their guards.

"Mon Dieu!" Father Gestang exclaimed, checking for signs of struggle. "These policemen...did you know them to be Tana police officials?"

"Oui, Officer Ejema, and his subordinates."

Philippe gasped and stepped aside when Officer Ejema rushed into the chaotic room.

"Where is she? What happened?"

"That is what we want to know, monsieur!" Brother Gestang said. "Where were you?".

"I have guarded her for the last two hours. I stepped out to use the water closet, leaving my men here."

"No one was here when we arrived."

"I left only ten minutes ago. The WC is downstairs. My officers sat in front of the door, and the foreigners were in their room at that time; I could hear the bathwater running."

Father Gestang walked to the bathroom to see the porcelain claw-foot tub half-filled with water—cold water. He felt the towels and found them dry. He saw no wet footprints on the tile floor, no discarded clothes. He stepped out.

Ejema walked in. "Oh, shit! I'll notify the inspector. We'll find Madame Askara and her husband and friend. Tana is a dangerous city for foreigners alone at night."

Philippe said, "Why say 'alone'? They must have accomplices. Possibly mercenaries are her friends?"

"She has committed no crime. What do you mean by accomplices, *monsieur*?" Ejema asked.

Philippe stared. "No? Why else would she flee the protection of the police…and the safety of my family's hotel? She must have enemies. Is she involved in a crime we haven't considered, smuggling perhaps?"

"That I question also," Ejema said. "She flees, but who—and why?"

Without looking at the priest, Philippe left the room to rush downstairs to alert Madame Tison. Within twenty minutes, ten police officers arrived to search the area and to question the stragglers who had been assigned to guard the door but had stepped out to grab a quick café au lait from the alley while Ejema was not present. The officers interviewed Madame Tison, Philippe, Priest Gestang, and even Officer Ejema.

As midnight neared, they dismissed Father Gestang, requesting him to appear at the station at eight the following morning to speak to the chief inspector. Two policemen escorted him back to the church, waiting for him to walk up the stone portico to his quarters before they left.

Gestang circumvented the rectory entrance and followed the footpath along the church's west side to the garden. He entered, not through the creaky, rusted ironwork gate but by the apple orchard path. Walking to the far end, where the wild woods began, he pulled open the wooden gate that separated the church grounds from the cemetery, taking care to make no noise.

A chilling breeze ushered from the darkness to surround him. The fatigue that had turned his limbs to lead lifted like a heavy mantle from his shoulders, making him buoyant, almost giddy. He focused on a small, glowing light in the distance. The light formed a halo around Madame Askara, hunched forward by a tomb, crouched beside her husband

Darian and friend Sara. Askara motioned Gestang over.

"I got a shock when I saw your room!" Brother Gestang said when he approached.

"Thanks to your friends, the Kalanoro, we escaped," Askara said. "They came to me in a vapor to show me a vision that men would arrive at our door. I had started a bath. Darian and Sara were visiting in the main room. I assumed it meant Officer Ejema's men. A terrible feeling of intense panic overcame me. I rushed out to Darian and Sara and said we had to leave immediately. To our surprise, no guards were posted outside. We ran down the employee's stairway to the rear of the hotel by the restaurant alley. The only place I could think of to hide was here by this tomb in the cemetery. The Kalanoro showed me in NoTime the men who tore up our room."

"You know them?"

"No! I don't know their names, but I have seen them before in the hotel's bar—mercenary soldiers. Ed Healy knows them. He once told me not to worry because if I ever needed help, they would help me. But Ed seemed scared of them. Later, he told me they were bad guys and to stay away from them."

The Kalanoro encompassed Brother Gestang with their cloak of silver mist. Askara knew every time physical people merged with the Kalanoro, they lost more of themselves. She had seen its effect already in herself. Vestiges of the group mind remained with her after the mist had receded, giving her perceptions humans usually don't have—thoughts bound in a web with others, voices from another time and place, and small hands touching her skin.

Following that terrible time in Kenya, when she experienced mind gaps after Nagali, the soothsayer, tried to

hypnotize her to bend her to his will, Askara felt trauma-
tized. The memory of Nagali's huge eyes staring into hers
still haunted her. Mentally, she couldn't afford to go there
again, but she needed the Kalanoro's help, fearing for the
safety of Darian, Sara, and herself.

Father Gestang slowly emerged from the Kalanoro.
After several minutes, he spoke. "Madame, these men, they
were hired to…."

"Kill me?"

"No, no, to protect you…from me."

Askara felt her skin crawl. "Do I need protection from
you, a priest?"

"Certain people think you do. They assume I work for
Father Devereaux. They have used you to bait him. He will
come after you, and they want him to. They search for a
treasure."

"What treasure?"

"The small vial I returned to Father Devereaux is only part
of the treasure. There is more—an ancient cross, papers, a
drinking cup, a key, things meant for another time and owner."

Askara gasped. "I know those things! I saw them in
NoTime. I helped smuggle them out of France when I was
a man named Anton."

"And?"

"That's all. I was hired to deliver those goods to an aristocrat's carriage. The nobleman paid me well. I watched
from the shadows. The aristocrat handed the package to
the captain of *Le Grand Serpent*, a ship sailing away from
Marseilles."

Father Gestang sat upright and shook Askara by the shoulders. "Be careful of what you say and to whom." The jolt woke
Darian and Sara from their stupor. "I understand the histori-

256   *Dyan Dubois*

cal reference in your statement. Captain Misson and Father Caraccioli, a dissident priest in revolutionary France, sailed here to start a utopian community named Libertalia. They stored items here in Madagascar. Madame Tison, the blood descendent of the captain and his Malagasy wife, want them. No wonder her great interest in you, madame."

"But Madame Tison thinks Father Devereaux tricked her out of her heirlooms. What's the big deal? They belonged to her family. She should deal with Monsignor Devereaux herself."

Father Gestang remained silent, crouched in the mist as if listening to someone. He said he was starting to understand now. Monsignor Devereaux's servant, a man named Antivo, took something, a small glass vial, which Gestang had given monsignor years back.

"Monsignor believed that vial a relic of Libertalia, and His Grace feels you, Madame Askara, know where the rest of those relics are."

"He can go look in the sand. This is not my battle to fight. It's bullshit! I know NOTHING!"

"Askara," Darian said, "madame thinks they belong to her family. Devereaux thinks they belong to him. Let them sort this out. There must be more importance to this than glass vials worn smooth by the sea, even if they have a revolutionary origin. We have to find out why they value those vials and why they accuse you."

"They mistake me for a player. I'm a stupid pawn," Askara moaned.

"Madame Askara, you are the pawn *en passant,* as we say in French, the special pawn with an enemy bearing down on you."

Sara spoke up. "Hey, Askara, ask those aboriginal blokes, those spooks. What do you call them, Kal-no-row?

Or maybe you can ask them to ask that ancestor that got dug up."

"Kalanoro," Askara said and thought about Sara's suggestion. Her mind drifted back to Mea's fear, the erased tapes, and Jean-Paul's sudden death and his words to her. What were they? She tried to remember; her mind felt fuzzy, like a black-and-white photo taking form in a chemical bath, the details slowly creating the image.

She saw Jean-Paul's words rise to the surface: I go to close the door. *Le Pierre est très important. Le temple est guarded.* Look to the house of Anjou. Like a phoenix, I rise.

She repeated his phrase, trying to dissect each sentence. Askara shook her head. "I still don't get it. Jean-Paul was old. Maybe his mind was going."

"We might lose our minds if you don't do something, Askara," Sara said. "Shit, everyone wants something. They blame their problems on you. Think. What pulls this together?"

"Come on, Sara, little glass vials and other pieces of junk?"

"People went to a lot of trouble to get that stuff out of France. Maybe it was worth a lot. Someone thought it precious enough to smuggle out during a revolution."

Priest Gestang broke in. "Mademoiselle Sara, yes, we need to find out who lost them. Then we may learn their value. Le Pierre was a society devoted to protecting the kings of France. They were a lineage of warrior aristocrats, like an elite secret royal army. Soon after King Louis XVI tried to escape from Paris, the ship sailed here, but the king was caught and jailed. I believe Antivo, the grandfather in the famadihana ceremony, Monsignor Devereaux's servant, knew something. But what? He used the famadihana ceremony to try to get help. Madame Askara, do you get any messages from that ceremony? Did your translator say anything that might help us?'

"Yes, Mea said the ancestor was angry because of the way he died…and he was filled with shame. He had been wrongly accused of something, but we couldn't figure out that part. No one accused him of anything that we knew of. He was so angry that he swore we have until, well, only hours from now, in the darkness of the new moon, to figure a way for his spirit to rest. Otherwise, no one will."

"That's the key!" Gestang exclaimed. "We must have Monsignor Devereaux, Madame Tison, her family, me, and you in the same place to call his spirit out again and ask what he knows on the new moon."

"How? The ancestor's family hates me. They would never let me near his tomb," Askara said and stopped abruptly to listen.

"The Kalanoro say they can usher his spirit here for a short duration, to their woods. If we don't help him, his spirit will become bewildered and drift into the abyss beyond NoTime, a place not safe for the Kalanoro, a place of destruction that will affect us all."

"Madame Tison?" Askara said. "What about her? Friend or foe?"

"She knows something. She also looks for something. She will come if you ask her," the priest replied.

"The mercenaries work for her?" Askara asked in disbelief.

Priest Gestang sat still in the mist as if listening to far-away voices. He continued after a few minutes. "Yes, some mercenaries do work for Madame Tison. They will obey her to get paid. Askara, you must stipulate that they cannot come. The Kalanoro don't trust them."

Gestang advised Askara that she must offer an incentive no one could resist, the little vial of worn silica. When Askara objects, saying she doesn't have it, he replies that doesn't matter. No one knows. She must let them think she does. They will jump to their own conclusions, he assured her. She must discover why Madame Tison and Monsignor Devereaux covet the vial, its true worth. He suggests Askara confront them, have them face one another, promising the vial if they explain what it means, and trick them into revealing their motives since they both hunt for treasure.

But, he poses, why involve Askara, a foreigner? She must discover how and why she suits their scheme. Gestang advised Askara they must meet here at the cemetery tomb. Madame Tison and Monsignor Devereaux are unaware the land lies within the ancient Kalanoro forest, a place of protection for Askara since the Kalanoro have contacted her.

"The Kalanoro will protect you and your husband and friend." Gestang assured her. "Bait Devereaux and Tison. Declare for a large sum of francs that you will lead them to what they desire."

"Then?" Askara said, looking at the slumped forms of her husband and friend. "They could kill us all."

"Mon Dieu, no. The Kalanoro will not allow that. But we must take the first step, n'est-ce pas? Neither Madame Tison nor Monsignor Devereaux would want to go to prison. Monsignor may not be ethical, but he is not a killer. He is greedy, driven by ego. Madame Tison, highly esteemed, may be dishonest, but she is no common criminal. Plus, she is clever. She feels her family honor rests on this. Pride goads her. Both will abandon their quests. I am sure of it."

"Okay, okay. I'm not so sure, but tomorrow night is the new moon. I've run out of time. Tell the Kalanoro they must protect my husband, my friend, and me at all costs," she said. Askara swept her hands to try to touch the dark shadows weaving in and out of the silver mist. "They must help me deliver some messages."

"Messages, madame? How, in EarthTime?"

"Transport me in NoTime, so I can impress thoughts on our enemies. The Kalanoro have done this with me. I must do this to others, but I need help."

"You know, Madame Askara, the more you transform with the Kalanoro, the more you lose yourself?"

"I have no choice. I will never do it again after this. I will never come this way again, trust me. We have no Kalanoro in India or America."

"*D'accord.*" Brother Gestang gazed into the mist. When his attention returned, he said, "The Kalanoro agree. I shall wait here in the mist with your husband and friend."

The silver fog set in, wrapping them in an impenetrable mist. Askara visualized Madame Tison. Soon madame's image floated before Askara's eyes. Askara saw her conversing with Philippe and Chef Pierre in madame's hotel suite. After the two men left, Madame Tison sat alone in her suite, in her tapestry wing-back chair, fumbling with a gold chain necklace, mumbling to the empty room. Askara felt herself grow weightless. A silver mist swirled around her.

CHAPTER SIXTEEN

The Closet Key

M adame Tison jerked her head up. She saw Askara
seated across from her in a chair.
"Mon Dieu, madame! You frightened me.
How did you get in? Madame... madame? Madame Askara?"

Askara found it hard to work her mouth. A chill glued
her tongue in place. Madame Tison pulled a shawl around
her shoulders and whispered, "Are you spirit or flesh?"

Askara replied, "Both and neither. I am here to tell you
this message: Meet me at the church cemetery in the new
moon darkness one hour before midnight to learn what
you lost and if you can reclaim it. Come to the vaulted
tomb at the back of the cemetery grounds in the shadow
trees. Do not contact me before."

"Bless you, madame; however, you came. Your safety
and freedom are at stake. Take care!"

Askara nodded. Before Madame Tison could speak,
Askara murmured, "Three vials, a gilt cross, paper in ancient
script, a cup, and a key."

Madame's eyes widened. "Mais oui, my family's heritage,
evidence of our lineage, our special calling. How could you

know these things?"

Askara's image fluttered and shredded like a ship's flag in a cyclone. She faded and dissolved into the air, leaving Madame Tison shivering in her tapestry chair.

———————— ⋄ ————————

MONSIGNOR DEVEREAUX KNELT, TENDING THE FLAME in his hearth, wondering at such coldness in his chamber on this night. He gathered his robes close around his thin frame. A breeze walked up his spine. Wheeling around to face the door, he saw the bolt fastened securely, as it should be. He picked up the Gnostic Gospel pages blown across the stone floor. Tirelessly, he had researched the Nag Hammadi scrolls, an anathema to church doctrine, convinced they would help him discover the treasure he sought.

The monsignor pulled up a chair, attributed his icy fingers to ill health and old age, and continued to read about the Persian mystic Mani, who claimed the same enlightenment from the same source as did Jesus, Zarathustra, and Buddha. The element of Mani's teachings—the startling claim that Jesus had not died on the cross—vexed and enthralled the monsignor. Although a Persian king flayed Mani to death, his teachings lived on and seeped into the Christian world like a poisonous balm, leaving the Vatican powerless to stop the heresy. Even St. Augustine, whom Monsignor Devereaux had long admired, was an adherent of Mani's teachings and drew inspiration from studying his works. Yet the monsignor questioned: Could Saint Augustine have been deluded?

When the monsignor contacted two Manichaean schools in the south of France for additional research, one caught his attention—the same one whose address he had found scribbled on a piece of paper in Brother Gestang's chamber. He wondered why they both pursued the same line of thought, especially one so unpopular with the church, yet kept it from one another. Monsignor Devereaux knew anti-Catholic writings would cast him as a heretic, yet his obsession goaded him on. His was not a crisis of faith, he reminded himself, but a crisis of scholarship only. But what of Brother Gestang? What could be his interest?

The monsignor prided himself on tenacity. He felt sure the writings would reveal a clue to recover the lost treasure he desired, the one sparked years back by a desperate young woman's confession. Over the years, he had amassed a small fortune from the church's coffers to help him with his plan. Under the guise of assigned church work, he had traveled, purchased ancient texts, and stowed enough money to bribe informers if necessary.

At a moment's notice, he could act swiftly and quietly to recover the treasure that Rome had been unable to find, a treasure beyond all else. Monsignor assured himself he coveted it not for material gain but for spiritual. These relics would guarantee his salvation, a seat at the hand of God. Treatises, holy wars, and sacrifices proved time and again that God supports a just cause. His endeavor, destined like events in the lives of martyred prophets, would play a unique role in Christianity's history.

Engrossed in thought, several minutes passed before he saw a flicker in the corner of his eye. Turning, he gasped and stumbled into the wall. The outline of a ghostly woman grew solid in front of the hearth. She pointed to a small fissure, a hairline shadow in the rock surface. Her voice hissed like steam.

"Your failure, Archbishop of Avignon, remember it? The king trusted you to protect his Bourbon lineage. In a tunnel vault lay hidden his precious relics. But you failed. You have one chance to redeem yourself. Arrive at the church cemetery tomorrow night at eleven p.m. Alone. You will find your treasure."

Askara's image faded into the stonework like a candle flame's final glow—flare, poof, gone. Stricken with fear, the priest slumped on the floor, panting.

ASKARA CHARGED UP THE HOTEL STAIRS WITH DARIAN and Sara in tow. They discovered the corridor clogged with police officers. Madame Tison blinked in dismay when she saw Askara approach.

Feigning a pleasant voice, Madame Tison said, "Bonsoir, mon amie." And turning to the policemen, madame said, "You see, she is well; our lovely guest is back." She grabbed Askara by the hand, squeezing silence.

Ejema rounded the door's corner and rushed to Askara. "We looked everywhere for you. How did you leave? Are you alright?"

"Yes, fine. I, um, we heard a noise, a scuffle down the hallway. We ran. What's the commotion?"

Madame Tison broke in before Ejema could speak. "Madame, I was told some men had taken you. I described them to the police. I had seen them in the foyer—foreigners. We all panicked. A silly misunderstanding. Tana is such a dangerous place at night. Foreigners do not know...."

"Please forgive me," Ejema said with a slight salute.

"You didn't do anything wrong, Ejema. No worries. Just misunderstandings, it seems," Askara said in a breezy tone.

Reaching for the door before anyone could stop her, Askara looked inside to see their room an upturned mess. "Our room's been ransacked!"

Ejema walked in, followed by Askara, Darian, and Sara, and declared it a crime scene, quickly slamming the door behind them. He whispered, "Those men the hotel clerk described— they are mercenaries. They often visited the bar downstairs. The bartender said you and the American Ed Healy are friends. He meets with them often. Is this true, madame?"

"Yeah, Ed Healy. He's a documentary filmmaker, not a mercenary," Askara said. "I know him, not well, though."

"Today, he left the country…on a late afternoon flight to France," Ejema said.

"So soon? Look at this mess!" Askara said and picked up her makeup from the floor. "It's not like I have anything valuable, except my camera, and it's here, untouched." She rifled through the camera bag. "Oh, shit!"

"What?"

"My film's gone, all the canisters I took of the famadi-hana ceremony."

"You must file a police report, madame."

"Okay. Weird, but Ed had offered to take them back for me. I said no. Everything else seems to be here. But without the photos, what can I do?"

Darian quickly searched his bag. "Nothing is missing, not even my money and passport."

"Someone wanted something. Why else go to this trouble? Maybe only the photos?" Ejema said, speaking to Askara with suspicion leaking into his voice.

"Photos make a news story. I'm ruined."

"I think that has been the problem all along—photographing the dead. The Malagasy don't like that. It brings a curse. Now, you will be left alone. You'll be safe. The images are gone. Maybe Ed Healy did you a favor. He knows how things work here. I'm sure further inspection will point a finger at him or possibly the deceased ancestor's family. If they are behind this, I will handle your problem. No worries, madame."

Sara broke in. "Will you let me go to my room?"

"Yes, mademoiselle. We will go now."

Ejema ordered Sara to follow behind his officers with Askara and Darian. He entered first, alone. No one had touched Sara's room. "Did you ever speak to Ed Healy?" he asked.

"Yes, at the bar. He flirted with me one night. His goons were there, in a corner, staring."

Darian interrupted, "That means nothing. Sara had nothing to do with Ed Healy or anyone else. She's our guest. I demand you go downstairs and get us new, safer rooms."

Ejema assured him that they would have new rooms and be safe because he and his men would stand guard on the street in front, behind, and at every entrance and exit of the hotel. He effusively apologized to Madame Askara, her husband, and their friend Mademoiselle Sara.

"Unfortunately, you are now under house arrest for your safety. Meals will be brought to you—anything you want. But you are not to have guests, not even the hotel proprietress and her family. Me and my men will escort you to the airport," Ejema said, checking his watch, "I return with your new room assignments in a few minutes. Meanwhile, my men will document everything in your rooms." He waved them in and motioned the foreigners to sit, "You will collect your things when I say you can."

ASKARA SLEPT THROUGH BREAKFAST; ASKARA SLEPT through lunch. Neither she nor Darian had fallen asleep until dawn. She saw that Darian had eaten breakfast already when she roused and walked to the front room of their new suite. Croissant crumbs lay on a plate, and an empty coffee cup sat on the table next to Darian, who was slumped in a chair, asleep, his book tossed to the floor. She walked to the front door and shouted, "Hello out there. I want breakfast, petit déjeuner, and lunch, and another pot of coffee."

Darian roused, looked at Askara, and whispered, "So, what now? We're stuck in this damn room until our plane takes off...if they release us at all."

Askara said, "Shh." She pressed her ear to the door and heard footsteps and Malagasy words, then the reply, "Oui, madame," but she wasn't sure if her request had been understood or if the food would come. Wondering what to do, she walked to the balcony window and looked out at piles of violet-gray clouds melting into the distant hills. She wanted to tell Darian she knew the Kalanoro, or someone, would come to free them; they had to because she must get to the eleven o'clock meeting tonight to confront Monsignor Devereaux and make him face Madame Tison. But how? She wondered what would happen to the deceased grandfather's spirit from the famadihana ceremony? Was all that true, or was it only a story to scare her? She didn't know who or what to trust anymore. If Ed Healy was a mercenary—a ridiculous thought—then anything could be true...or false. The one thing she knew was how fragile she felt, like a leaf on a breeze, blown away, fragmented, lost.

When a hard knock on the door made her jump, Askara started toward the bolt, hearing the lock on the other side slid open. A female voice called out, "Petit déjeuner, madame."

Askara opened the door to see a young girl quickly shove the large food tray at her and retreat immediately, armed police watching every move. She heard the same repeated at Sara's door down the hall.

Askara removed the dish covers to see crusty bread, soup, roasted chicken, and herbed vegetables next to a silver pot of coffee and pats of white butter but no pastries. Weird. *Petit déjeuner?* she wondered. The aromas reminded Askara how long it had been since she had eaten. She sliced into the roasted hen to serve Darian a piece. She cut down, working the knife back and forth. When she withdrew the blade, a soggy piece of wax paper clung to its serrated edge. Askara pulled gently, extracting a small envelope wrapped in another layer of wax paper. She opened it cautiously. A key fell onto the serving plate. Thready script blurred by grease spelled one word: *cabinet.*

"What's that for?" Darian asked, pouring the coffee. Askara nodded, scrunched her shoulders, and said, "Who knows. But I'm gonna find out."

She looked around the room for any lockable drawer or cabinet but found none. She tried the key in the bathroom keyhole. No luck. The channel had been partially painted over long ago. She rifled through the small clothes closet next to the bed where she had hung her two dresses. Leaning in, she groped around in the dark recesses. Under an upper shelf at the back left side, she felt a thin ridge. She ran her finger along a raised, large rectangular perimeter until she felt a metal keyhole. She leaned in closer, inserted the key, turned it side to side, pushed it in further, and finally heard a click.

With a one-finger push, the door swung open. Askara coughed to mask the creaking sound when she forced the door to its fullest extent. Dank air, the smell of stagnant, moldy earth made her nose twitch. In a small voice, she whispered into the darkness: "Hello? Bonjour?" Quietness gulped her words.

"Hey, Darian, it's a passageway. Should we try it?"

"Probably a trap. You never know where and when we will show up again in this crazy country. Forget it, Askara."

"Right. I'm starving anyway," Askara said and pulled out of the closet to return to the table. She plowed through the food like she hadn't eaten in days, pondering the key, eyebrows arched. She washed down the last bite of rice and a roll with strong black coffee. She fidgeted in her chair. "Wish we had cake, napoleons—that would be some compensation for being locked up."

"You're thinking of going in there, aren't you?"

Before Askara could answer, Darian walked over and inspected the opening. "Obviously not built with adult height in mind; it's probably a child's secret hideaway."

"No child wrote 'cabinet' in English and stuffed it into our food. Look, I'll go first, so you don't hit your head. Are there matches anywhere?"

Darian searched and found a glass ashtray with a pack of matches in a dresser drawer. Askara lit one to see where to place her foot before she stepped through the opening. She stood upright in the narrow passageway. "Too short for you, Darian. Bend forward before you get in. Better yet, why don't you wait here. Let me walk down a little and see what this is, might be for plumbing or something."

"Could be a rat trap."

Askara poked her head through the closet opening, cobwebs tangled in her hair. "Thanks for that. You know I hate rats." She climbed back into the bedroom to exchange her sandals for tennis shoes and eased through the tunnel opening again. "This is gross. Stinks."

"Don't go far. It's not worth it. No one cooks with a key. This is a setup."

"Or is it setting us free?" Askara said.

"Seriously, Askara, don't get out of range of my voice. I'm right here, at the opening. Let me know what you see. Got the matches?"

"Yep. Well, here goes."

She struck a match and felt along the chiseled wall until she reached a slope. Cautiously, she probed with her foot before taking a step down. She felt a small drop, then another. "Narrow steps," she whispered back to Darian. She descended one step at a time, balancing against the inner wall. The air cooled as she dropped.

She called to Darian that she was going ahead, but he didn't answer. When she dislodged a few loose stones, they fell a long way before hitting. Askara realized the tunnel's right side dropped away, so she leaned into the rock wall on her left and felt a metal cable bolted into the rock surface. She followed it. Further along, she heard muffled noises and realized that she must be near street level or slightly below.

Wings swooshed by her, making the hair on her neck stand up. "Bats! Yuck," she complained to the darkness. The stench of guano filled her nose. Going slowly, gripping the cable, she leaned into the wall and tested every step before committing her weight. The stone steps of uneven heights made the descent unnerving. If she hit a surface too hard or dropped too low, she feared she would lose her balance and fall off the right side.

Darian could not hear her now, she assumed. She was too far down. After several very irregular steps, she stumbled onto rough horizontal ground, a plateau. More bats fled, whisking overhead, stirring the dank air.

When Askara felt something graze her hair, she jerked up, hitting hard on a pocked rock that dripped water down her hair. Or was it blood? She felt her scalp and couldn't find a cut. Running her fingers around the rock, she realized it was a stalactite. The odor of sulfur irritated her nose and reminded her of a cavern she had explored in California, a maze of columnar rocks hanging from the ceiling and stalagmites protruding from the floor. It was like navigating the teeth of a monster.

She figured she would have to traverse this cave like a minefield. She couldn't see the downward or upward forms until she hit them. She lit several matches at once. In the dim glow, she saw a maze of protrusions. Askara stopped to listen to the gentle clap of bat wings into the distance and dripping water. She realized the cave was huge. She wanted to surface and report to Darian, but he was a long way up, and she, a long way down. Too far to turn around now, she knew.

Inching along the bumpy ground, testing every step, hands overhead for obstructions, feet gingerly stepping forward, she sank into sticky material, the kind she preferred in her garden, not clotting her tennis shoes treads. She moved toward a sound, the steady plunk, plunk, plunk—of water hitting stone. Her knee scraped a stalagmite. She stumbled but regained her balance. When the matchbox fell into the muck, she didn't try to retrieve it.

In absolute darkness, Askara couldn't figure which way she was headed, so she backed away from the dripping. The pungent odor of rotten eggs burned her nose. Vast darkness weighed down on her, making Askara whimper. She wanted out of the labyrinth, wondering if this was the reason for the key, to lure her to her death, making it seem an accident.

When she slipped on loose stones, she got her balance and froze to listen. She slowly stooped to gather a handful of pebbles under her shoe. Then Askara methodically turned clockwise very slowly, tossing a pebble every twenty degrees, to listen to the pings. She followed the direction of the stones that took the longest time to strike an opposing surface with the clearest ping.

She trudged along, hands raised overhead, feeling for protrusions. The rocky ceiling scraped her head where she could barely stand upright. A timid breeze like a delicate finger touched her face with fresh air. *Thank God*, she thought. She ran her hand along the rocks on her left and again found the cable leading away from the bat cave. The air grew warmer and less stale. She felt a minute stirring of air. In several more paces, Askara spotted in the distance the sickly yellow glow of an electric bulb. Hearing muffled sounds overhead, she approached carefully, taking care to make no noise. She saw anemic stars like milky dots in the night sky beyond the dangling incandescent bulb when she looked up through a metal grate.

Askara tried to pry open the grate with her fingers. Scratching along the metal to loosen the dirt, she stopped abruptly, hearing two men speak French creole overhead. When their voices faded into the distance, she resumed, figuring she was under an alley in the restaurant district. She knew she couldn't navigate her way back to Darian and the closet, having come so far. She needed to reach the street to return to him.

After an hour, her fingertips abraded from digging around the grate, Askara managed to carve a small channel along the metal lip. She wedged her fingers into a corner and yanked with all her strength. Dirt fell into her eyes and hair, but the grate didn't budge. She caught the edge and tried pull-ups, but her fingertips couldn't hold. She tried over and over, causing an avalanche of pebbles and soil to give way. She jumped back just in time before the heavy metal grate crashed at her feet, nearly hitting her in the shin.

The sound of the dull thud rebounded in the cavern and echoed along the walls. Panicked bats flapped in the darkness, creating an echo of swooshes. She strained to hear sounds from above. Nothing. She stood on her tiptoes and tried to hoist herself up. She couldn't get a grip. Her fingers slipped, her grip gave way, and she collapsed with a dull thud. She tried again. On the third attempt, she heard a muted voice call out.

"Madame Askara? Is that you?"

"Father Gestang! Help me. I'm down here."

"One moment, I will throw you a rope ladder. Step aside." Soil and rocks fell on her head when Gestang threw the ladder down. "Hold the outer ropes taut. Keep your weight in the center. This end is secured now. Climb."

Askara grabbed the rough rope, placing her left foot in the center of the lowest rung to leave her bruised right foot to dangle. Above, she heard Father Gestang groaning to stabilize the rope. She inched upward. When she was high enough, she flopped forward from the waist and clawed to pull herself out of the hole.

Gestang dragged her by the arms away from the opening. Askara found herself on the grounds of The Church of

Immaculate Conception. Stained-glass windows flickered soft colors in the distance.

Gestang whispered a faint *shh* while he helped Askara to her feet. Walking uphill but keeping to the shadows, they passed into the cemetery. When they reached the large sarcophagus, they crouched in the shadows of ornate angels.

"You are clever! Madame Tison guessed correctly."

"She hid the key for me?"

"Oui, with the help of Chef Pierre, a cousin."

"What?"

"Oui, Madame Tison, Chef Pierre, and I, we are family. Secrecy is a blessing, not a sin, madame."

"The monsignor doesn't know you are related to her?"

"Not exactly, he may suspect."

"But you are a priest in his church. I thought he would know everything about you."

"A priest, yes, but one with an obscure past even the Vatican could not trace. You see, I was born here in Madagascar. My mother did not do well in her pregnancy. She almost lost me, but a village healer cared for her, a woman wise in the way of herbs and decoctions. During that time, my mother had a visitation, a message."

"From God?"

"Yes, we believed it to be, but it came in the form of a silver shadow, a vapor, that formed before her eyes. She realized many years later it was the Kalanoro, the original people of this island, who are now consigned to mist and shadow. They warned that her child must be preserved. He must be nursed and raised by a village woman and then sent to a seminary in Arles, France, where he would train as a priest to protect the family heritage. So, here I am."

"Family heritage, as in related to a king? Is that it?"

Priest Gestang looked at Askara with dismay and compassion. "Why would you think that? Let me explain. I will speak, but you will not remember. The Kalanoro will see to that."

Askara shrunk back. "Do they plan to kill me?"

Gestang considered her words and stifled a laugh. "Madame, neither the Kalanoro nor my family are killers. But there is someone who hunts you. Have you not guessed?"

"Mercenaries?"

"No. Madame Tison hired them to protect you, just as she employed the young policeman Ejema, although those two do not know of one another's specific roles. No, your foe is far more clandestine and dangerous, and he has men at his disposal for certain tasks."

"Let me leave with my husband and Sara. Please. We don't want to be involved in whatever this is."

"You deserve to know; you should know. I will tell you only as much as needed so that you can leave. The Kalanoro inform me certain information will help you."

Priest Gestang asked Askara to describe the vials to him. She felt a chill come over her. She was surprised at how clearly the image of them appeared in her mind. First, she saw herself as the man Anton who carried them to the nobleman's carriage in Marseilles. Askara described the three vials accurately, even down to the worn embossed design of a fleur-de-lis topped by a crown still visible on their rounded bellies, although she couldn't recall seeing them. She heard these words impressed on her—the vials and other objects were precious to the King of France, Louis XVI.

"What are these vials for?" Askara asked in a dreamy voice.

Priest Gestang smiled and said, "If I tell you everything, you are no longer safe. These vials once held potent healing

Dyan Dubois

ointments made from frankincense, myrrh, and honey, and they were used for a holy task. That is all you need to know. Is that all you saw?"

An image floated into her mind's eye of a jeweled gold candle holder shaped like a cross with a raised relief crucifix on the front, an old metal cup, a key, a roll of parchment paper secured by a leather string, and three glass vials embossed with a crown and a *fleur-de-lis*.

"The jeweled candle holder-cross with a crucifix has three arms with shallow depressions for candles. The cup is old, looks like bronze, a key with a filigree head, a roll of yellowed papers tied with leather, and three worn glass vials," Askara replied.

"The Kalanoro must have trouble communicating with you, or possibly they don't trust you. You are withholding. The papers have meaning. What do they refer to?"

"They are only papers in a roll held by a leather string. Could be blank. They're old and stained. They look brittle."

Gestang sighed, seemingly disappointed, but then he described to Askara a terrible battle at sea in which a ship sailing out from Marseilles said to carry these very items was attacked by the famous pirate Captain Misson. The ship took a severe beating. Many men were lost or forced into slavery by Misson when he took command of *Le Grande Serpent*. She became a much-feared pirate ship, but ultimately the sea kept her secrets.

Years later, while Captain Misson was trolling the coast of Africa near Morocco, *Le Grand Serpent* came under fire by one of Napoleon's military ships. The captain perished, as did many of his men, but some swam to safety. Years later, Misson's family in France received his captain's log saved by a loyal sailor who desired to pay him tribute.

According to the record, the king's inheritance had survived, kept safe in Libertalia by Misson's native wife. Only one object—the captain's favorite drinking cup, one he never traveled without—accompanied him always and was with him on his tragic final voyage. The Vatican surmised the cup had found its way to Napoleon after that skirmish because he became Emperor Napoleon in 1804. But no island descendant of Misson knew where the treasure had been hidden by his native wife or if there ever was one.

The Misson heirs' secret rested peacefully, held in obscurity. Until one day not so long ago, a small vial washed ashore where the utopian colony, Libertalia, had stood. A village boy, digging in the sand where Libertalia had once stood, gave his catechism teacher, Priest Gestang, a small glass vial. Yet, the priest did not recognize it at first. When he showed the vial to his superior, Monsignor Devereaux, the monsignor recognized its historical importance immediately and snatched the vial from him, saying it would be displayed in a museum exhibit.

"Madame, the vials you see in your vision and the vial I speak of are one and the same."

"Why did Jean-Paul mention a vial to me?" Askara asked. "I have no relation to this."

"Jean-Paul believed in many things that were often hard to verify," Gestang said.

He recounted that most believed Jean-Paul to be a good man but misguided. He abandoned the church after his wife Paulette died and never came back to the fold. Like others, Jean-Paul believed *Le Grand Serpent* had sunk with treasures. It was, after all, a pirate's ship. The wreck, as it was referred to, ignited everyone's imagination. People thought the captain had stolen important things from Libertalia, the utopian community he had tired of, and sailed home to France to sell them. Yet, the colony owned nothing of value. After World War II, when Monsignor Devereaux arrived on the island, a lover of history and especially objects relevant to Catholicism, the story of a priest, Father Caraccioli, joining a pirate, Captain Mission, to leave revolutionary France and create a utopian colony in Madagascar, fascinated him.

"Add to that a treasure hunt the historian priest could not resist and *voilà*, here we are tonight. But I imagine all this confuses you, Madame Askara. Do not worry, for you will not retain this. Your visions are nothing more than a film you watched at some time, in someplace, and it will fade like a dream that seems fresh and evaporates in the light of day. It is safer that way."

When the Kalanoro fog lifted, Askara respectfully said that she had come on a journalism assignment and the island's history meant little to her. She apologized for sounding rude. She explained the custom of walking the dead—well, that did interest her, but the Captain Misson legend sounded like BS, a tourist gimmick.

She pushed Gestang to clarify why the ceremony scared Jean-Paul so much? And his granddaughter Mea? Askara lamented she had been very fond of Mea and wished her well, but the other stuff "just wasn't her thing."

"Ah, yes, Mea, another black sheep. Everything scared her. Did she help you, or did she run away as she did when a child, chased by her own shadow?"

"Helped me. I liked Mea a lot. She had reason to run if you ask me."

Brother Gestang quickly shifted blame to Monsignor Devereaux for Askara's present mess, contending that none of this would have happened if the monsignor had not tricked

Clarisse Tison when she sought her confessor's help as a young, frightened woman. The two have been bitter enemies since, and now, they grow old with enmity. But when the Tison family arranged for a new priest, Gestang, to come from Arles to head the local school instead of him, Monsignor Devereaux knew Madame Tison's family, the island's most influential, had no confidence in him, much less respect. And that was when the war between them escalated.

"I am sorry, madame, you have stepped into a hornet's nest. But I feel it is no happenstance. Yet I have only added to it."

Gestang surmised that when the monsignor's devoted servant, Antivo, a man of robust nature, died unexpectedly, people began to suspect the monsignor of having mistreated him and possibly even caused his demise. Upon hearing the local gossip, Gestang investigated. He retraced every step Monsignor Devereaux had taken previous to Antivo's death and discovered the monsignor had requested from a fishmonger on the north coast a fish known for its deadly poison. The stonefish brings on swift death, one difficult to detect. But in a minute quantity, the toxin can help with the pain. Only a trained compounder would know how to prepare the formulation; most would be too afraid to try.

Gestang realized the monsignor had discovered the fish because he suffered greatly in his joints and had tried many remedies. Gestang met the local compounder who lived north of Tana on the coast. The man explained he had made formulations for the priest for years, yet the joint pain never left, so in the last years, he increased the amount of the dried fish in the curative powder, which seemed to help the priest. The compounder stipulated that Monsignor Devereaux purchase the fish himself and bring it to him. Gestang searched the monsignor's chamber for poison and found none, only a bottle labeled Joint Curative Powder, which the compounder acknowledged as his formulation for pain.

"Why are you telling me this stuff?" Askara said. "I want my husband. He'll be worried. I need to return to him. It's late."

"Madame, your husband stands here, in this cemetery, beyond a veil of vapor, as does your friend Sara. The Kalanaro escorted them. They came to search for you, but do not fear, they are protected. Yet, they do not know you are here. Let me explain further.

"Listen to me. On monsignor's request, you came here to Madagascar, approved by the coalition, to report on the famadihana of monsignor's servant Antivo for a reason. His family accuses you of disgracing them and of causing the deceased anguish. They fear Antivo may never go to the spirit realm of the ancestors because you photographed his face. Antivo's death was not accidental, in my opinion, nor was it the family's fault."

"I did NOT photograph his face!"

"Yes, I am well aware. But what you did threatens the Kalanoro and the monsignor. You allowed that poor ancestor's cry for help to be heard. His anguish holds open the door to the world of spirit, which must close to preserve the Kalanoro. Oddly, you, a foreigner on a journalism assignment, have provided a way to discover if Antivo was murdered and why."

"Priest Gestang, the grandfather ancestor, Antivo, could have told you what happened to him. You should consult with the Kalanoro. I have nothing to do with this."

"No, Antivo could not have. That you must understand. The famadihana jolted his spirit from where the poor man's soul drifted, confused and alone, for many years. None could reach him, not even the Kalanoro." Brother Gestang checked his watch. "We must go now deep into the Kalanoro woods. The time arrives."

Askara hobbled silently behind Brother Gestang as he led the way beyond the cemetery to the adjoining woods shrouded in darkness. She trudged along as if to her execution. She worried for Darian, who had waited by the closet, listening for any sound of his wife's return. She feared for Sara, held like a prisoner alone in her hotel room, not knowing who would come for her. Now here, they were hidden behind a veil of fog. Askara wondered if they would live through this.

A vapor rose from the ground. The Kalanoro mist enveloped them. Brother Gestang hurried, walking in a rigid, clipped gait, Askara trailing behind him. When they reached a small clearing in the forest, the night sky, brilliant with vibrating silver stars, felt heavy like a wet curtain sagging on their heads. Askara couldn't remember ever seeing such a night sky, especially one that pressed down on her. The Southern Cross moved overhead and retreated to rush in again like the sky was breathing. The noise of twigs breaking underfoot shattered her fascination. She squinted to see into the darkness. Her heart pulsed in her throat; she swallowed to steady the errant beats that grew wild when she saw who was approaching.

Madame Tison and Chef Pierre appeared out of the dynamic blackness like specters, followed by silvery images of Darian and Sara. Madame, with her finger placed on her lips, commanded Askara to silence. Askara felt a surge of anger burn her face while acid etched her stomach. She wanted to run, screaming through the night. Tree roots

Dyan Dubois

wrapped her feet, tethering her in place. Unseen hands balanced her shaking body. Seconds stretched to hours and snapped back together as thin as a piece of paper. The Kalanoro silver mist birthed dark, human-like forms.

"The time has come," a Kalanoro elder said.

CHAPTER SEVENTEEN

Epiphany

S omeone knocked hard on the front door. Darian
shouted, "Who is it?" and stepped back. He looked
around the front room, shaking his head, debating if
he should open it, and trotted to the bedroom. He quickly
replaced the sheetrock panel, pushing clothes to that end, and
closed the closet when another knock, this time harder, made
the front door quake. A man's voice bellowed: Open up. Now!

Darian pressed his ear to the front door and could hear
a man arguing with Madame Tison. She called to others:
"Quickly." The sound of several footsteps crowded close.

"Please, monsieur, open up," Madame Tison said, her
voice strained. "There is a serious problem. Where is
madame?"

"Sleeping. Don't bother us," Darian replied through the
jamb seam.

Then he heard Sara's Australian accent. "Darian, me,
Sara. Something's gone terribly wrong. We're worried about
Askara. We know she's not in there. She's fallen into a trap.
Open the door, please; trust me. I only want to help her.
This is serious."

Darian's resolve melted. The fear in Sara's usually confi-dent voice shook him. He knew Askara had been gone way too long. It was nearing eleven. Darian had tried to follow the tunnel when he could no longer hear Askara, but he had gotten confused in the dark and struggled to find his way back to the closet in the dark. Now, all was quiet in Tana, except in their hotel hallway.

He unlatched the bolt and stepped through the door to see several people: Madame Tison, her nephew Philippe, Chef Pierre, Sara, policeman Ejema, and six large men he had never seen before and hoped he never would again. Mer-cenary soldiers, he guessed—Madame Tison's hired hands.

Madame Tison pushed Sara in first, then followed. She rattled away in French to her men but switched into English, calming her voice when she faced Darian.

"Your wife is in danger. Our plan fell through."

"What plan?" Darian snapped. "Hiding a key for Askara to escape, and now she's in grave danger for doing so—that plan?"

"We planned to meet her in the underground tunnel. Something went wrong. My men heard her voice, but she did not surface where she should have. The soldiers were ready to protect her, to bring her back. Someone led her away. We couldn't find her. I fear she may have fallen into a trap."

"It seems we all did—a trap you set, madame."

Sara patted Darian on the back. "Listen to her. She's not the enemy like we thought. Neither are her relatives. It seems the true enemy is the monsignor, and nobody can find him either, or Priest Gestang. You need to tell them what you know."

Darian shook his head. He couldn't figure who was playing which side. Had they tricked Sara? Had they tricked Askara? What about the policeman? Was Ejema in on the game? He studied their faces, stopping at the mercenaries' cold stillness. Darian understood they would do whatever they were paid to do. The game didn't matter; winning and getting paid did.

Darian rattled off that Askara had read the message in the stuffed hen, took the key, found the plaster seam in the rear of the closet, unlocked the small door, and crawled in to see where it led. Against his better judgment, he let her go.

Askara had asked him to stay, saying the tunnel was too low for him and that she would come back in a few minutes. He heard her for five or ten minutes, and then no more. He waited. When Askara didn't return, Darian crawled into the passageway, but he had no light since she had taken the matches and couldn't see anything.

"The path grew steep, and the right sidewall fell away, so I climbed back into our room to wait for her. Askara didn't come. But you have. Where is my wife?"

"We don't know. This tunnel leads to the downtown restaurant area. My family built it long ago, a secret passage if there was a food shortage or a way to hide if the Nazis made it to Madagascar. There was a rumor that Hitler was sending a force to subdue the island. People gossiped he sought something of value here, the same thing Mussolini had searched for in Ethiopia. Who knows what? Whatever the reason, the gossip faded. Hitler never came, and neither did Mussolini. The war ended, and we were safe again. And we need to make sure Madame Askara is safe tonight," Madame Tison said. "The hour is late."

Although Madame Tison's family had used the tunnel only once, for a practice run in the early days, she explained that it terminated at the old school in the restaurant area, now a warehouse. But how could a foreigner have known?

Askara didn't show up there. The family had searched the warehouse. The exit, covered with loose soil, remained as it had been for the last thirty years. When policeman Ejema visited the family who had threatened Madame Askara over the failed famadihana, they had no news of her, nor would they continue to blame her, they said. They mentioned that Priest Gestang had offered them money for an additional silk shroud to end the conflict, which the family refused.

"The deceased ancestor, Antivo, had been Monsignor Devereaux's personal servant at the church. Did you know that, Mr. Timlen?" Madame Tison said.

"Dalal is my last name, madame."

Madame Tison, annoyed, resumed. "Antivo had told his family years back that he had never liked Brother Gestang, who once beat him severely with a stick for being late, and he doubted that the monsignor liked him either. We also cannot find Priest Gestang tonight."

"Gestang? I believe Askara respects him very much," Darian countered. "She does not like the monsignor, that much I know."

Ejema spoke up. "I had a meal at the Hilltop Café with Madame Askara. She mentioned she was going to the church to speak to the monsignor, but my men couldn't find him either."

"But we were put under house arrest by Madame Tison's family, and you, the police, guarded our door. Why?"

"For your protection, monsieur." Madame Tison broke in. "We feared something might happen on this night of the new moon. This is the night my dear friend Jean-Paul spoke of to your wife, the night the angry ancestor would take his revenge. We have little time. We must find her. We must find the priests."

"Has anyone seen Monsignor Devereaux?" Darian asked the group.

The captain of the mercenaries stepped forward. "Yes. We scared him a bit yesterday. He had no information to offer. If he knew anything, he would have spoken, believe me."

Darian had no trouble believing this man could scare anyone into confessing any crime, even one he had not committed. Darian's reasonable opinion of Madame Tison faded. Her flamboyant, spicy-red personality appeared sinister now. No longer the charming entertainer he had met in Toamasina, Madame had become a devious crimson bloodstain.

Madame Tison took control. She ordered her soldiers to walk the hotel and restaurant district to find any mention of an American woman or priests and meet her at the Church of Immaculate Conception in thirty minutes while she and Chef Pierre would question restaurant owners in the area. Philippe was to remain at the hotel counter. She started to assign Darian and Sara an area to patrol, but Darian stopped her.

"Madame, we do not take orders from you. It is your fault my wife is missing. Sara and I will go our own way."

"How is it my fault, monsieur? I did not hire her to report on that ceremony, nor did I encourage her to come all this way for the job. The blame lies with you."

Darian flushed prickly hot at her words. "You placed the message with a key to the damn closet in that hen—you or Chef Pierre!"

"Monsieur, we did not. The first I've heard of it was just now. We would never have suggested she take such a dangerous tunnel, much less cook a message in a dinner you were to share when we could knock on your door—a door guarded by our men. Part of that tunnel collapsed not three months back. The rock gave way to mud. You and everyone else in this hotel and those down the avenue would have heard if such a calamity had occurred tonight. Be at ease on that point. And take care who you accuse. There is more at stake here than you realize."

Sara lunged close to Madame Tison's face. "Don't speak to my friend like that. Know what a bitch-slap is, madame? I got one reserved in your name. Right here," she said, holding up her hand. "I'm watching you."

Madame Tison stepped back, turned, and rushed down the hall. She called out from the landing, "Thirty minutes. Meet at the church."

——— ✂ ———

ASKARA FROZE, HEARING SOMEONE APPROACH. PRIEST Gestang motioned for her to crouch and remain still in the shadows of the Kalanoro forest. Through the mist, a tall man in flowing robes evolved like a phantom. He spoke to Madame Tison, who had arrived only a minute before him.

"Madame, why feign surprise? I am here because of you! I saw you approach. Meeting on this sacred ground, especially at night, does my church injustice."

"No more injustice—in fact, far less—than you pretending to be a monsignor when you are a robber and a murderer! You stole my family heritage, our sacred right, when I was a scared, vulnerable girl. I am no girl now, and you are no priest. I mean to reclaim our legacy."

"For what reason? Personal gain, madame?"

"For the sanctity of the objects—something you cannot understand!"

"You judge me severely. I do know my preservation rests with me procuring the vials, as does my eternal salvation. I had the opportunity to protect one object from a reckless girl—you madame, a silly, pregnant girl—and I did. I have saved another from squander.

For years they have rested with me until Lucifer whispered into Antivo, my servant's ear, to steal a vial, one of my holiest of treasures, my passport to heaven. And for that, I have suffered daily. But tonight, we shall discover in the darkness of the new moon when the portal opens, where my servant Antivo hid that treasure and others if they exist. The temple is guarded…by me. You shall not challenge the sanctity of church ground upon which we stand. The door to the ancestors' world will close with Antivo's admission of guilt."

"Monsignor, you have lost your senses. Eaten by guilt and driven by remorse, you have become a vile creature," Madame Tison said and spat at him.

"You and Gestang conspired against me. Or should I refer to him as your bastard child, nursed by a witch after her herbs did not release his soul from your womb, and later shunted to a church orphanage in France for education. You were young and foolish. Now you are old and no less a fool. But power has grown in you. I have seen its corrupt nature."

Madame Tison rocked on her feet. The others stared at her in confusion. "You have a devil's forked tongue."

Devereaux continued needling her with accusations about her family, calling her the spawn of a simple Malagasy whore bedded but never married to the illustrious Captain Misson, a pirate who hijacked a ship, *Le Grand Serpent*—a braggart, a robber, a louse.

Monsignor, unaware of forms hidden in the shadows, continued his tirade against her family. "But Clarisse, it seems you had a plan of your own. You returned one vial to me, a peace offering of sorts, handed to me by your bastard son, who claimed a village boy had gifted it to him. Was your intention to rope me in with trust, to lure me with renewed hope, and use me for your own gain?"

Madame Tison broke in. "I never gave you a vial, nor did I give him one. What do you hope to win from this? The Vatican will condemn you; the brotherhood will forsake you. My family will hunt you. Remember—above all—this is my family's heritage."

In the Kalanoro Forest, shadows skimmed the ground, rushing in all directions. The mist grew heavy in places, thinner in others, causing one soldier to see what he couldn't accept. When he tried to tell his captain that he had seen a small naked man running in the shadows, the captain waved him off.

Brother Gestang motioned to Askara. They stepped forward from the shadows.

Madame Tison stared at Askara. "You are here? From where? Unlucky girl! You stumbled headlong into a trap, snared by a priest you consider a friend and duped by a priest who is your enemy.

"Which is which, you ask? Let me help you. Monsignor Devereaux requested the Christian Coalition of Catholic Churches to hire a reporter to document the famadihana. Monsignor paid your salary since the coalition had rejected his initial request. Monsignor paid for the ancestor's silk shroud, the least he could do for his loyal servant. Monsignor paid for the famadihana feast, not out of respect for his departed servant Antivo's poor soul, but to try to discover a treasure's hiding place.

"Think how Antivo wails from limbo at the thought that the man who people whisper killed him should profit from his death. Anguish and disappointment haunt the poor man's soul. Priest Gestang had used Antivo to procure the vial under the guise of him, Gestang, helping the monsignor in his research. How frantic you must have been, Devereaux, when you realized the only link you had to the treasure had been severed by the poor man's death. *Imbécile!*"

Priest Gestang stood next to Sara in the circle of accusers. "Am I correct, monsignor, in what I have conveyed to Madame Tison? I realize I haven't given all the details of your treachery, the one omission being the fisherman who sold you a certain poisonous fish. He recounted your visit to the northern part of the island to see the Church of the Annunciation and to purchase the deadly stonefish. Unfortunately, typhoid fever ended the poor fisherman before he could be questioned by the police."

"You insult the Church with these erroneous accusations. Priest Gestang, you came here on behalf of the society that desires to reclaim France's royal relics, did you not? Yet you have no idea of what you seek. You only began to understand when I accepted the vial you gave me. You have long hated me because I revealed your mother's sin, eighteen and pregnant by a married man. Their child, born out of wedlock, nursed by a villager until age three, was shipped to Arles to be raised in a church orphanage. Your shame is hers, not mine! I am a historian who stumbled upon a treasure and did not know its worth at the time. I do now. I have done nothing wrong. The Vatican will stand behind me."

Madame Tison straightened her back and lifted her chin to look Devereaux squarely in the face. "I have learned to live with my shame all these years. I have realized one crucial fact. What you revealed from my confession was said in sacred trust. I sinned; that is true. My unforgivable sin? Girlish ignorance, a trusting heart, and clouded judgment.

"You sinned against the church itself, Monsignor Devereaux, against God, and against what your holy order stands for. You abandoned a young girl in need. You misled me. You found that herbal witch. When her herbs failed, you arranged for her to house me under the pretense of teaching me herbal medicine until the delivery, and then she took my child to nurse. You blackmailed my influential parents into building the church addition you wanted, your personal library, in exchange for your silence.

"On Judgment Day, which sin will be more severely punished, yours or mine? You kept a small vial, part of my family's inheritance, for personal gain. I would not want to stand before God in your holy robes. But I shall stand and declare I was wronged twice! Once by the man I loved, once by the holy father I trusted—the second more grievous. I ask God to damn your soul!"

When Madame Tison turned to challenge Brother Gestang, who was standing beside Askara, he shrank in his robes. "And you, do you think our family is unaware of your role in this?"

"What do you mean, Clarisse? I informed you there was another vial in the monsignor's possession, the one he made me hand over to him years ago, the one I later retrieved. I did not know you had paid him with one when you were a pregnant girl, Mother. I gave you hope, did I not, that we would find the missing third one? If it is missing...or do you possess it yourself?"

Father Devereaux wheeled around to face Brother Gestang. "What?"

"Had I not entered prematurely for vespers, had my timing been different, I would have never known about you, monsignor. Your excuse was a lie—what was it? Ah, yes, you said the vial was a relic from the *Republic de Libertalia*, the early French settlement, something of historical interest only, and you would put it in an exhibit at a museum."

"But that is true. I am a historian. I have planned an exhibit."

"A lie is something not wholly true. There is more you left unspoken."

Madame Tison broke in. "Is that when you contacted the Vatican, Gestang, my clever bastard son?"

Indignant, Gestang shouted, "I never contacted the Vatican! Do not call me bastard!"

"As I suspected," Madame Tison replied. "Why would you not? Are you not bound by duty to tell the Vatican and your society's superiors? After all, a great treasure of Christendom, an ancient candle holder-crucifix, assumed lost to the world since King Louis XVI's death, had been mentioned in a dead captain's log, and a small fleur-de-lis vial had appeared on the shore. Surely the Pope would be interested, n'est-ce pas?

"But you never saw such a treasure. You had read about it in Misson's captain's log. Fool, do you think something like that would be kept on this small island? Did you not read his last entry when Napoleon's ship fired on *Le Grande Serpent*: 'The ship is going down. This is my end. I take lovely treasures to lie hidden at peace beside me in the sea. May God bless my soul.'"

Priest Gestang answered in a surly voice: "You talk too much, madame."

Askara backed away from him. She looked at Darian and Sara, who appeared as baffled as she was. Askara started to speak when Madame Tison broke in.

"Oui, Madame Askara, it is well you back away from the men in robes beside you. But you must comprehend their purpose to realize their deception."

"My purpose, Clarisse," Priest Gestang said, "is as it has always been—to protect our family and uphold our family name."

Askara and Father Devereaux stared open-mouthed at Brother Gestang.

"Shall I tell who brought you here from Arles, son? It was not I, be clear on that point. The man next to you in church robes, your mentor Monsignor Devereaux, wanted it to appear he found offense in a novice priest coming to take some of his duties when, in reality, it was he who initiated the request. That is something he would have never told you because his aim was to use you," Madame Tison said.

"My mission was of noble purpose." Father Devereaux hissed. "I knew his worth."

"Worth? Me of illegitimate parentage? You could glean no personal advantage from that, monsignor, unless you sought to blackmail me, or my mother. Yes, I was raised decently in a monastery in Arles, one established under the patronage of King Rene d'Anjou in the fifteenth century. I received an excellent education from the monks. I had no mother or father. I had scores of brothers, members of a society dedicated to protecting secrets so powerful that only the noblest would be chosen for appointment. Yet, oddly, I—the illegitimate—was chosen. I endured rigorous training that made me the man I am now. Do not be tricked, Madame Askara. I am here to help you, and I am here to help Clarisse Tison."

Gestang explained he had studied several subjects in the monastery, but his interest lay in the Cathars, the Knights Templar, and the Holy Crusades, noble warriors waging holy wars. He had joined a society of men dedicated to the preservation of Christian relics who pursued a treasure that disappeared during the French Revolution, one entrusted to the Bourbon lineage of King Louis XVI. The fraternity, sworn to noble purpose, escorted the valuables from Varennes to the Papal Palace in Avignon and later in Marseilles safely delivered them on board a ship, *Le Grande Serpent*, bound for Ethiopia's sacred city of Axum for safekeeping.

But an industrious revolutionary-turned-pirate, Captain Misson, and his men overtook the ship while en route. Misson freed the hostage sailors if they agreed to work for him as pirates. Their ship, *Le Grande Serpent*, became famous for raids along the coast of Africa. The pirates plied the waters, capturing male slaves and stealing women to be wives and workers for them.

Thus, Captain Misson populated a colony in Madagascar he named the *Republic de Libertalia*, fulfilling his dream of liberty, fraternity, and equality, yet his settlement had none. Local Malagasy women married the pirates by force, or by choice after seeing their riches, while local men conspired against the intruders and much later drove them out. One young beauty became the famed captain's most valued property and wife, a great-great-grandmother of Madame Tison.

"I have guarded our family's history well," Madame Tison countered. "Captain Misson proved to be a man of integrity, no matter what else may be said."

"Do you have integrity, Clarisse?" Gestang asked with a wry smile. "Pride drove you to confide in a wayward priest to help you conceal an illicit pregnancy. For that, you paid him with a small vial, the only thing you had, an object your parents valued highly, although you couldn't understand why at the time. Unfortunately, the priest was as devious as you were naive. Much later, when the sea offered a vial to a small Malagasy boy, I used it to bait the monsignor."

Madame Tison shook with rage. "You killed one of your own society's members, trying to obtain information, n'est-ce pas? Poor Jean-Paul, such a decent man, my dearest friend. He wanted only to protect his granddaughter from further involvement," she said, her voice snapping like a shattered twig.

"You killed Jean-Paul?" Askara shouted at Brother Gestang.

"No, Madame Askara, Clarisse tries to confuse you. She listened to gossip. But she did hire that idiot American filmmaker—Ed Healy—to find out about you, track you, befriend you and your husband and friend. Seems he served no real advantage, so they got rid of him."

"What does that mean?"

"They shipped him back to Ohio, I believe. We have little time. The ancestor's spirit soon will arrive in the Kalanoro Forest," Priest Gestang said, pointing to the shadows where swirling fog wrapped long fingers around quivering tree trunks. "Let the tormented ancestor Antivo speak of midnight tears."

"The time of judgment, the time of vindication," Madame Tison said.

Before Askara could reply, the Kalanoro formed from the mist. A clear voice declared the Kalanoro had come for only one purpose—to secure the spirit realm portal, to protect their domain. The Shadow-Being explained that worlds would collide if the famadihana ancestor, Antivo, became wedged between the disembodied and the material worlds in a gap where disgruntled souls desire to inhabit weak-willed humans, the last battleground.

If they gather strength, the disembodied will wedge open the portal to NoTime, the Kalanoro's flowing ocean of goodness and inspiration. Since primordial creation, the Kalanoro, the Shadow-Being continued, have been responsible for NoTime's protection of temporal Africa to Australia. As guardians of the gate, they demanded the ancestor's anguish be resolved. His soul must be put to rest immediately to stop the portal membrane from dissolving. Antivo must face his soul's anguish, so he could step through the portal, thereby closing it.

The Kalanoro Shadow-Being warned them, "Antivo's anguish is two-fold—a lesser one in the present, a greater injustice from long ago when he served the Archbishop of Avignon."

Askara shook her head in despair. "How?"

A blast of dry, fetid air swept across the woods. Trees tossed and moaned. Kalanoro shadows dissolved and formed again. The night sky swirled, hurling stars into the gray-green distance. Lush trees withered in the desiccating air. Crimson lightning created a sickly, bloody glow.

Madame Tison stumbled backward and collapsed into the arms of Chef Pierre. Father Gestang held his cross to his forehead, mumbling prayers while he planted his feet firmly beneath him. Monsignor Devereaux, attempting to run, stumbled on a gnarly tree root and fell to the ground, his voluminous robe fluttering around him like a murder of crows. With each new blast of death-wind, the Kalanoro, standing like charred trees after a great fire, pulled closer to encircle the humans.

A low rumble vibrated through the moaning trees, growing louder as it reached the human circle. The sound of women screaming, animals howling, and wild dogs yapping threaded together like a barbed-wire fence to prick them.

Askara's knees buckled. She crumpled like a paper doll, weightless, on shifting ground. A mass of anguished, pleading faces—men, women, and children—beckoned her with outstretched hands through a fissure in the portal, trying to touch the horrified onlookers.

The monsignor stood and shouted, "Do not be deceived! They are the enemy. Do not let them touch you."

A dark figure inside the membrane cried, "I am here." He looked directly at Askara and said, "Anton, I see you. Friend, help me now. Release me. Set my spirit free."

"If I am Anton," Askara said, "your friend in France who called you Michel, and you are the wronged ancestor Antivo from the famadihana ceremony, prove this to me. Show me you are one and the same. Call on Jean-Paul; only he can verify you."

"Jean-Paul is not here. Like a phoenix, he rose." The ancestor's outline wavered. Gray light shot through the membrane as blood-red fingers ripped at the seams.

Antivo spoke. "I am the reason you came to Madagascar. I am your exit visa as you are mine. To rest in NoTime with my ancestors, my soul's torment must end. Reveal who poisoned the Archbishop of Avignon, for it was not me, although I died in shame from the many curses that fell upon me. I have carried this burden for too long, waiting to see you again. For all our sakes, speak now."

"I don't know who killed you, Michel. When you left and ordered me to run from the tunnel with the leather bundle…that was the last time I saw you, my dearest friend. I died with deep regret, feeling I had deserted you. I only learned someone poisoned the archbishop that night, nothing more."

Antivo looked at the horrible forms approaching the membrane, pushing, shoving, leaning out to break the effacing, slimy substance. He tried to hold them back while he recounted his understanding of the night that damned him, the night the archbishop died.

———————— ✿ ————————

MICHEL AND ANTON WERE CHIPPING ON THE STONE vault when Michel heard angry voices from the archbishop's chamber. He wanted to rush to him, but he knew it was not his place as a servant to barge in on His Holiness. Michel begged his friend Anton to deliver the bundle to Marseilles as planned.

Running to fetch warm cognac for the archbishop, Michel chose the quickest path to the larder, the one that skirted the nightsoil pit. When he returned, sweaty from running and smelling of sewage, guards accosted him at the archbishop's door. Panicked by what he saw, the archbishop lying on the stone floor, Michel attempted to rush past them but was stopped short when a soldier grabbed him by the shoulder. Michel screamed and struggled to free himself, longing to embrace the archbishop.

The captain accused him of murder, yelling the Archbishop of Avignon would never let a lowly servant whose pants reeked of sewer water serve him cognac. The captain took the warm cognac from the tray and commanded Michel to drink. He complied. Nothing happened. Enraged, the captain ordered Michel to drink from the second glass. Again, under the searing glare of the captain, nothing happened. The captain ordered his men to drag the servant below and lash him to the tree in the courtyard and fetch the other monks to bring them up to view the body.

Michel's fellow monks, his friends, spoke up for him, but two did not. They said hateful, condemning things: Michel was an orphan, the discarded son of a whore. He stole from the kitchen, a fornicator too vile to live in the monastery. Michel knew they were jealous of how much he loved his adoptive father and how the archbishop loved his foundling son. They declared Michel had killed the archbishop. Shame stunned him into silence. He could kill no man, especially one he loved and served with devotion.

The captain threw Michel into jail, saying they had found a powder near the archbishop's water basin, later identified as the poison. He was dragged away like an animal with hands and feet shackled. In the Kalanoro woods, Michel confessed he had died by his own will, starving himself in that lifetime, a grievous sin he knew damned him, but now with Anton's help, he could find redemption from torment by revealing who did poison the Archbishop of Avignon.

Michel blurted out, "That person is here among us tonight. And once again, he wears the cloak of the priesthood. And once again, as his servant, Antivo, I beg for mercy. Force monsignor's confession. Stop this madness."

The Kalanoro mist thickened. The figures of Madame Tison, Chef Pierre, Darian, Sara, Brother Gestang, Monsignor Devereaux, police officer Ejema, and the mercenary soldiers vanished from Askara's sight. She felt liquid mist swallow her.

---------- ⚬ ----------

ASKARA LOOKED DOWN AT HER DIRTY LEATHER BOOTS, smelled horse sweat on her clothes, and heard Anton's gravelly male rasp. Her eyes flared.

"Anton, go," Michel commanded.

Hearing the brawl, Anton looked down the tunnel. Someone hit the stones with a groan. Crouched in darkness, he slipped the leather bundle under his vest and cinched a leather strap to secure it. The door creaked. In dim torchlight, he witnessed a man slip out the archbishop's chamber and run in the opposite direction, his monk's cassock too short to hide fine riding pants and boots. Anton raced down the vault tunnel to another passageway that descended to the opening next to the nightsoil pit and glimpsed a rider on a fine white horse running away through the trees.

Anton recalled that same powerful lead horse, a pale gray almost silvery-white Percheron, pulled the elegant carriage up to the dock in Marseilles. He did as Michel instructed and handed over the leather bundle to the aristocrat, but then he waited, crouched in alley shadows, to witness the nobleman hand the package to the ship's captain, who rowed back to board his ship, *Le Grande Serpent*.

When Anton returned to his home in Avignon, his wife informed him an aristocrat's fine carriage pulled by six Percherons had been attacked on the road from Marseilles. The man was robbed and stabbed to death. Locals gossiped he was an Austrian spy. Two days later, Anton learned his dearest friend Michel had been sent to jail, suspected of poisoning the Archbishop of Avignon, where his friend died.

"I was not the killer," the spirit of Michel cried out. "I failed my master that night. Possibly I could have stopped the killer, but I had been with you, Anton, doing as the archbishop commanded, retrieving his possessions from that vault. The archbishop must have known someone was coming for him.

"Set me free, Anton. Anguish strangles my spirit; redeem me. I made a mistake. Challenge Monsignor Devereaux to free me from my past as Michel and acknowledge me his loyal servant Antivo in this life. Twice wronged, I am caught between NoTime and EarthTime because of him. He holds the key. This new moon is my last chance. Soon the portal…."

Monsignor Devereaux dropped to the ground, crushing his head between his veined, trembling hands, and wailed. "I never meant to harm you, Antivo, not in the present and not in the past. You were my trusted servant. You nursed me when I was ill, protected me, served me with honor. I realize that now, Antivo. Forgive me."

The ancestor slumped into the thinning membrane, pressing his form closer, stretching the membrane toward the monsignor to try to touch him.

"Father, I did nothing to harm you. Not then, not now. Not ever."

The monsignor sighed. "I was misled. Antivo, I feared a man I met years ago on this island who came from France to escort a young orphan boy to Arles for his education. I trusted him. In that, I was fooled, but you suffered for it."

Antivo pushed harder on the gray membrane. The gristle snapped back, throwing him deeper into its folds. A network of delicate cracks appeared where his hand had been. The lines raced out like cracking ice. His words sounded muffled.

"The worlds, they cleave away," Antivo moaned.

Monsignor, trying to calm him, said, "Antivo, do you remember in France when I asked you, Michel, my beloved son, to bring two warm cognacs to my chamber that evening? I intended we share a toast. I wanted to thank you for your loyal service."

The ancestor lifted his head and pressed his forehead on the barrier. "Yes, Your Grace," he gasped. "I remember. That was the first time you had ever asked me to share a drink with you. I knew you were afraid."

"Yes, son, I was afraid…of you. I thought it was you who conspired against me. I was mistaken. I fell into a trap like an unwitting rabbit. It is little wonder we met again here in Madagascar, me your priest superior once again. I faced my enemy that night in Avignon, relieved he was not you.

"That night in France, I set a simple trap. I would offer a quick face wash before cognac, a habit I enjoyed, as a refreshment fit for a traveling guest. But the man who visited me pressed my face into the basin to mute my cry for help. My last image was of the aristocrat watching me choke on poisoned water. Yet my last prayer was for you, Michel. At that instance, I realized I had judged you wrongly. I died grateful you were not the enemy. I hoped we would meet again; I prayed. In this life, when you stole a vial from me, I cursed you Antivo. We both have been wrongly used by others. Forgive me."

———————— ✂ ————————

ANTIVO SCREAMED, "I CANNOT HOLD THIS BACK." THE monsignor looked at Antivo's opaque form adhering to the weakening membrane. A fissure opened and oozed brown liquid onto the ground.

Madame Tison screamed. "The portal is giving way! Save us!"

Kalanoro shadows rushed forward, trying to hold back the putrid water that ran in rivulets onto the forest floor. Writhing figures behind the membrane lurched forward, clawing to free themselves. A foul wind whipped the acrid air. The Kalanoro screamed, their weightless bodies dropping like black moth wings onto the sticky ground. Anguished moans reverberated in the sky. Constellations fell like shattered glass.

Madame Tison roared, "Monsignor if you have ever done anything decent in your life, do it now! Spare us. Stop the breach!"

The monsignor looked at her with dispirited eyes. "Madame, I wronged you also. You trusted me as your confessor. I exploited your trust to search for treasure. I beg your forgiveness."

"Who murdered you?" Madame Tison pleaded. "Put an end to this."

"I cannot say, but now I know it was not my beloved Michel. He is innocent."

Askara tried to step closer to the priest, but her feet sunk in the black ooze. "Monsignor, who could have known about those vials?

"Madame Askara, you told me Jean-Paul had shown you a vial," Monsignor Devereaux said. "How did he obtain one? I do not know. Was he at fault?"

"Monsignor, I...I lied. It was not Jean-Paul. It was Brother Gestang."

Gestang spoke rapidly. "Sometimes one must lie to protect someone or something. I understand that is not always the answer. I tried to protect my mother, Madame Tison, Clarisse. Turning to face her, he said, "Your *ravageur*, my sire, was a married man when he came from France to seduce you specifically to blackmail your parents."

"You deserve to understand the forces that were at work in your shaming, madame," Monsignor Devreaux groaned. "I tried to spare you. I wanted to protect you."

Madame Tison gasped in horror when Monsignor Devereaux explained the sire of Gestang had not come to Madagascar on business. No. The man belonged to a secret society dedicated to protecting the French royals.

The society sent him to discover if there was any truth to a rumor that certain valuables spirited out of France during the revolution existed and were buried on this island.

Adventurers had come over time, primarily pirates, but several years ago, when the Vatican showed renewed interest in the rebel colony Libertalia, that interest sparked a storm. The son born from the illicit union of a descendant of Captain Misson and his island wife, a boy who grew up in France, seemed a place to start—a boy raised in Arles' church orphanage and educated for the priesthood, a boy who received unique training from a society dedicated to guarding treasures of the Merovingian rulers of early France.

When the boy grew to a young man—yet no progress had been made in locating the treasures—the Vatican investigated a priest, Monsignor Devereaux. Although respected for his historical scholarship, he had alarmed the Vatican and piqued the interest of the pope when he requested documents related to the colony Libertalia in Madagascar, established during the French Revolution.

In his communique, Devereaux used language, an unfortunate choice of words—"there appeared to have been a treasure of sorts stored at the colony, the locals contend"— a sentence that rang the alarm bell for the Vatican and the secret society. Soon a young priest, Gestang, arrived to serve under the monsignor and watch his every move, to discover his superior's motives.

Years passed. Nothing happened until one day when a small boy handed Priest Gestang a little glass bottle embossed with a flower pattern and crown that he had found in the sand where Libertalia had once stood.

Madame Tison looked from Gestang to Devereaux and said, "Mon Dieu! Two snakes, both betrayers."

"Your seducer and your son carry coveted blood, madame, royal blood from both parents. Do you find this of interest, Mother? I did when I learned of it."

"Monsignor, is this true? The man who seduced me was related to me?" Madame Tison said, her bracelets quaking in the stale air.

"Yes, a fifth cousin, on the paternal French side, I believe."

Devereaux discovered the seduction had been planned to both disgrace Clarisse's parents and to shame them into silence while ascertaining what they knew of their bloodline. The plan worked to shame them, and it revealed an object of lineage, a small glass vial. The order from Arles stated that the monsignor must surreptitiously shelter the girl and have her live with a village herbalist to save her and the child from public scorn. The woman—no witch, but a wise woman versed in herbal medicine, a healer— would care for the child until three when he would come to Arles.

"In return," Monsignor Devereaux said, "I earned Clarisse's wrath although her parents knew the truth. Her *ravageur* met an untimely death in France. Clarisse, your son was spared, and your parents, madame, funded and built my personal library at the church out of appreciation, not blackmail, as you believed."

Madame Tison broke down in tears. "Why was this done?"

"To ensure the society would be appointed the only protectors of the treasure once recovered," Gestang interjected. "You must understand the history behind their decision."

Captain Misson left France for Madagascar on a mission, using the utopia story as a pretense, even employing a priest the Vatican had suggested, Father Caraccioli, a renegade, to accompany him. They were to establish a haven for the crumbling house of Louis XVI and his Austrian wife Marie Antoinette, a safe place to hide their treasures.

But time ran out. It was rumored the Austrian Holy Roman Emperor, Leopold II, Marie Antoinette's brother, stood ready to secure the goods as soon as they crossed the northern frontier into Austria. But God had other plans. Count von Fersen, and other members of the society, proved too astute for the emperor.

Hearing her shame explained like a chess game, Madame cried. "I had no idea."

"Just as God found a way to get the treasures out of France, I was sent back to Madagascar to protect you, my mother, from Monsignor Devereaux and others deemed a threat."

The monsignor tittered and lost his balance. When Sara rushed over to support him, aided by Darian, they lowered him to the ground. Sara felt his wrist, saying, "His pulse is weak, bumpy, out of step. Monsignor needs a doctor, fast. This has been too much for his heart."

Madame Tison knelt next to him, bowed low, and whispered a prayer: "May their souls and the souls of all the faithful departed, through the mercy of God, rest in peace. Amen. I am sorry I judged you so harshly. Forgive me."

A silver light engulfed Antivo. Through a slit in the membrane, he reached out and touched his master's hand, causing the membrane, like a diaphanous curtain, to collapse on the ground. Silver mist enveloped the monsignor, with his servant Antivo kneeling beside him. Antivo placed his translucent hands under the monsignor's back to lift him. Madame Tison backed away.

Heavy boots marched toward them from the cemetery gate. Brother Gestang bolted from the circle before anyone could stop him when the rusted gate screeched loudly. A man bellowed: "Halt!" Pigeons, roosting in the crypts, exploded into frantic wings whipping the humid night air.

Darian rushed toward the gate, yelling, "Stop! He's a pr…"

A deafening gunshot cracked the air. Askara and Sara rushed to join Darian who stood over Priest Gestang's motionless, face-down body sprawled on the walkway.

A uniformed man stepped over the inert body and holstered his pistol. "He charged us."

"That's Priest Gestang," Askara cried. "You killed a priest!"

Ejema rushed in from the crypt shadows. "You're under arrest. You are not the law here. I am! Back off."

"No, sir, private security, Officer Ejema. The monsignor hired us to guard the church grounds at night. When I saw this man running at us, I shouted. He didn't stop, so I fired. I didn't aim at him. He fell, knocked hisself out is all."

Ejema looked down at Gestang's body, turned him over, and felt his neck. "He'll be okay. Concussion. Hail a taxi. Take him to hospital."

"Monsignor's back there, dead. Heart attack, I think," Sara said as Madame Tison and Chef Pierre trotted up. "There was a thick fog."

Ejema shook his head in confusion, his back rigid. "Here? You saw the fog here? Wait for me inside the church. Bad things happen back there. Ghosts in these woods don't like priests on Kalanoro sacred ground. I'll meet you in a few minutes."

Officer Ejema ran to the monsignor's body, trailed by others, and felt his thready, weak pulse hanging on but barely, weak like the last drop of water from a faucet, "Tragedy," he said and leaned in closer. Monsignor's closed eyes fluttered. Ejema lowered to listen to his heart.

Faint words tiptoed on the priest's last breath: *Clarisse, ravageur. Le Pierre.*

Ejema felt the pulse in his neck cease. "Monsignor is dead," he announced as Madame Tison and Chef Pierre stepped closer. "Madame Tison, his last words, they were not clear, but I think he said, *Clarisse, ravageur, Le Pierre*. I will get Priest Gestang to the hospital and take monsignor's body. I am very sorry for this, but you all must come to the station to file a death incident report. You will cost me my *très bonne reputation* if you don't come tonight. Comprenez vous?"

They nodded in stunned assent and looked at one another. Madame Tison spoke. "We were looking for Madame Askara and her friends. We will be happy to come with you for the paperwork; you understand we want no trouble, no attention. This is a sad day for us all. Monsignor Devereaux was a noble priest, a guardian of the church. We must honor him and assist Priest Gestang in his healing and in his mission of tending to the flock here. We are at your service, Policeman Ejema, as always."

She looked at the others, and with a slight touch, pressed her index finger to her mouth and tightly closed her lips.

CHAPTER EIGHTEEN

Exit Visa

T he hotel lobby was quiet when Ejema escorted the foreigners in. Philippe must have fallen asleep. He was not at the front desk, but there would be no work since no one would show up so late with restaurants and bars closing at midnight. All hotels warned their guests Tana wasn't safe after taxis stopped working for the night.

Upstairs, when they approached, the guard propped against Askara's door, dozing at a gravity-defying angle, woke with a jerk but straightened quickly when Ejema gave him a quick rap across the shoulder. "*Attention,*" Ejema said and spat a series of Malagasy words like daggers at the guard who hung his head in shame while his boss motioned for two police escorts to check the room. After they searched every corner and looked behind every door, Ejema walked in, repeating the same pattern, plus locking and relocking the bathroom's small window and scanning the closet. Trying the tunnel entrance, he found it securely locked.

"The key to the tunnel opening—where is it?" Ejema said to Darian,

"Ask Madame Tison. She must have it. I'm glad it's locked. We don't have it."

Ejema nodded. He ordered two policemen to patrol the hall and four others to guard both stairways.

"I will speak with madame on this matter. I believe you are well protected now. No visitors, none—but me—and if my superior comes, I will be with him. Otherwise, do not open the door to anyone unless I tell you. Mademoiselle Sara, I will lock you in your room next door and return to escort you all to the airport. Get sleep. Food will be brought to your door when you call for it. *Bon nuit*, or should I say *bon matin*, as it is now four in the morning."

When Ejema stepped out and bolted the door from the hallway, Darian turned the lock on the inside. He started to speak to Askara but stopped short, watching her withdraw the closet key from her bra.

"He asked you, Darian, not me. Too embarrassing to reach into my bra in front of an officer, plus we may need it."

Darian shook his head. "At this point, what does it matter? I'm sure madame has several keys. And what do you intend to do anyway? We're flying out in several hours. That's good enough for me."

Askara tiptoed to the closet's small opening, feeling for the crack in the plaster. "Must be swelled," she said to Darian. She picked along the edge. "It's locked, thank God."

But Askara froze, hearing a faint noise inside the tunnel. She held her breath. The sound of swooshing bat wings made her arm hair stand on end. She quickly unlocked the tunnel door, pushed it hard to force it into alignment, and started to turn the key when she heard a muted whisper.

"Wait! Madame, please."

Askara recognized the voice of Madame Tison's nephew Philippe. "Wait, I am coming. Please turn on the light by the closet."

Askara switched the light on and stepped back. In a less than a minute, Philippe appeared at the opening.

"Madame, I must speak. May I come in?"

Darian, standing behind the closet door, shook his head, no. Then he stepped in front of Askara to prevent Philippe from entering and growled in a low voice: "The police are at our door. Leave us alone!"

"Turn off lights now, monsieur. I must speak to you. I mean you no harm."

Askara whispered to Darian. "I want to hear what this is about," so Darian grimaced, hit the lights in the bedroom, and closed the bedroom door.

Philippe struggled to hoist himself through the opening without making a noise. His panting echoed in the night, but only the bats stirred a little. He brushed the dust from his shirt while motioning for them to walk into the bathroom. He followed and shut the door behind him, whispering, "Shh." He turned on the shower and pulled the window curtain closed before turning on the light. Philippe's clothes were dirty and crumpled, his face haggard. He smelled like dank earth.

Askara backed away from him and said, "We're leaving Madagascar. You can't stop us."

"Thank you from all my family, madame, monsieur, for what you have done. We now have two small relics safe, where they will stay away from the eyes and ears of the world. They may seem like nothing to you, but you have given us a great gift, our family's *raison d'être*. We are in your debt, madame, monsieur. My Aunt Clarisse and Uncle

Pierre wanted to thank you in person, but the cave approach is très difficile—which you must agree—and they must appear visible to the police downstairs for verification of their alibi. As a child, this cave was my favorite playground. I know it well."

"I'd like to say we appreciate the gesture, but we do not," Darian said.

Philippe continued. "My message may alarm you, but we believe there are those who will try to stop you from leaving the country. You see, Monsignor Devereaux had friends in the police department and in the government. When he lost a small vial from the historical settlement of Libertalia, he paid for any information he could glean. Also, the monsignor sent communiqués to many officials on another date, declaring a valuable cross and a communion cup had been stolen from the church. Evidently, he followed a misguided, fruitless hunch, based on gossip, that some treasures Misson pilfered related to the French royals.

"Although none were found, people told stories handed down from generation to generation about the colony Libertalia concerning the famous captain's treasures. If he had some, the booty probably would have sunk when *Le Grande Serpent* went down off the coast of Africa, but Monsignor Devereaux became obsessed with a naive folly that influenced him so powerfully that many wondered at the educated monsignor believing in such a fable. Was he going mad? Frankly, even I questioned his sanity.

"Some members of his congregation went so far as to write to the Vatican to request his transfer from Madagascar. Well, that is over now with his untimely, tragic death. God rest his soul. He was a good man, despite the disagreement he had with my aunt Clarisse.

"Unfortunately, erroneous whispers linger among certain government officials. We received word early this morning that certain individuals now claim that you two have the cross and the communion cup he claimed as stolen and will attempt to leave the country with them. I know this sounds absurd, but we must take care. For this reason, we have discovered you may be prevented from departing the airport this afternoon. Your friend, Mademoiselle Sara, evidently will not be detained; only you, madame, and you, monsieur."

"Oh, God, I thought this nightmare was over," Askara said, starting to shake.

"Madame, my aunt—our family—has a plan to help you. She has learned that an army officer from the President's Special Forces will come here this morning to interview you. You are to give him this," Philippe said, unrolling a length of canvas securing two objects.

"Beautiful! The missing communion cup and cross? Did Devereaux steal them from the church?" Askara asked.

"Not exactly," Philippe replied and explained the meaning.

Three years back, Monsignor Devereaux enlisted the government to help recover the church's missing cross and cup. He implied Philippe's Aunt Clarisse had something to do with it, an absurd notion by most standards, yet the family understood it as a ploy since Monsignor Devereaux and Clarisse Tison had long been enemies. As a confessor, he failed her when she was a young woman in need of help. She, three years back, repaid that insult when the monsignor intended to purchase the forest that adjoins the church cemetery. She quickly made a bid before the notice of the sale went public. Madame Tison and family purchased the forest plot. She had thwarted him.

"Monsignor Devereaux hates—excusez-moi—hated my aunt for this. So, anticipating a problem, my aunt Clarisse ordered a jeweler in France to make an imitation of the items—the cross, in the description the monsignor had given the police, and the communion cup. Although facsimiles made of inexpensive materials, gold leaf and semiprecious quartz stones for the cross and simple bronze for the communion cup, the craftmanship was *par excellence*. We never had to use the replicas. That day didn't come in monsignor's lifetime, but it may be upon us now."

"Why bother?" Askara said. "He's gone."

"Insurance. Monsignor Devereaux, his lawyer informed us, left a will that specifies the possessions for his pet project, the history of Libertalia, the first French settlement in Madagascar, go directly to the French Embassy Historical Museum, a nonprofit agency under the auspices of the embassy. This could prevent your getting an exit visa today and may embroil you in years of investigation and possible litigation.

"Things move slowly here in Madagascar. The facsimile cross and cup are your exit visa. You must have them with you, unhidden, when the Special Forces Officer comes later this morning. You must give the package to him willingly. Tell the government officer, his name is Monsieur Johann Alatsinainy, that Monsignor Devereaux, before his unfortunate demise, had requested you to deliver a package for him to the French Embassy. But you were unable to because you have been locked in this guarded room, for safety reasons, until your departure. That is all you know. That is all you need to know. Request Monsieur Alatsinainy to deliver the package himself."

"Why don't you give your aunt the cross and cup and tell her to do it? Better yet, you do it. Here, take it back. This is crazy."

Darian broke in. "What assurance do you give that the government won't blame us for the theft? Madame Tison and you should handle this. We want nothing to do with this craziness."

"There is a problem, yes." Philippe's brow furrowed. "You must realize how delicate the matter is. You learned of my aunt's shame. Let it be. She made the mistake of passionate youth, which has haunted her life. Let her enjoy her elder years. No one here knows of Gestang's—well, their relationship. Leave the priest that much dignity. He is a good man. He and madame may not be on the best of terms, but they are blood. We all are. Our family will work it out. The items will be returned to the church with Priest Gestang to watch over them. No harm done. They are facsimiles of objects copied from a famous medieval cathedral in Arles, France. To the eye, they are pleasing.

"The police searched your room when it was ransacked. Yes? So, why did they not find these items if you were harboring them? Because Monsignor had not yet asked you for help, that's why."

"They will assume that is true," Darian replied with a quizzical look, his eyebrow cocked like a mountain peak.

"Yes, they searched," Philippe said, "but Madame had stored them inside the tunnel entrance, out of sight, in case the need for them ever arose. I know Madame Askara lied about the key. She has it. And we know that. How would it look if we filed a police report stating that? Be reasonable sir, do you want to take your flight home with your wife?"

"I get it. The government official doesn't know about the tunnel…yet. We give them what they want by playing your game, and we leave the airport today to go home. Correct? Case closed."

"Police Officer Ejema knows the details. He has investigated the monsignor for some time—undercover, of course. Ejema is family, a distant cousin. Americans say no harm, no foul, n'est-ce pas? You return the genuine lost items that had been in the monsignor's possession all along, no charges shall come against a respected dead priest, the police drop their search for the missing items, the church gets back its cross and cup, you go home, breezing through the gate with your exit visas. Win-win."

Askara's stomach lurched at the thought of what would happen if they refused. She held the canvas bag, nodding in agreement without enthusiasm. Philippe placed the canvas bundle on the nightstand, stepped into the closet, and slipped from their room as stealthily as he had come, only the swoosh of bat wings signaling his disappearance.

Darian hugged Askara and watched the rising sun drench the city's red-ochre roof tiles in a rosy-amber glow, assuring her it was almost over. Askara collapsed on top of the bed, closed her eyes, and fell into a coma sleep.

Tana's bustle woke Askara mid-morning. She lay across the bed, fully dressed from the night before, and heard Darian in the shower. Looking at the mirror, she sneered at her crumpled blouse, wrinkled jeans, and matted hair—evidence of a night she wished had been just a bad dream.

Activity stirred in the hallway, animated Malagasy conversation. Askara called through the bolted door to request breakfast, heard someone reply oui, gathered her dress, kissed Darian on the cheek when he entered the room, and went in for her shower without another word. When she came out, her braided hair still dripping, she stared through the balcony's dusty glass door to the Zoma Market's white umbrellas. Darian, too exhausted and too worried to speak, poured her a cup of coffee from the silver pot. Askara sipped silently, feeling like Marie Antoinette ascending guillotine steps.

She mulled over the plan, too simple to be effective, in her opinion, and too complex to go right. But what options did she have? Walking to the bedside table, she lifted the canvas-wrapped objects to look at them in the sunlight. Their heaviness caught her attention.

No expense was spared in creating these facsimiles, she thought. The gold leaf luster of the cross—set with red garnets, squares of rough-cut yellow tourmaline, and a chunk of pale blue quartz—caught the morning light. She noticed the indentions on the cross clotted with remnants of candle wax. *Such an odd design*, she thought, *must be a Catholic thing.*

She ran her finger over the raised crucifix on the central axis. Askara's face constricted. She choked on her coffee.

"Oh, God. I've seen this before."

Darian tipped over his coffee cup, hearing the panic in Askara's voice. "What, Sweetie?"

Askara walked to the balcony slider and angled the cross so that the pale blue chunk of stone touched the pane. With moderate force, she dragged the cross several inches along an inconspicuous area near the frame. She reduced the pressure to look. Her heart stopped. A neat score in the glass caught the morning light. She inspected the stones closely. Ruby, yellow sapphire, blue diamond.

"Oh, shit! Darian, this isn't a facsimile," she gasped. "I'm positive these are precious stones, and that gold leaf is twenty-four-carat gold." She nicked the candle holder with her tweezers. A hairline indentation appeared, but no flecks fell. "Nothing about this damn cross is fake; everything about Philippe's story is."

"Tell me you're wrong, please."

A knock at the door made her jump. "Yes?" she shouted. "Bonjour, madame, petit déjeuner."

Askara stuffed the cross and cup into the canvas bag and shoved it under her pillow. She rushed to unbolt the door. A Malagasy serving girl from the café smiled as she lowered the tray onto the table. Askara tipped her and followed the girl to the door to relock when two guards stepped in front, rifles in hand, to block Askara after the girl stepped out.

Askara smiled weakly, glanced up and down the hall to see more guards, and said, "Merci, mademoiselle," to the girl. "Can you knock on my friend's door and tell her to join us for breakfast?" The serving girl looked at the men for permission. A guard nodded and walked to Sara's room to knock on the door.

Askara heard Sara shout: What the hell do you want now?

Askara yelled to Sara it was okay. When Sara poked her head out the door, Askara leaned through the guards to smile and wave her over. "Food, petit déjeuner. Come on." The guard motioned another man to escort Sara to Askara and Darian's room. Once she got in, they slammed and locked the door from both sides.

The aroma of strong coffee permeated the room. Darian poured Sara a cup. "Glad you're here with us, Sara. I want to apologize for putting you through all this. We would never have guessed the mess Madagascar has become. Askara wanted me to meet her dearest friend, and I am delighted I did. I would never have wished this on anyone, not you, not us. Please, accept our apologies. When you visit us in India, we will treat you like a queen."

"No worries, friend. Make it Betty Windsor, please. No need to apologize. It's been a real trip. If I get out alive, well, I reckon it's been fantastic. If I don't…no comment."

"We're in deep shit, Sara. All of us," Askara whispered. She led Sara by the hand into the bathroom and turned on the shower. Darian followed and closed them in.

"See these damn relics," she said, holding them out to Sara. "The cross and the cup are genuine; this cross is valuable, the cup looks genuinely old, an antique for sure, but not valuable, just bronze. I think it is a knockoff of a historical cup. Not sure, though. The soldered seams look relatively recent. But it has a definite allure. I love holding it. It feels warm to the touch like it can take you on a walk back in time. Odd.

"Anyway, we fell into Tison's trap. A government officer will show up soon. I am supposed to hand these over like a fool, supposedly on a request from Monsignor Devereaux before he died, to clear up some church theft he had reported years back. What do we do?"

Darian held the items. The cup felt warm from Askara's touch, the cross cold. His face fell. "We do what they want. It's our only chance to leave. I don't care who's right or who's wrong here; I care about getting out. That's all. Let these people play their silly games, their family vendettas. I'm never coming back, neither are you, so we do what we have to do to get out of here now. Luckily, Sara, your flight goes before ours. We were assured no one would prevent you from leaving. Evidently, they don't include you in their weird scheme."

"Who said that?"

"A family member. The less you know, the better."

"Well, I'm with you two," Sara said. "Madame Tison… something's wrong with that dame; I don't trust her or her family…if they really are her family. The only person I like is that Ejema dude, the policeman. He's cool. I think he knows more than he lets on, though."

"I like him too, but guess what—he's family too, some distant cousin. They're all freakin' family," Askara said. "But maybe that's all a setup, even Priest Gestang, with his poor-me bullshit story about being Madame Tison's illegitimate son. They look nothing alike."

Askara grabbed a croissant and stuffed it in her mouth, angry she had trusted Madame Tison and her family, starving since she hadn't eaten in many hours. As she chewed, she realized she wanted to slap the old lady across her rouged face.

Askara gulped down more coffee while Darian and Sara ate omelets. Caffeine-crazed, she imagined how this would end. She would be caught with a genuine gold cross and an antique metal cup, so why all the government officer stuff? Askara intended to tell the Special Forces man how Madame Tison's nephew Philippe had set her up. If she was going to prison, she wouldn't for an imbecile like Philippe! She knew the cross wasn't fake, and the cup was pretty worthless but truly old. Other than Darian and Sara, she wondered, *Who else knew?*

They shared a meal before Askara told Sara to return to her own room before the officer came. At one o'clock, when a hard rap made Askara break into a cold sweat, Darian reluctantly opened the door to see three men—one in a police uniform wearing a badge, another in a Western suit, and the third officer in Special Forces military attire.

"Bonjour. I am with the president's office. My name is Mr. Alatsinainy," the military officer said. "I am assigned to your case. I have questions to ask to complete your exit paperwork."

"Come. Sit down," Askara said in a subdued tone. "What do you want to know?"

"I see from the report, madame, you came to write a story on the Walking the Dead ceremony, the famadihana?"

"Right. The Christian Coalition of Catholic Churches hired me to write the article.

"Your contact for this project here in Madagascar?"

"Well, Monsignor Devereaux. He's dead now. But I worked with Priest Gestang too. I hired an interpreter, Mea, but she returned to England."

"Madame, have you received payment?"

"For my article? Not yet. I thought I would get an advance, half payment here. Not sure that's going to happen now that the monsignor passed away. When I submit the article in America, I hope to get paid."

"Did the priests, or anyone else, give you anything here in Madagascar that you plan to take out of Madagascar? Anything you did not declare upon entry?"

"Yes," she said as she walked over to her bed to retrieve the canvas bag from under the pillowcase. She pulled out the cross and small cup and saw the man stiffen. "I was supposed to deliver this, but I've been locked up. Couldn't."

Mr. Alatsinainy took the items from her. "Who handed you this, madame?"

"Monsignor Devereaux. He asked me to deliver them for him…then he passed away."

"Oh," Mr. Alatsinainy said as he held the heavy cross in his hands. And, I believe your room had been searched previously, yet these were not found. How is that possible, madame?"

"Um," Askara said, swallowing. "Well, sir, I found a little compartment inside the closet and stashed it in there for the monsignor, so the maids wouldn't see it. Unfortunately, he had that heart attack. I was told a government official would come for it."

"And did the priest ever explain his strange request to you, madame?"

"Well, he said…he said he couldn't give me my advance for the article if I couldn't do this small thing for him, turn these things over to a government official when that person showed up. He questioned leaving them at the church. He felt that wasn't safe for some reason. Guess he meant the President's Special Forces official, you."

"Oui, madame. The priest was correct on that score. But someone—we are not sure who—wants it to appear you intended to take these out of the country, I am afraid."

"Shoot the messenger, right? Look, I've delivered the monsignor's church things for you to officially replace at the church, something I'm sure he intended to, but God called him home first."

"Oui, *exactement,* but the monsignor, did he say the items were of little value—facsimiles, a fake cross, and old communion cup that he had made for church display?"

"I don't remember exactly. He implied they were."

Mr. Alatsinainy scrutinized the objects. "Yes, just as he said, gold leaf and paste jewels. Funny, the monsignor had caused such a stir, had the police search the island, saying how valuable they were. An old man's folly, I suppose. His research into Libertalia and the treasures of Captain Misson, the famous pirate, upended his reason and his ability to judge what is real."

"Fakes, wow, how silly," Askara said with forced astonishment.

Mr. Alatsinainy's eyes lit up. "You have been very cooperative, madame. I know you need time to get ready for your departure. I will fill out the appropriate exit paperwork, so you have no difficulty in leaving. You didn't come with this;

you didn't leave with this. Just as it should be. I will handle the rest. Forgive the intrusion—madame, monsieur—and thank you for your cooperation. Bon voyage. Your exit will be a smooth one, and we will meet again when you return for your next pleasant holiday with us in Madagascar."

Mr. Alatsinainy stood and straightened his jacket, informing them that Officer Ejema would assure their safe passage to the airport and that he regretted this inconvenience and hoped it had not marred their stay in Madagascar.

When Darian asked about Priest Gestang, an officer replied it was only a slight concussion and that the priest would be back at his church duties within a few days. Mr. Alatsinainy wrapped the cross and cup in the canvas cloth and stuffed it inside his mud-brown uniform jacket. The officers said good-bye and closed the door behind them.

"What the hell? That was crazy."

"Very worrying, indeed," Darian added. "Askara, did that make sense to you?"

"I'm dumbfounded. There's some double game. I hope Ejema shows up soon. We need to get out of here; can't trust anybody."

———— ✤ ————

ASKARA CONSIDERED TELLING EJEMA ABOUT THE MEET-ing when he first arrived but decided not to, remembering he was family. When they descended the carpeted stairway to the foyer, escorted by Ejema, Madame Tison approached.

"Madame Askara," she said, leaning close to kiss Askara on both cheeks. Askara recoiled, puzzled by the glimmer of a smile that flashed across the old woman's face. Madame greeted Darian in the same affectionate way, with pecks on the cheek. Sara yanked backward before Madame Tison could reach her. "You watch over them, Officer Ejema, especially Madame Askara. She is a precious gift to us all. We look forward to hosting you all again."

Philippe and Chef Pierre stepped out from behind the counter. Philippe smiled and said, "Good luck, and thank you. Bon voyage until we meet again."

Chef Pierre gave them a small salute, and tipping his head, he took Askara's hand in his to kiss it. "The house of Anjou thanks you, madame," he said and gently squeezed her hand before releasing it.

Askara felt her face burn, her stomach drop. Jean-Paul's words rushed into her head: "Look to the house of Anjou." She started to speak but shut her mouth and followed Ejema to a waiting police car. Askara climbed in first and turned to see Madame Tison, Philippe, and Chef Pierre waving enthusiastically. Sara and Darian scooted across the back seat next to her when she spotted Imboule run up to join Madame Tison and her family at the Hotel du Parc's entrance to vigorously wave good-bye. Askara wondered if Imboule were family too.

They rode in silence for twenty minutes through the busy roads of Tana. Askara stared out the window, dreading what would come next. She didn't understand madame's oddly affectionate behavior, much less the rest of the morning.

Sara couldn't hold back. "What the hell is that old dame about?"

Ejema spoke up. "The monsignor, it seems, he was not playing a fair game."

"What do you mean?" Darian asked. "Will we be able to leave?"

"Mr. Alatsinainy's official inspection of monsignor's chambers this morning showed evidence, sketches of artifacts from the Cathedral of Arles of a jeweled cross and an antique cup of the same description that existed there in the Middle Ages. I believe the monsignor may have lost his way a bit. He displayed fakes at the church, wishing them genuine. Possibly he repented. He might have wanted you, Madame Askara, to return the facsimiles to absolve him of impropriety. Or possibly his own manservant Antivo had some hand in the deception since his soul found no peace in the famadihana."

Ejema recounted how the cross caused a big problem three years back when Monsignor Devereaux reported it stolen from the church. Many officers, including him, searched across the island for it. "And for what?" he sighed.

Askara listened to Ejema like he was the judge who would deliver her sentence. She wasn't sure of the verdict if things didn't go well at the airport. All she wanted was to leave Madagascar with Darian and for Sara to return safely to Lesotho for work.

She pondered their situation. The communion cup seemed a common thing to Askara, except, she assumed, for the way the metal alloy had been formulated. It glowed and felt warm to the touch. It convected body heat quickly. Possibly it was special metallurgy of an earlier time?

Thinking of it, she lapsed into a daydream of an old stone temple in a dry landscape, a different world where she touched the small cup and images appeared. She saw a young girl standing next to an elderly man in a flaxen robe. He placed his hand on her shoulder. The girl looked up and smiled. The man cradled a small metal cup filled with pale yellow oil, taking care to not disturb the floating wick flame.

He spoke to the girl. "Uphold your duty, Asha. Fire is holy. The cup will always find its way back to you for as long as you remember, you are…."

A taxi horn blared. Ejema swerved, snapping Askara back to the present. For a brief second, the young girl's image lingered in her vision. She felt the girl's innocence, her strength, her familiarity. Askara wondered what that scene meant. It felt so real. She longed for the peace that enveloped the old man and the girl, whoever and wherever they were.

Staring out the police car window, she watched women walking along the road with baskets of fruit balanced on their heads, and envied their graceful gate, their uncomplicated lives. *They know what their days will bring. How reassuring that would be*, she thought. *I am not sure of even the simple things anymore. I thought this assignment would be interesting, simple, and straightforward. Riding to the airport, I feel I might as well be marching to my death. Anything and everything could go wrong from no fault of my own. What a tangled web this turned out to be. Fake crosses, real crosses. What's the point? If ignorance is bliss, bring it on*, she sighed.

Renewed anxiety tightened her neck. *Maybe an impending noose?* Askara realized her thoughts had plummeted from serene to macabre, so she tried to pull out of it and focus on Ejema's words.

"Monsignor Devereaux claimed the items were worth a fortune," Ejema continued. "He filed a recovery claim saying the pope had instructed him to offer a reward. But no one found the cross or the small communion cup until this morning. Mr. Alatsinainy, the Special Forces Officer, is also a respected evaluator of antiques. He swore in his communiqué to the President's Office that the cross is a fake, gold leaf on brass with mediocre garnets and colored quartz stones, and the communion cup is crudely cast bronze of no value. The police department closed the case of the church's missing cross and cup shortly after."

"That was quick," Askara said, feeling slightly nauseous.

Ejema clucked disapproval at the whole affair but defended the monsignor as a man who wanted to impress, but not a bad man, only a man with ambition that did not fit the priesthood, in his opinion. That was his downfall. Devereaux had a library built for himself from tithe money, people gossiped.

Brother Gestang never agreed with the monsignor on the running of the church, yet now Priest Gestang would be elevated by the Vatican and hold a greater position than the monsignor ever held. Monsignor Devereaux's pet research project on the French settlement in the southern tip of the island, Libertalia, ended with his death. He doubted the priest's replacement would follow in his footsteps because, in Ejema's opinion, Devereaux's folly led him to the Kalanoro forest and to his death. Malagasy shadow people never accepted the Catholic invaders. The monsignor should have understood that and not stepped into their woods, especially at night. His domain lay within the church boundary only.

"*C'est la vie!*" Ejema said. "The priest is at peace now."

Askara mumbled, "Huh," and slumped into the car seat, uttering a feeble, "yeah, interesting." Darian grimaced at his hands, gripped tightly in his lap, and remained speechless while Sara grinned at the passing scenery en route to the airport.

———————— ❧ ————————

EJEMA ESCORTED ASKARA, DARIAN, AND SARA INTO THE airport departure lounge generally used for VIPs, as requested by Madame Tison. After a routine search of their luggage, they walked into a small room where a man in a starched khaki uniform with green trim greeted them cordially. Ejema excused himself. When Askara saw Ejema walking out, she grabbed his arm.

"A formality, madame. I wait outside. I will see you off at your departure gates."

Two armed guards stood behind the official while he pored over Darian's and Sara's exit paperwork and quickly approved them, ordering the guards to escort them to the next waiting room. He took more time with Askara's papers—her passport, money exchange receipts, sales slips, and the police reports—one related to the robbery of John's necklace in the Zoma Market, and one related to the death of Monsignor Devereaux.

"You must settle your account, madame, to move on," he said, holding up the papers.

Askara felt the blood rush from her face. She remembered those words from a dream, a nightmare.

"How?"

"Well, there is much here. Your exit visa must be complete as to what you owe."

"Owe to who?"

"Balance of stubs, madame," the uniformed official said, taking a report handed to him by a guard. He looked at her, his impassive face solemn like weathered stone, sun-dried and bleak. "There is a discrepancy."

"In what, sir?"

"In your possessions. Your entry report lists one camera and twenty canisters of film. The customs officer's slip states you have no film in your luggage. You must have sold it on the black market, a serious offense."

"No, sir, my film was stolen."

"Did you report it?"

"No. Since I bought it in the US, I didn't think it mattered. I only recently realized it was gone."

"You must account for each and everything to get an exit visa, just as your husband and friend did. We don't take our laws lightly. We work hard to curb black-market commerce. I cannot grant your exit visa without proper documentation."

Askara burst into tears. "I'm sorry! I didn't sell the film. It was stolen from me!"

"But you failed to report the theft?"

A hard knock at the door interrupted the official's interrogation. Askara slumped forward, kohl smearing with her tears. When she heard Ejema's voice, she looked up.

"Madame," Ejema said in a professional voice, "it seems you forgot something at the hotel. The proprietress Madame Tison has come on your behalf." He turned to the immigration official, "Sir, may I lead the woman in?"

"Yes, yes. Hurry. I am busy!"

Madame Tison entered with a flourish of gold jingling bracelets, wearing a mink stole clipped at her neck and rose perfume that saturated the room.

"My poor, poor girl. I rushed, hoping to catch you. My maid found something that had fallen under your bed, something I knew you would want," she said, pulling a paper bag from her large, shiny snakeskin purse. "Your film canisters. You cannot complete your feature article without your photographs, n'est-ce pas?"

Askara stared, momentarily speechless. "Thank you, madame. I thought I had lost them."

"You did, but now they are found." Madame Tison leaned in to kiss Askara on both cheeks. "An innocent mistake," she said, turning to the official, "as you can see, sir. Bon voyage, mon cher amie, until we meet again. My son sends his fond regards to you, your husband, and your friend. We close the door on your visit with sadness and joy. Like a phoenix, your plane rises to the sky with our deepest gratitude, now and forever friends."

Askara, dumbstruck, looked into Madame Tison's playful eyes. She watched the grand dame leave as she had entered, a swirl of bracelets, fur, and perfume.

"Well, Madame Askara Timlen-Dalal," the immigration officer said, stamping several papers in quick succession, "that completes the process. Here is your exit visa; your account is settled. You may leave Madagascar. We look forward to your return."

Askara's vision rippled like river water flowing over pebbles. She saw into the ocean of her past. Seated behind the customs officer appeared a kindly face she remembered with love from long ago, her adoptive father, her teacher, the Respected One. His words floated in gentle arcs like a feather on a breeze, touching her memory softly, filling her with courage. His words imprinted on her heart.

"You have done well, daughter. You cleared an impediment in your destiny. Now you can complete the process set before you. Remember who you are, Asha, the Protector of the Cup.

"Emperor Haile Selassie died in an Ethiopian prison only days ago. You must face the man you feared the most. Prepare. The soothsayer Nagali comes for you. His hopes of retrieving what he wanted through Emperor Selassie are forever broken. He seeks The Cup of the Shining Sun. He turns his attention back to you, the one he knows who last touched its power.

"The cup searched for you, remembers you. You didn't recognize it, yet it recognized you. It did not remain long with the old guru in India. The cup is a shapeshifter more powerful than any. It played its role on this ancient island where it had rested before, but when the cup wants to return to a person, it finds a way.

"Your greatest challenge lies ahead. Remember the lessons I taught you when you were my temple acolyte. I am with you. Be with me. Listen to the quietness where wisdom dwells. Go forward with Darian, return to India, prepare for your long-awaited honeymoon, the beginning of the end."

THE END

Author's Note

Thank you for reading *Exit Visa*, Book Two in the trilogy "The Cup of the Shining Sun." This book takes place initially in India but primarily in Madagascar, a fascinating island. I visited there in 1992 during a break from my Fulbright research work in Mauritius. A fellow Fulbrighter, John, and his wife Elaine asked me and my two-year-old daughter to travel with them. (A brave act!) I would not have taken it on myself, although I loved Madagascar, its people, and its wildness.

As I had written earlier, real life is my jumping-off point for adventure stories that weave between worlds. True for this second book and true for my life. Skating realities is more fun than jumping puddles. You can't see the other side until you land…if you land.

I hope you enjoyed the story. Since I do not have a "big house" behind my efforts, I would appreciate your writing a review if you are inclined.

Also, check out my website at www.dyandubois.com.

The final book in the series holds unexpected twists as Askara develops further in the understanding of her role as the Protector of the Cup. I hope you'll join me for the finale of the series. We'll go back to Mother India to conclude her journey.

Thank you!
Dyan Dubois

Acknowledgements

A big thank you for encouragement, editing assistance, and for "being there" to Tricia Dulaney, Rajinder Gill, Rentia Humphries, Janet Switzer, and last but certainly not least, Jan Weir. Without creative support, the journey would be a dry exercise. And thank you to the excellent team at Luminare Press who make the publishing process enjoyable and educational.

Made in the USA
Monee, IL
15 August 2024